The
STONE
TRAVELER

OTHER BOOKS AND AUDIO BOOKS
BY KATHI ORAM PETERSON:

The Forgotten Warrior

An Angel on Main Street

The STONE TRAVELER

A NOVEL BY
KATHI ORAM PETERSON

Covenant Communications, Inc.

Cover image: *Jaguar* © mb-fotos, *Close-up of the Waxing Moon* © Manfred_Konrad, *Aztec Calendar* © Ulga, *Spherical Crystal Orbs* © jamesbenet. For more information on these images, visit www.istockphoto.com.

Cover design © 2010 by Covenant Communications, Inc.

Published by Covenant Communications, Inc.
American Fork, Utah

Printed in Canada
First Printing: July 2010

16 15 14 13 12 11 10   10 9 8 7 6 5 4 3 2 1

ISBN-13 978-1-60861-039-6

With great love and heartfelt appreciation,
I dedicate this book to my family:

~my husband, Bruce

~my children, Kristina, Patricia, and Benjamin

~my son-in-law, Gregory

~and my two grandsons, William and Jonathan

Acknowledgments

SOME MAY THINK A WRITER works alone, but most writers are influenced by events, places, and the people they meet along the path of writing a book. Such is my case.

My parents, John and Edna Oram, had a profound influence on my life, not only as I was growing up but also later in their twilight years. My parents served two missions: one in Columbia, South America, and the other in Roanoke, Virginia. They built a cabin above Palisades Reservoir in Idaho where our family would gather. Dad wrote stories, and Mom painted many beautiful pictures that hung in the cabin. My folks passed away, and we sold their cabin, but I have tried to capture in the story of this book their testimonies of the gospel, their talents, and their love of family. I will always be eternally grateful to my parents.

To my writers group, The Wasatch Mountain Fiction Writers, I owe my undying gratitude for listening to my stories week after week and year after year. A warm thank you goes to Michele Ashman Bell, Dorothy Canada, Ann Chamberlain, Tina Foster, Kerri Leroy, Charlene Raddon, Peggy Ramsey, Nikki Trionfo, and Roseann Woodward. Three members—Brenda Bensch, Katheen Dougherty, and Maureen Mills—read this book cover to cover. Thanks ladies for becoming this book's special guardians!

I want to thank my dear friend and mentor, Elizabeth Lane. We've worn a path in the park plotting our stories and sharing our lives.

Of course, I want to thank my publisher, Covenant Communications, and especially Kathryn Jenkins for supporting this book. I owe another big thank you to my new editor, Samantha Van Walraven, who helped me trim and keep my story on track. Thanks for all the help, Sam.

I'm extremely grateful for the wonderful people of the Book of Mormon. They were men and women of great courage. Some went to battle for what they believed, some spent years away from their loved ones doing the Lord's work, and others led exemplary lives with their devotion to the Lord.

Most of all, I have a deep gratitude and love for my Savior and His atoning sacrifice. I am humbled by His perfect example. Such love and devotion the world has never known.

Disclaimer

THIS IS A WORK OF FICTION. I have woven a fictional tale around events that took place in the Book of Mormon and in the New Testament to create this story. I have invented certain details and created characters to embellish this work.

My hope is that after finishing this novel, readers will compare it to the Book of Mormon and the New Testament to learn the true details of what actually happened.

1

Traitor

AD 33—Northernmost part of the land Bountiful
Sabirah

I WATCHED AS KEI TRIED to outrun my men. He thought he had escaped. But we had tracked him most of the day and knew if we could capture him, he could lead us to Princess Jamila's camp. Staying hidden from view behind the trunk of a large rain tree and giant fern fronds, I waited for the young Lamanite, who ran as fast as a white-tailed deer, to fall into my trap.

The Lord had guided me—a Lamanite woman of only ten and nine years—and my devoted, small army of men, some old, some young. They were believers of God and followed me because they loved and revered my father. Now I had to prove my worth.

My hand reached for the sling at my waist as I quickly surveyed the ground for rocks. I saw several at my feet. Then my fingers touched the ivory dagger. Asim, my elder brother—who left our people more than a year ago—had carved it from the tusks of a giant curelom, saying that when I fought, the blade would give me the strength of the mighty beast. He wanted me to use a real weapon and abandon fighting with rocks. So denying what came naturally, I pulled the dagger to the ready and waited. Without knowing, Kei headed straight toward me, dodging hanging vines and massive ferns.

Patience . . . patience . . .

And then he was in front of me. No time to think, only time to attack. I leaped onto his back, catching a firm hold on his shoulder. He grabbed my hand—as I tried to place the white tip of my dagger to his throat—and flipped me to the ground. I landed hard on my back.

"Sabirah?" Leaning over, Kei reached to take my weapon. I kicked him in the head, making him reel backward. As I rolled over, I noticed he had recovered and had already pulled a knife from his leg strap.

"Kei, why have you betrayed your people?" I had to know his reason, but he didn't answer.

With his eyes locked on mine, I knew he thought his only threat was my knife. Good. I would let him think so. I hid a rock in the palm of my hand without him noticing. Then quickly scrambling to my feet, I threw my dagger at him as he expected.

The handle hit his body instead of the blade and fell worthless to the ground. He cackled, thinking I'd failed. With deliberate purpose, I threw the stone and hit him between the eyes. He stumbled backward and dropped to the ground unconscious.

Recovering my dagger, I knelt beside him, waiting for him to awaken. As his eyes opened, I placed my knife to his throat and said, "I know of your treason."

He didn't dare fight. One move and I would stab the life vein in his neck. He stared at me with hatred in his gaze. I pressed hard on the blade. "Why did you join Princess Jamila's people?"

Realizing he was trapped, yet not wanting to admit defeat, he said, "I give no credence to a god I cannot see, nor do I fear him." He stared at me with loathing in his eyes.

His answer caught me off guard more than the flip move he had used earlier that had brought me to the ground. Kei had been a devoted follower of my father. And though Father had been gone many years, how could Kei so easily forget his teachings? Sorrow filled my heart, though I would not show weakness, not to him . . . or to my men, who had now come to stand in a circle around us. Despite my concern about Kei's treachery, I had to learn all I could about Princess Jamila and why she was here. "What do you know of Jamila's mission?" I asked.

Kei said nothing at first. I threatened him by pressing the dagger's blade along his throat. With eyes wide and fearful, he said, "She searches for more followers of her father."

Rage tore at my chest. How dare King Jacob, the wicked Nephite ruler of Jacobugath, send his daughter into our lands? Worry filled my heart for my people. All at once, Kei grasped the talisman hanging from my neck, and I panicked. He knew how special the token was. My father had carved the small wing-spread eagle from jade with his own hands. Kei's spite for me must run deep; there was no other explanation for why he would risk losing his arm and maybe his life by daring to take it.

My men stood breathlessly, still waiting to see what I would do. With serpentlike reflexes, I grabbed his wrist with my free hand, twisted his arm, and broke the hold he had on my necklace.

Disgusted with his pathetic attempt and betrayal, I stood and motioned for my men to bind him. Mahir, my second, quickly took charge.

Kissing the flying-eagle talisman, I let it rest again on my chest. Though my father was but a memory, the eagle kept him close to my heart. I sheathed the dagger and nervously rubbed the band tied about my middle as I straightened the ragged doe-skin tunic that hung to my knees. The nagging fear that both my father and brother had been captured by King Jacob haunted me. But why else would the king so brazenly send his only daughter to seek supporters for his cause? How arrogant and pompous the king had become to think she was not in danger.

She was!

What I had planned would surprise not only the king but also the princess, though I had to be patient. When I was a little girl, my father told me I would be tested while in my youth and that through my trials I must remain as strong as an ocean wind while waiting for God's guidance. The Lord would send a young wayfarer to aid me when all seemed lost. This wayfarer would be a healer and foreign to my people in every way, yet he would believe in Christ.

As time had passed with no word of my father, I'd felt abandoned. His wise counsel had given our people hope that a Messiah would save us. The sign of the Redeemer's birth, which my father foretold, happened many seasons before I was born, but I remembered my father warning the people of Christ's death and that great suffering would fall upon the land. I knew this time was close, for trouble brewed both near and far. Turmoil between believers and nonbelievers grew stronger with each passing day. My people desperately needed Father's loving guidance. Ashraf, my uncle, assumed the role of counselor for our village, yet he lacked the mantle of authority and caring that had resided in my father.

So did I.

We needed the wayfarer.

ᑲᕊ

AD 2015
Idaho Falls, Idaho
Tag

"YOU'RE GOING TO BE LATE, TAG," Mom called from the kitchen. She'd just arrived home. Mom believed in the motto "Do it, or get out of the way so I can." As an emergency room nurse at the Idaho Falls Hospital, she was a strong, take-charge woman.

Nothing bothered her.

Nothing made her lose her cool.

Except me.

"Coming," I yelled. Making sure I had Dad's sketchpad and drawing pencil in my hip pocket, I quickly locked my bedroom door. I hadn't always locked it when I wasn't home, but things had changed. I had changed, too. Things weren't normal anymore. This sixteen-year-old guy needed privacy. I was no longer a little kid, and I didn't want anyone, not even Mom, snooping around in my stuff. Not that she ever had, but a guy couldn't be too careful when dealing with a well-meaning parent.

As I entered the kitchen, she handed me an oatmeal power bar. She still wore working scrubs. Small blood drops stained the hem of her pant legs where most people wouldn't have noticed, but I did. *Must have been a bad night in the ER.* She eyed me up and down, taking in my freckled face, formerly red hair now dyed jet black, black eyeliner, black nail polish (yeah, guys wear it), black T-shirt, and black baggy jeans with chains dangling from the pockets—very fly, and all of which she'd seen before, but she still looked at me as if I were an alien from the third ring around Saturn.

Her eyes grew even wider as she noticed my latest addition—a black dog collar with spikes. My persona was finally complete. I was impressed with the new me.

Mom wasn't.

"Tag, you might dye your hair and paint your face, but you can't change your blue eyes." She smiled as if remembering the kid I'd once been and then said, "I might not say too much about your appearance, but I'm letting you know right now there'll be no tattoos. You can get infection, you can . . ."

"Sure," I said over my shoulder as I left, glad she couldn't see beneath my T-shirt and find the newly applied henna tattoo of a skull with spider legs on my chest. It was temporary and would only last ten to fifteen days. Thought I'd try it out and see if it looked as good on my skin as it did on the computer screen before I went beneath the needle and made it permanent. It was four inches high and wide and fit nicely on my sternum. Glad that she hadn't insisted I lose the collar, I didn't look back to say good-bye or have a nice day. I'd come to believe that using one-syllable words was the best way to communicate with her. No arguing that way—plus, no actual conversation.

I had tried to avoid talking with her at all. But then she forced me to talk with Doctor Kenyon Bradford—the tall creep who wormed his way into our lives. His height could easily intimidate the average person, but not me. I saw right through him from day one. He might have believed he could reason a pit bull into not biting him, but he couldn't reason with me.

A few months ago, the man had started having Friday night dinners with us. Not many mixed-up kids could say their mothers were dating their therapists. But me, I'd become "special." All I knew was I wanted to be left alone, not only at home but at school, as well. I'd come to feel I didn't belong anywhere. I actually felt like I should be somewhere else. I just didn't know where . . . so I started dressing this way, thinking everyone would leave me alone. My plan backfired with my mother and with a group of dudes who wanted me to become part of their gang called Prime.

They were a bunch of losers who wanted other losers to join them.

Recently, they demanded I skip school and meet them in back of the football stadium, which was really no big deal. Skipping school was no problem. I hated sitting there talking about things that were easy and unimportant; though, I was totally cool with honors lit and the library. I loved to read books—science fiction, fantasy, even Shakespeare.

As I hurried by the seminary building, I remembered I was supposed to meet with Bishop Carpenter last night. He tried to keep a close eye on Mom and me since Dad and Tyler left. Talking with him never solved anything. Besides, whenever there was a big lull in the conversation, the bishop would encourage me to serve a mission, like my father had. Going on a mission was not on my list of things to do, especially since Dad had ditched us.

Heading for the stadium, I decided I was going to put an end to the Primes bugging me. I'd just tell them they were boring as dirt. I was sure that would go over well. Of course, since these guys weren't really a hard-core gang yet, I might have pull it off.

I continued down the worn, grassy path flanked by cottonwoods and an old wooden fence.

Stepping out near the meeting place, I saw that the Primes had someone cornered. Some poor, pathetic person was in trouble. As I neared, I stopped dead in my tracks. My heart machine-gunned against my ribs. For a brief moment, I thought the person they had trapped was my brother, Tyler: same sandy brown hair, same thin body. I did a double take. No, it wasn't Tyler; it was my stupid, always-do-what's-right cousin, Ethan.

Ethan Gordan was Aunt Crystal and Uncle Lee's son. He was the bane of my teenage existence and seriously threatened to screw up my day. Though we were both sixteen and attended the same school, we rarely had much to do with each other. Many kids didn't know we were related because of our different last names; his mother was my father's sister. Cousin Ethan, the Ivy-League-snob type, couldn't ruin his reputation by being seen with me, the whacked-out cousin.

What was I going to do? On one hand, I couldn't let the Primes torment Ethan. Technically, he was family. Besides, he looked clueless, standing there in his golf shirt and Docker slacks. On the other hand, I didn't want Ethan to know I planned to ditch the Primes.

Dino, their leader, leaned against the car, swilling a beer and smiling. His dimpled grin could make girls blush or make rival gang members shiver in their Nikes. He liked me and what I could do with a can of spray paint. He'd seen my work on the cinderblock fence near the hospital. I'd drawn the Grim Reaper taking money from a patient's wallet. Didn't take the hospital long to whitewash it. Word spread fast that I was the one who did it. Many thought my name was my moniker and stood for Turf Artist Graffiti. They didn't know my dad had named me Tag because he didn't like Taggert, which was the name my grandpa Quincy wanted to call me.

Skids twirled his pocket chain. He drove the wheels for the gang. Gordo, the muscle man, who looked as if he chewed broken glass for a snack, didn't think I had what it would take to be a member of Prime. Pirate, the skinny, nail-biting lapdog gave his hyena cackle as he circled the victim.

"Don't tell me what I should and shouldn't do, Mormon boy," said Gordo as he flicked cigarette ashes on Ethan.

"Smoking and drinking is against the Word of Wisdom." My cousin's tanned face turned pale as he swallowed hard, but he still had a self-righteous glint in his eyes. What was Ethan thinking? Probably that he was a prophet of some type.

I tried to remember Book of Mormon prophets. My grandmother used to tell us stories from that book. All at once I realized which one he reminded me of. Ethan probably thought he was like Nephi, the prophet who preached repentance to the people before Christ appeared in America. And he probably thought God would send down an angel to protect him. Like that would ever happen. Well, I was no angel, but I *was* Ethan's only hope for escape.

"Us Primes—" Gordo grabbed ahold of Ethan's shirt collar right up against his throat "—we got our own words of wisdom."

"Hey, whats up?" I walked up to Gordo and stared him straight in the eyes.

"Choir boy—" Gordo gave Ethan a shake, "—thinks smoking and drinking is bad and said we shouldn't do it." Gordo blew a puff of smoke in Ethan's face.

My cousin immediately started coughing and wheezing. Gordo let go of him as the coughing fit grew into a choking frenzy. Ethan frantically searched his pants pockets for his inhaler, pulled it out, held the device to his mouth, and pumped. Instant relief came to his face.

"You some kind of junkie?" Gordo jerked the inhaler out of Ethan's hand, tossing it to the ground.

Ethan looked at me. Hope filled his eyes. And then the most curious thing happened; pure disappointment and sadness claimed his face.

Like it or not, cuz, I'm your only hope.

"Know what I think?" Dino walked over and took ahold of Ethan's ear, pulling hard. "I think he needs a taste of what he's missing." Dino shoved his beer can up to Ethan's mouth.

Great! Now what do I do? Finally, something came to me. "Not here. If you're going to teach him a lesson, you ought to do it at the tomb and not where Coach Madsen can find us."

"See, Gordo! We need this dude." Dino punched my arm as he let go of Ethan and headed for the car.

Now Ethan could escape. I just had to find the right moment. Skids was already behind the wheel of his souped-up Honda Civic with mag wheels, racing stripes down the sides, and a big spoiler on the back. Dino rode shotgun. My stupid cousin began to crawl into the backseat. I shoved him to the ground and spat out, "Baby-faces get in last."

Gordo kicked Ethan as he passed and then crawled into the car. Skeleton snickered and followed his idol.

Ethan slowly stood, glaring at me as if I were a traitor. I snatched his inhaler from the ground without anyone noticing and shoved him hard against the fender. Acting as though I was roughing him up, I leaned against him, planted the breathing device in his hand and, at the same time, whispered, "Take off."

He sprinted away. I stepped back and doubled over, pretending he'd punched me. Making a show of chasing him and still clutching my gut, I gave an Oscar-worthy performance of suddenly giving up. Dino jumped out of the car and came over. "You all right?"

Rubbing my stomach, I said, "Yeah."

Dino patted my shoulder. "It's okay. We have more important things to do. Today we start the ritual of initiating you into the gang."

"About that—" I dropped the charade. Now was my chance to break free of these creeps. With Ethan safely gone, I could tell them what I thought. "I've decided not to join."

Dino glared at me. "What?"

"Sorry." I started down the path Ethan had taken.

"Think again!" Dino yelled. "I know that loser was your cousin. Why do you think we singled him out? You don't come with us . . . well, I don't believe he'll keep that innocent face of his too long. He might even lose it all together. The choice is yours."

Gritting my teeth and clenching my fists, I stared at Dino. He grinned. The Primes could and would make Ethan's life miserable. And mine. If I joined, at least I'd be able to protect Ethan. Dino turned and walked away. Not knowing what else to do, I followed him to the car.

Skids drove to Eriksen's Funeral Home and stopped. Dino turned to look at me and said, "Did you know that that old maid librarian, Miss Birdsell, died?"

Poor Miss Birdsell. She'd worked at the school forever. To think that her age-bent body that shuffled books from shelf to shelf would never be in the library again was sad. She'd been nice to me, even though I'd changed. The way Dino said "old maid" made me angry.

He continued, "Old Biddy Birdsell's laid out for her viewing with no one to kiss her good-bye. So that you know I'm the boss and to kick off the beginning of your initiation, you're going in to plant one on her stone-cold lips."

Kiss a dead person. My stomach roiled. I stared at Eriksen's Funeral Home. The thought of stepping across the threshold of that place made my skin crawl. The building's aging stucco and gothic windows made me think of Edgar Allen Poe. At any moment, I expected a raven to fly by, bats to swarm above the roof, and lightning to appear in the sky. I read too much.

I stole a glance at Gordo. A sly smile creased his hockey-mask-like face. He was enjoying my discomfort. My palms became sweaty, my mouth turned dust-dry. A quivering started deep in my gut and was fast moving to my arms and legs. A multitude of ghostly fears grabbed for me. I dodged them, knowing I had to keep things in perspective. After all, this was no big deal. Wiping my sweaty palms on my pant legs, I opened the car door and crawled out.

Gordo followed. "Someone needs to see you actually do it." He folded his arms as if he were my master.

Great. I glanced at the other Primes. Dino and Skids appeared comfortable, sitting in the front seat of the Civic. Pirate waved from the back, and I knew he was glad I was the one chosen for this fun. At least the entire gang wasn't coming with us.

I took a deep breath. A whiff of lilacs in the air signaled the last of spring and beginning of summer. I should be planning what I am going to do during the summer break that would start tomorrow instead of "playing nice" with these creeps to save my cousin's neck.

"Are you coming or not?" Gordo started toward the building.

I walked down the sidewalk and trudged up the steps. Before I could reach the door, it opened. A tall, elderly man said in an overly kind mortician's voice, "Welcome, Tag. It's been a long time. You've changed."

I didn't know why he knew me, but I could play along. "Yeah, well . . . sir, I understand Miss Birdsell, the school's librarian, is here. We'd like to pay our respects."

"Oh yes." He slowly nodded and stepped back so we could enter. A large, sparkling chandelier hung in the entryway. Overstuffed chairs and couches lined the walls. The mortician wrung his hands together, giving Gordo a good once-over as though trying to guess his coffin size. He finally said, "She's down the hall to your right, in the mourning comfort room."

I muttered a thank you and started down the plush carpeted hallway with Gordo by my side. The walls closed in. The scent of funeral flowers turned my stomach. I had a strange, déjà vu feeling.

Stepping inside the mourning comfort room, I stopped short. There it was—the casket.

Miss Birdsell was in there, quietly waiting. A nervous quaking started deep inside me. I took a quick breath as I stepped forward.

My legs were rubbery gelatin, yet I kept my focus on the coffin. All at once, the single casket blurred and became two. The room turned into the tilt-a-whirl ride at the amusement park. Nausea boiled in my stomach, tightening my throat. I couldn't take it. Surreal images swarmed me like bats frantic to escape. I held my arms in front of my face, blocking them out. Spinning around, I ran into Gordo.

"Hey!" he yelled.

I didn't stop, determined to get away before I made a fool of myself. As I burst out the back door of the funeral home, I could hear Gordo cackle. "There goes Quivering Quincy, the spineless wonder."

His words didn't stop me.

I ran . . . and ran . . . and ran.

After a while, when I was sure I was safely away from the Primes, I slowed down. Bending over, I took a few deep breaths. The nausea had left. Perspiration trickled down the sides of my face. I wiped my brow and took a cleansing breath. That was too close. Out of nowhere the thought came, *What would Doctor Bradford think of my running away?*

I didn't care. And I certainly wasn't going to tell him. Yet, a small part of me wanted to. *Stupid, confusing thoughts!* I looked around and found I was near the school.

Oh, snap! I couldn't run somewhere else? Kicking a rock, I figured I might as well go in. I'd already missed so much the principal was bound to call Mom unless I attended a few classes. I didn't need her nagging me again.

I'd planned to sneak in through the gym. Walking up the concrete steps, I pushed on the bar that opened the door. Standing before me was Principal Kinghorn—a beady-eyed, bald-headed man who seemed to have a sixth sense when it came to trouble and me.

Before I could back up and put distance between us, he placed his arm around my shoulders and ushered me inside. "Mr. Quincy, are you having a good day?"

I knew that was a trick question, so I didn't answer. I just looked at the stern-faced man who held my fate in his giant bowling-ball sized hands.

"No answer?" He waited.

I kept my mouth shut.

"I understand you were smoking and drinking on school property."

"What?" How in the world did he come up with that one? I'd never smoke and drink living with *my* mother, the nurse, who described in graphic detail lung and liver diseases. Someone had sold a bill of goods to Kinghorn. And that someone must have seen me with the Primes earlier and assumed I was one of them. I replied, "Sir, I can honestly tell you it wasn't me. I don't do that, sir."

"An eyewitness says you did." He guided me down the hallway.

My bacon was fried, drained, and crumbled. Someone had seen me. Coach Madsen? But I didn't think he was the type to rat on a student. Madsen would have dealt with me himself.

The blare of the buzzer signaling the period end vibrated up and down the halls. Swarms of kids left their classrooms. They gawked and stared. Of course, they weren't surprised Tag Quincy was headed to the principal's office. But the fact that the man whose job it was to make me miserable had his arm around my shoulders was humiliating.

Nearing Kinghorn's office, I peered through the large windows which allowed the "ruler" to see everything inside and outside of the school. He must have seen me walking up to the gym. Coach wasn't in there, but someone was. Another student? He wasn't facing me, and I wondered if one of the Primes had turned me in.

Gordo! He hated me as much as I detested him. As Kinghorn opened the door to his office, I saw the person wasn't Gordo. For a wild millisecond, I again thought my brother stood there, and then I realized who the person was.

Ethan! Backstabbing, bootlicking, double-crossing Ethan. And sitting beside him, still dressed in her scrubs with bloodstains from the ER, was my mother.

2

Backstabber

Sabirah

WE TRAVELED MOST OF THE DAY. With Kei's reluctant help, my men located Princess Jamila and her entourage camped outside Tlalocan, a small Lamanite settlement. My first instinct was to attack, using the shadows of twilight to our advantage. Such bold actions would startle Jamila's men, and we could take them without bloodshed. Yet, the Spirit whispered for me to wait. My mother had taught me long ago to listen to that still, small voice from within.

One of the best life experiences that taught me this was when I was a curious six-year-old and I'd noticed a nest of baby hawks on the branch of a needle tree. I watched as each one courageously leaped from the nest and flew away. I wondered if I could fly. As I climbed a large, craggy rock to use as my perch, a voice from within told me not to jump. I didn't listen. Instead, I bravely spread my arms like hawk wings and leaped, crashing to the ground below. I tore the skin on my knee, bloodied my nose, and bruised my young pride. As I explained to my mother what had happened, I told her of the warning voice. She smiled and said the Great Spirit often spoke to us from within. Our job was to listen. From that moment on, I'd learned to follow the promptings even when I didn't understand them.

So instead of attacking Princess Jamila's camp, I had my men rest a short distance away while I stood watch. At dawn, we'd take action.

After many hours, Gian, a young man in my army, came to relieve me. I liked him because even during hard times, he'd find a reason to smile. In the darkness, I saw his toothy grin. Then he asked, "Has there been change?"

I shook my head.

"Forgive me for asking." Gian nervously bit his bottom lip; his smile disappeared. He said, "Some of the men are concerned that the longer we wait to capture her, the more difficult it will be." His face turned uncharacteristically serious.

"Yes, I know." I patted his shoulder. How could I tell him I wasn't sure what we should do, that I had doubts of my own? He stood there staring at me with faith and confidence in my ability to lead, despite my youth and gender. His belief in me, as well as the other men's, was due to their loyalty to my father.

Stay strong as the ocean wind. My father's words rushed to my mind. Praying that the Spirit would help me say the words that would calm Gian's worries, I said, "By dawn we shall have our answer."

His smile returned as he nodded.

Grateful, I left him. As I drew nearer the others, I couldn't help but wonder why I believed the answer would come when the sun broke on a new day. But a warmth spread through my body, as comforting as a llama-hide blanket, and I knew all would be well.

The wayfarer would arrive on the morrow.

જી

Tag

MY MOTHER NEARLY RUPTURED A gut, she was so mad at me for pulling such a stunt on the last day of school. I was sentenced to spend the summer with Grandpa Quincy at Palisades Lake. She lectured about how bad cigarettes and beer were for the body. Even though I swore I didn't use them, it didn't stop her rant.

As I watched my mother expounding upon my health, the old, haunting hurt recaptured her face. I hated it when she got this way. Seeing that pained glint in her eyes melted away my pledge to keep Ethan safe from the Primes. Ethan was going to pay for putting my mother through needless worry. His real danger was now me. When I finished with him, even the Primes would pity the guy.

All too soon, Mom was taking me to Grandpa's. Her SUV pulled onto the long dirt road leading up to his mountaintop cabin. Shadows of tall, stately pines flickered over our vehicle, reminding me strangely of fleeing blackbirds. A creepy feeling skittered over my skin, the same one I'd felt standing in the mourning comfort room staring at Miss Birdsell's casket. Impending doom waited for me at the end of this road. If I looked closely, I was certain I'd see the eye of Sauron from *Lord of the Rings* glaring down, condemning me.

Mom's car chugged, climbing up the last curve, and finally we turned onto the grassy driveway leading to the cabin.

Kicking open the screen door, Grandpa stepped out on the dilapidated deck. Waving to us, he shouted, "You made it!" He wore his old fishing cap strewn with dangling lures and hooks. Under his bib overalls, he wore a plaid flannel shirt. One cuff of his pants was crammed into one of his worn cowboy boots. Grandpa had forgotten his teeth again, and when he smiled, he looked like Jed Clampett, a character from an old TV sitcom.

Great, just great. Welcome to the Beverly Hillbillies. *Y'all come back now, ya hear?*

By the time I crawled out, Grandpa had reached the car. He hadn't seen my transition from the freckled, redheaded idiot to what I was now. His eyes trailed from my too-black hair, to my makeup, to my collar, and then to my clothes and nails. He cleared his throat and muttered something. He was probably talking to Grandma, a habit he'd taken up since her death.

"You haven't seen Tag for quite a while, have you, Grandpa?" Mom got out of the SUV and grabbed my duffel bag.

"Can't say I've missed much." Sarcasm coated his words. Again, Grandpa's eyes did a probing assessment of me.

"Well—" Mom walked up to him, dropped my duffel, and gave him a hug, "—the packaging may have changed, but he's still our Tag inside."

I rolled my eyes and looked at the cabin Mom had sentenced me to stay in. The logs looked freshly painted. Yet, the deck was old and sagging in spots.

Grandpa seemed to read my mind. "Tag, thought you could help me replace the deck this summer. I could sure use someone with your muscles." Grandpa had decided I wasn't so bad and gave me a nudge with his elbow. I guess that was all the welcoming hug the new me deserved. "I also thought we could use some help." He yelled to someone in the cabin, "Come out here and join us!"

Out stepped Ethan.

⌘

Ethan stared at me. I glared back. I didn't think my life could get worse. Of all the dirty, rotten tricks Mom had played on me, condemning me to a summer with Ethan was the lowest. I tore my gaze from Ethan to look at Mom.

She smiled and said, "Your Aunt Crystal and I thought you two needed to spend more time together and become better acquainted. After all, you are cousins."

Mom thought entirely too much. I grabbed my duffel and stomped into the cabin, escaping their gawking and condemning stares. When we had been in the principal's office, I should have told her what had really happened between Ethan and the Primes. I should have told her how I saved my cousin, the kid she said I didn't know very well. And I should have told her Ethan lied about me.

I couldn't back then when she'd stared at me with that haunting-hurt look in her eyes . . . and I couldn't now, either. I don't know why. Maybe it was because she should know I would never smoke cigs or drink beer. She should know me better than that.

She should know me like she knew . . . Tyler and Dad.

But she didn't.

I dropped my bag next to Grandma's old Naugahyde rocker, which had been repaired many times with Grandpa's miracle cure: duct tape. The blue afghan she'd made years ago was draped over the back. The rocker looked as if it were waiting for Grandma to sit down.

Glancing around the room, I realized I'd forgotten so much about this place: the dilapidated hutch Grandpa built for Grandma's chipped pieces of china, a neglected bamboo fishing pole, the "Welcome to the Lake" sign with a carving of a moose and fish nailed to a log wall, and Dad's oil paintings. They hung on almost every wall: some of the lake, some of Grandma and Grandpa, some of Dad and Aunt Crystal, and some of Tyler and me.

The one Grandma loved the most hung by the Franklin stove. The scene was of Jesus appearing in the land Bountiful after His crucifixion in Jerusalem. Dad served a mission in Mesoamerica when he was nineteen. He believed that part of the world where he'd served—down by the Yucatan—was where the land Bountiful was and where Christ appeared in America.

Grandma had hung the painting by the fireplace long before she had died. She believed people were more reflective when watching a fire burn, and if they looked up and saw Jesus, He might warm their hearts. She loved the Book of Mormon and at every opportunity would tell me stories from it. Maybe it was her scratchy voice or the way her eyes lit up at the most exciting parts, but Grandma could really make those stories come to life.

I walked over to the Franklin stove and stared up at the picture, gazing at Jesus' face. Dad had an amazing talent. He'd often told me an artist expresses inner feelings about himself through his art. Dad truly cared about this piece because he'd captured an expression on Christ's face that I couldn't quite define. Love, caring, forgiveness? I wasn't sure.

As I gazed at the details, I realized the coppery-colored eyes, rich with dark flecks of amber, gave strength to the piece. Their shape and color made me feel as if Christ were gazing into my soul. My stomach churned. I felt unworthy to even look into those eyes.

How ridiculous! Over the last couple of years, I decided I didn't know what to think about religion. If the Savior watched over everyone, why was there pain and suffering in the world? Why did He let Dad and Tyler leave us? Religion just didn't make sense to me anymore.

The screen door opened, and I stepped as far away from the picture as I could. Everyone filed in.

"Thought I'd fix some lunch before I leave. How does everyone feel about BLTs?" Mom said, heading for the kitchen. I grabbed my duffel and escaped upstairs until Mom called me down to lunch.

After we ate, Mom gave me a hug, told me to mind my manners, and scurried back to Idaho Falls as if she couldn't wait to be rid of me. I was stuck in purgatory with Grandpa, Grandma's ghost, and worst of all: bootlicking, bottom-dwelling Ethan.

No sooner had Mom left than Grandpa declared he needed to take his afternoon siesta, which left me alone with my cousin. Now I could start my revenge on the creep.

He put on a good act of ignoring me, playing a golf game on his laptop. Every once in a while he'd nervously steal a quick glance my way. Guilt flushed his face. I walked up close behind him, leaned over him, and said, "You owe me, and before this summer's over, you'll pay."

"Oh, I'm scared," Ethan countered, barely taking his eyes off the screen.

"You should be. I saved your butt when the Primes had you cornered." I was warming up for a good knock-down-drag-out.

"I wouldn't say I was cornered." He kept playing his game.

"I should have let Gordo have at you."

"Which one was he?" Ethan turned from his game. Why was he suddenly giving me his full attention? And then I knew. He was pumping me for their real names, not their monikers.

"Fat chance I'm telling you. Here's the deal. I saved you, and you thanked me by lying to the principal and telling him I was smoking and drinking on school property." I couldn't wait to hear his explanation.

"I didn't lie! You were with them; therefore, you are guilty by association. Besides, I did it for your own good."

What a self-righteous creep! At that moment, Ethan deserved to have his face smashed into his computer screen. I reached to take hold of his head but stopped, teetering on the edge of doing something I'd regret. No, this was what he wanted, what he hoped I'd do. Grandpa would side with him. I wasn't falling for it. "Watch yourself, cuz. A lot of things can happen in the time we're stuck here. You'd best sleep with one eye open."

"Oh, now I'm really terrified." He made a good show of pretending to shiver with fear.

We'll just see who gets the last word on this deal. Nobody, not even my cousin, could get away with making fun of my threats, even though I did wonder what I would do to the jerk.

I had to get away from him before I did some real damage, so I left the cabin, letting the screen door slam behind me. I walked out onto the rickety deck where we'd had many parties in happier days.

Dandelions and thistles grew up through the spaces between the deck boards. The picnic table was in its usual spot, but the tabletop was warped and sunstained. The barbeque grill looked like squirrels had set up a nice house inside. Before Dad went away, we used to come to the cabin several times a year. Summer was when we had the most fun.

Dad and Grandpa'd barbeque, which meant they'd stand by the grill and talk about politics, cars, and sports. Mom and Grandma would set an elaborate table with wildflowers for the centerpiece. They'd make potato salad, Jell-O (the green kind), and baked beans. Grandpa was in charge of assigning everyone a turn at cranking the ice-cream machine. He refused to buy an electric one, said it brought families together to put muscle into their dessert. Tyler and I always fought over who'd lick the beater. Thinking about it, I guess we'd actually had the dream family.

But then everything had changed.

One summer night, Grandma unexpectedly died. Grandpa said she was sitting on the couch talking about what she was going to fix for supper, and then she slumped back, peaceful like. He said she looked as though she'd up and decided to take a nap. Grandma hadn't been sick a day in her life. She was always fussing over everyone else, making sure they were comfortable and happy.

A couple of years later, Dad and Tyler left. We haven't heard from them since. They were just gone, and I couldn't remember why, which was embarrassing. They could have at least called or something. That's when I realized I must have done something to make Dad mad at me, or maybe he thought I wasn't good enough to be his son. It was my fault they were gone; Dad didn't want me anymore, so he just left and took the son he loved with him. He left me behind. So why would he call me?

I remember Mom cried a lot after they were gone, and I didn't want to make her cry more by bringing them up and asking stupid questions that I should know the answers to. She had enough on her plate. Shortly after they left, Mom asked to be put on the night shift in the ER so she could be home with me before I went to school and when I came home. She felt that was important. Except, she was never really home, even when she was there.

That first year, every time she looked my way, I saw blame in her eyes. I tried to be the best kid ever: cleaning the house, washing dishes, doing my own laundry. But it didn't seem to matter. She never smiled, never seemed to care if I was there or not. She'd spend hours gazing at the family photo album.

I started having problems concentrating in school, and that's when my math teacher, Miss Gouch, suggested I go to a therapist.

Enter Doctor Bradford. He made Mom smile again. And I felt worse than ever. Why couldn't she smile when it was just me? There was something serious going on between Doctor Bradford and Mom, and I just couldn't stand it. Mom belonged with Dad. Dad and Tyler belonged at home with us.

The squirrel in the barbeque grill started chattering. I yelled back, "Hey, look, buddy, you're the one trespassing."

I trudged up the hill, stepping around haw and dogwood bushes. The ground was covered with wild strawberries. Farther up was where Grandpa put the salt lick for the deer and Bruce, the moose.

Grandpa had given the moose a name because the animal came around every year as regular as spring rain. Every day in the summer Grandpa filled the water bucket for this awesome "critter." He was a big thing, an animal you'd see on the Discovery Channel. And many times, the beast would walk right up to the deck as if to say, "Thanks, Grandpa," and then he'd lumber around the cabin like he was a watchdog or something. Right now Bruce wasn't at the salt lick, but I could see the grass trampled flat where he'd been.

Taking in the scenery down the hill, I realized I'd missed this place that was filled with aspen trees, pines, and a view of Palisades Lake.

Yep. There it was . . . the lake.

The sun's rays shimmered on the water like a spotlight hitting a chandelier. I felt a stab in my gut and took a deep breath. Grabbing Dad's sketchpad and pencil from my pocket, I quickly drew the scene. But something was missing. Frustrated, I flipped the page and started again.

I heard the screen door slam, and Grandpa bellow my name. Glad to be taken from my frustration, I slipped the sketchpad and pencil into my pocket and hustled down the hill.

As I walked near, I heard Grandpa talking to Grandma. "I know the boy needs help, Teddy."

Grandma's name was Edna, but Grandpa called her Teddy. He spied me. "Tag, we need to go to town and pick up lumber for the deck. I've laid out some clothes for you in the loft. Hurry on in and change. Wash your face while you're at it." He tossed a sunflower seed in his mouth. He kept a supply in the front pocket of his bib overalls. Obviously, he'd found his teeth.

"I'm fine the way I am."

"Nope. Grandma says you need to change. What?" He paused a moment as if receiving instructions and then continued, "Oh, and lose the dog collar."

"Huh?"

"You want to argue with your grandmother, be my guest. I'll wait." Grandpa folded his arms.

Argue with Grandma? Sure. I looked at the old guy, trying to see if he really knew what he was saying. He winked at me and popped another seed into his mouth. "Hurry up." Grandpa cleared his throat and yelled, "Ethan!" Grandpa turned his attention back to me. "He'll help me figure out how much lumber we'll need while you get yourself ready."

"Yeah?" Ethan walked out of the cabin, rubbing his computer-dazed eyes.

"Need your help while Tag changes. Grab some paper and a pencil." Boot Licker disappeared inside the cabin. Grandpa walked down the steps and started inspecting the deck. Ethan reappeared. I growled as he passed. He yipped, "Don't touch my laptop."

On my way to the loft, I unplugged his computer and chuckled because I hadn't touched his precious computer, only the cord. This summer might be more fun than I'd thought. As soon as I stepped into the loft, I realized how wrong I was. On my bed, Grandpa had laid out one of his flannel shirts and some bib overalls.

The shirt was at least in dark blues and black, so I'd wear that, but no way was I putting on those overalls. And I wasn't going to wash my face, either. I had to get away. At least Mom let me be myself. Here . . . Grandpa was trying to change me into someone

I wasn't, Ethan was waiting to squeal on me, and I just didn't fit in here. I didn't fit in anywhere! If I remembered right, the grocery store in Alpine had a bus schedule. While in town getting the lumber, I'd somehow find a way to check out when the next bus would arrive.

Tomorrow I'd be long gone.

3
Searching for Answers

Sabirah

As I made my way through the dark jungle to my small army, thoughts of my father came to my mind. He'd taught me how to track in the night using fronds and fauna as a guide. Some of my most cherished memories were of walking with him in jungles thick with vines, though those moments were few.

During most of my childhood, he was away preaching in other lands. And when he was home, he seemed as restless as a jaguar. My mother told me that he was eager to do the Lord's work because before the happy day when the resurrected Christ would appear, there would be much sorrow and destruction. My father's calling was to warn the people and inspire them to repent.

He had even gone to the Nephites in Zarahemla, under the Lord's direction, and explained what was about to take place. They tried to kill him with stones, spears, and arrows. But the Lord protected my father. After narrowly escaping with his life, Father never preached to the Nephites again. He said he was devoting his time to our people, the Lamanites.

Our people. I hated the sting of jealousy that bit my heart and wondered why they needed him more than his family did. I shouldn't question. I should dwell on the times when he was home. After our evening meals he would take a walk. I was always afraid he was leaving again, so I'd often tail him like a desperate red-faced monkey. My father always knew I was there and, after a while, would call me to walk beside him. I felt highly honored to have that privilege.

I remember the last walk we shared when he warned me of hard times to come. He wanted me to always take care of my mother, for he loved her and sorrowed for the time he had to be away. He also told me how much he loved me and my brother. As he spoke, I realized he was unsure if he'd return from his next journey. Oh, how I wanted to beg him to stay, but I knew he wouldn't. He was called by our Father in Heaven to warn His people. And I knew my father would always obey the Lord.

Now as my men saw me approaching our makeshift camp, they came to greet me, anxious to hear what I wanted them to do next. Portly Sahan, who cooked and cared for us, spoke first; his gruff voice softened as he said, "I dared not start a cooking fire." He handed me a guava.

I nodded thank you as I took it, though I wasn't hungry.

"What should we do?" Strong and solid, Mahir stood ready to do whatever I asked. His eyes took in my every move, patiently waiting. Mahir was often by my side, silently watching me, there to help when I faltered and there to strengthen my sometimes fading courage. Mahir was more to me than just a good warrior. I could easily grow to love him. And why not? He had charcoal-black hair, eyes dark brown as the meat of black zapotes, and a heart the size of the great condor. What woman would not want such a good-looking and compassionate man by her side? But what I needed from him was respect. I couldn't hesitate and give in to emotional weaknesses. He stood ready to do what I asked.

"We shall wait," I said, trying my best not to show my misgivings, least of all to him. "Get some rest. On the morrow we will need our strength."

Turning about, I left Mahir with the others as I prayed I was right to not take him into my confidence but to trust that inner voice I had learned to obey.

✲

Tag

AS WE RODE INTO ALPINE, I saw the town had grown since my last visit: a new community center, a beauty salon, even a car wash. Grandpa pulled up to the hardware store. He planned to buy the deck lumber here. As we started into the building, I saw some grocery items on his list.

"Hey, Grandpa, I can go to the market while you and Ethan take care of things here. That way maybe we can stop at the Blue Max's for milk shakes. I saw a sign that said they have huckleberries." A huckleberry shake was Grandpa's favorite.

"Huckleberries aren't in season yet," Grandpa said under his breath, as if thinking to himself.

"They're probably frozen," said Ethan. Of course, he had all the answers.

"Well, a frozen huckleberry is better than no huckleberry." Grandpa winked at me.

Ethan gave me a look of skepticism, but Grandpa seemed happy with the idea. "Don't forget eggs and bacon. They're not on the list. Oh, and if you see a brownie mix, grab one of those, too." Chocolate was also one of Grandpa's favorite desserts, second only to huckleberries. I nodded and took off.

The market's parking lot was full of out-of-state cars: Utah, Colorado, and California. The place was surprisingly busy for the middle of the week, but with the arrival of summer, I knew many people came to the lake for vacation. I quickly grabbed the items we needed and checked out.

I had two very large bags and a gallon of milk in my arms. Near the door I saw the American Tour Bus schedule. With the grocery sacks secure in my arms and the milk tightly gripped in my right hand, I studied the different routes and times. A bus would stop at the market around eight in the morning.

"Do I see travel in your future?" asked a deep, melodic voice from behind.

I turned and came face to chest with a tall man who was probably in his late thirties. He wore a Stingers baseball cap, Wrangler jeans, and a sweatshirt. His eyes were the most unusual blue, like aquamarine. He smiled and a dimple pierced his right cheek. Why would this complete stranger speak to me—a mere kid who wore a plaid flannel shirt, black eye make-up, and nail polish?

"Maybe. Why?" The grocery bags in my right arm began to shift. I didn't know if I could hold the milk and the bag much longer.

"Curious, I guess. Here, let me help." He grabbed the bag before it fell to the ground. "Not from around here, are you?"

I shook my head.

"Didn't think so." He headed out the exit. "Let me help you to your car."

I reluctantly followed, wondering why he wanted to help me. Something wasn't right.

He stopped. "Where's your car?"

I nodded at Grandpa's truck across the street.

"Oh, you're with Quincy. You must be his grandson." He held out his free hand to shake mine. "Name's John Doe."

"John Doe? Yeah, right." How dumb did I look? I ignored his hand.

He gave up on the handshake. By now we had come to the highway. He studied the traffic flow.

"No one is named John Doe," I told him.

"I get that a lot. Wish someone would have told my parents." He smiled at me and headed across the street. I didn't know why, but despite my misgivings, I kind of liked him. I followed.

John Doe set the groceries in the truck bed and turned to me. "You know, I think you need to give your grandfather a chance before you hitch a ride on a bus to who-knows-where."

"Huh?" How did he know what I was thinking?

"Come on. No kid studies the bus schedule as intently as you were without thinking of taking one." He casually slung his thumbs in his belt loops as though he always gave free advice to strangers without asking. He looked at me, waiting for my answer.

"Why do you care?" My good feelings toward him turned to mistrust.

"A lot of people care about you, Tag."

I hadn't told him my name. But before I could say anything, I heard the forklift coming from around the building. Grandpa and Ethan led the way. They had an entire bundle of lumber, enough to build a deck clear around the cabin. All that wood was going to keep those two busy, since I had no intention of sticking around. I turned back to John Doe to ask him how he knew my name and what business it was to him what I did.

He was gone.

I quickly spun around. John Doe had totally disappeared. Impossible. Grandpa motioned for me to move the groceries out of the truck bed. I set them inside the cab while the forklift loaded the wood. The old truck jostled and moaned from the weight.

We crammed into the truck's cab, groceries and all, and headed to the Blue Max. I ordered a chocolate cashew shake, Ethan went with strawberry, and Grandpa had the huckleberry special. As we sat doing fish faces sucking on the overburdened straws, I thought I'd ask about the stranger.

"Hey, Grandpa?"

He glanced at me as he quit his war with the straw and grabbed a plastic spoon. "Hey, Tag."

"Do you know a guy named John Doe?"

He chuckled. "Can't say I do. Why?"

"Nothing." I wasn't about to tell them about the stranger who helped me carry groceries to the truck and then disappeared. Because of my recent physical transformation, my credibility was already in question; no need to add more to the heap.

When we finished the shakes, Grandpa started up the old '53 Chevy truck, and we began the journey back to the cabin.

We worked hard on the deck until dusk. Grandpa gave us a dinner of bread and milk with green onions. I really didn't think this could count as a dinner, but it didn't matter because as soon as everyone was asleep I was getting out of here. Alpine was a good ten-mile hike, and I wanted to get there in plenty of time.

"Well, I'm ready to say good night to the stars. Anyone want to come?" Grandpa always made a point of stargazing before turning in, a family tradition. Both Ethan and I followed him out onto the main deck.

A blanket of twinkling stars filled the coal-black night. The moon was a mere sliver, making the Milky Way shine brightly, though I did notice clouds moving in. Each of us stood in silence. I glanced around, forming a plan of how I would sneak out later.

I couldn't use the north door where we'd removed the deck. Took us most of the afternoon once we'd returned from Alpine. Unfortunately, the main exit was right by Grandpa's bedroom door. Might be tricky escaping without waking him but worth trying. I could always say I wanted to stargaze some more.

"Tag, your father had a hard time locating the Little Dipper. I pointed the stars out to him most every time he came up here. Do you know where it is?" Grandpa stood stone still, taking in the majestic scene above.

"The Little Dipper pours into the Big Dipper, right over there." I pointed, remembering what Dad had told me. My father knew where the Little Dipper was, but he loved having his father show him. He said his asking made Grandpa feel important. Now I wished I hadn't answered so quickly.

"Ah, you haven't forgotten. Been so long since you've visited, I wasn't sure if you remembered." He yawned. "Well, boys, Teddy says it's time to turn in." Grandpa blew his nose in his bandana and then stuffed the cloth in his pocket. "Night all."

The old, bent man didn't even double-check to see if we followed. He was really tuckered out. Good. Maybe he wouldn't hear when I made my escape.

༄

As quietly as I could, I unlocked the main door and turned the knob. The door swung open, and I stepped out into the darkness. The wind had picked up since we'd been stargazing. A fading, surreal, silvery glow from the dim moonlight outlined the trees. Pine boughs and quaking aspens tossed in the wind.

I'd never been outside in the forest in the middle of the night by myself. I'd been out a lot in town. That's when I did my artwork with a spray can, but with streetlights and the occasional car it was never this dark. Here, the only lights were the stars, and they were quickly being eaten by heavy clouds. I'd never really noticed how clouds swallowed the stars when a storm was rolling in. I was tempted to draw a sketch, and then I panicked. Where was Dad's sketchpad? I felt my back pocket. Pencil and pad were safely there, as always.

Sneaking off the deck, I flipped on the flashlight and quickly ran down the grassy driveway onto the dirt road leading to the main highway. As I walked, I wondered if Bruce the moose was nocturnal. I hoped not.

But I'd heard skunks were.

I remembered one night long ago when my little brother, Tyler, found a skunk in Grandpa's garbage can. The poor kid was sprayed from top to bottom, and, boy, did he stink. Grandma bathed him in tomato juice, but his clothes had to be buried. After that, Tyler got nervous jitters when the subject of skunks came up.

Creeping down the dirt road, I kept the flashlight beam ahead of me. Every once in a while, I heard a rustling in the bushes near the road and hoped squirrels or mice were about. Not a skunk. And not Bruce the Moose.

The evening air was chilly. Of course, my jacket was deep inside my duffel. I didn't want to take the time to mine it out. I came to a fork in the road and couldn't remember which to take. How stupid! I'd walked this road so many times in the daylight, but not alone and not in the middle of the night. Finally, I made my decision and took the road on the left, and just as I was headed in that direction, I dropped the flashlight, and the beam went out. Grabbing it, I clicked the "on" button. Nothing. I shook the thing, took out the batteries, and put them back in. Still nothing happened.

Great. Using the meager light from the moon, I journeyed forward, tripping on hidden rocks and ruts. I scratched myself pretty good on a dead pine tree, but I still kept going. I readjusted my duffel bag several times, trying to move the bulk of the weight to a different spot.

I'd hiked for what I thought was at least a couple of hours, heard all sorts of rustling and once I could have sworn a snort—a big-animal snort. Possibly Bruce. But I kept walking, nervously peering into the darkness, very aware that at any moment a moose or, much worse, a bear could stumble into my path.

The wind kicked up more seriously, and I felt raindrops. Rain in the mountains could lead to a good soaking. Thunder and lightning could convert you to religion.

No sooner did I have the thought than lightning streaked across the tree line and thunder cracked, echoing off cliffs and shaking the ground.

Scared? Nah.

Terrified? Definitely.

I heard the worst thing you could do in a storm was to stand under a tree. Well, I was pretty much surrounded by trees. So what should a person do in a case like that? I had no answer except to keep moving. Rain soaked me, and though I didn't think it possible, suddenly, the rain felt harder, like pellets being shot from the sky.

Hail.

Man!

I became disoriented while hail bullets pinged off my back and head. I didn't know which way was up or down, where I'd been, or what direction I needed to go.

Then, in the distance I saw a light. A cabin! Must be the one over the mountain from Grandpa's. I didn't know who owned it, but right now, I didn't care. I hoped whoever lived there wouldn't mind if I stayed with them until it quit hailing. Chances were they would know Grandpa and would probably call him, but I didn't care. I quickly raced up the wooden steps, wiped my muddy shoes on the mat, and knocked on the door.

No answer.

I knocked again.

The door creaked open.

Poking my wet, dripping head inside, I saw a fire glowing in the fireplace. "Anyone home?" I asked, stepping farther in.

No answer.

I became brave, went in, and shut the door behind me. The place was pretty bare—a futon couch with sleeping bags and pillows stacked next to it, and a table in the kitchen corner with a couple of chairs. A bathroom door and a bedroom door. Whoever was staying here had probably gone to bed but had forgotten to lock up. But what about the sleeping bags and pillows? Hmm. Well, I wouldn't stay long. Just needed to get warm and wait for the weather to clear. That was all.

Water dripped from me and puddled on the floor. Setting my duffel down and shivering in my shoes, I put my hands up to feel the warmth of the dwindling fire. I stood as close as I could to the fireplace grate. I would have moved the grate and crawled inside if I could. I glanced at the table in the kitchen. Looked like a map of some kind had been left spread out. My stomach growled. I was tempted to look for something to eat, but that would definitely be overreaching my welcome.

All at once I heard someone at the front door. Frantic, I looked for a place to hide. Too late to do anything, I stayed where I was and braced myself for—I didn't know—screams or yells.

The main light flipped on, and in walked John Doe. As soon as he saw me, a smile split his face. "Tag! I'm glad you're safe. We've been looking for you." Behind him were two other men. They quickly came in. John held an old-fashioned lantern. He blew out the flame and hung it on a peg on the wall near the door. "As soon as we heard you were out in the storm, we went looking."

Grandpa must have called everyone on the mountain. I glanced about looking for a phone. Didn't see one, but that didn't mean anything. They could have their cell phones in their pockets. Except I thought cell phones didn't work on the mountain.

They had obviously heard I'd run away, and now, here I was in their cabin. They hung up their jackets. The two men I didn't know went to the table and sat down. Their heads were bent as they studied the map. The one with short, curly blond hair glanced at me. Freckles dotted his fair complexion; his kind eyes were welcoming. The other one had a crew cut. His facial features were sharply defined by a large nose and calculating eyes that were wary . . . wary of me. I waited for John to turn around and say something.

He nodded toward the bedroom. "I'll see if I can find something dry for you to wear."

Awkward silence hung in the air.

I decided to introduce myself to the other men. "I'm Tag."

"They know who you are," John said from the open doorway of the bedroom.

The blond guy smiled. "Don't mind him. He gets a little grumpy when one of his charges does something stupid like wander out in the dead of night during a storm. My name is Steve Smith."

The one with the crew cut nodded and said, "Bob Jones."

My mind caught on "one of his charges," but it didn't make sense, so I dropped it. I nodded back to the men. Holding my hands in front of the heat, I asked, "You guys own this place?"

Steve shook his head. "Borrowing it. We don't stay in one place for very long."

"So are you three buddies on a vacation or business trip?" I was more than a little curious.

Bob answered this time. "You could say traveling is our business."

I noticed they studied the map on the table. "What do you do, other than help lost people in the middle of the night?"

John Doe came back and handed me an old poncho. "This should keep you warm until your clothes are dry." He moved a chair close to the fire.

I turned my back to them. For some reason, I didn't want them to see the henna skull-and-spider-legs tattoo I'd put on a few days ago. I'd been careful in the shower, not scrubbing it. Quickly peeling off my wet clothes, I left on my Fruit of the Looms. Dad's sketchpad and pencil dropped to the floor. Scooping them up, I could see many of the pages were wet: the sketch of Dad's dog, the one of Grandma crocheting, and the one of Mom. But the most damage was to the lake scene I'd sketched earlier. I set the pad next to the fire where the pages could dry and slipped on the poncho. It hung past my knees. The material was scratchy but warm. There was a pocket on the front.

Moving closer to the fire, I slipped on the wet floor but didn't fall. John draped my clothes over chair backs and handed me some sandals. "These might keep you from falling until your shoes dry."

The thin leather straps were worn. No buckles or Velcro. The straps needed to be tied to keep them on. After securing the sandals, I straightened. "I look like I stepped out of the Bible or something."

"Except for the dog collar," John Doe pointed out. "And the make-up and nail polish."

"No, remember the Gadiantons? Some of them wore make-up." Steve Smith smiled at his friend.

"Oh yeah." John Doe nodded. So did Bob Jones.

I felt like I'd missed an important part of the conversation. Gadiantons? The only time I remembered hearing that word was when Grandma told me of the Gadianton robbers in the Book of Mormon. I shrugged. All three men smiled at one another but said nothing.

John filled a teapot with water and set it on the stove. "Thought I'd make you some cocoa. Like cocoa?"

"Sounds great," I said sitting at the table.

"Tag." John turned serious, folding his arms and leaning against the counter. "Why were you out on a night like this?"

I wasn't explaining anything until I had some answers myself. "How do you know my name? We met today at the market, and I know I didn't tell you."

"Long story." John dragged a chair over to sit near me. "But believe me when I say I know all about you."

"All?" I said. Gooseflesh rose on my arms. This guy was creeping me out.

He nodded.

"You can't know all." I laughed nervously.

"I know you've been struggling. After tonight, though, I think you'll find answers."

Now I knew the man was delusional. I glanced at the other two. They smiled as if they were in on some kind of secret. These men were up to something. I'd landed in a far worse situation than at my grandpa's.

4
Would-be Hero

Sabirah

I AWAKENED MY MEN JUST before dawn. I had made up my mind. Whether the wayfarer appeared today or not, we were going to capture the princess. I couldn't let this chance slip through my hands. The Spirit hadn't cautioned me away from this idea, so I felt as though this was what I was supposed to do. We needed to be well hidden near the pathway so when the princess and her procession passed, we could take them by surprise.

"Nabi." I called the young boy who was our watcher. "Scale the mother tree." I pointed to the tallest ceiba. "From there, you can see her entourage coming. As soon as you see them, climb down and signal us with your birdcall."

Without question, he set about his task, scurrying up the hill to the tree.

The others took cover throughout the jungle glade. I knew Mahir was behind me because I felt his eyes on my back. I was glad he couldn't see my face; he would have seen the shadow of doubt in my eyes. As we waited in the predawn light, I began to worry that I might be wrong. Had I risked my men's lives on a plan that was doomed to fail? Was I too daring in our preparation, hoping the wayfarer would miraculously appear?

I had to maintain my faith. I had to be strong and unwavering.

He would come!

Of that, I was certain.

ↀ

Tag

I GLARED STRAIGHT AT JOHN Doe, like I did when Gordo tried to intimidate me. If John was trying to scare me, I wasn't going to let him succeed. Plus, how could he possibly know my struggles?

He smiled.

The teapot whistled. He quietly rose from his chair and made my cocoa. As he set it on the table in front of me, I looked at the brew and then back at him. He could have put something in it. Maybe these men were some wacko rednecks scouting for new members to join their cult.

As if reading my mind, John took the mug and sipped. "See, it's all right." He placed it in front of me again.

Taking a sip, I found it wasn't the usual run-of-the-mill cocoa. It tasted as though cinnamon and a hot spice had been added. I didn't usually like spicy stuff, but I drank it slowly as I watched him sit near me. Steve and Bob rose and folded up the maps they had been studying. Steve yawned as he grabbed one of the sleeping bags and started to undo it. Bob stretched as he disappeared into the bedroom. He returned droopy-eyed, but in his arms was a huge stone box. Obscure carving and writings were chiseled on it. He carefully put the heavy load on the table, as if the contents inside were eggs.

"Finished?" John looked at my cup. I drank down the rest of the spicy chocolate liquid and handed him the mug. John rinsed it out, placed it in the sink, and came to stand beside me. He leaned over and looked me straight in the eye. "Tag, it's almost two thirty. You must be tired. The three of us will bunk out here." He nodded at the sleeping bags near the futon. Steve was ready to climb into his. "You can sleep in the bedroom."

Something about the man's aquamarine eyes bothered me. They were kind and caring, but there was something more. I couldn't find the word to describe them. It bugged me that he knew my name and that he supposedly knew all about me. I remembered earlier today he had said he knew my grandfather. But Grandpa said he didn't know anyone named John Doe. Maybe Grandpa forgot. That was possible. After all, he was in his eighties and talked to a ghost every day.

Besides, what did any of this matter? I planned to crawl out the bedroom window as soon as I thought it was safe and would probably never see these three clowns again. The whole night would be a footnote on my history page.

I finally replied, "Thanks. I appreciate everything you've done."

I rose to my feet, nodded good night to Steve and Bob, grabbed my sketchpad and pencil, and went into the bedroom, closing the door. Slipping my stuff in the poncho pocket, I checked the window. The latch at the top was rusted. Trying to pry it open, my hand slipped and just about went through the glass. I quickly glanced at the door. A light shone beneath, but no one was coming.

Trying again and using both hands while bracing my foot against the wall for leverage, I managed to pry the latch open. Glad for the success, I pushed up on the window. It wouldn't budge!

What the . . . ?

It was almost like—my fingers felt the top and found what I suspected—like someone had nailed it shut. Man!

Now I had to wait and sneak past the Three Musketeers in the other room. Might as well lie down on the bed and wait for them to fall asleep. Shouldn't be long. They seemed plenty tired.

A brilliant light framing the door drew my attention. What were those nut-jobs doing? As quietly as I could, I rose from the bed and made my way toward the door.

A board in the floor squeaked. I froze midstep. Did they hear it? As if answering my question, I heard someone walk near the bedroom door and stop. I hardly dared breathe, afraid they might come in. After what seemed an eternity, the person outside the room walked away. I pressed forward.

Cracking the door open a sliver, I pressed my eye to the slit. The light was near blinding at first, but I kept looking and finally saw John, Steve, and Bob standing around the small kitchen table. In Bob's hand was a stone that shot off radiant light, flooding the room with a glow that was as strong as a thousand sparklers. Gazing at it, I was filled with a sense of peace I'd never felt before. I was overcome with a strong need to see the stone up close and hold it in my hands. As I was about to walk out there, the light suddenly faded. The feeling of peace faded, as well. It took my eyes a moment to adjust, but soon I could see that the stone now looked as transparent as glass. *Must be some type of magic stone.*

Bob carefully placed the gem inside a sphere about the size of a soccer ball. The orb was intricately covered in carved golden trees with inlaid jade-stone leaves. Closing the tiny clasp on the ball-like object, Bob placed it inside the stone box and set the heavy lid on top.

The three of them talked a little longer, as if discussing something of highest importance. Then they bowed their heads and folded their arms while John said a prayer. I couldn't hear everything he said, but I heard my name a couple of times.

Why were these guys praying for me? What if they were a cult of some kind and were going to sacrifice me or something? I had to get out of here, and the sooner the better. Their prayer ended, and they started for their beds.

I eased the door shut, dove under the covers still wearing my sandals and poncho, and jerked the blankets over me just as the door opened. I faked sleep the best I could. Must have worked; the door shut. Footfalls retreated. Glancing down, I saw the light under the door blink out.

I had to wait a little bit to make sure they were asleep. Lying there, I thought of my mom. She had no idea where I was. Nobody did! No rescue was being planned for me. I was on my own. A deep, quiet gloominess that every once in a while found me in quiet moments settled on my shoulders, except this time fear and panic had hitched a ride. My surviving this ordeal was up to me. Once I got out of here, *if* I got out of here, I was heading for . . . ? Where would I fit in? Not Grandpa's, that was for sure.

My mind turned to the stone. Then, almost beyond my control, I again felt an urgent need to hold it. I couldn't explain why, but I knew I had to have it. I had never stolen anything in my life, but maybe that stone could help me somehow. I had to get my hands on it. The thought of stealing filled me with regret, but, again, that weird yearning to hold it took over, and I pushed the regret aside. I could do it! The words made me feel powerful, like I'd discovered an aspect of the new me I was creating. I had to be careful, though. Taking the time to snatch the gem with those three sleeping in the same room would be dangerous, but I hoped the payoff would be worth the risk.

I slipped out of bed. As I opened the door, the hinges groaned. I stopped instantly and listened. No sounds of movement, which meant I hadn't disturbed anyone. I pushed until there was enough room for me to squeeze through without causing another hinge groan.

Standing in the dark, I tried to remember where everything was situated in the room. The table was close to the kitchen and to my right. The futon was to my left; the sleeping bags on the floor were just beyond.

A green glow from the digital clock on the wall allowed a little light in the room. Enough for me to make out body shapes. The snoring of the three men had increased enough to awaken a grizzly.

I tried to spot the stone box. Impossible! Despite the new feeling of power at the thought of stealing, I felt relieved when I couldn't see the box. I really couldn't waste time looking for it, either. I was finally thinking straight again. I really couldn't figure out why the stone was so important to me a minute ago. I had to find my clothes and duffel. I crept past the kitchen area where earlier John had laid out my stuff, but the chairs he'd draped my clothes over were empty. And where my duffel had been was a stack of wood.

Where had they put my things?

Snap! Now I'd be stuck wearing this weird biblical getup. But I had to get out of here. Deciding to cut my losses and leave, I opened the door. The rain had stopped. The moon's glow crept into the cabin and spotlighted the stone box beneath the futon where one of the men slept.

Should I chance it? Before I realized what I was doing, I crept over and got down on my hands and knees. The marble box was on a rug, so I was able to tug it out without much trouble. I pulled up the bulky lid. As I set it down, the heavy stone slid from my grasp and clunked to the floor.

I froze.

Whoever slept on the futon mumbled something, turned over, and continued snoring. I stole a glance at the other two. No movement. All three innocently slept undisturbed. Maybe they weren't the bad guys I'd dreamed up. If they were truly planning to hurt me, would they just go to sleep? They could be nice, though very stupid, leaving a valuable gem where anyone . . . where *I* could take it. Even if they were harmless, I felt again that I had to take this for me. I'd be an idiot not to take a chance and look out for number one. I had to.

Not wanting to pull out the round object holding the diamond and risk it rolling away from me, I felt for the opening clasp. Fumbling for a moment or two, I finally found it. Ever so carefully, I tilted up the dome lid and quickly snatched the glasslike stone.

Slipping it into the pouch pocket of my poncho where the sketchpad and pencil were, I swiftly placed the lid on the box. With great care, I slid the container back into place under the futon.

I gazed at the three sleeping men. A deep, nervous trembling began inside me. I had to get out of here. Fleeing to the open door, I quietly stepped out, closed it, and tore down the trail leading away from the dilapidated cabin. The ground was slick from hail and rain, and I slipped several times, nearly losing my balance. But falling wouldn't hurt me.

I'd done it!

Me, Tag Quincy, major screwup, had actually stolen.

I stopped.

Taking the magical stone from my pocket, I saw that it almost filled my palm. I wanted it to glow like it had in the cabin. I wanted to feel that peace once again. As I gazed at the stone, I wondered what kind of traveling business Bob, Steve, and John were doing to have come upon something like this. Had to be shady to deal with gems this size. Only billionaires could afford something so valuable, and those three did not look like billionaires. No, they looked like—their kind, caring faces flashed before me—well, they looked like nice guys, who even gave up their bedroom so I could be comfortable and sleep.

My throat was dry.

What had I done?

I had to take the stone back. What was I thinking? Talk about a major screwup! Ashamed, I held the gem tightly in my hand and started up the hill toward the cabin, toward the scene of the crime.

The gem felt warm. My hand tingled as if it'd fallen asleep, which was really weird. I stopped and looked at the stone. The stone was no longer clear; it was white as a cloud. The whiteness within the gem turned so bright I could no longer look directly at it. The radiance grew bigger and bigger like a bubble, and before I knew it, I felt as though I was encircled in an incredible warm brilliance. The tingling in my hand crawled up my arm, through my body, to my legs, toes, head, and hair. Every inch of me was filled with radiance until I thought I couldn't stand it any longer.

And then I blacked out.

℘

MISTY RAIN FELL ON MY FACE. I opened my eyes and found I was lying on the ground. The consuming light was gone, but the magic stone still rested in my hand. I must have passed out from the brilliance of the thing.

Maybe the stone I held wasn't magical but was filled with some type of nuclear fission. Maybe those three "good" guys were really terrorists selling illegal uranium or something. This stone had some type of powerful mojo. I had to return it. I quickly stuck it in my pocket, not wanting to hold it because I was afraid of what it might do.

Through the stillness of predawn, I started up the trail in the direction of the cabin. I noticed the bushes and trees were different. Instead of pines, quaking aspens, and mountain brush, I was surrounded by huge, gnarly trees with long-limbed branches that canopied over the top of me, only allowing splinters of light through. Tentaclelike tree roots burrowed into the ground, crisscrossing in every direction. The brush was no longer mountain ash and chokecherry plants but instead big leafy ferns and giant flowers in the most awesome colors of cadmium orange, cobalt blue, and alizarin red—colors my artist father had taught me. He would have loved to have seen this striking scene.

How strange!

Was I dreaming? Hallucinating? Maybe there had been some kind of drug in that spicy cocoa John had given me, and now I was seeing things. Was I really in a jungle? The air was thick, heavy with the scent of moss, earth, and sweet flowers. This was a tropical rain forest, not the forest that surrounded Grandpa's cabin. I heard the rush of flapping wings and looked up in time to spy a red parrot fly overhead and rest on a tree limb not far away. I caught a glimpse of a strange little rodent scurrying beneath the brush.

I heard someone running down the mountain, crashing through bushes, heading right for me.

The men from the cabin!

They must have awakened and discovered the gem missing and were coming after me to tear me apart with their bare hands. I had to hide. Once they passed, I'd sneak to the cabin and leave the stone.

No harm. No foul.

Dodging behind a huge mahogany-colored tree, I watched as a young Native American boy dressed in a poncho similar to mine and sandals scurried down the trail. He stopped not more than ten feet away, cupped his hands to his mouth, and let out some kind of birdcall. Then the kid quickly hid behind a tree.

Huh?

I scanned the foliage and saw other Native Americans. Old and young men hid behind trees, ferns, and bushes. They were armed with spears and swords.

What was going on?

What drug had they slipped into my cocoa? how long was I going to be seeing things? but if I were under a drug's influence, wouldn't things be distorted? These guys were crystal clear, though I could hardly believe what my eyes were telling me. They weren't like the Indians of the Old West. They looked like . . . well, they looked like the Lamanites I'd seen pictures of at church.

Below, I heard a lot of movement, people talking, and it sounded like horses. Something was coming on a pathway not more than fifty feet down the hill. The noise grew louder, and then I saw them: an entourage of soldiers who wore breastplates and headgear of leather. Some rode on horses and packed swords and shields. They were followed by burly men dressed in diaper-type underwear—decorated with symbols of some sort—and around their ankles were beads and seashells. They wore turbans on their heads, and on their shoulders they carried an elaborately carved wooden litter painted in colors of turquoise and crimson. On top of a canopy rested the large head of an angry dragon. Long peacock feathers made up the body.

Inside the litter sat a woman. From where I hid, I couldn't see her very well. I craned my head for a better view, and at that split second, she looked in my direction. As I ducked down, I caught a glimpse of her.

A major hottie! Her honey-colored hair hung to her waist and shimmered in the sun's morning rays. On her blond head was a feathered crown of deep royal blue and emerald green. She must have been some kind of royalty dressed in a halter-top dress with gold bands on her upper arms.

All at once, a tall Lamanite-type woman stepped beside me.

I gazed up at . . . a warrior goddess!

She looked like a character in the comic book series *Amazon Warrior Woman:* flawless dark complexion; long, shiny, ebony hair hanging freely about her shoulders as if it were black water pouring over her skin; and mesmerizing doelike eyes. A leather tunic clung to her shapely form. Dad had introduced me to the *Warrior Woman* series. Man, he'd love to see her. Hanging around her neck from a leather strap was a small jade carving of a wing-spread eagle. It rested on her chest. I quickly averted my eyes, not wanting her to see me staring at her, and that was when I noticed the white dagger beneath her waistband next to a rock-throwing sling. She carried a spear in one hand and a very long, sharp sword in the other.

She stared down at me with eyes dark as Hershey's chocolate and started to speak. At first I couldn't understand her, and then her words blended into meaning. "My father told me you would come. Follow me."

My father told me you would come? Follow me? She had me confused with somebody else.

All at once, she let out a piercing battle cry and charged. I was so shocked that I stood rooted in my tracks. Stunned, I watched as other men who had been hiding followed her. Some swung from trees like Tarzan to the rescue. Others leaped, agile as deer, to the attack, clearing bushes and rocks. There was no way I was following her into a battle scene. I couldn't figure out where I was, but even in my confusion, I knew I wasn't going to get myself killed in some super-hero-like battle dream.

The battle boiled in earnest. Yet, time crept by in slow motion. I caught snatches here and there: horses rearing up, swords clanking against shields, and men yelling battle cries.

I couldn't take it all in. I'd seen battles in movies, but that didn't compare.

I heard screams and saw blood smeared on their bodies. What kind of nightmare was this?

I quickly looked for the Amazon beauty who had spoken to me. She chased after the hottie who had been in the litter, which was now in pieces on the ground. Two of Hottie's men tried to shield her.

Amazon Warrior Woman leaped up on a rock and then jumped, body slamming the two guards. Regaining their feet, they scurried off like cowardly rats, leaving the two women to duke it out.

I pinched myself a number of times. It all seemed too real to be a dream, but I couldn't figure out what I was doing in the middle of a jungle. That just doesn't happen. But no matter what was going on, I felt like I needed to protect the unarmed Hottie. She looked as pathetic as my cousin, Ethan, when the Primes had cornered him. If I didn't step in, there was a good chance Amazon would tear her apart. If this was just a dream, I figured I could manipulate the outcome and stop a senseless death. And if not, I guess stepping into the face of danger would prove to me that I was in the middle of something way out of my control.

5
The Riddle of the Wayfarer

Sabirah

PRINCESS JAMILA FLED LIKE A peccary seeking cover. I prayed I could capture her before she got away. My father's and brother's lives depended on it. I knew King Jacob had taken them as prisoners, or they would have returned home long ago. Too much time had passed without word from them. And if I were going to get them back, I would need leverage. I would need the king's daughter.

As I ran, I glanced back to be sure the wayfarer was on her trail, too. I felt such a huge relief knowing he'd come, that the prophecy had been fulfilled, and that the wayfarer was going to help in the conquest . . . until I noticed that he stood where I'd found him, as though he were a confused tlacuache awaiting direction. Had I been wrong? Was he not the wayfarer? Was I so hopeful that the help my father had promised was this stranger that I'd made the wrong decision? I'd been wrong before when I agreed with my brother, Asim, that he should go search for our father. Such a huge mistake had touched all of our lives. I longed to take back my words and demand he stay. Wishing didn't take away the hurt, nor right my wrong. Asim was gone.

I quickly glanced over my shoulder at the young man. He fit the description my father had given. And the Holy Spirit had confirmed his identity to me as I spied him behind the majestic tree. It was such a strong impression, one I couldn't have made up on my own. No, I knew in that instant God had intended for me to find him and that he was supposed to help our cause. Clearly, he was a foreigner in every way: black painted eyes, hair, nails, yet his skin was the lily white of a Nephite.

It was frustrating to watch him just stand there, but I didn't have time to solve the riddle of the wayfarer. The princess would be mine with or without his help.

℃

Tag

As I LOOKED AT HOTTIE, I thought of my cousin Ethan and how the Primes had him cornered. Back then, I knew my cousin needed my help. But in this case, I really didn't know who the "good guys" were or who the "bad guys" were. I ran toward the women as if I were some great warrior. As I charged, I realized I had nothing to fight with except my bare hands. Just then I saw a dead branch on the ground, and I grabbed it. Armed, I ran ahead.

Amazon ignored me as I swung the branch in front of her. Stepping past, she grabbed Hottie's arm and wrenched it in back of her. I stopped hollering when I realized Amazon had no intention of killing her but stood there looking at me.

"Are you all right?" the Amazon beauty asked, as if she expected me to say something profound.

"Uhhh," was all I could manage.

"You're a man who speaks few words." She turned to the defeated lady, whose arm she held in a viselike grip. Amazon said, "Forgive me, Princess Jamila. Your father left us little choice."

I finally found what I wanted to say. "Why are you taking her prisoner?"

"I shouldn't have to explain my actions to you. Father said you'd arrive in time to help." Shaking her head as if she couldn't put words to her thoughts, she turned away.

What was she thinking? I knew the entire scene was some whacked-out dream brought on by either a drug in the cocoa or the magic of the stone. What did I care what this beautiful woman—who looked as though she'd stepped from the cover of a superhero comic book—thought? Even though she was one of the most striking women I'd ever seen in my life, I didn't need her. What I needed was for the stone to take me back to the forest near Grandpa's cabin, to some place normal.

Reaching into my pocket to take it out, I gazed around at the wounded. A few of the princess's men lay dead on the ground; those who lived had already run off. Amazon's men had suffered many wounds. One of the older ones held a small boy—the one who had made the birdcall before the battle—in his arms. Tears streamed down the child's face, his arm hanging awkwardly. His small shoulder joint was in front of him. The arm had been dislocated. This had happened to me in a fluke accident during a soccer game. Remembering what Mom had done, I forgot my need for the stone and went to them.

"You're going to be fine," I said and stroked the boy's forehead as I quickly scanned him for other injuries. There were none. Gazing up at the man holding him, I said, "Lay him on the ground."

The man glared a *who-do-you-think-you-are* look at me.

Still holding onto the princess, Amazon said to the man, "Trust him." Without further questions, he carefully laid the moaning boy on the ground. Gently, I took the child's arm and bent it at the elbow, rotating the arm and shoulder inward. The boy gasped.

"Hang on." I glanced up and saw that we were surrounded by all of Amazon's men. Wounds on their arms, legs, and heads didn't stop them from making sure I wasn't harming the boy. I gulped. Then I took ahold of the injured arm lying on the boy's stomach and began slowly rotating the arm and shoulder outward.

The boy cried and tried to pull away, yet I continued making certain the arm was stationary as I turned it. All at once the shoulder popped into place. The boy's cries immediately stopped. Glancing at him, I saw relief in his eyes. I quickly gazed up at the crowd around us. Amazement stared back at me.

Amazon nodded and smiled, as though to say, *Yep, I knew it.* What she'd said before, that her father had foretold of my coming, made me wonder. Without realizing it, had I automatically fulfilled some whacked-out prophecy? Who the heck was Amazon's father anyway? And how did he know someone was coming to help her in this Neverland? I wasn't even sure where I was. Baffled and not knowing what to think, I noticed Amazon's attention had shifted to her other men now.

I could tell immediately that they were a rag-tag bunch who looked to her for guidance. She was very young, maybe only a few years older than me. Since I was sixteen, that might make her eighteen . . . yet older men awaited her words. How odd.

"We will take the princess to Pagog," she said. The men nodded in agreement. I stood there awkwardly wondering where Pagog was and what it looked like. But I hoped I'd never know because as soon as I could, I was going to sneak off, pull the stone from my pocket, and disappear from here. Though I knew I'd have to wait for the right moment.

"During the fight, Kei escaped," said a man who glared at me. "Who is this?" He looked as though he could lift hundred-pound weights with one arm and not break a sweat.

Amazon smiled. "Someone who will help us! Don't concern yourself over Kei. He will meet his fate." She glared at the weightlifter as if to say, *Don't question me further.* The others caught her drift and readied themselves to leave.

As they started walking, the princess's skyblue eyes stared at me, pleading for help. She stirred my conscience. The war between Amazon and her had nothing to do with me. I shrugged my shoulders and gave her a sheepish *I'm-sorry* look. Realizing I would do nothing, she gave in to her captor's demand and moved forward.

Amazon relinquished control of the prisoner to the guy who had asked who I was. With brawny muscles and a broody expression, he looked as though he'd take great pleasure in snapping the princess's neck if she blinked. But he gave the princess's care to an older man with a noble brow and only a slight wound to his arm. Amazon spoke with a couple of the young warriors who were not badly injured. When she finished, they took off running ahead of us. The brawny guy took the lead, followed by the older man and the princess. The rest of the men trailed after them, everyone except Amazon. She turned to me. I remained where I was.

"Are you going to walk the path of your destiny, Wayfarer? Or would you rather become a suckling ceiba planted in the jungle?"

Suckling ceiba? I didn't know for sure, but that sounded like an insult. What did she want me to do, go with her? She stepped nearer, as if to herd me forward. That was enough. "Look, I don't know who you are or who this wayfarer dude is, but I do know it's not me. This is all some big mistake."

She waited for me to move with teeth clenched and patience close to breaking. Then she glared at me with deep disappointment, as if I'd done something wrong. And for some reason, it bothered me. Finally, I thought of a possible way out of this situation.

"I need some alone time." I hopped from one foot to the other as if I had to go. "If you know what I mean." Surely she would understand. Everyone needed to be alone every once in a while.

"I shall wait," she said as a questioning eyebrow rose upward. "Though the princess's men have fled, they may not be far. I've sent two scouts ahead to seek them out, but there is no one at our flank. I'll not risk something happening to you."

Though I'd only known her a short time, I knew Amazon would not turn away and give me privacy. No, she would stand there and watch. I thought of pulling the stone out and escaping right then and there, but what if she stole it from me? She very well could. I mean, the way she'd captured the princess, I knew this woman could cause real damage. And if she took the stone, I'd never get it back. I'd be stuck in this twilight zone. Nah, it would be best to keep the stone under wraps until I had time to myself. I could walk for a while with them. What could it hurt?

"Never mind," I said under my breath.

I planned to trail behind, and when she wasn't looking, I'd sneak off. Wanting to appear polite, I motioned for her to go first. She ignored me and nudged me forward so I would go. Some of her men ahead had stopped, waiting for us to catch up. I gave in.

We walked for a ways in silence. I tried to think of what we could talk about, but what could one say to a woman who could very well tie a guy into a square knot? Many questions circled my mind. Finally, I decided to blurt one out. "If your father told you I was coming, why don't you know my name?"

"My father gave few details of God's revelation. He only told me a young wayfarer would arrive who would save not only me but many others when the time was right."

Glimpses of my helping the young boy came to mind. But I only did it because I knew what to do. Obviously, her dad had a few mental screws that needed to be tightened. Revelations from God! What was that all about? And I'd save his warrior daughter and others? Whoa! Was that a wrong number!

But Amazon appeared quite serious. Her intense glare was downright spooky. I had to move the conversation away from the subject of her father and revelations. Deciding to introduce myself and find out who she was, I said, "My name is Tag Quincy."

A puzzled expression crossed her face.

"You can call me Tag."

She nodded, still wary.

"What's your name?"

She ignored me.

I kept after her. "Come on, you say you knew I was coming, and I know nothing about you other than you could break a brick with your pinky."

A smile tugged at the corners of her mouth. "What is a pinky?"

I showed her my little finger.

She chuckled and said, "I am known as Sabirah."

I held out my hand in a gesture of friendship, like I'd seen Dad do so many times when he would meet strangers. Her eyes became alert as if she thought my movement threatening. Taking my life in my hands, I reached over, grabbed her hand, and shook it. "Sabirah, nice to meet you." She squeezed my hand hard, giving me the message that one wrong move could mean I'd be minus a limb. I quickly released my hold. Reluctantly, she did the same.

Nervous, I blabbered on, "This might sound a little strange and all, but where do you come from?"

"My village was near Zarahemla, but many years ago Giddianhi and his robbers made it impossible for us to stay. And though Giddianhi is dead, we are still at war with the Gadiantons. If given the chance, they would slit our throats as we sleep. When our chief judge was murdered by *her* father—" She pointed to the princess up ahead. "—the self-proclaimed King Jacob, my people moved nearer to the land Bountiful. We call our village Pagog."

I stopped, feeling as though a boulder had dropped on me.

Zarahemla . . . Giddianhi . . . Gadiantons . . . land Bountiful.

Cold, certain knowledge came to me. I was not only in a different land but also a different time—Book of Mormon times. Time travel only happened in the movies, not to major screwup Tag Quincy.

"Tag, are you all right?" Sabirah asked as she stopped and motioned for her followers to wait.

Though she was a good thirty feet away, I felt Princess Jamila's pretty blues on me, as well. Her gaze was cold, no longer pleading for help but full of hatred. I swallowed hard, hoping the growing lump in my throat would disappear, hoping *all* this would disappear.

No such luck.

"I thought I was having a dream or a hallucination," I said, unable to take in what had happened. I stared at the others. They stared back as if I were an alien, *which I was.*

I started walking. They followed.

Sabirah patted my shoulder. "You are awake, my friend."

"Oh no, I'm not!"

"Your coming was foretold."

I stopped, sucking in long drags of air. "By your father, right?"

She nodded.

I continued, "Just who is your father?" I had to know.

"Samuel."

My mind whirred, trying to find data on the name. I remembered Grandma telling me about Samuel the Lamanite, who foretold of Christ's birth and death. Couldn't be the same Samuel, could it? I asked, "Did your father preach to the Nephites of Zarahemla?"

"You know of him?" Hope showed in her gaze. She didn't wait for me to reply. "He spoke to the Zarahemlans over eight and thirty years ago. Before I was born." Pride for her father lit her eyes.

"I thought your father died after his visit there."

Worry and fear clouded her once-happy face. Stopping, she took a firm hold of my upper arm. The others traveled on, not seeing that we no longer kept pace. Once they were farther away, Sabirah and I followed, hanging back as if she didn't want anyone to hear us talking. She asked with great urgency, "My father is dead? How do you know this?"

"No, no, no. I didn't mean to say that." I had to reassure her. "I don't know if he's dead. The Book of Mormon says he was never heard of more among the Nephites. Which doesn't mean he's dead. I mean, obviously he lived after that since you're—how old are you?"

"Ten years and nine," Sabirah said.

"Well, see, your father disappeared from the Nephites five years before Christ was born. And if King Jacob is on the scene, that means . . . well, that was long after." I wished I had listened better to my grandmother's stories. "Your father is probably still alive. I mean, you're here."

"How old are you, Tag?"

Sixteen was on the tip of my tongue, but remembering how she had stated her age, I said, "Ten years and six."

Her eyebrows rose. "You are younger than I thought the wayfarer would be." She closed her eyes as though thinking and then said, "I was also concerned because you're a Nephite . . . and dressed as you are." She gazed at my dog collar and painted fingernails. "You don't fit the image of a wayfarer. Though you healed Nabi, and to hear you speak of Christ, I know that you are."

I had to set her straight. "Okay, maybe I am a wayfarer because it's true I have traveled a ways . . . quite a ways actually, but as for believing in Christ, well—"

"Yes, I know you do. What is the 'book' you spoke of? Is it a scroll?" Sabirah was assuming I believed in Christ, which was no longer true. When Dad and Tyler left, that part of me went with them. Too much had happened; too many questions had gone unanswered. But now as I stood in the jungle speaking to the daughter of Samuel the Lamanite, I realized—I could have been wrong. Sooooo wrong.

Wait a minute! My rethinking was based on this entire scene being real. And though this world had texture—people talking, birds flying, bugs biting—it was still very surreal. I wasn't sure of anything anymore. Should I stop Sabirah's rambling and set her straight? Or should I just play this out? After all, I didn't really know what the heck was going on. And it probably wasn't worth the hassle. Better to just go along and see where this ride ended.

To answer her question, I said, "No, it's not a scroll. The book is a record of your people's history written on gold plates." I didn't want to explain more about the book, so I asked, "When did you last see your dad?"

"Dad? You mean my father?"

"Yes."

The brawny, broody man who had asked Sabirah about me walked toward us with a determined look on his face. As he neared, he said to her, "We need to talk. There is a good place for everyone to rest up ahead."

She nodded to him. "I need to go with Mahir and see to my men. We will talk more later, Tag." And Amazon Warrior Woman— daughter of Samuel the Lamanite—left me.

The man she called Mahir shot me a look that would have made even Gordo think about disappearing. I had the perfect chance to take out the stone and try to return to my own time and reality. But, strangely, I didn't want to. The dirty look from Mahir stirred something within me. Before coming here, I'd been running away from my life with no destination, no purpose. Here it seemed I was needed. I realized I didn't want to go back home, not right now anyway. Nope, I wanted to stay here and talk with Sabirah.

With renewed purpose, I followed her men.

6
Guard It with Your Life

Sabirah

LEAVING THE WAYFARER, I ASKED Mahir, "What's wrong?"

"Who is that jumil bug who healed Nabi and has claimed your attention?" He nodded in Tag's direction. His eyes were full of distrust . . . and jealousy? Jealous of my time spent with the wayfarer? As I thought about the situation, I realized Mahir didn't know of the prophesy.

Father had warned me against telling anyone about the wayfarer until he'd actually arrived. I had kept the secret to my family, sharing it only with my mother, uncle, brother, and grandfather. But now, Tag, the wayfarer, was here. I could tell Mahir and ease his mind. As my second, he should know. Deciding to take him into my confidence, I solemnly said, "He is the wayfarer."

"Wayfarer? What are you talking about?" He quickly studied my face as we walked, only taking his eyes from mine to avoid vines and rocks on the trail.

"Before my father left, he told me the Lord would send a wayfarer to aid me when all seemed lost. He said this wayfarer would be a healer and foreign to my people in every way, yet he would believe in Christ."

Mahir seemed to think for a moment and then asked, "And your father said he would have the white skin of a Nephite?"

I shrugged. "Father didn't describe the wayfarer." By the suspicious look on Mahir's face, I wondered if I had made a mistake by telling him. The men needed to accept Tag, treat him as if he were one of them, not look at him with a wary eye. "Please don't tell the others."

"As always, you have my pledge." Mahir gazed back at Tag, staring at the young man with a doubtful look. "You are certain that he is the one?"

I nodded.

Mahir continued, "He could be a spy of the king's."

"Would a spy of the king's so readily have helped to ease Nabi's pain? He left little doubt that he is a healer," I challenged. Truth was, I'd hoped Mahir would argue with me because that would make me defend my claim and reinforce my decision to follow that still, small voice from within. Debating with Mahir took away any hidden doubts I might have had toward Tag. That was the role of a good second, to question, to reinforce, and then to accept. Yet, in front of our men, we were always of one mind.

I couldn't help but wonder if when my father and brother returned safely home and if I decided to become Mahir's wife as he'd like, would we argue over important matters behind our children's backs only to be of one mind to their faces? For many months, Mahir had wanted me to commit to him, but with my life in turmoil and my father's and brother's lives uncertain, I couldn't. And deep down, I didn't know if I should, for I wasn't like the other women of our village. Mahir stood silently in front of me, waiting for me to say more. I finally said, "He'll help us. Don't be concerned."

I walked away, letting Mahir know I wouldn't discuss the matter further. The decision to believe Tag was the wayfarer was mine and mine alone. And that was how it should be; that's how my father wanted it. A leader had to make decisions, but a leader also had to be right. But oddly, talking with Mahir had not relieved my worries as I'd hoped it would. It had only multiplied them.

Glancing behind at Tag, I wondered how such a white, scrawny young buck could help in my quest. I needed to look past what I could see with my eyes and listen to my heart—listen to the still, small voice telling me my father would never mislead me.

❧

WE CONTINUED THE JOURNEY, AND I left Tag to himself, hoping he would think about his role among my people. I also kept my distance from Mahir. Instead, I walked and talked with my men: wise one, Tzuriel, a man of nearly sixty years and a friend of my father's; Elan, a man who had left his expectant wife at home and remained loyal to our cause; and Gian, my smiling friend who could make me laugh when I needed it most. These were but a few of my faithful followers . . . no, my father's followers. They relied on me to guide them. And guide them I would.

As we came to Sisal Springs, I told my men to take a well-deserved rest. Many drank eagerly of the clear water, gulping from the palms of their hands. I could tell Tag wanted to, but he held back. Perhaps he was not accustomed to our ways. Mining the drinking gourd from Sahan's cooking pack, I offered it to him. Hesitatingly, he accepted, filled the cup, and waited.

"What's wrong now?" I asked.

"Are you sure this is safe?" He gazed into the gourd filled with water. "My mother told me how dangerous the water is south of the border."

"South of what border?" If he came from the north lands, he should know all water to the south was the best for drinking: the sparkling waters of River Sidon and beyond that the Waters of Sebus. Those waters gave Ammon mighty strength, enabling him to smite off his attackers' arms.

For a moment, Tag seemed at a loss for words, and then he said, "Strike that. There's no little beasties in here, right?" He swirled the liquid in the gourd.

Confused by his fighting term and wondering what kind of beast was in his cup, I peered into the hollow gourd expecting to see a bug of some type, but the water was clear. I shook my head and motioned for him to drink. "There is nothing in your water. Drink."

"Of course, you don't know about microbes and diseases that would make you sick." He stared into the water as if to see something hidden from his view. All at once, he drew a deep breath, raised the gourd, and said, "Bottoms up."

Though I knew we needed Tag for what was ahead, I still couldn't help but wonder if he was a little crazy. I wished my father would have been more specific in regard to how Tag would help me. He had a healer's knowledge, of that I was certain. And he believed in Christ, but I wondered how a young man who saw beasts in his clear drinking water would help me when all seemed lost. Perhaps the wayfarer needed to rest from his long journey. Sleep would do everyone some good.

Leaving Tag muttering to himself, I decided to make camp here for the night. We could push on to Pagog in the morning. Mahir was now watching over the princess. I relieved him and asked him to help the men build a fire. Sahan's cooking would refresh us all. We'd gone for several nights with a cold camp.

Finding a sturdy sandalwood tree, I lashed Princess Jamila to the trunk. Several men took off their traveling ponchos and laid them on the ground, claiming their areas for the night. Beneath their ponchos, they wore tunics. Tag didn't remove his, and I wondered if he was self-conscious, realizing he lacked the muscles of those around him. As I thought about his role, I realized the wayfarer didn't need the physical strength of my men. His mission was to aid and heal. Tag watched as Sahan stirred the fire, pulling burning wood near his flat cooking stones. Sahan didn't take to Tag, almost growling at him as he watched. This didn't deter the wayfarer; instead, he appeared fascinated.

Tag pulled out of his poncho a small bundle. It looked like very thin papyrus leaves bound at the top. Flipping through them, he seemed to find one he liked, and then he began to make markings on the papyrus with a writing stick. His hands and fingers worked feverishly as he divided his time between watching Sahan and the work on his lap. How curious was our wayfarer. How strange were his ways. He watched as Sahan mixed ground maize with water. Perhaps Tag had never eaten flat maize cakes and had never seen them made. He'd like Sahan's food because his strong hands could mix the meal like no other. He flattened several cakes and carefully laid them on the cooking stones heated by the fire.

Tag finished using the papyrus and drawing stick and returned them to his pouch. Curious about what he'd been doing, I joined him as he walked about studying the trees. "What are those tools you store in your pouch?" I asked.

He patted it. "You mean, my father's sketchpad and pencil?"

I found this very interesting. "Yes." Perhaps if I knew more of the wayfarer's family I would understand him better. "I told you about my father; now tell me about yours."

"His name is Matthew." Tag became watery eyed with remembrance. "He's an artist. Paints beautiful pictures, but he makes his living drawing a comic strip called *Chump Change*."

I didn't know what a comic strip was, but I didn't want to interrupt him, sensing that Tag needed to talk.

"He came up with the idea for the comic because of my brother, Tyler, and me. When we were kids, we were always getting into trouble. Dad would see the humor of it and put it in his work." Tag grew quiet.

"You miss your father, don't you?" I understood his pain of being separated from those he loved.

He nodded and said no more. Looking up at the ancient trees that surrounded us, he stared at the long growing vines that had attacked the mocou mocou trees and crisscrossed above us.

"Do you have snakes here?" Though he tried to hide it, his voice rose in fear.

"Yes. The jungle is home to many." I couldn't lie. I found it odd that he'd fear a serpent. I'd been taught that man could so easily crush the head of a belly-crawling snake.

"Poisonous?"

I hesitated only a moment, wondering if I should tell him, but he needed to be warned. "Yes, very. The great boa, however, will not kill you with his venom. Still, he can squeeze the life from you. Near my village, I saw the great serpent eat an entire goat."

Too late I realized I shouldn't have said quite so much. Tag's eyes grew wide with alarm as he scanned the area around us.

"Don't be afraid; the boa moves slowly. With the noise of our group, they've left." Though I knew this wasn't completely true, I felt Tag needed some extra assurance.

"Good, 'cause snakes and I don't mix," he said, swatting at a biting gnat. Then another and another.

Realizing Sahan had finished some maize cakes, I decided to take a few to the princess. "My duties call." On my way, I passed Gian, who had a small vessel of soothing salve. I asked him to share with our new friend.

〜

Tag

I HAD BEEN BITTEN BY yet another mosquito. They were everywhere. I'd had a few bites before, but now dusk had fallen and night was coming. The critters were having Thanksgiving off me. Noticing some of the men rubbing ointment on their skin, I realized they weren't getting bitten. A friendly fellow with a toothy grin must have seen me scratching.

He came over and handed me a small gourd with some type of salve in it. I nodded thank you, and he went away. I remembered learning in history class that some pioneers used bear urine on their skin to fight off biting insects. Sniffing the tarlike cream, I decided that whether there was animal urine in this or not, I was using it. I wasn't proud. Rubbing the gooey stuff over my arms, I noticed the mosquitoes, if that's what they were, immediately left.

Grateful, I returned the medicine to the smiling fellow. He took it from me and then left me standing alone. Feeling like a dope because he hadn't included me in his circle of friends, I decided to sit by myself on a large, flat-topped rock near the fire.

I watched Sabirah trying to feed Princess Jamila, who had been tied to a tree. When Sabirah saw me, she motioned to the cook, my cue that dinner was ready. After collecting my food, I kept watching Sabirah and how she took great care, coaxing the princess to eat. The proud woman took a few bites then refused any more. I quickly pulled out Dad's sketchpad again and captured the scene.

I knew Sabirah hadn't eaten yet. She must be starving. When finished with the princess, she laid out a blanket for Jamila to sleep on. The princess glowered with deep resentment. But Sabirah paid her no mind.

Done with the task, Sabirah came my way. I slipped my art pad into my poncho. She sat beside me. The cook immediately brought his leader supper. Great admiration shone in the man's eyes for Sabirah. She thanked him, calling him by name. Sahan. Interesting. I supposed I'd eventually learn all their names, bit by bit. I wondered how Sabirah had earned his respect because from the looks of him, that was not something this man would give away freely.

I held my tongue, though, letting Sabirah eat in silence. The other guys came and ate their fill and then began to bed down while the cook stored away his food supplies. Soon it was just Sabirah and me left sitting next to the dwindling fire.

No moon shone tonight. The heavens were filled with stars in formations I didn't recognize. I remembered Grandpa asking me if I could find the Little Dipper. In this sky, I couldn't even find the Big Dipper. I was definitely in a different hemisphere. Again the question of why was I here came to mind. "Sabirah."

"Yes, my friend?"

"I know your father was a prophet. But tell me more about him." I wanted to learn what I could of the man who had had so much courage . . . and for some reason knew that I'd come here.

"He has never been home much. Our family knows the Lord needs him, and we're fortunate to share a small portion of his time." In the firelight, I saw Sabirah's dark eyes reflecting distant memories. "I have always liked his hands. Words can't leave his mouth without his hands moving, as if his thoughts are attached to them. I really believe if he were bound, he couldn't speak. They are strong hands, though, with long fingers and clean, short nails. When he gave me a father's blessing and placed them on my head, I felt his soul."

I remembered Dad had given me a blessing when I was sick with the flu and running a 104-degree temperature. I didn't remember feeling anything but sick. I tried to imagine Samuel the Lamanite placing his hands on me and feeling his soul, but I couldn't. "When was the last time your father gave you a blessing?"

"Before he left, four years ago. God told him the time was fast approaching when Christ would die. Father had to be about God's business. He told me trouble would come while he was away. And that you'd arrive to help me."

So we were both without fathers. On this Sabirah and I had something in common. Then I remembered she'd said her brother went after her father a year ago and hadn't returned. Sabirah and I were both missing our brothers, as well. How odd that we had these two things in common. As I thought about her father telling her I'd arrive and help her, a strange feeling that what she said was true washed over me.

I didn't want this burden! Why me? "I can't imagine what I can do to help *you*. You're the most capable person I've ever met."

"Though I have abilities you lack, you will fulfill needs that will come. You have already." She glanced over where Nabi lay, smiled, and patted my shoulder.

Gazing into her brown eyes that seemed to reach into my brain and read my thoughts, I realized I liked being around her. I liked having her look at me. And I liked that she thought she needed me.

A question popped into my mind. "Why did you kidnap Princess Jamila?" I glanced over at the sleeping enemy, who was leaning against the tree trunk, huddled up with Sabirah's poncho.

"My father should have returned long ago. I believe King Jacob has captured him . . . and my brother. My mother is ill and needs them. I will use the princess to barter for their freedom." She glanced at her captive, her face determined about her quest. I couldn't blame Sabirah. If there had been some way I could bargain to have my father and brother returned, I'd do it.

Sabirah turned her attention back to me and said, "I have answered your questions. Now tell me about this Book of Mormon."

Keeping my voice low so as not to disturb her men, I said, "Well—" I stole a deep breath and let it out, hoping I could put the facts in the right order. Grandma had told me this story, but so had my seminary teacher and Bishop Carpenter. I should know how to explain it. Finally, I said, "The Book of Mormon is a record of the Nephites and Lamanites written by several prophets on those gold plates I told you about. Moroni hid them in the hill Cumorah before he died."

Sabirah's face was scrunched with disbelief. She said loudly, "Captain Moroni led a great army and defeated the king-men. He didn't die on a hill called Cumorah."

Oh, I'd forgotten that there were two Moronis. "Shhh! Your men are tired from hiking; you don't want to wake them, do you?" I quickly glanced around to see if her raised voice had bothered anyone. Their snores drifted to the sky with the campfire smoke.

Sabirah nodded and said in a quieter tone, "But you have to explain yourself."

"Different Moroni altogether. See, the Moroni you're thinking of fought at the battle of Zarahemla."

"Yes, he was a brave chief captain." Sabirah seemed to grasp what I was saying.

"The other Moroni was born much later, hundreds of years after your time."

Again she looked confused. "Your time? You keep saying 'your time.' I don't understand your meaning."

I realized I'd really goofed. How could I explain time travel to Sabirah? "You know about prophets and warriors who lived long ago, right?"

She nodded.

"They lived in a time in the past. Everyone has a past and so does time. In past times, Lehi and Nephi came to the promised land."

She nodded. "Yes."

"Your time is the present. And future time is ahead of us." I knew this was a simple explanation, and if I kept talking about this topic, this conversation could go on for quite a while. She was smart and seemed to understand.

"This Book of Mormon you speak of is in future time?" Sabirah stood, looking down on me. Her voice raised a little as she asked, "What 'time' are you from, Tag?"

Yep, Sabirah was one smart cookie. I knew I had to tell her more. The daughter of Samuel the Lamanite should be able to handle the truth, right? Her father received direct revelation from God. Surely Sabirah would catch on.

"Please sit down." My voice held a sternness, which surprised even me.

She tentatively sat in a different place, leaving space between us. Already she didn't trust me. I swallowed and said in a voice only she could hear, "I'm from a land and time far, far away. A place called Idaho Falls, Idaho. The year I left was AD 2015."

"What is aye dee?" she asked.

"I'm not sure. I think it's Latin and means in the year of our Lord, but most people believe it means after Christ's death or something like that." I waited for her to take in that chunk of news.

Sabirah's Hershey-brown eyes grew wide. Her face, despite her dark complexion, paled. "What is the present year?"

I wanted to impress her, so I thought out loud. "You said your father spoke on the wall of Zarahemla eight and thirty years ago . . . that was five years before Christ was born . . . so minus those, and I think it is the year AD 33." Whoa, that meant Christ was alive right now. My mind started to reel, but I couldn't really get a handle on that thought, so I pushed it aside and concentrated on Sabirah.

I couldn't tell whether she completely believed me or not. She gazed into the dying fire, and then she looked up at me and asked, "How did you journey through the years?" Her eyes probed me as if checking to see that all my parts were still attached.

I pulled the clear stone from my pocket. "I think this had something to do with it."

As soon as Sabirah saw it in my hand, she panicked. "Quick, put it away." She glanced around the camp and at the princess. She appeared to be sleeping, though I thought I saw her eyes flutter. Satisfied that no one had seen, Sabirah said in a heated whisper, "Where did you get that?"

I couldn't tell her I'd stolen it, so I fudged a little. "A man named John Doe."

She pushed a lock of silky black hair away from her face, focusing on me.

I had to explain. "I borrowed it from him. I didn't realize it would send me here."

She said, "Long ago there lived a people called the Jaredites."

Excited that she'd changed the subject and that I wouldn't have to confess, I said, "I know this story." I could hear Grandma's voice as she'd rocked me on her knee when I was little. "They lived in the city of Babel thousands of years before even your people came to the Americas."

Sabirah squinted a skeptical eye at me. "Americas?"

"Yeah. That's a place, not a time. See, in the future this is called America. Well, actually this is Mesoamerica, but that's getting real picky."

Sabirah thought for a moment. *America.* She sounded more comfortable with the word.

I continued to tell her what I knew of the Jaredites. "The brother of Jared prayed to the Lord that his family's language would not change." I stopped. Thinking of language, I began to wonder. How was it that I could understand Sabirah and speak with her? During Book of Mormon times, the people spoke a different language. What had happened to me? I remembered when she had first spoken to me, I didn't understand her, but then after a few words, I did. My hand went to the bulge in my poncho pocket. The magical stone.

"Are you all right?" Sabirah asked, as she reached to pat my shoulder.

"It's just that all of a sudden I realized how amazing it is that we understand each other. See, my people speak English." I remembered Grandma telling me about the gift of tongues. That had to be it. But why would God give me the gift of tongues?

Maybe He thought I was special. But why give me special gifts now? Why not when I lived with Mom? Why not before Dad and Tyler left? *Why not give me special gifts when they could make life bearable—when I needed them?*

I glanced at Sabirah, who patiently waited for me to continue. "What was I saying?"

"Your people speak English. What tongue do you think my people speak?" she asked, and I knew she was testing me.

"I'm not certain. I think some kind of altered Hebrew."

She nodded.

I smiled and said, "What's important is we're able to understand one another. Anyway, back to the brother of Jared."

"Yes, the Jaredites." Sabirah gave me the look a teacher gives a student, waiting for an oral report. Usually that look made me really nervous, but not now. I knew this story. It had been one of Grandma's favorites.

"The Lord told the brother of Jared to take his family and friends and leave Babel." I paused a moment, trying to remember. I continued, "He told him to build barges to take his people across the sea."

"And what were these barges like?" Sabirah tested me.

"They had no windows."

"How could the people see inside these barges? They had a long journey to cross the ocean." Sabirah was up to something.

Cautiously, I pressed on, "Well, the brother of Jared worried about that, too. He chiseled small stones from a rock. The stones were clear." I kept an eye on Sabirah as I spoke, waiting for her to do something. I didn't know what, but something. She only nodded.

I continued, "The brother of Jared took these stones and carried them to the top of a mountain. He prayed, asking the Lord to touch the stones so they would give—" Suddenly my stomach felt all queasy. I thought of the stone in my pocket. Had the Lord touched that stone? "—they, the stones, would give off light inside the barges."

"And did the Lord touch the stones?" Sabirah quizzed me.

I gulped and said, "He did." The gravity of the moment crowded in on me. My hand trembled as I rubbed my chin. I said, "That was a long time ago . . ."

"Yes, it was."

"And I got this—" I patted my pocket, "—from John Doe."

"Tag, it doesn't matter who gave it to you. The stone in your pocket could very well be one of the sixteen the brother of Jared carved. *That* stone was touched by the Lord and has special powers. *That* stone is what brought you here. And when the time is right, it will take you home. Wayfarer, guard it with your life."

7
Appearances

Tag

I FELT LIGHT-HEADED WITH the weight of my new knowledge.

Great! Not only had I stolen for the first time in my life, but I'd stolen a sacred object the Lord had touched. How could I ever be forgiven for such a crime? *And* I had lied about it to Sabirah. Told her John Doe let me borrow it. I was going to hell, straight to, do not pass go, do not collect two hundred dollars.

I realized my actions were those of a true Prime, something I didn't want to be. How in the world did I get into this mess? Well, I knew how to get out. And maybe, just maybe, I could repair the damage.

I would go home, return the stone to John Doe and his buddies, and then go back to Grandpa's. Though I still had questions about God and why things happened the way they do, I knew I had to get this right. All I had to do was wait until Sabirah fell asleep, and then I'd have the stone work its magic and send me home. Once home, I'd return the stone to John Doe.

"Tag." Sabirah took ahold of my arm. "Tell no one you have this stone. If word spreads that you possess such a precious gift, only God will be able to help you."

If she only knew the extent of my situation, Sabirah would probably . . . well, I didn't know what she'd do, nor did I want to find out.

She continued, "My people have been fighting those with secret combinations and those who have joined King Jacob. Princess Jamila's journey to our land was to seek new converts. It is an ongoing battle. My people grow weary. Some have fallen under her spell. Trust no one."

Great! If she wanted me scared, she'd succeeded. I quickly looked around. All of Sabirah's men appeared as though they were sleeping. Movement near the tree where the princess slept caught my eye. Maybe she'd turned or something. Or . . . it could have been my imagination gone wild. Like that was a stretch.

Sabirah rose. "There is more I want to ask you, but we need our rest. Tomorrow will be a long day, though we should reach Pagog by nightfall." She flattened ferns, lay down, and quickly fell asleep.

I thought about our little talk. Knowing that the stone could be one of the sixteen stones the brother of Jared had carved made me wonder about John Doe and his buddies. Just who were they, and where did they get the stone? I would never find out stuck here in ancient times. I pulled the crystal-like orb out of my pocket. I had to get this back to John, and the sooner the better. Holding the stone in my hand, I waited for the glowing to start.

Nothing.

Maybe I needed to rub it. As I reached to do so, I thought of how the Lord had touched it. I was not worthy to even hold such a gem, let alone rub it. I said a silent prayer. *Please, Lord, if this stone has your special power, please make it work. Send me home so I can make everything right.*

I opened my eyes and saw that nothing had happened. The stone remained clear. That strange feeling of belonging here overcame me. I fought it. I needed to go back. I couldn't understand why I kept feeling like I needed to stay here; I didn't want to understand. Determined, I readied myself to wait all night for the stone to work; though, as I stared at the dwindling fire, I became very tired. My eyelids felt heavy. I forced them open. My back ached. My head pounded. What would it hurt if I were to lie down? I could hold the stone in my pocket. Who said I had to be awake to have it work? Who said it had to be out of my pocket for it to light up?

I found a grassy space near the fire and stretched out. As I leaned my head back, the dog collar around my neck choked me. I unbuckled the clasp and tugged it off. Gazing up at the stars again, I thought of Grandpa. If only he could look at this sky. Uncontrollably, I yawned and closed my eyes. Making sure the stone was within my grasp inside my pocket, I turned over and drifted off to sleep.

ᴄ∘

Sabirah

DURING THE NIGHT, I RELIEVED the sentry, allowing him to return to camp. As I stood watch, I noticed Mahir sneaking toward me from behind, like a crouching jaguar. But he was not as soft-footed as he thought. As he drew near, I asked without turning around, "Why have you come?"

Giving up the surprise, he walked to my side. "I want to know what you want me to do."

"What you always do." Why did he question? Mahir knew the duties of a second.

"The wayfarer seems to have taken my place. He sat near the fire talking with you for quite a while." He gazed at me, waiting for an answer.

Even though I would trust Mahir with my life, I couldn't tell him Tag's story of time travel. I was still trying to understand it myself. I said, "Everyone has their own place. Last night mine was talking with the wayfarer." I thought of something I could tell him. "I learned that Tag knows of my father."

"That's good. Has he recently seen him?" Mahir loved my father almost as much as I did. He, too, had been worried, as had all the people of our village.

"No, he has only heard of how he preached on the wall at Zarahemla. Tag wants to help us find him." I knew this was true. Tag said my father was a prophet, and I could tell that deep inside him, he wanted to help me find him.

"Oh." Mahir seemed disappointed. I felt bad that I didn't have better news. He placed his hand on my shoulder. "I don't trust the newcomer, and I don't believe you should, either."

"Why?"

"He looks like a Gadianton," Mahir scoffed. "Black nails, blackened lines around his eyes, and that spiked wrapping around his neck. It could be new armor or one of their new weapons."

"I agree, Tag doesn't look like us, though that doesn't mean he is a Gadianton. He is merely from a different land."

"A different land, yet he knows of your father?" Mahir was confused, and I hated to admit it, but so was I. Usually I shared my misgivings with Mahir, but not this time. I needed to pray and ponder to understand more.

"I wish I could explain, and I will later but not now. Now we must prepare to break camp. We shall reach Pagog today. Perhaps later tonight, after we have supped with our families, you and I can meet." That would give me time to think about how to explain Tag's presence, not only to Mahir but to the others, as well. All at once, an urgency befell me, as though a waterfall of trouble flowed in my path and was about to swallow me.

"Our usual place?" he asked softly.

I nodded, unable to put my sudden apprehension to words.

℮ℑ

Tag

WHEN I AWOKE, EVERYONE WAS milling around the muttering cook, who was handing out leftover tortillas from last night's supper. Disappointed that the stone hadn't taken me home in my sleep, I put my dog collar back on and rose to my feet. Making certain the stone was secure in my pocket along with my father's sketchpad, I joined those in line to receive food. I couldn't help but wonder what these guys would think if they knew I had the stone.

Of course, they'd be impressed. I was certain they knew of the stone's history. But then I wondered which one of them would try to take it from me. Someone would. In all the movies and stories I'd read, whenever there was something pricelessly valuable, someone always tried to steal it. I thought of *Lord of the Rings* and how Frodo had to guard the ring with his life. I realized I had pretty much the same burden—though the stone was not making me sick—I was responsible for its well-being and safe return to John Doe. That I'd stolen it proved my point that when word leaked out, I would be in as much trouble as Frodo was with the Nazguls that were after him. Sabirah had warned me to keep the stone a secret, and I would. But I also had to learn how to make the stone work so I could go home. I wished I could put the stone on my finger like Frodo did the ring to activate its power. The burden of keeping the stone safe weighed heavily on my mind.

I'd almost forgotten I was standing in line for food when Sahan handed me a tortilla. I think I nodded a thank you. I was hungry and some food, even though it tasted like the sole of Grandpa's fishing waders, would be better than no food. I moved out of the way for those who followed.

As I ate, I glanced around, searching for Sabirah. She was talking with the princess, placing the feathered crown back on her head. It struck me that even though the two of them seemed to be about the same age, they were very different, and it wasn't just because one was a Lamanite and one a Nephite. They were contradictions of what most people back home thought. Some thought only Nephites were good and Lamanites were bad, which was the total opposite here. I studied the beauties more closely.

Jamila, the Nephite, should be a strong supporter of her ancestors: Nephi and Lehi. But she wasn't. Sabirah, the Lamanite, humbly followed those prophets. Jamila dressed immodestly, wearing a halter-top minidress; Sabirah a modest tunic, crudely cut and a little bit tight, though anything she wore would have enhanced her shapely curves. The princess wore golden armbands and a crown to show everyone she was important, but she wasn't. Sabirah wore only a necklace of a flying eagle, no outward signs of her position, yet she was the most important person.

Sabirah checked the leather straps that tied the princess's arms and then guided her over to the rest of us. The princess came begrudgingly. As she drew near, Jamila sneered at me as though I had betrayed her and her people. Whatever! Let her think what she wanted of me. The Lamanite and Nephite battles were history, which I couldn't undo.

Anyway, I didn't think I could. I thought about time leaps and how Samuel the Lamanite foretold of my coming. So, was I supposed to steal the stone? Was I supposed to be a mental screwup? If I thought about this too long I'd get a headache. What I needed to focus on was keeping the stone safe. That was it. And, hopefully, if I did my job well, the rest would right itself.

We broke camp and started the march toward Sabirah's village. Mahir took charge of Jamila, which was fine with me.

After walking a couple of hours, the path became overgrown with thick, tall brush. Mahir tied the princess to a red-barked tree. He joined several other men in the lead, hacking a pathway through the overgrown, tangled bushes. Progress was slow. Those of us waiting became targets for mosquitoes and all sorts of biting bugs. They didn't seem to bother Sabirah.

"What gives?" I asked swatting a mosquito about the size of a dragonfly.

"What?" She had no idea what I was talking about.

"Why don't these flying critters bother you?"

"The 'critters' don't like my blood." Sabirah smiled.

"Maybe you're a vampire and have no blood," I teased, knowing the word *vampire* would be a stumbling block.

She shook her head, "I am uncertain what a 'vampire' is, but a Blue Viper is rumored to have no blood."

"Blue Viper?" Okay, I couldn't help but ask, "What is a Blue Viper?"

"A woman by day, but at night she seeks a silk tree where she sheds her mortal body, becoming a blue light. She preys on humans, seeking sweet-tasting blood. Once she finds it, she feasts until her victim is dead."

"Soooo, are you one?" I asked, knowing full well she wasn't.

"What do you think?" she said with a teasing smile.

I pretended to ponder, looking around as if I'd find the answer in the jungle. Princess Jamila seemed to enjoy our conversation. I chose to ignore her and turned to Sabirah. "I don't believe you are, but she's a definite possibility," I said, pointing to the princess.

Sabirah chuckled. "True . . ."

Suddenly, a pain-ridden scream filled the air from up ahead. We froze in our tracks.

Deep concern washed away Sabirah's happy expression in an instant. She said, "Watch the princess." Then she took off.

Alone with "her majesty," I didn't know what to say. I'd seen her kind in action at my high school. She was a replica of the I'm-the-center-of-the-world girls. Gals like her rarely spoke with guys like me.

Word finally filtered down through the men that the one who had screamed had accidentally sliced his leg with his sword. Because of the help I'd given Nabi, Sabirah sent word that she wanted me to see what I could do. Mom had taught me a little first aid, so maybe I could help in some way. I untied Princess Jamila from the tree and dragged her along as I tried to remember what Mom had told me about deep cuts. It would certainly need to be bandaged, but what could we use? As I hurried, I fought through brush and passed some of the other men. The air grew thick as the humidity closed in like a sauna. My poncho smothered me. Out of the corner of my eye, I noticed movement on a branch. Looking closer, I saw a boa constrictor.

Oh, snap!

Just keep going!

I quickly skirted around it, dragging the princess along.

Princess Jamila tugged on my arm. "The snake is our friend."

There was no time to stand here and argue with her. Harshly pulling the princess, I said, "Yeah, well, I'm not surprised."

Trying to find the way and worried over the injured man, I said without really thinking, "The next thing you're going to tell me is the scorpion is 'our' friend, too."

She jerked back, making me stop. Her pretty blues gentled as a smile brightened her face. "You are right. The scorpion is our friend as well as the caiman and the jaguar."

"Princess, you hang with some pretty strange friends." I had no clue what a caiman was, though I got the drift of what she was saying. But this conversation didn't matter. We had to keep going.

She laughed. It wasn't a usual laugh but sounded more like a hyena. "Tag, how well do you know the people you travel with?"

The fact that she remembered my name told me she had paid more attention to Sabirah and me than I'd thought. I jerked her along and said, "I know Sabirah very well."

At the sound of her foil's name, a cold glint grew in the princess's eyes. She stopped. "Remember, no one is what they seem. Even the mighty Sabirah has her flaws. That she has taken me hostage is a *very* grave mistake." She said it with such determination and conviction that I wanted to abandon her.

Yet, Sabirah was counting on me to keep an eye on this spoiled brat and see to the injured man. I dragged the princess as I forged ahead. I spat out, "Your father has captured Sabirah's father. What do you expect her to do?"

"Her father is a crazy man who wanders the land preaching of old legends and stories. If my father has captured him, the world is a better place. I hope her father is dead."

The word *dead* made me stop. Despite the heat, a cold chill breathed over me. How dare she wish that on anyone? I turned and stared at her, and for a moment, her face looked like a serpent's, her eyes mere slits. What kind of hatred consumed a person so much that they had no feelings, no sense of compassion? At first I couldn't think of a comeback. Her words didn't deserve a reply. She was full of hate and rage, and why? I glared at the princess and said, "You are a very small person."

"Thank you."

"That was not a compliment. It means behind your pretty eyes and good looks, there's not much left."

She cocked her head like a puzzled puppy.

I added, "You are shallow."

"Shallow?"

Again her face creased with confusion.

"All right, look, you're a rude, hateful, spoiled brat who only thinks of yourself. You wouldn't know a prophet of God if he walked up and shook your hand. How dare you wish Sabirah's father dead."

Anger fueled my words. "Let me tell you something, Miss Plastic. Samuel the Lamanite beats you hands down when it comes to being a good person. You're not worthy to walk on the same sidewalk as Sabirah or her father." Boy, did that feel good.

Princess Jamila rolled her eyes and gave me the *what-a-weirdo* look that I'd seen so often in my life. This time it didn't bother me in the least. This time I was right.

A rustling in the foliage concerned me at first, but Sabirah broke through. "What's taking you so long?"

"It's not important. How is the man who was hurt?" I asked, genuinely concerned.

"Gian has lost a lot of blood." Worry slanted her brow.

Gian was the smiling fellow who had shared the bug ointment with me. "I don't know much about wounds. My mother is a nurse . . . a healer, and I might be able to think of something."

Sabirah motioned for me to follow. I grabbed ahold of the princess and tugged her along. We burst through the foliage close to where several had gathered around the victim. Blood splatters were on the leaves, and there was a growing pool of blood on the ground near Gian . . . more than I'd ever seen.

Handing the princess off to Sabirah, I went to Gian. They'd wrapped his tunic around the wound on his upper thigh. I had to take a closer look to see how deep. Pulling the blood-soaked material away for only a second, I saw the muscle had been cut to the bone. An artery spurted blood. I quickly covered it again. I knew this was bad, very bad. Mom had told me about a fellow who had come into the ER with a similar cut. She'd said if he'd been alone he would have died, but someone had put a tourniquet on him and probably saved his life. When he arrived at the hospital, they performed surgery. She had been worried he would still lose his leg.

So, what did I do now? I doubted there was a surgeon in his village. But maybe some healer would know what needed to be done. At least I could save his life for a while. I had to rewrap the bandage and apply pressure to stop the bleeding. Looking up, I saw Mahir and said, "Hold his leg."

Mahir quickly did what I asked as I reshaped the material. I wrapped his wound, twisting excess cloth on top like Mom had shown me as she'd prepared for a triage seminar. I needed to tie it off, but there wasn't enough material. Trying to think what would hold it tight, I rubbed my neck. My fingers touched the dog collar. Perfect!

I quickly unbuckled the leather strap and began to put it on Gian. He moaned. I was tempted to stop but instead forged ahead as if Mom were giving me instructions, buckling it over the twisted knot exactly where pressure was needed. When finished, I checked Gian's face. He'd passed out either from the pain or lack of blood.

Sabirah patted me on the back. "Good work."

I shook my head. "Not really, but it will have to do."

She nodded. "We must hurry." She handed me a sword. "But we need your help."

I took the weapon and noticed blood smeared on my hands. Wiping it on a broadleaf plant, I realized that back in my time, a stranger's blood on bare hands would be cause for alarm with the threat of HIV. Here, I knew I was probably safe.

Sabirah guided the princess and me to the others and motioned for Sahan, the cook, to watch the princess. I followed Sabirah to the head of the trailblazing line. Mahir was already there. He scowled at me and glared at Sabirah.

She started whacking at the brush and vines, ignoring Mahir. Okay, I may be slow, but if I didn't know any better I'd think Mahir had a bad crush on Sabirah and was jealous of the way she turned to me when she needed help. He watched her every move and had all the signs of wanting a serious relationship with her. The dude needed to get a grip or he was going to lose her. I didn't know much about girls, but I did know you need to keep your cool.

I put Mahir out of my mind and concentrated on following Sabirah's lead. The sword was awkward in my hands, but as I kept working on the path, I found I could whack a sword through jungle vines with the best of them. I knew the muscles in my arms would ache for days, but I didn't care. As we worked, a few men tied together a makeshift litter with limber branches to carry Gian.

After many hours, we broke through to a clearing. Besides my arms smarting, hunger was another problem, but I wasn't about to complain. Although my stomach growled so loudly Sabirah heard. She pointed to a stand of trees. The other men had already seen it and were heading that way. Catching up to the others, I found they'd discovered an avocado tree. Grabbing a piece of fruit, I peeled off the tough skin and ate it like an apple. No crunch, but, oh, it tasted good.

Glancing around, I noticed Sabirah had taken fruit to first Gian and then Jamila, but she refused to eat. The princess seemed even more belligerent than before. I'd like to think it was because of the conversation she'd had with me.

We didn't rest very long, needing to get Gian to the village. We pressed on. The sun was setting when I saw a large settlement in the distance. I guess I thought Sabirah's people would live in teepees or something, so I was surprised to see their homes were made of tree limbs tightly tied together for the walls. Each had a thatched roof.

Lamanite children rushed to greet us. Little boys and girls were dressed in tunics and leather-type moccasins. Some of the girls carried infants strapped to their backs with cloth. I wondered where their mothers were. No one seemed concerned for the babies. It must be an everyday thing to see a little sister packing her momma's infant around. Large smiles brightened the children's faces. Some toted spider monkeys on their shoulders; others were followed by what looked like gray-spotted pigs but not quite. I really didn't know what kind of animals they were. The children giggled as they found their loved ones and ran into their waiting arms. Soon it seemed as if the entire village had joined us.

When Gian's family came upon him, Sabirah calmly told them what had happened and how brave their son was. His father unbuckled my collar and studied the wound. The bleeding started again. He quickly wrapped it with a shawl. Gian was semiconscious and smiling, though he was very pale. His father came over to me and gave back my collar. With his hand over his heart, he nodded a thank you. Tears welled in his eyes, and I knew his emotions had choked him up. I nodded in acknowledgement of his gratitude. With grave faces, Gian's family took their wounded son home.

Wiping smears of blood from my collar, I put it back on. The crowd continued to follow Sabirah as we walked through the village. Since eating the avocados, Sabirah had left Princess Jamila untied and made sure she stayed by her side. I wondered if this was wise, but Sabirah seemed to know what she was doing. I turned my attention to my surroundings.

Some homes had pens with small, fat dogs. The animals tried to bark, but their barks were more like a very odd yodel. Other homes had bird perches with colorful parrots, parakeets, and cockatoos.

We continued to trek through Pagog and finally stopped at one of the larger huts. A tall, stout Lamanite dressed in a plain tunic greeted us.

The stately man smiled at Sabirah and her army. Then he saw me and frowned, but when he spied the princess, his expression changed to stone. He turned to Sabirah. "We have waited for word of you and your men. You are late by several days."

"Sir, we came upon the enemy. In the battle, we captured Princess Jamila," Sabirah said.

"And also captured her aide?" He was looking at me, assuming I was with the princess. Well, why wouldn't he? She was a Nephite, and my white skin told him I was, too.

"No, sir. He helped us." Sabirah gave me a slight smile, probably in the hopes of easing my fear.

Worry slanted the man's brow. He motioned for Sabirah and the princess to step inside.

Sabirah dismissed her men and grabbed my arm, making me follow. Mahir noticed and scowled. This guy was going to make mincemeat out of me if she kept singling me out. But for once, I didn't care. The pretty girl had chosen me over the big, brawny captain of the football team. I was loving it.

Leaving Mahir behind, I entered the hut. Positioned beside Sabirah, I leaned near her and asked, "Who is this guy?"

"The leader of our tribe and my father's brother, Ashraf."

The man motioned for us to sit on what looked like short snack-bar stools, except these were made of stout tree limbs latched together. A tall, slender girl, who turned from my view as soon as we came in, rose from the cooking area. Ashraf motioned for her to take the princess out the back door.

"No." The princess stood defiant against his orders. "I deserve to hear what my captor says."

"You will do as I say." Ashraf clapped his hands. A beefy man who reminded me of my favorite wrestling champion—all muscle and no nonsense—entered the room.

"Ravid, take her to the hut in the back and watch her," Ashraf said.

The princess leaped at me, hugging me as if I were some type of lifeline. I could hardly stand to have her touch me. Pushing her away, I handed her over to the guard. Princess Jamila smiled like the Cheshire cat. She was a total psycho.

"Daughter, take her to the stream to freshen up before she is imprisoned," said Ashraf. The shy girl guided the guard and the princess from the room. As Sabirah and I sat down, Ashraf looked at me and said, "Why do you want this stranger to join us?"

"I trust him. He healed Nabi and helped Gian."

He gazed at me as he sat down. "We are indebted to you." The man neither smiled nor frowned, and I wondered if he really meant it. Then he turned his attention back to Sabirah and said, "Why did you bring the princess here? Your mission was merely to find a new valley to hunt food and to protect us from the Gadiantons."

"Princess Jamila and her men have enticed many of our people to join them. Besides, King Jacob has my father and probably my brother, as well. Why not capture her?" Sabirah clenched her teeth; a blood vessel over her right eyebrow protruded.

Ashraf shook his head. "You assume too much. I have counseled you against such actions."

"Yes, but I believe it is true. I had to do something." Sabirah's gaze studied her uncle as if pleading to be understood.

"The Gadiantons attack, not us. Your father and brother would *not* want you to endanger the village by bringing her here."

Sabirah jumped to her feet. "Why don't you allow me to search for them? Why must we wait? At least now we can bargain."

The uncle motioned for Sabirah to sit. She seemed slightly hopeful as she returned to her seat.

"What do you suppose King Jacob will do once he learns of his daughter's capture?" Ashraf's left eyebrow quirked upward; he pressed his hands together in a steeple.

"They will come looking for her. That is what I want. We can trade for my father and Asim." Sabirah seemed sure of her conviction. Her brown eyes sparkled with hope.

"You are correct. They will come. Though they will not bring your father or brother. If they have them, they'll kill them and come after us for revenge. Many of our people will die." He paused a moment, taking a deep breath as he thought. He said, "You must take the princess to her father and beg forgiveness."

"Beg?" Sabirah's face clouded with anger. Her hands bunched into fists. "I will not beg."

"You will!" Ashraf's determination stiffened his back. "And pray the king shows mercy."

Surely her uncle must know that King Jacob would very likely sentence Sabirah to death. The king had no mercy. He was ruler over the Gadianton robbers, whose evil doings were so horrible they couldn't be written down. No way would the king let Sabirah walk away even if she did beg. I couldn't sit there like a gecko on the wall. "He'll kill her."

Ashraf shot a stare at me as if I'd stepped across his line in the sand. "God will keep her safe." He looked at my dog collar, saying, "My niece may trust you, but that doesn't mean I do. Are you one of the king's men?"

Sabirah answered for me, "No, Uncle. He isn't. I couldn't explain before in front of the others, but this is the wayfarer, the one whose coming father foretold." Fire still lit Sabirah's eyes; her rage glowed red on her face.

"Yes, he told me of this revelation. You think he is the one the Lord sent to help you?" Ashraf didn't believe it. "I thought he would be more—" His eyes trailed over me. "—like us."

I wondered what he meant. Then I knew. So their skin was dark and mine was white like the princess, but that didn't mean I was on her side.

Ashraf stared at my collar again. "His adornment is that of the king's." He shrugged. "Yet, perhaps it is good. I am glad he has finally arrived. He can go with you."

Go with her! I wanted to help Sabirah, but I knew my limitations. I would only slow her down. Besides, I wasn't a fighter. I didn't know exactly what I was. A medic? an artist? Though the thought of spending more time with Sabirah was very appealing, I knew I didn't have time to go traipsing through the jungle dragging around a spoiled princess. I needed to set things right with John Doe by returning the stone. Yep, I had to hightail it out of here as soon as the stone and I had some quality alone time.

And I was determined to have that time tonight.

8

Be Wary

Sabirah

MY UNCLE'S ORDER TO TAKE TAG with me to deliver the princess to King Jacob was what I'd hoped for.

"You will leave in the morning. Tonight, your mother needs you." Uncle placed his hand on my shoulder. "She's been worried."

An urgency to go home possessed me. I quickly rose. Tag did, as well.

Uncle followed us to the door. "I'll keep the princess here tonight safe under Ravid's guard. We'll see you when the sun rises."

As Tag and I walked away, I stole a glance back. My uncle was staring not at me but at Tag. What had bothered Uncle Ashraf about the wayfarer? Tag looked back, too. He waved. Uncle did nothing but turn his back and walk into his house. Ignoring his rude behavior, I kept walking, with Tag by my side. He was only three years my junior, yet he seemed much younger and gangly, like a monkey. He scratched at the belt around his neck.

"Does King Jacob wear a collar?" he asked.

"I don't know." I was angry at my uncle for making Tag feel bad. But hopefully once he thought about what I'd said of Tag's healing abilities, he would accept him.

"Okay, so that was weird," Tag said.

I stopped for a moment and asked, "What does 'weird' mean?"

"It means strange or unusual."

I started walking again and added, "What was weird?"

"Just the whole scene in there: your uncle demanding that we take Princess Jamila back to her father and that I need to go with you. I mean, don't you find it pretty weird?" Tag was practically running to keep up with me.

"No. Actually, it's exactly what I'd hoped for." I waved at some people of my village as they passed us. I could tell they wanted me to stop and introduce Tag to them. Word must have spread about his healing knowledge, but I didn't have time to talk. I needed to see to my mother.

"Wait a minute." Tag stopped for a moment.

But I kept walking. He sprinted to catch up. "You planned the whole thing?"

"Yes. I knew Ashraf wouldn't want the princess here, and he would demand I take her home. My uncle wants to keep the peace, work in Grandfather's corn, and wait for word from his preaching brother. I am tired of waiting. Now I can see for myself if King Jacob has my father and brother." I stopped for a moment, placing my hands on Tag's shoulders. "Besides, you'll be with me. Everything will be all right." The moment had come for Tag to accept his full wayfarer calling, that of aiding me. Yet, as I gazed into his eyes, I realized something was shadowing Tag, something from his past.

"See now, this is what I want to talk with you about." Tag appeared frustrated. "How can I make you understand I am nobody special? I'm an artist. I don't fight. I mean, not like with swords and stuff. I make statements with art. That's about as gutsy as I get. See? So if you're thinking I can protect you, you're wrong. I mean, give me a can of spray paint, and I'll make you proud, but I really don't think you have spray paint, do you?" Tag looked up at me. Spray paint? Though I didn't understand many of his words, his new argument wouldn't change my mind. I knew what his true mission was.

"Stop it," Tag said.

"What?"

"You know, that I've-already-made-up-my-mind baloney."

I chuckled. "You use odd words. But you speak the truth. I have made up my mind. My father told me to watch for you, and here you are. Everything will work out. But I don't understand *baloney.*"

He rolled his eyes and said, "It's not important, but making you see reason is. I know your father was . . . is a prophet and everything, but how in the world would he have known I was coming?" Tag looked as though he would like to eat his words. He continued, "Okay, so he receives revelation from God. I'll give him that, but for the life of me, Sabirah, I don't know how I can help you."

"I watched you with Nabi and Gian." I had seen how caring he'd been to my loyal followers. "You healed them. My father said you would be a healer. Much goodness resides within you. During this journey we'll know why you were sent to aid me. Until then, I'll teach you how to fight." I had to build up his confidence. That's what my father would have done. That's what he would expect me to do.

Tag exhaled as though extremely frustrated. "I was only able to help them because of what my mother taught me. Look, I don't understand why your dad told you I was coming. And I must admit, for a little while, it kind of made me feel good to be needed. But your dad must have got his wires crossed."

I folded my arms. Ignoring his foreign terms, I knew Tag needed to convince himself. I needed to wait until he had settled the war within and had accepted his calling.

As if he were a mind reader, Tag raised his shoulders and said, "You make it hard for a guy to say no. All right, already."

This small victory was mine, though I knew something shadowed him from his past. The battle haunting Tag from within was far from over.

☙

Tag

Sabirah pointed to a house, one of the smallest I'd seen. "My family's home."

A very small thatched-roof hut was all it was, smaller than Ashraf's. Who would have thought prophet Samuel would have lived in such a humble dwelling?

"Grandfather will know of our arrival and will have prepared something for us to eat. Whatever he offers you, tell him it is good. He believes he is a great cook, and sometimes he is, but most often he isn't, and he'll press you to tell him the truth. Whatever you do, don't tell him what you think of his food. He is what I believe you would call 'weird' about his cooking."

I knew Sabirah wanted to get in there and see how her mother was, so I didn't ask her any more questions. I'd delayed her long enough by arguing, which was stupid and a waste of time. Before we reached the door's threshold, Sabirah's grandfather stepped outside. It seemed as though light beams shot from his cheer-filled eyes. He was bent with age, and I would have thought he'd be slow to move and speak, but I would have been wrong.

Like a mighty chief, her grandfather reached up to the sky. "Great One, you have brought her home!" His teary eyes gazed with love at his granddaughter. "Angels have smiled on us and blessed us once more." I stole a glance at Sabirah. She gave me the *remember-what-I-told-you* look and then gladly went into her grandfather's arms. "I missed you, old one."

While they embraced, I noticed tears leaked from the elderly man's eyes. "And I you, young one."

I couldn't help but think of the welcome Grandpa had given me when I'd arrived at the cabin. Of course, I wasn't the strong, capable Sabirah. Nope, I was the problem grandchild who was being dumped on him for the summer.

"Grandfather, I caught her. Our plan worked." Sabirah was quite proud of herself.

More joy filled the old man's face. "Thrice good! Just as I knew Samuel would preach to the Nephites in Zarahelma, I knew Ashraf would send you to the king. To have outfoxed your uncle, you are a woman of great bravery and courage." The elderly man reached up and cupped Sabirah's cheek in his gnarled hand.

The tenderness of the moment made me envious. I thought about what the old man had said. So he was Samuel and Ashraf's father. Their family dynamics reminded me of Mom and Grandpa Quincy. My mother always turned to my father's father for help.

Sabirah's grandfather then focused on me. His smile broadened. "And Wayfarer! Saints be praised! My Samuel told of your coming. Doubly blessed we are. Come, come, you must eat. I've made something new." He leaned toward me as though to share a great secret. "It is the best food of the village. I am sure you'll agree." I was surprised that he, too, knew of the wayfarer prophesy. Made me wonder if Samuel had left a description of me or something. But Sabirah didn't say so. I remembered she'd mentioned that her father said I'd be an aide to her when she needed me, that I'd have a healing hand, and that I'd believe in Christ. Yet, how could anyone think I fit that description soley upon seeing me?

The grandfather stepped back to allow us to enter his home. "Come, let us feast and talk, but first, my Sabirah, you must pay your respects to your mother, our precious Lena. She's been most anxious for your return. Your absence has not helped her condition, and I fear she'll not take your leaving again so soon very well."

"She grows worse, Grandfather?"

"She will be much better seeing you, my girl. And maybe after your visit, you can take the wayfarer to see her. With his healing touch, he may give her comfort. But while you visit your mother, our wayfarer can test my cooking." He wiggled his graying eyebrows at me.

"His name is Tag," Sabirah said before disappearing behind a curtain that acted like a door to the next room.

"Tag? A simple name." The old man nodded his head. "My name is Hashim. Come." He motioned for me to sit on a mat as he walked to his cooking area. A pot tooled of copper was nestled in a small fire. I sat cross-legged, concerned about what was in the concoction, wondering if I could get amoebas or something. But cooking food should kill any microbugs.

Maybe.

Hashim ladled up my dinner into a handmade pottery bowl. I stared at the contents. Some kind of mushrooms, peppers, and corn in a dishwater-colored base. Didn't look too tasty.

Tipping the bowl up to my mouth, I courageously took a mouthful. At first there was a fresh, woodsy taste, though the flavor turned to fire on my tongue. I wanted to spit it out, but remembering what Sabirah had said, I quickly swallowed, and the flaming food burned all the way past my throat to my stomach. Looking down, I totally expected my gut to glow through my clothes. I blinked several times to keep tears from clouding my eyes. The fire on my tongue grew more intense. Looking up, I gasped, "Very good!"

"You truly think so?" He skeptically studied me. I turned aside, hoping to avoid eye contact. He kept on. "I have eaten too many fire peppers so my tongue betrays my taste much of the time. Do you think it needs a quail egg to help the base?"

He appeared to earnestly want the truth. Sabirah must have been mistaken about her grandfather. He really seemed like he wanted to know what I thought, and he wanted to make his stew/soup/whatever it was the best he could, so I answered, "Maybe a little."

"Oh, stars in heaven! Give me that slop, that poison." He grabbed the bowl from my hands. "I will not feed such hogwash unfit for a tapir to my guests." Dumping the remains of my bowl into the main pot, he placed rags on his hands and hefted the pot from the fire. Dashing to the door, he threw the contents out on the ground. Then he hustled back to the kitchen area, muttering to himself. "Maybe more . . . lots more squash, peppers." He grabbed the vegetables, as he named them, from baskets near the fire. "Sweet potatoes, yes, yes. Oh, and I know what might help, a dash of the juice of the agave. Yes, this will make it much better. Wait and see. Thank you, thank you, thank you. It is so refreshing to have someone tell me what is wrong with my food. Lena, bless her soul to heaven, tries to eat whatever I give her, barely making a peep. Sabirah will eat anything. But Wayfarer, Tag, you are rare." The old man was chopping vegetables and talking at the same time. He didn't bother wiping out the pot he'd dumped the contents from but just started filling it up again with his new recipe.

The way Sabirah had spoken about her grandfather becoming upset if someone critiqued his food, I had imagined the opposite reaction. I thought he would become angry, have a tantrum, but not this old guy. He'd rather work himself silly trying to please a person. I wondered which was worse. I felt horrible.

Sabirah finally came out of her mother's room. "You were right, Grandfather, she was relieved to see me. Though she fell asleep as we talked."

"Take the wayfarer in to her. Maybe he can help." Her grandfather feverishly worked over the food.

"I think his healing hand is more for physical ailments, not diseases or broken hearts." She noticed her grandfather fussing with the food. "I thought dinner was ready."

He stopped a moment as though reassessing what she had said about "healing hand." Then he set to work again. "Our kind friend made a suggestion of what I needed to do to make our meal better. You deserve the best food for your homecoming." He scooped the chopped vegetables into the pot and then squeezed juice over it. When finished, he wiped his hands on his tunic.

I felt Sabirah staring down on me, and I didn't want to meet her gaze. I could say nothing in my defense. She sat on the mat beside me, grabbing a tortilla from the stack. She handed me one and then turned to her grandfather. "Have you any news of my brother?"

The old man stopped his fussing and looked at Sabirah. He sadly shook his head. "No, courageous one."

"You never told me your brother's name," I said as I took a bite.

"Asim. He is a year older than I. As I told you before, when Father failed to return, my brother waited until he could wait no longer. I, too, thought he should search. He left a year ago. Some fear he has become a Gadianton."

"What you say offends my ears, Granddaughter." Hashim's cheery face was now somber.

"Grandfather, forgive me. Asim knows what is right. My brother would give his all for our father and for the gospel." Sabirah's voice filled with conviction.

Hashim seemed to take comfort in her words and busied himself with the meal.

"My father and Asim—" Sabirah turned to me. "—shared a special bond. I fear having both my father and brother away has broken my mother's heart. She's grown much weaker."

Except for her mother possibly dying of some illness, I couldn't help but think again how our families were alike. Our brothers and fathers who were gone. Vanished. Both our mothers suffered from broken hearts.

Dad and Tyler had left and now me. For sure, Mom would know I was gone by now. I tried to remember the last time I'd seen my father and brother, but I couldn't. That memory had been sucked into some type of black hole. Had I done something so horrible that I could never remember? Fear needled me away from the thoughts.

Wanting to talk about something entirely different, I changed the subject and asked Sabirah about the city of Zarahemla. Though her people were Lamanites, she spoke of the Nephite city with great love. Many of her people who had converted to the gospel had lived there but left when most of the people in the city began to reject the gospel. We talked until dinner was ready.

We had a late supper. Sabirah's mother was too ill to join us by the kitchen fire. I praised Hashim's meal and gave no suggestions, only told him everything was perfect, even though the food tasted like fire with lumps of charred vegetables. Sabirah ladled a bowl for her mother, probably thinking the heat in the food would liven her up . . . or kill her. Nah, she had to be used to it by now.

Hashim stacked the dishes and pots in preparation to wash them.

"Let me do the dishes," I said. "Where's your water?"

"The stream is out back. But be cautious," Hashim warned.

Sabirah, with her mother's dinner in hand, glanced up and said, "He speaks of the caimans. They are quite fond of our stream. Beware of anything that moves in the water. Caimans are quick." Sabirah's forehead wrinkled with concern before she disappeared into the other room.

"Caimans?" I muttered, taking an empty water gourd and heading for the door. I remembered the princess had mentioned them before. What were they?

Hashim patted my back and asked me once again if I really liked his food. And again, I said it was fabulous and then escaped to the stream.

The moon was full and lit my way. For a moment, I thought Hashim and Sabirah had been teasing me about the caimans. They were probably like "snipes" in my time, the mythical creatures that Scouts tricked newcomers into hunting. Snipes didn't exist. Still, every bump in the trail, every rock in the stream, seemed threatening.

I nervously knelt down on the soggy bank, scooping water into the gourd. Now that I was alone, this would be the perfect time and place to see if the stone would send me back home. I'd healed two of Sabirah's men, so I hoped I had done what I was supposed to do. A twinge of guilt caught hold of me at the thought of leaving Sabirah before she squared off with King Jacob. But she was a very capable warrior. She didn't need me. I'd only hold her up, seeing as I'd never fought with a sword. I needed to get out while the getting was good.

About to pull the stone from my poncho pocket, I saw someone creeping in the shadows of nearby bushes. At first, I thought of caimans. Then common sense kicked in. Whatever caimans were, they surely didn't walk on two legs. But who would be out here sneaking around?

I needed to warn Sabirah. To reach the house, I'd have to pass whoever was hiding. And that person probably planned to jump me as I went by. I had to counter attack. I could do this. Besides, I had the element of surprise on my side.

Leaving the gourd by the stream, I doubled back. Sneaking up behind the person, I leaped and knocked him down. We wrestled, turning over and over, but finally I gained the upper hand and straddled my would-be assailant.

The moon shown down on Ashraf's daughter.

9
Duped

Tag

"YOU! WHY ARE YOU SNEAKING around?" I was totally surprised. When we'd been at Ashraf's house, I hadn't really looked at his daughter. My attention was divided among her father, Sabirah, Princess Jamila, and the guard.

I gazed down in the moonlight on high cheekbones that underscored dark frightened eyes staring at me with sincere regret. Long, dark hair framed her oval face. Full lips trembled as she tried to decide whether to speak or not. She didn't have the striking beauty of Sabirah, but she was good looking in a quiet sort of way.

She softly said, "The princess has escaped. I have come to tell my cousin." Her voice was soothing, even though her message was not.

"This isn't good." I jumped up and headed straight for the house. She followed close at my heels. Upon entering, we found Hashim had fallen asleep, sitting on a floor mat and leaning against the wall. Sabirah must still be feeding her mother. "I'll get Sabirah," I quietly told the cousin so as not to disturb Hashim.

Pulling back the drapes, I saw Sabirah next to her mother. A candle glimmered between them, softening their features and giving the room a rosy glow, even though her mother could possibly be dying. The woman's fragile body on the sleeping mat looked so very small and pale and weak. Her dark-rimmed eyes saw me before Sabirah's did, and she nodded in my direction. "Is this your friend?"

Sabirah turned, the bowl in her hands still full of food. She looked discouraged, as though she'd tried to get her mother to eat without much luck. Glaring at me, she appeared upset that I had intruded, but then she smiled. "Yes. This is Tag."

"Come here, young man. Let me have a closer look at you." The older woman's eyes, though sunken and framed with dark moons, were warm and inviting. I stepped closer.

"Ah, yes. You are right. He is the one."

Did she also believe, as her daughter did, that I was sent here to help them? Such a thought made me feel important. I said, "It's a pleasure to meet you."

"Sabirah says you are to go with her in the morning to take the princess to King Jacob. You'll meet my Samuel and my Asim." A sure knowledge shone in her gaze, and I remembered why I'd barged in on this private moment.

"Sabirah, we need to talk."

If a look could growl, hers would have. Still, I anxiously motioned for her to follow me out. "She'll only be a minute," I said, hoping to give the ailing woman comfort.

She nodded and closed her eyes. Sabirah followed me to the next room. As soon as we entered, she saw her cousin.

"Rasha, why are you here?" Sabirah handed her mother's bowl of uneaten food to me. I accepted it without concern, my thoughts on the cousin. I'd been so worried over the princess's escape, I'd neglected to ask the cousin's name. Rasha was a pretty name, sort of musical. I answered for her. "She says the princess has escaped."

"Uncle promised he would have Ravid guard her." Sabirah's angry voice awakened her grandfather.

The old man quickly scrubbed sleep from his face. Scratching the top of his graying head, he staggered to his feet. "Rasha, my sweet angel."

Then I realized I had Sabirah's mother's bowl of food in my hands. Not wanting Hashim to see his daughter-in-law hadn't eaten his food and worried that he might become offended, I turned about and gulped it down. New flames from the spicy peppers ignited in my throat. Willing tears away from my eyes, I turned back.

Rasha nervously looked from her grandfather to her cousin as if wondering whom to talk to first. Speaking to Sabirah, she said, "Ravid helped her and fought off the guards. My father is seeing to the injured and has some men looking for them."

"They won't catch her," Sabirah said. She had that far-off look in her eyes, a look I was learning meant she was thinking of a plan.

"My father sent me to tell you." Rasha wrung her hands together as she studied her cousin, as though they shared something more than Hashim knew.

He growled. "I warned your father not to place his trust in Ravid. That guard has always had shifty eyes. My son is entirely too trusting. Last month when we learned marauders were close, he told me I needed to be more *trusting*. They stole half of my corn before Ashraf could see the truth," he huffed.

"This time it is my fault." Rasha defended her father.

Hashim shrugged as if her words made no difference.

Rasha continued, "My father trusted me to watch her, too. I have failed."

Hashim put his arm about her shoulders. "This is not your fault, fair angel. He should have doubled the guards."

Sabirah drove her fingers through her long, thick hair, pulling it away from her face. The glow of the kitchen fire played over her high cheekbones and thin nose. Again, I thought of how drop-dead gorgeous she was, even though her dark eyes were clouded with anger as her long fingers swiped across her brow. "So many have fallen under King Jacob's spell." She glanced at Rasha with what looked like sympathy. That was odd. Then she added, "What is to become of us?" She looked at her grandfather, and I knew she was worried about her brother, Asim, wondering if he, too, had accepted the ways of the Gadiantons. I wanted to take the worry from her, tell her everything would be all right; still, who was I to make such promises? But I wanted to. I wanted to do whatever I could to take away Sabirah's worry. I liked her, liked her a lot. She turned to me and said, "We must leave now."

"Yes, Granddaughter," said Hashim. "Your keen sense and reliance on the Lord will keep you safe." Though his voice was firm and certain, his stooped shoulders seemed to droop. "The princess will cover much ground by morning's light." He went to the kitchen area and started packing food. He looked up at us as he worked. "Take my boats. Our stream flows into the River Sidon. Worries me that you go without guards." He placed several corn cakes in a pouch.

Sabirah stopped before going in to her mother. "Don't worry. The Lord will guide us."

I hoped so.

"I shall go, as well," said Rasha.

Wow, such love and loyalty from a cousin. I thought of Ethan.

Love, never.

Kinship, doubtful.

Full dislike, probably.

"No," Hashim said to Rasha as he tied the pouch he'd packed.

"Princess Jamila trusts me, Grandfather. She bragged that she took something from this one." Rasha pointed to me.

I couldn't imagine what she was talking about.

And then I knew! The world screeched to a halt. Panic pulsed through my veins, hammering to my brain. I frantically felt the pocket of my poncho, pulling out my sketchpad, pencil, and a rock.

A plain old rock!

I'd been duped.

The brother of Jared's stone, the stone that Christ had touched those many years ago, the stone that was my only hope of returning home, was gone. The princess must have switched them when she'd grabbed ahold of me at Ashraf's. Why hadn't I noticed? I was so stupid. Horrified, I gazed up at Sabirah.

She knew immediately what I'd lost. I would have done anything I could not to see that look of pure disappointment on her face. She gave a heavy sigh and shook her head. "So our journey will have twice the urgency."

Rasha looked between Sabirah and me, as if knowing something more was wrong. "You need me to help with the princess, and I can be of much service should anyone become injured." She pointed to a small bag strapped to her waist. "I have my special poultices."

Sabirah said, "You will follow us anyway, won't you?"

Rasha crossed her arms with a determined *what-do-you-think* glare.

"My uncle would never forgive me if something happened to you." By the tone of her voice, I could tell Sabirah was giving in.

Hashim added, "Let me deal with Ashraf. I will make everything right with him. He may be the leader of our village and foreman of my cornfield, but I am still his father, and he has to listen to me. Besides, I can remind him of his duties to his family. Though there's a high probability he will whine because Rasha won't be here to fix his meals. Not to worry. I shall fill his belly. You need her. I am completely certain I can convince my son of that."

"But, Grandfather, you're too busy seeing to my mother to cook for him, as well." Sabirah's concerns were just.

"Ashraf will have to break bread with us. He is of able body and can make the small journey across the village to our home. And . . . I will have yet another person to try my recipes on. It has been a long time since he has supped with me. Strange, he always finds a reason to leave just before we eat. But now, it will be as it should. Besides, he needs to visit his brother's ailing wife. A family should stay close during hard times."

The word *family* echoed in my mind. I thought of my mother. She worked alone and always seemed to have reasons to be busy. Mom was on the go, involved with life, and helping others. Until the available Doctor Bradford arrived on the scene. Thinking about how it was with the three of us, I should have been happy Mom had found someone since Dad had left, but I wasn't. I wanted her to myself. I wanted to be the one to help her. But I'd messed up there, too.

I gazed at Sabirah. If Mom had had her for a daughter when Dad and Tyler left, she would have turned to Sabirah for help. She looked like she could fix any problem. Plus, she was sort of like Mom, a take-charge person. I wondered if the two would get along. What was I thinking? Mom could get along with anyone.

Except me.

I yearned to see her and Dad and Tyler. For a moment, I pictured my family in happy times. Smiles. Laughter. I missed them. And I knew Sabirah had the same longing for her dad and brother. I had to help her. We were both desperate to keep our families together. Maybe, in a strange way, by helping Sabirah, I would be helping my own family, too.

"Sabirah?" The weak voice came from her mother's room.

She gratefully patted my shoulder before going to her. "We shall leave as soon as possible." And then she disappeared behind the drapery door.

10

Exposed

Sabirah

AFTER VISITING WITH MY MOTHER, I went to meet Mahir. He was waiting for me beneath the canopy of the great mother tree near our village. He looked up as I approached. A smile gentled his worried face. "It's late."

"I know. I have bad news." I told him of the princess's escape and that at this moment, my grandfather was preparing a boat for me to leave with Tag and Rasha.

"In the dead of night?"

I nodded.

"I should be the one to go with you." He looked determined. I took his hand, feeling his calloused knuckles and feeding on his strength.

"I need you here," I told him.

He pulled away, but I still reminded him of his duty. "I don't know how long I'll be gone, and I need you to watch over the village. My uncle means well, so does Grandfather, but it will fall to you to keep our people safe. I leave with a heavy heart, not knowing what will happen to my mother in my absence. Grandfather will see to her comforts, but he'll not be able to keep our enemies away. Nor will my uncle."

Mahir paced as though he could hardly abide what I said. I continued, "You are my second. Your place is here."

He came to stand very close in front of me, so close that I felt his breath on my face. He said, "If this is truly what you want." He tilted my chin up. In the moonlight, I gazed at him, knowing he wanted me to say something I couldn't. Not now.

I remained silent.

"I'll do it, but know that when you return, I will expect the answer to the question I asked you long ago. I, too, have needs, Sabirah. I am alone and need a woman by my side. I want *you* by my side. I want you to be the mother of my children." He reached to touch my cheek. He wanted to kiss me. A kiss would only add more confusing thoughts to my already troubled mind.

I stepped back. "I promise. You will have your answer upon my return." I left him standing alone under the tree, leaving a piece of my heart with him. He wanted more from me than I could give. Why must he make our lives harder than they already were? My first obligation was to my father and family. At this moment, their needs came before my own. Their very lives hung in the balance.

I also needed time to sort out my feelings for Mahir. They were as tangled as creeping vines and much harder to understand. In my heart, I wanted to be his, but in my mind, I wondered if such a union would be wise. I wasn't the usual girl men wanted. They wanted women who stayed at home fulfilling the traditional role of wife and mother. And as much as I yearned to, that wasn't who I was.

My father had taught me how to hunt, how to fight, and how to lead. He'd told me he had known I was to be different from the other girls of the village, that mine was a different life mission. Until Asim failed to return, I'd not fully realized what my father meant. And though the village sought my uncle's advice, they still came to me to find game to feed their families. They came to me to defend their homes. Now with the princess's escape, my plan of saving my father and brother and restoring my family was in jeopardy.

Doubts flooded me. How could I reason with the king for my father's return without a ransom? What leverage did I have to sway his mind? Added to my burden was the fact that Jamila had stolen the sacred stone from Tag. I should have taken the stone from him and cared for its safety myself. Would the Lord forgive my oversight?

Yet, I knew the stone was Tag's burden. He was the one the Lord had picked as guardian for the stone. The wayfarer would need my full attention and help to retrieve it. Together we'd see this through or die trying. I couldn't be delayed over worry of Mahir. I couldn't even pause over my mother's weakened state. I had to trust that the Lord would strengthen Grandfather to see to Mother's needs and make peace with my uncle.

As for Mahir . . . nothing would soothe him except an answer I couldn't give.

❧

Tag

GLAD FOR THE FULL MOON, I peered through the darkness at the other side of the stream, searching for the dreaded caimans Hashim had mentioned. I'd decided the creatures had to be real. Sabirah had mentioned them, too, and she was serious at the time. I was sure they were out there somewhere.

Hashim's boats bobbed in the water, waiting for unsuspecting victims. I'd been told the canoes were dug out of ceiba trees. They appeared none too safe. A collage of possibilities flooded my mind: boat rolling over from a sneeze, big river water washing over the sides, those caiman critters attacking. The possibilities were endless. I fought the overwhelming desire to run away.

Sabirah came to stand beside me, an armload of supplies in one arm, a torch in the other. She placed the supplies in the canoe she would paddle. Grabbing a tunic, she handed it to me. "Mother said you needed this. You also need this." She handed me a sword, the same one I'd used to hack through the brush yesterday.

"This belongs to Gian." I should have given the sword to his parents when they returned my collar. "When he gets better, he'll need it."

"No, he won't." Sabirah said in a rather solemn tone.

"Do you mean he's too ill to use it, or that he . . . really doesn't need it because he's . . . dead?"

"He no longer needs it," Sabirah said. "No one survives such wounds. When his parents took him, they knew his fate. They were grateful for your help. You kept him alive until they could say their good-byes. His sword is now yours."

Taking the blade from her, it weighed heavy in my hand. I felt as though I was being sucked into that black hole in my brain where forbidden memories hid. I was freefalling into a nothingness darker than the night around me. I felt smothered. I couldn't go there. Not now! Terrified, I grabbed ahold of Sabirah.

"Tag, are you all right?" Her voice seemed far away, yet it pulled me back. I willed her to keep talking.

"Tag?" She placed her hand on my shoulder and peered into my eyes. The smothering sense left. The inky blackness lightened until I focused on her. There stood Sabirah, brave Sabirah, warrior woman. She cupped her hand to my face. "Don't worry, Tag. I'm here."

She'd saved me. Sabirah had pulled me back. I felt dizzy and dropped Gian's sword. She picked it up. Handing me the torch, she tied the weapon to my waist. She then gave me a dagger and leather bindings. "Strap the dagger where it can't be seen but where you can easily reach it."

Though she may have thought the weapons made me nervous, they didn't. It was what was hidden in my mind that did. As the cloudiness of the moment passed, I wanted to act normal, so I glanced at Sabirah to see where she'd placed her dagger. I couldn't tell. Her sword hung at her waist. I was sure she had a dagger, as well. Noticing my perplexity, she pointed to the weapon strapped to the inner calf of her leg and smiled while taking the torch from me.

As I laced the weapon to my leg, I watched Sabirah arrange the other supplies in the boat. She took meticulous care in covering the supplies.

Glancing at me, she said, "I talked Grandfather into only sending us cornbread for the journey. We'll eat fruit we find on our way."

"Wise." I nodded in agreement. My stomach churned from the two spicy helpings I'd eaten—mine and Sabirah's mother's.

Rasha and Hashim walked down the path toward us. As they neared, Hashim said to Sabirah, "Don't worry. I shall take good care of your mother. She's stronger than she thinks and will wait for your return before she takes her journey to heaven. You've given her much hope, courageous one.

"And you, Rasha, my precious angel, I'll handle your father. He will not dare to be cross with me. It's I who has a score to settle with him." Hashim tweaked Rasha's nose. She hugged her grandfather and then placed her supplies in the other canoe.

She would paddle the boat I was to ride in. I knew nothing about canoeing, and truth be told, I didn't like boats, paddles, or anything that had to do with water. My wish for this moment was that they had life preservers in Book of Mormon times. I thought of the abandoned orange life preserver in back of Grandpa's cabin.

Darkness began to gather in my mind again. Rubbing my forehead, I willed the image from my mind and stared at the Tootsie Roll canoes the moon light shone upon. I felt doomed to my fate.

Sabirah handed Hashim the torch, kissed his cheek, and wasted no time pushing her boat into the stream and hopping in. Rasha motioned for me to get in the water and help start us on our way. Swallowing hard, I entered the stream. The cold liquid crawled up my legs to my torso. I lunged into the safety of the boat at the same time as Rasha.

"Wayfarer," Hashim called from the shore. "Take good care of my loved ones." He waved to me. I waved back. If he only

knew my brain's crazy state, he'd not even ask me to watch over a
sleeping turtle, let alone take care of his loved ones.

Our boats glided easily through reeds and deadwood. The only
noise in the quiet night was the paddles dipping into the river and
the trickle of water as the paddles were lifted forward.

After what seemed like a couple of hours—but it must have
been longer because of the metal tones of dawn that crept upon
us—the stream we rode in poured into another river, much larger.
As the sun climbed higher, the green of the jungle dripped into the
wide river on both sides. I pulled out Dad's sketchpad and quickly
caught the scene.

I wanted to put more detail in the water and the sky, but I
knew I'd become too absorbed in my art and would probably miss
something important, like a floating snake or caiman. On second
thought, it might be a good thing if I were occupied. No. I flipped
shut the sketchpad and slipped it and the pencil into my poncho
pocket.

Sabirah stayed close to the east shore, which was curious since
she was in a hurry and the main current was near the middle. But
near shore was where I wanted to be.

"Our boats were not meant for this large water." Rasha had a
worried look on her face. I'd hardly given her a thought.

"I'm sure Sabirah knows what she's doing." I glanced at Rasha.
She was much more plain than Sabirah. That's not to say she was
ugly, by any means. She reminded me of a sparrow, a small, fidgety
but determined bird. Wanting to take her mind from her worries, I
asked, "Where do you think the princess is going?"

"Jacobugath, north of the land of Desolation." Her eyes
nervously scanned the water, watchful and wary.

"Does the river go there?" I asked.

"Oh no. We have to journey on foot much of the way. But the
river will take us past much of the dense jungle. Don't worry, we'll
catch them." She said it convincingly as if to help herself believe. I
wondered now if she regretted coming.

"Tell me again. Why did you want to come?" I was more than a little curious. If she was so scared, why was she putting herself through this?

"To help my cousin."

So she was sticking to that story. I knew she had more reason, but I was in no mood to probe. When she wanted to, she'd tell me. For now, I wondered what she knew about my stone the princess had stolen. I asked, "Did Princess Jamila show you what she took from me?"

"No. She kept it hidden. But she had me fetch a small basket. And when I brought food to her, she'd bound the basket shut with leather straps Ravid had given her. It must be very precious."

"Yes, it is. I'm such an idiot."

"Idiot? What is an idiot?" Rasha asked as she paddled smoothly through the water, her eyes constantly scanning our surroundings and coming back to Sabirah in the boat ahead.

I tried to think how to explain the word to her. "A person slow in the mind."

"Oh. Yes. Maybe so."

I didn't like the way she had accepted the meaning and applied it to me, even though I'd said it. She didn't have to agree. I decided talking with her was not a good idea.

The air grew hot and muggy with the sun beating relentlessly down on us. I wanted to take off my poncho and put on the tunic Sabirah had given me, but too much rocking might pitch us overboard. With no hat or sleeves, I knew I'd have one blazing sunburn. Sweat trickled down my back and the sides of my face. Of course, Sabirah and Rasha hardly suffered. Their clothing was light and their dark skin was more adapted to this climate than my red freckles.

Sabirah motioned across the river and started out into the main current.

Rasha followed paddling madly.

"What's going on? I thought we were staying close to shore because it's safer. We really should stay close to the shore, don't you think?" I hoped she'd agree and turn about.

"We have to cross somewhere. The land of Desolation and King Jacob's city lie on the other side. We have no choice. Sabirah has picked a good place to cross. The river flows slowly here."

If it flowed slowly, why were they both paddling as if the devil chased them? Then I realized that out in the main current, we were exposed and might be spotted by the princess. I wanted to help, but there was only one paddle per boat. I leaned over and tried to aid using my hand. The canoe tipped and rocked. I was slowing us down. Glancing back at Rasha, I knew she was thinking of the new word I'd taught her. I might as well just write "idiot" across my forehead. I limply smiled and settled back where I would do less harm.

As we neared the shore, I saw the bank was littered with logs . . . logs with big, round eyes.

"Caimans!" Rasha said.

So they *were* real. And caimans were crocodiles! Though I knew Sabirah could probably hold her own with one of the beasts, I also knew I'd be croc bait if I fell in the water. Luckily, we paddled past their resting area and finally came to an eddy that was crocodile free.

Sabirah went ashore, and we followed. Trees shaded the bank. It felt nice to get out of the boat and stand up. Sabirah stretched and then stopped and studied me as if I'd grown another head.

"What?" I was more than a little self-conscious. Did she see a poisonous bug on me?

"Your face is as red as the setting sun."

I reached to touch my face. She grabbed my hand. "So are your arms. We should rub the meat of the calming plant on you."

Rasha walked up beside her. Her eyes grew large as coconuts upon seeing my skin. "I have some in my pouch." She ran back to the canoe where she'd left it.

"You're going to hurt tonight, my weird friend." Sabirah chuckled.

"I should never have told you what *weird* meant." I cleared my throat, straining against my dog collar.

At that moment, Rasha screamed.

I whirled round in time to see a crocodile headed straight for her. Doing a double take, I realized there wasn't just one. The entire herd we'd seen upriver had migrated to our spot.

We were croc bait!

11

Caught

Tag

IMMEDIATELY, SABIRAH GRABBED HER SWORD. I pulled mine to the ready and started running away from the river.

"The jungle is too thick to run through here. We need the boats," Sabirah yelled.

I wanted to yell, *"Forget the stupid boats,"* but there was no time to argue. Both Rasha and Sabirah were heading for the river. Remembering the cornbread Hashim had sent for us, I yelled to Rasha, "Throw the bread so they'll go after it."

She promptly grabbed the bag containing the food. Untying the bundle, she hurled the entire contents as far away as she could. The crocs weren't distracted and kept coming. Rasha narrowly dodged a croc as she jumped into her boat and launched it. Swords in hand, Sabirah and I raced to the other canoe.

One of the larger crocs was hot on my tail. Sabirah whirled about and with one mighty swipe of her blade whacked the reptile's head clean off. Crocodile blood spewed everywhere.

"Get in the boat!" she yelled at me.

Once I reached the water's edge, I dropped my sword into the canoe. Sabirah was beside me and leaped swiftly into the boat. I pushed with all my might to help launch it.

As I tried to crawl in, my foot got tangled in the roots of a tree beneath the water. Falling under the water, I panicked beyond reason. I tried to stand using my other leg, but my foot slipped in the mud, keeping me beneath the water's surface. I tried to see where the surface was, but I kept kicking up mud, blurring the water. I jerked and jerked on my leg, praying some miracle would happen, hoping help would reach its hand down into the water and save me.

No help!

No air!

I had to fight. At any moment a croc could get me. Trying with all my might, I couldn't break free. My limbs were losing energy. Water pressed in on me, filling my nose, stinging my eyes. Through the murky water, I wondered, *Will I die here today?* My arms and legs moved slowly. A sense of hopelessness clutched me. Then I thought of Mom. If I died, she would have no one except Doctor Bradford. I couldn't let that happen. I had to prove to Mom I was strong, I had courage, and I was a survivor. No way was I going to give up my life here in Book of Mormon times. As if in answer to prayer, a picture came to my mind of me strapping a dagger to my leg. Reaching down, I tried to pull the weapon free. With one last thrust, I yanked out the dagger and then sliced at the tangled root mass that held me captive.

As I surfaced, my head bumped into Sabirah's boat. She reached over and with both hands pulled me from the water, sopping wet poncho and all, just as a crocodile glided past.

"Are you all right?" Sabirah dropped me in the canoe and started paddling hard, escaping from the pack of hungry carnivores.

I sucked in long drags of air. "Yeah. Got hung up," I said, swiping water from my sunburned face and kissing the dagger in my hand. I was amazed that the camains weren't following us, but maybe the oars in the water frightened them away. Whatever stopped them, I was grateful. Quickly securing my dagger to my leg, I grabbed my sword that I'd dropped in the boat, tying it to my waist. I had learned a valuable lesson. Always keep your weapons with you.

ço

Sabirah

RELIEVED THAT WE'D ESCAPED, I felt the tremendous weight of my mission. I'd been so concerned about rescuing my brother and father that I'd nearly killed the wayfarer and my cousin. I had to be more careful and think through my actions more clearly.

I stared at Tag. My world was a new adventure for him, and I realized that his coming wasn't only to help me find my father, but it was also to benefit Tag. A darkness had followed him here. At some point, he would have to turn and face it. I hoped when he did, I could help him. Though he hadn't told me a lot about his private life, I knew the darkness he fought wasn't of his own making. When Tag was strong enough and had learned the lesson he needed here, I knew he'd contend with the darkness. I would stand beside him through it all. The words *stand beside him* made me think of a wife and husband. My thoughts drifted to Mahir.

He'd been patient thus far; yet, how long would he wait? To expect him to wait for my life to be resolved was asking too much. He was a man of needs and wants that I couldn't fulfill. Better for him to find another to make his wife. Though he might think he'd only be happy with me, his happiness would fade as I continued to hunt by his side, continued to run about the jungle where my heart soared as the eagle. My hand went to the necklace. I'd used my father's absence to keep Mahir at arm's length. In truth, I didn't know if I could be a wife to anyone. With God's guidance, I'd make my own path because I knew He gave me these desires for a reason. Deep in my heart, I wanted Mahir as my husband, but what was best for him? I answered my own question.

Someone else.

His future didn't include me.

☙

Tag

WE DRIFTED WITH THE CURRENT for quite a while, all of us quiet and thankful. My mind played over and over the scene of Sabirah whacking off that croc's head. She really did have the strength of an Amazon. She was like no woman I'd ever known. She was so beautiful, strong, and independent. I knew I could tell her anything and she'd understand. I was glad she was on my side. And I sure wouldn't want to be King Jacob, especially if he'd captured Sabirah's dad and brother.

By late afternoon, we'd traveled a good distance downriver. We hadn't seen a croc for a long time. Sabirah decided we'd be safe to put into shore again. As we pulled our boats up the bank, she studied me and winced. "Oh, my friend, you are now the color of a red pepper." I knew my sunburn was bad. When I'd raise my eyebrows and wrinkle my forehead, it hurt. Luckily, only my face, neck, and forearms had been exposed. I'd hidden my legs under my poncho. But my sunburn wasn't my main concern. Though I was glad Sabirah considered me her friend, I hoped that one day her feelings could grow into something more. Whoa. What was the matter with me? She'd never look at me like she did Mahir. Would she? Hmm. An interesting thought.

Rasha brought the green stems of the calming plant to me. It looked like an aloe vera. She cut it open and gently rubbed the green, slimy insides on my face. Mom had used aloe vera on me many times when I'd been burned. As Rasha coated my skin, I felt a slight relief, and I knew this was about the best medicine available for my burn.

"Take off this band around your throat, and I'll rub it on your neck." She pointed to my dog collar.

I quickly unclasped it, and immediately I heard Rasha inhale deeply.

"What?" I asked, touching my throat.

She moved my hand. "Your burn is more brilliant against the white of your throat." Her tender touch rubbed more plant meat on me. I imagined my neck looked like a strawberry Oreo with a white creamy center. When she finished, I tried to put the collar back on, but now the edges of the leather irritated my sunburn. Giving a sigh, I tossed the collar into the canoe. Rasha handed me the plant meat so I could rub it on my forearms.

She smiled. "I think I could easily find you in the dark. You are as bright as my parrot."

Not only was I smarting from the sunburn, but I was being compared to a bird. Well, it served me right. I'd compared Rasha to a sparrow. At least she made me a parrot.

She patted my shoulder and said, "You will heal."

I noticed Sabirah had disappeared. Rasha stored away the rest of the plant in her pouch. I glanced around, wary of any type of threatening creature that might come traipsing out of the foliage, wanting us for dinner. Thinking of food reminded me that lunch had long passed. People really didn't eat on a regular basis in this era. Unfortunately for me, my appetite was still on Rocky Mountain time. My stomach growled loudly.

"Sabirah is searching for food," said Rasha as she unloaded more things from her canoe. "Though it's early, she may have us camp here for the night."

"But won't the crocodiles find us? I mean, we're right by the water."

"I believe they are far away. Besides, they will not want you. You are burnt." She smiled as she began to unload the supplies from her canoe.

"Very funny. Ha, ha. For all you know, there might be a croc who likes his food extra crispy."

"Maybe crispy but not scorched." She smiled again and suddenly the entire jungle brightened. Even my sunburn didn't hurt quite so much when Rasha looked at me with her soft and tender eyes that could hypnotize a cobra. I had to snap out of it. What was wrong with me? I was thinking like one of the jocks back in my own time. And that wasn't me. So why was I attracted to Sabirah and Rasha?

Thinking about Sabirah, I realized she probably had feelings for Mahir. And I was probably confusing my feeling of gratitude for her with attraction. She was really like a sister to me. I had to remember that. Rasha, on the other hand. Maybe. No.

This was one whacked-out world. I turned away.

As if she knew my thoughts and was embarrassed, Rasha busied herself scouting out an area to set up camp.

Wanting to change into the tunic Sabirah had given me, I untied the belt that held my sword. I stole a quick glance at Rasha. I didn't want her to see me in my briefs. She'd probably never seen underwear like mine; besides, a guy needs his privacy. I realized she was too busy searching the bushes to even notice what I was doing. I carefully tugged off the poncho so as not to irritate my burn. I glanced down at my chest. My henna tattoo was starting to disappear. All that thrashing in the water had rubbed most of the spider legs away and parts of the skull. It made it look like some creepy voodoo something or other. It wouldn't do for Sabirah to see this. I quickly slipped on the light tunic. This material was much cooler than the poncho. I retied the sword to my waist and started unloading the supplies from Sabirah's canoe.

Suddenly, Sabirah came running through the brush. Though out of breath, she managed to say, "I spotted the princess and Ravid. We have to keep moving." She grabbed the supplies from me and slung them over her shoulder, positioning the bulk on her back. Spotting them had pumped fresh energy into her. I wished it had done the same for me. I was beat.

Rasha abandoned her attempt to set up camp and immediately followed Sabirah's lead by gathering her supplies.

I slipped on my poncho, not wanting to carry it, and then grabbed a bundle.

Sabirah motioned toward the canoes. "We'll need these for the return journey. We can hide them in the bushes."

I hefted one end and she the other. First we hid Sabirah's and then Rasha's, placing the paddles inside each one. I took one last look at my dog collar inside Sabirah's canoe. I yearned to take it because it reminded me of home, but I couldn't wear it on my sunburn, and I didn't want to take the time to pack it in the bundle I held. It would be safe here until we returned. With the boats well hidden, we headed out.

We power walked with Sabirah at the lead. I knew she wanted to run but held back because of me. After about an hour and as the sun was setting, I could tell she was upset and nervous because we hadn't caught up to the princess. Trying to console her, I said, "Maybe they saw you."

"No." Sabirah scanned the area as we trekked on. "Ravid is very cunning and has a keen sense for trouble. Be alert."

I remembered the guard Ashraf had summoned when we were in his home. I had been impressed by his muscles and even thought he looked like a pro wrestler. Great.

As we traveled, the jungle trees became more sparse, the bushes less dense. Grass was no longer green but yellow. And it was getting darker. Since suppertime had long passed, I felt as though my stomach were gnawing a pathway past my backbone and on to King Jacob's city.

I pulled Sabirah aside and asked, "Don't you think Rasha needs something to eat? She hasn't had anything since we left."

Sabirah dug in her supply bag, pulled out what looked like some type of jerky, and handed a piece to Rasha. "Thank you, Tag, for reminding me." My eyes followed the hand off of food. Rasha nodded a thank you. Sabirah closed her bag and started walking away.

That was it? no food for herself? no food for me?

Seeing my dilemma, Rasha called, "Sabirah, others are hungry, as well."

An *oh-yeah* look crossed her face. She once again dug in the bag, pulling out another stick, which she immediately chomped down on. She glanced at me and, with a teasing smile, said, "Tag, you want one?"

I nodded. Sabirah chuckled and threw a stick to me as she

started up the trail. I bit down, expecting the tang of jerky, but instead it tasted more like chicken or—something that definitely wasn't jerky. The flavor was unlike any meat I'd ever eaten. "What is this?" I asked as I chewed, enjoying the taste of food while I hustled to keep up.

"Dog," Sabirah replied over her shoulder.

"What?" A picture of Mom's Yorkie came to mind. I hated that little rat-dog, but I'd never eat it. "You're kidding, right?"

Sabirah stopped, looking at me all puzzled. "Kidding?"

"You know, saying something that makes someone laugh."

She shrugged. "I enjoy 'kidding' you, but I don't laugh over food. Barkless dog is very good. Only a few families in the village are fortunate enough to raise them."

"Dogs are pets, not food!" The stick in my hand became the front leg of a Yorkie.

"Maybe where you come from they aren't, but we eat them. And if you're smart, you will, too. This will be the only food we have today. I'll not risk a fire, and I haven't seen a fruit tree or a pepper plant." She started walking again. Rasha smiled at me as she passed, chewing on her dog jerky.

I didn't care what Sabirah said, I couldn't eat dog meat. My hunger wasn't that bad . . . yet. I caught up with Sabirah and returned my piece. She gave me a puzzled look but took the meat and placed it in her bundle. "Didn't you say Hashim sent some corn cakes?"

"Remember the caimans?" And that was the end of that.

We journeyed another couple of hours and came to a nice grove of trees. Creeping slowly into the foliage, we found a campsite. A fire crackled and popped. No one was about. Sabirah pressed her finger to her lips to keep us silent. She had grown very quiet in the dusky glow of sunset as she studied each bush and tree. She paused as if listening to something and then slowly reached for her sword.

All of a sudden, out of the brush walked Princess Jamila, cool, calm, and collected, as though we were her invited guests. But where was the servant who had run away with her? I couldn't see him.

In a low, throaty voice, Jamila said, "Sabirah, where is your man, Mahir?"

Sabirah looked at the princess as though stunned by her nerve and surprised that the princess would speak of her second-in-command. At any moment, I knew the warrior in Sabirah would take over, but right now the woman in her had been taken off guard. Because of Mahir's jealousy over Sabirah spending time with me, I had a feeling there was something going on between them. Obviously, the princess had picked up on it, as well.

"Princess Jamila." Rasha drew her attention. "We came looking for you." She appeared scared and brave at the same time.

"I know. But I have grown weary of this cat-and-mouse game and decided to put an end to it. That's why I allowed you to find me." Though she was answering Rasha, the princess had locked her sights on Sabirah and wasn't about to be distracted.

Sabirah latched onto her arm, sword to the ready.

Undaunted, Jamila continued her badgering. "Your man, Mahir, and I had a good talk on the way to your village."

"One more word and I'll take a corpse back to your father," Sabirah spat out as she jerked Jamila to her, placing the tip of her sword to her throat.

Despite her life-threatening situation, Jamila smiled and said, "Your man needs a real woman to make him happy, not a horsewoman who roams the hills."

Pure hatred gleamed in Sabirah's eyes. What was wrong with the princess? Did she have a death wish?

Rasha looked to me as though expecting me to do something. If someone didn't say something real soon, there was no telling what Sabirah would do.

A noise from above drew my attention. In the branches of a far-reaching tree was Ravid. He was a mountain of muscle. With a sword in one hand, he made ready to leap toward Sabirah and the princess.

I yelled, "Look out!"

12

Numb

Tag

SABIRAH WHIRLED AROUND, STILL HOLDING the princess close to her. Ravid was already in midleap as he came crashing down on them. His blade missed Sabirah but caught the princess in her upper thigh. He immediately withdrew his sword. Blood ran down Jamila's leg. Disbelief shone on her shocked face.

"What have you done?" she yelled at the man who had forsaken his own people to side with her and run away.

Sabirah let her go. Even in the meager glow of the campfire, I could see anger reddening Jamila's cheeks as she stared at the astonished guard. But pain demanded her attention as she sank to the ground.

Ravid dropped his sword, reaching out to the princess. I quickly retrieved it, passing it to Sabirah. With a sword in each hand, she glowered down at her captives.

"Princess, I meant to kill *her* not stab you. Please believe me," Ravid begged for forgiveness.

Sabirah motioned with one sword and said to Ravid, "Carry her to the fire. Tag might be able to save her." Blood dripped to the ground, leaving a trail as Ravid followed the Sabirah's orders. Though in pain, the princess didn't cry or utter a word, just pointed her loathing stare at Sabirah and Ravid.

The guard laid her down on a poncho. Must have been his. All of us huddled close to see how badly she'd been hurt. I knelt beside her.

I could hardly see the wound. "I need more light."

Looking back at the fire, I noticed a smaller log, a branch really, with only one end aflame. "Sabirah, would you grab that?" I pointed to it. With quick understanding, she handed one sword to Rasha, picked up the torchlike tree branch, and came back to us. With the light shining directly on the wound, I could see much better.

Pushing up the princess's short tunic to gain a better view, I found the large gash ran down the outside of her thigh. Ripping off the corner of my poncho, I wiped oozing blood away from the injury. The wound was longer than Gian's but not as deep and had not cut the artery. True, the skin was split, but surprisingly not much muscle had been damaged, and I could not see bone.

"I have seen worse," I said to the princess. She glared back. For a moment I was tempted not to do anything more. I glanced up at Rasha and Sabirah and knew I had no choice.

Kneeling at Jamila's side, Ravid appeared relieved. He said to her, "Please, forgive me." His concerned eyes pleaded with her.

"Clumsy fool," she hissed, refusing to even glance at him.

Trying to think what Mom would do in this situation, I gazed down on the wound. "It needs to be cleansed and stitched up."

Ravid quickly grabbed the water gourd, handing it to me. The water wasn't exactly sterile, but it was all we had. As I poured it over the injury, Rasha dug in her medicinal pouch and then gave me what looked like large dried red chili peppers. "This will numb the skin."

I rubbed them on the wound. Next Rasha handed me a cactus needle threaded with a long strain of hair—probably from a horse's tail. I remembered watching medical procedures on TV with Mom. One was about how doctors made stitches. As I recalled, they knotted with each stitch.

Okay . . . I could do this.

Sabirah caught my eye and slightly smiled as if to say, *Go ahead. I believe in you.* Taking the needle in my hand, I began to stitch. I nervously glanced at the princess. She barely flinched, keeping her eyes on me. Either the chili peppers were working or she had a mighty high pain threshold.

I set my mind on the job before me. After I finished, Rasha handed me a healing poultice and ragged strips of cloth she'd torn from the hem of her tunic. I wrapped the wound and said to the princess, "This should work. Don't put much pressure on your leg, though. You don't want to tear your stitches and bleed."

The princess examined my work. "Your artist's hand works well on skin." Her eyes sparkled in the firelight. She must have seen me sketching as we journeyed to Pagog.

With Princess Jamila taken care of, I remembered the stone. "Since I have helped you, would you return my property?"

"You talk as though you are the boss," said the princess as she leaned back on her elbows.

Sabirah's right eyebrow rose. She tossed the branch we'd used for light back into the fire and then turned with the sword firmly in her hand. "Are we not?"

"No." Jamila motioned. "While you were preoccupied, my father's men arrived."

An entire regiment of soldiers stepped from behind the cover of trees and bushes.

13
Desolation

Sabirah

KING JACOB'S SOLDIERS SURROUNDED US. Many snarled in the darkness as if eager to rip us limb from limb. In the campfire glow, I could see some were Lamanites, some were Nephites, and some were even black skinned. I had heard of such people but had never seen them. The army was at least twenty in all. And they were big men. It would be difficult to make a stand against them. Upon their heads were leather helmets and across their chests, breastplates. Most held spears with obsidian tips, yet some brandished swords and crude axes with very sharp blades.

One brawny fellow jerked our swords from our hands and quickly laid claim to our daggers. I gave them no resistance, mainly because I didn't want Tag or Rasha to resist and risk harm. They were no match for these men. We were sorely outnumbered and surrounded. Tag stood close to me and Rasha as if to protect us. I supposed that was an instinct of men. If only I'd listened to the small voice that had prompted me to use caution moments ago as we entered the trees, we wouldn't be in this sorry state. I glanced again at Tag and Rasha.

Tag stood tall. The wayfarer had truly stepped into his role. I could tell by the determined air about him. Rasha, though afraid, tried her best to remain calm.

A big, strapping, dark-skinned soldier who looked as mean and tough as all my men put together came forward and bowed to the princess. His hands were massive, his fingers as thick and round as large tree roots. He could easily break rock with one fist. Weapons of all sorts dangled from his belt: daggers, a double-edged ax, and what appeared to be two lethal sticks fastened together as one. If thrown at an attacker they would do great damage. Would the enemy always make new weapons to harm us? Strapped to his back was a spear.

"Princess Jamila." He bowed on one knee. "We met a coward named Kei, one of the men from your entourage who fled when you were captured. I killed him for his desertion. We were on our way to rescue you. I should have known the daughter of King Jacob would not stay captured long." His jaw was as big as a thighbone. His bottom teeth overlapped his upper ones.

"Bomani." The princess smiled warmly. "Not only have I escaped, but I bring gifts for my father . . . prisoners."

He swiveled around to have a closer look. At that moment, I knew how it felt to stare a demon in the eyes. Red-hot hatred simmered in his gaze and mingled with crazed pleasure. He was envisioning what tortures he'd use on me. His eyes turned to Rasha. I stepped closer to my cousin, blocking his view. He'd have to get past me before laying a hand on her.

A ghoulish grin spread over his face as though he were accepting my challenge. This Bomani man was pure evil. I'd seen such a look before, and I wanted to jab his animal eyes from his head.

"Oh, you have seen the younger maiden," Princess Jamila said, bringing his attention away from me and back to Rasha. "She is rather fresh and innocent, just as you like them. And though I'd like nothing better than to reward you by turning all of them over to you, I feel it my obligation to offer these three to my father. You understand, don't you, Bomani?"

"You know best, Princess." He refocused his full attention back on her and then saw her leg. "What has happened to you?" he asked.

"This one—" She pointed at Ravid. "—fool that he is, tried to stab one of the prisoners but missed."

Bomani's big chopping jaw protruded as he ground his back teeth. He glared a deathwish at Ravid. The traitorous guard fell to his knees, bending his head until his chin touched his chest.

"Shall I behead him now?" Bomani asked, reaching for his double-edged axe.

The princess appraised Ravid, clicking her tongue as she eyed him. "He did help me escape their village. I shall wait and decide later."

"Thank you, Princess Jamila. Thank you." Ravid groveled on his knees. I couldn't blame him. He'd forsaken us, his people, for this viperous woman, and now he would pay and pay dearly. Bomani spoke of killing as if it gave him great pleasure, as though it were part of his daily ritual.

Bomani placed his foot on Ravid's back and shoved him forward, making him fall to his hands. "Crawl like a dog." Ravid, as big as ox, cowered to the ground, a broken man.

Next Bomani turned to me. "This one looks entirely too proud of herself." He slugged me in the stomach. Pain sharp as quills stabbed through my midsection. Reflexively, I doubled over, though as soon as I could breathe, I rose and glared back.

"If you'd like, I could tame her for the king." Bomani spoke to the princess while staring at me.

As though he couldn't bear to see me injured, Tag quickly came to my side.

Like a bolt of lightning, Bomani punched him on the side of his head, forcing him to collide with me. We both fell to the ground. I quickly gained my feet and reached a hand to Tag, helping him up. A welt rose on the side of his sunburned face.

Jamila said, "Bomani, they are gifts to my father. I can't deliver them battered and bruised. Especially him." She pointed to Tag. "My father will want him unblemished." I wondered what devious plot she was up to. Why would she single out Tag? There had been rumors about the king's satanic rituals. I couldn't bear to think of the wayfarer becoming his victim.

"Just gaining a little respect, Your Majesty. These gifts will give us no problems now."

Tag rubbed the side of his head and seemed glad the princess had stopped Bomani's assault, oblivious to the wicked tortures that could befall him when we reached the city.

"Princess, if we're to cross the land of Desolation, we should do so at daybreak. We shouldn't cross the wilderness at night. It's too dangerous." Bomani stood waiting for the princess's reply.

Tag leaned into me, saying softly, "I've heard everyone talk about this land of Desolation, but what is it?"

Before I could answer, Bomani turned about, zeroing his malevolent gaze on Tag. "The narrow neck of land making up Desolation is filled with shifting sands, the most barren wasteland on mother earth. Set your foot in the wrong place and you will sink out of sight. Very few can read the sands as I. The passage is ever changing."

Tag swallowed hard. I could tell he was terrified at the prospects of walking on shifting sands. Our wayfarer had many fears. I remembered he'd asked me about snakes as we made our way through the jungle to our village. At least the boa didn't reside in the sands. Poisonous pit vipers liked the heat, but they mainly sought shelter in rocks and caves. I'd keep Tag safe.

Bomani took great delight in strapping Tag's arms together. As he did so, the curious, small papyrus bundle fell from Tag's poncho pocket. Bomani scooped it up.

Jamila called out, "Let me see that." Bomani handed it to her. She thumbed through Tag's bundle, stopping when she came to something that obviously interested her. "Ah, a good likeness," she said to Tag. "Father will be pleased I am bringing him one with an expert hand. Tag, you continue to surprise me."

Hate reflected in the young man's eyes as he clenched his teeth.

Afraid Jamila might see his rage and have Bomani torture him more, I said, "Jamila, give it back. You have no need for it."

I had diverted the princess's attention away from Tag and back to me, where it belonged. After all, it had been my fault we'd been captured by showing the heartless she-wolf mercy. I should have left her to bleed.

The princess laughed. "I shall do as I wish. So will my father. He doesn't take kindly to people kidnapping his only daughter." She handed Bomani Tag's bundle and motioned for him to store it.

Tag fought against the binding cords. I could see his wrists quickly turning red and raw. Hate and what could be a sliver of fear fed him energy. By stealing the stone from Tag, Jamila had made a powerful enemy. I knew his bundle meant a great deal to him also, but the stone was his salvation and his pathway home.

"I don't know, though," Princess Jamila now looked at me and continued, "Maybe I'll ask my father if you could be my personal slave." She motioned for Bomani to turn me around as if I were merchandise she was inspecting. I did so begrudgingly. She continued, "I captured you, which will sway him. Might be fun to have Samuel the Lamanite's daughter fetch and carry for me." She began to laugh and then abruptly stopped, holding her leg.

"Princess," Bomani said. "You need your rest. Let me tie these jungle rats on the other side of camp. Morning will come quickly."

"As you wish. But, Bomani, remember I am to give them to my father." She lay down on her mat and closed her eyes.

Both Tag and Rasha grew quiet. And though our capture wasn't what I'd planned, at least we were going to Jacobugath, where I might at long last find my father and brother.

14
Holding On

Tag

WHEN I AWOKE THE NEXT morning, I found Sabirah staring at our captors, who were busily getting ready to leave. "What is it?" I asked, sitting up and trying to itch my nose even though my hands were tied together.

She shook her head. "I don't trust them." Sabirah watched them like a lion watches prey, mindful of their every move.

"That's an understatement," I replied without thinking that she might not understand what I said. Sabirah didn't say anything.

Rasha had awakened and sat up, too. We all had our hands bound and legs tied. Made for a bad night of sleep, though Rasha was bright eyed. "What is *understatement?*" she asked, clutching her medicine pouch to her. I was surprised they had not taken it from her. They'd taken our swords and daggers.

Determined to somehow reclaim my possessions and the stone, I forgot to answer her question before I asked my own. "So what's the plan?"

"Plan?" Sabirah looked at me as though I was mad.

"Yeah, you are thinking of a way we can escape, right?"

"The plan is we do exactly what they ask us to do," she said. "The princess should feel better today. If we are more willing, it may insure the release of my father and brother."

Rasha added, "And help find my mother."

"What?" That was the first I'd heard anything about her mother. Rasha gazed at me as though confessing a great sin.

Sabirah nodded. "Her mother ran away to join King Jacob's tribe years ago when they headed north. She no longer believes as we do. We'll find her." She tried to put a comforting arm around her cousin but only managed to nudge her because of her tied hands.

"So, that's the real reason why you insisted on coming and why you—" I nodded at Sabirah. "—let her."

"Yes. Grandfather does not know of his daughter-in-law's betrayal. Nor does my father." Rasha let out a deep sigh. "They believe she disappeared while hunting for healing plants. Only Sabirah and I know the truth. I am hopeful I can see her and maybe convince her to return to her people." For a millisecond, the sadness in her eyes reminded me of Mom's.

I wondered if my mom felt sad about me because I had run away. Was Mom hopeful I'd return? Did she miss me the way Rasha obviously missed her loved one? I yearned to see my mom's face, even Grandpa's. And even though I didn't want to admit it, Ethan's, too.

My thoughts turned to Dad and Tyler. Oh, how I wanted them to come home. If only I could see them again and talk with them. It's tough having loved ones gone and out of your life. I understood what Rasha was feeling. I also understood Sabirah. If I could be patient and help these two, I might be able to hang on to the hope of my family being reunited.

But for that to happen I had to get my hands on the stone. "Sabirah, when we arrive in the city and you demand they release your father, can we demand they return the stone . . . and the sketchpad?"

"I'm afraid we're in no position to demand anything right now. Yet, the Lord will make a way." And despite our being captives about to walk through miles of sand in the hot burning sun, she smiled, and I felt like everything would be all right.

❧

Sabirah

BOMANI'S MEN CONSTRUCTED A MAKESHIFT litter to carry the princess on. As we were about to set out, his men untied our leg bindings. When they left us, Tag asked, "So, what's with untying our feet?"

"They want us to walk freely through the desert and not hold them back. Tag, you must help me watch Bomani. We need to learn how he reads the sand for our return journey."

As they prepared to leave, Ravid joined my little group. Bomani had sent him to walk with us. Why, I didn't know, other than Ravid could spy and overhear us talking. I thought Rasha would not treat him kindly because of his betrayal. But she warmly smiled at him. All was forgiven.

"Welcome, Ravid." Rasha nudged him with her shoulder. To my amazement, he smiled and seemed genuinely appreciative. His ability to quickly shift allegiance made me wonder where his loyalties truly lay.

We finally set out. As we traveled north, the jungle disappeared. I looked toward the horizon and saw no trees, only sparse plants: prickly cacti and sagebrush amongst miles and miles of sand.

The wind swirled sand granules, rolling them over the ground like writhing snakes. The winds grew more and more intense as the day wore on, and we soon found ourselves in a sandstorm. Bomani's men wrapped their heads in scarves, leaving a slit for their eyes.

Ravid left us and went to the princess. I watched as he spoke with her. He seemed to plead. Finally, she opened the bag Ravid must have packed for her before they escaped. She pulled scarves from it. He bowed and returned. He untied our cords and handed me the scarves to pass around. Grateful for the protection, I quickly gave them to the others and then wrapped my head. As I finished with my own, I noticed Tag struggling with his scarf. The cloth sagged in front of his eyes and draped down his back. He'd done his best. I was about to go to him when Rasha beat me to it. Her hands worked magic with the material as she looped the cloth around Tag's head and finished by tucking the end piece behind his neck. She'd expertly left a slit for his eyes.

Despite the winds, the two stood there gazing at each other. They were a good fit, and the thought crossed my mind that if Tag should have to stay with us, he might find happiness with my cousin. Though Tag was haunted by his past, Rasha could help him face it. They would both be of marriage age within a year or so. Tag appeared befuddled by her kindness, as if he didn't know how to thank her for her help.

Rasha was no different. She, too, seemed uncertain. Tag gazed into her eyes and smiled. Rasha returned the favor and then came to me. Tag followed her.

A line formed so we could continue our journey and keep track of each other. I had to position myself to watch Bomani and make mental notes of the directions, what kind of ground he stepped on, and so forth. Ravid seemed to know my concern and made the soldiers make room for us close to the front. Bomani looked at him, skeptical, but he must have thought Ravid was positioning us where Bomani could keep track of our whereabouts. And he possibly was.

We followed the princess's procession. First in our line was Ravid, then me, Tag, and Rasha. Bomani led us farther into the land of Desolation. The winds were brutal and unrelenting. As I strained to keep up, I noticed in the distance a figure walking toward me. The sands did not affect the personage. Some type of force kept the winds at bay. As the person drew near, I became paralyzed with joy. The man had a familiar, purposeful gait; his shoulders were squared and straight. His black hair was pulled behind his ears and that smile . . . that marvelous fatherly smile I had yearned to see for years filled his chiseled face.

My heart quickened. Father was but a few feet from me. How could he be here in the middle of the land of Desolation?

About to run to him, I stopped. Father had warned me of the powers of evil and how those who worked with such forces could at times manipulate the mind. Remembering the remedy, I thought of Christ, and the image of my father disappeared.

My heart nearly broke. Anger boiled in my veins. I looked ahead through the blinding sands, trying to see the princess. She was the only one with the mental capacity for such deviousness. Barely able to make out her litter, I couldn't clearly see her, but I heard her wicked cackle.

She was toying with me, torturing me with the image of my father. For a moment, I wanted to pull her down from the litter and make her pay for such cruelty. Then I remembered how Father had taught me the pitfalls of revenge and how it gave great joy to the evil one. Vengeance on Princess Jamila was in the Lord's hands. I'd put my trust in Him. Bending my head into the fierce wind, I kept walking.

❧

Tag

HOT, BURNING SAND PERPETUALLY SEEPED into my sandals as I walked. Granules stuck between my toes. With each step, I tried to kick it out, but soon the action became too much, so I tried to ignore it the best I could. Blinded by the sun, I stumbled along. The wind became more intense. Sand stung my eyes. Grit crept into my mouth, sticking to my lips and teeth. I could hardly see Sabirah. She stopped and had me grab ahold of her poncho. I made Rasha grab mine. Sabirah took ahold of Ravid's.

We trudged along through ankle-deep sand for hours. My hand grew weary and numb, but I held tight.

And then it happened. I felt Rasha let go.

15
Building Courage

Tag

"Rasha!" I yelled. Grit blew into my mouth. The sandstorm grew more intense. I jerked on Sabirah's arm to make her stop. She swung around. Through the blinding wind, we saw that Rasha had stumbled off the trail and was hip deep in quicksand. Ravid leaped and grabbed her hand, digging his heels in the shifting sands, madly trying to pull her out. But he, too, was being sucked into the pit and was up to his hips.

"Bomani!" Sabirah yelled. His army quickly drew their leader's attention. The brute brought everyone to a standstill. The men carrying Princess Jamila eased her litter to the ground. Bomani fought against the wind on his way to us. Several of his soldiers followed.

Wasting no time, Sabirah grabbed ahold of Ravid. Bomani latched on to Sabirah. The other soldiers took ahold of Bomani. They pulled hard, dragging Ravid out, but in doing so, his grip on Rasha weakened. All at once, Ravid's hand broke free.

Panicked, Rasha struggled to grab ahold of something, anything, while sinking up to her chest. She would die if someone didn't do something quickly! The soldiers stood back, seeming to know that their weight would be too much on the quicksand. Fear drove through me faster than Skid's Honda Civic.

All at once the sand became ice-covered water. A hand reached from the waves—a hand needing help. I froze, unable to think, unable to move. My world spun with snatches of images. Faces blurred together. A chill surged through me as though the breath of winter and death tried to claim me. I blinked and shook my head. Why was I seeing water in the middle of a desert?

I needed to focus on Rasha. Sand replaced the water. Desperate to help, and without really thinking of anyone else except her, I moved to a different spot than the others. The ground was firmer here. Using my body like a plank, I stretched out over the sand, grasping Rasha's flailing arm.

Sabirah immediately latched onto my legs, acting as an anchor.

"Give me your other hand," I shouted at Rasha.

She fought against the sucking sand and turned, reaching toward me, barely missing. In the struggle, her body slipped farther and farther down. Suffocating sand edged up to her chin. Fear shone in her eyes. I could barely touch her fingertips. I needed both her hands to pull her out, or I was afraid I'd break her arm, though one was better than none. Finding a hidden strength from deep within, I lurched forward and safely secured her free hand.

From somewhere in back of me, there came a mighty pull. I glanced behind and saw that Ravid had repositioned himself behind Sabirah, and Bomani had clamped onto him. They gave a mighty tug. Inch by little inch, Rasha's body slowly eased from the sand until she finally broke free.

We collapsed, lying on the sand. Rasha, laughing and crying, crawled to my side. Through our scarves, she pecked my face and head with kisses, stopping briefly to say, "Never have I seen such bravery!" She gazed into my eyes.

The winds had died down and a strange calm hung in the air, which only made this moment even more surreal. Rasha had said I was brave. Me, Quivering Quincy! Without thought of my personal well-being, I'd grabbed for her. I'd reached out for life. Overwhelmed by the moment, I couldn't speak.

All at once Sabirah stood me on my feet. "Tag, though you are small, you are a warrior." Rasha gave Sabirah hugs and kisses like she had me as well as Ravid and even Bomani. But Bomani didn't let go. He clutched hold of her as if he had other notions on his mind, which had me more than a little concerned. He was a man who took advantage of any situation, especially if it had to do with women. He'd made that plain before we started on this journey.

Bomani's men rallied around us, leaving the princess to herself on her litter. As soon as Bomani realized their abandonment of her highness, all niceness ended. He dropped Rasha and yelled to his men to fall back in formation. Turning to Rasha, he latched onto her arm. "You walk with me."

I could tell she regretted showing appreciation to this hulk. She couldn't even look at us as he dragged her to the head of the line. I started to follow, when I felt Sabirah's hand on my shoulder.

"She'll be safe with him until we are out of the desert."

I knew she was right. I could do nothing but watch Rasha's little form try to keep up with her captor.

℘

Sabirah

WE MARCHED THROUGH THE HOT sand the rest of the day. At times the wind was merciless, and at other times, the sun fought with the wind to torment us even more. Those in front passed along a spare ration of water, but by the end of day, there wasn't much left, only enough to wet our tongues. I didn't take any, wanting to make certain there was enough for the others.

As the sun began to set, distant palm trees came into view.

We'd made it through!

No more sand punishing our every step. It covered me from my hair to my toes. Where trees grew, there had to be water. I longed for a bath. Surely the princess wouldn't want her prized captives to be dirty for her father. I wiped grit from the corners of my eyes. A layer of sand not only covered my tunic but seemed to coat my tongue.

Once within the comforting protection of the trees, I found I was right—the palms protected a large pond. Water-skaters skimmed over the glassy surface. Frogs croaked from thickets of cattails. A gentle breeze drifted through the fronds and ferns. Everyone drank until they were full.

Bomani's men passed around cornbread, peppered with sand, for dinner. I knew the bread would be a welcome change from dog meat for Tag. I smiled at him as he ate.

When Bomani busied himself with settling the princess for the night, Rasha found her way to us. "I hope he forgets me. I want to stay with my family." She looked at me and Tag as though to include him as her family, too. He beamed at the prospect. Then Rasha glanced at Ravid and smiled. Even though he was the guard who had betrayed her and her father, she included him, as well.

I had Rasha sit on the ground out of sight of the guards. I could tell she was nervous now that we were out of the desert. I knew her worry was Bomani and what he would do to her.

"How far are we from Jacobugath?" Tag asked.

"I don't know," I answered. "Only members of King Jacob's tribe know the way. The city is well hidden in the mountaintops northward. Years ago, rumors were that the Gadiantons had begun building their city there. It is impossible to approach without being seen. Many have tried and were never heard of again. Jacobugath holds nothing for my people, except maybe my father and brother."

"And my mother," Rasha piped up.

"Yes, and your mother." I glanced down at her sitting near my legs. I stroked her head.

"I do believe we are close. Might be a day or two away." I gazed at the mountains on the horizon.

"Two," Bomani interrupted. The brawny man had sneaked up behind us. "I plan to take our time because of the princess's wound." Though he spoke of the princess, his eyes were on Rasha. She cowered behind me.

Bomani snaked her out, bringing her to her feet.

Trying to save my cousin, I said, "Surely you're hands are full caring for the princess. You don't want this little mouse in your way."

"I am a man of many duties and needs. Perhaps you would like to take her place." He said, glowering at me.

I wouldn't back down as he expected. I knew his kind preyed on the young and defenseless. But a grown woman would give him the fight of his life, which I fully intended to do.

He grabbed my arm. With my free arm, I reached for the dagger my brother had made but remembered it had been taken. Still, I didn't cower, matching his stare. The breath in my lungs came ragged and rode on fear I had to hide. I thought of Mahir. He'd never look at me the same if Bomani had his way. No man in the village would want me. Yet, that didn't matter, not now. Better me than Rasha.

Bomani threw my arm aside. "The princess wanted you for her father, or I would teach you a lesson you would long remember."

Relieved beyond words, I stood my ground. Satanic eyes settled on me. I stiffened my spine, building courage.

The beast studied me and then looked over at the princess. Finally, he uttered, "Very well." Pointing to Ravid, he said, "It will be your head if any of them escape."

Ravid bowed. Bomani marched away, joining his men.

A sigh escaped my lips.

Rasha hugged me. Tag held the flat of his palm up. "Give me five."

I had no idea what he was talking about. He grabbed my hand and slapped my palm. "Five," he said, rolling his fingers. I nodded, knowing that this must be some high compliment.

Embarrassed, knowing that my true saving had been the Lord's doing, I said, "We had better sleep while we can." Everyone nodded and found a space to lie down. Rasha found a place next to me, Tag next to her. I wanted them close so I could keep them safe. But I planned to slip away and take that bath in the pond that was calling me. I might be a hero in their eyes, but I longed to be clean.

☙

Tag

Sabirah leaned against a palm tree with her eyes closed. Rasha curled up beside her and quickly conked out. Ravid's bull-like snores clued me in that he'd nodded off. In fact, the entire camp had grown silent, except for the rumble of more snoring from the troops. As quietly as I could, I sneaked over to Ravid. His broad shoulders were a good yard wide. He'd have been a star on the wrestling circuit. Too bad he was stuck here and would possibly die because he had mistakenly slashed the princess's leg.

His big, beefy arm lay across his bag. I wondered if in all the confusion, the princess had left the stone in his care. Maybe? Definitely worth checking out. Ever so carefully, I inched it from his hold. He snorted and turned over, freeing the bag entirely.

Delighted at my good fortunate, I grabbed it and walked a ways from camp. Riffling through the contents, I finally felt a small basket. Could it be the one Rasha described? Hope filled me. I pulled it out. My fingers fumbled over the leather straps as I untied the knots. Taking a deep breath, I opened the box.

Nothing! Of course the princess wouldn't leave the stone with Ravid. She didn't trust him anymore.

"Looking for this?"

I turned to find Princess Jamila leaning on her makeshift cane, standing behind me. In her outstretched hand was the stone.

16

Tangled Vines

Tag

THE MOONLIGHT HIT THE STONE, making it shine bright as lightning. There, only a short distance away, was my ticket home. My hands yearned to touch it, to feel its smooth surface. As much as I wanted to help Sabirah, I still wanted to go home. It had been so long since I'd left. I said, "The stone doesn't belong to you."

"Oh, I think it does. My father will be very pleased. Not only am I delivering to him Samuel the Lamanite's daughter but also two slaves and this." The princess smiled. "I am sure he shall reward me in many ways." She stopped a moment and then said, "And this." She held my father's sketchpad.

"Princess, Your Majesty," I groveled, hoping somehow I could think of something to say to make her give me the sketchpad and the stone. "Why would your father be interested in stupid little drawings and a rock?" I had to make her think they held no value. "Your father has plenty of riches. He doesn't need an old worthless pebble. You could give the stone and drawings to me, and I won't tell anyone."

She clutched the gem and pad to her. The moon's rays caught her blond hair. Using her cane, she walked around me. Her cold, calculating eyes appraised my body while her thoughts judged my words. She stopped in front of me, closed her eyes, and seemed to go into a trance.

I heard rustling in the bushes. A jaguar broke out from behind a fern. The feline crouched low as it, step by step, crept closer ready to spring to the attack.

Swallowing hard, I uttered, "Th . . . there's a big cat sneaking up behind you." I didn't want the princess to panic, but she needed to know her life was in danger.

She opened her eyes and smiled, not looking behind. Stepping aside, she left me as the animal's sole target. "Like the snake and the scorpion *and* the caiman, the jaguar is my friend."

This woman was a certified nutcase. At any moment, this "friend" was going to pounce on me, tear off my arms, and chew on my face. Friend, I don't think so. Knowing the princess was absolutely no help, I very carefully moved backward.

With each of my steps, the cat crept forward. My heart thudded up my throat. My mouth was as dry as the desert we'd just left. No way could I outrun this beast. Why was it every time I thought I was close to going home, something horrible, something absolutely rotten happened? The only thing I could think to do was pray.

Help me, God, and I promise to help Sabirah find her father, help Rasha find her mother, and if you send me home, I'll even play nice with Ethan if only you'll get me out of this mess.

"Princess!" Sabirah stepped into the clearing. "What kind of mind games are you playing on him?"

Instantly, the jaguar disappeared, completely vanished. Relief left me weak as if I'd just run from Eriksen's Funeral Home clear to my house.

"Why must you always spoil my fun?" Princess Jamila skulked past Sabirah, sneering at her as though to say, *"Curses, foiled again."* She hobbled away and then stopped and said, "I should send Bomani after you, but perhaps you two will escape. Go on, I'm sure he would relish hunting you down." She turned again and walked back to camp.

"You have come to my rescue again."

"Not me. The Lord."

Of course, she would never take credit. I thought of all the promises I'd just made to my Father in Heaven. The jaguar wasn't even real. It never would have attacked me. I was never really in danger, and He had to know that, so He had to know all those promises didn't count, did they?

"What did she conjure for you?" Sabirah put her arm around my shoulders.

"A jaguar." I felt foolish. "How did she do it?"

"She has pledged her life to serving her father and following Satan. Satan has armed her with a gift that manipulates minds. She would have used it on us when we first captured her, but she was too far away from her father. The closer we come to Jacobugath, the stronger her powers grow."

"Oh, that's just great! How in the world am I ever going to get the stone back?" I looked up at Sabirah, and the odd expression on her face made me feel selfish. I quickly added, "How are we ever going to find your father and brother, fighting odds like this?" The impossibility of it all left me deflated like a blown-out tire, all hope lost.

"We have the Almighty on our side. Nothing is impossible." Sabirah nudged me to follow her.

She guided me toward the pond. "Stand watch while I bathe."

Oh, man! Wait—what was wrong with me? How could I think like that? Only moments ago I was begging the *Almighty* for help, and Sabirah had saved me.

"Tag, I'm counting on you." Sabirah left.

She would have to say that. No way could I try anything risky now. Besides, she was Samuel the Lamanite's daughter and like a sister to me. I'd probably be hit by a bolt of lightning if I tried anything. And though the little boy in me still wanted to, the young man in me thought of Rasha and my growing feelings for her.

Sitting on the ground, I listened to the sounds of Sabirah bathing and wondered why God had sent me here. Though the stone had been the catalyst, the Lord was in control of my destiny . . . or was I? My life had become one confusing puzzle.

❦

Sabirah

THE NEXT TWO DAYS WERE filled with mind-numbing exertion as we steadily climbed. When we reached a pass, I looked over the mountaintops. Along the spine of the range, I saw a huge mountain with vapors escaping the peak. Wafts of smoke from its large mouth coiled into the sky. It was an amazing sight and something I knew would be burned into my memory. All too soon, we moved on and scaled the next mountain.

The jungle was filled with spider monkeys swinging from rain tree to rain tree. Macaws mocked us. Pecas and aganits of every size and shape scurried from our path, hiding beneath fire brush and tail flower. The air hung heavy with the scent of orchids and moldering leaves. Tangled vines and ferns brushed against my legs and felt like spiders and snakes. Snakes made me think of Tag. I turned to see him carefully studying the vines, wary of each. He had confided his fear to me, and I understood his fears and how a giant boa could intimidate him. Many were probably watching our every move waiting for some defenseless person to fall back so they could wrap their coils around him. I would not share such knowledge with Tag. After his encounter with Jamila and her mind game, he seemed even more jumpy than usual.

With Rasha and Ravid well ahead of us, I decided to talk with Tag, hopeful to help him forget his fears. I waited, and he caught up with me. "I want to understand your fear of snakes."

Right away he tensed. "Did you see one?" He searched the ground with his worried gaze.

"No." I shook my head.

Tag relaxed. "Well, it started when I was very young. The kids in our neighborhood liked to float down the Burgess Canal in the summer. Whenever I swam in the sun, I wore a T-shirt; otherwise, with my freckled complexion, I'd burn up."

I nodded, remembering his sunburn on the first day of our journey. By now his skin had peeled but was still pink.

"One day Ronny Rasmussen put a water snake down the back of my shirt." Tag's face reflected the fear of the distasteful memory. "I can't tell you how creeped out I was when I felt the snake wiggle against my skin, trying to inch out. I jumped around like army ants had attacked me. Tyler came to my rescue and jerked the snake from my shirt."

Such mischief was frequent in my village, but I didn't want to tell Tag. He seemed too upset. We continued to climb and talk at the same time. "Tyler is your brother?"

"Yeah." Tag didn't seem to want to talk about him.

I grew curious as to why, so I asked, "Tell me about your family."

"Well, I have a brother named Tyler. He's two years younger than I am. Though he's always seemed older. See, I'd rather draw or read a book while Tyler goes nuts sitting at home. He has to be out doing something all the time. He used to get us in so much trouble."

"Any sisters?"

"No, just my mom and dad, Tyler, and me . . . and Grandpa. Oh, I have an Uncle Lee and Aunt Crystal. See, Aunt Crystal is my father's sister. But we don't see them much anymore, not since my father and Tyler left."

"They left?"

"Yeah." He fell oddly silent.

We walked a little farther. "Is your father a preacher like mine?" I wanted to understand his odd expression and silence.

"No."

His face grew somber. I could tell his father and brother's absence wasn't a subject he wanted to talk about. "Then your family is really you and your mother?"

Tag nodded. "And Lizzie, her Yorkie."

"Is a Yorkie a slave?"

Tag chuckled. "No. It's a dog, a little, tiny rat-dog that I hate but love, too."

"No wonder you didn't want to eat the dog meat I gave you."
Such different worlds we were from.

"Yeah."

Now that he seemed more relaxed, I went back to the sore
subject. "Why did your father and brother leave?"

We climbed the trail in silence.

He finally said, "I don't know." He seemed to search for words,
though soon emotion claimed him, making it difficult for him to
speak. I said nothing, wanting Tag to overcome this problem on
his own. He finally said, "One day they were just gone."

"Like my father." Though I had a feeling the situation was
somehow different, especially since my father had said good-bye,
had kissed and hugged me before leaving.

Again Tag struggled for words. "See, my memory has these
blank spaces." He stopped and looked at me. "Doctor Bradford is
trying to help me fill them in."

"Is he a healer?"

"Sort of." Tag bit at his bottom lip and then added, "I've never
told this to anyone. But . . . I don't *want* to remember."

"Why?"

He stared at me, and I could see fear fighting within him.

Tag turned away. "Just don't want to." He walked ahead. I
followed, feeling his heavy turmoil. Wayfarer's journey was so
much more than even I'd imagined.

We'd reached the top where everyone was catching their breath.
They were looking down at the valley below.

Tag grabbed my arm. "Look, Sabirah."

Below us was the mighty city—Jacobugath.

17

A Cool Dude

Tag

JACOBUGATH SEEMED BATHED IN WHITE, a stark contrast to the jungle that edged the bulwarks. The bulwarks were huge, white walls with bold primitive paintings along the top, but I couldn't tell what they were from this distance. These walls framed the entire city. As an artist, I was fascinated with the design. I don't know what I expected the place to look like, but it wasn't this. This was something that would rival the Egyptians.

In the center of town was an extremely high alabaster temple, tall as a mountain. The peak was hidden behind scaffolding. Workers were busy on some type of sculpture. Near where they worked at the top, it looked as though small white balls were stacked. Hundreds of steps in the middle of the temple climbed to the uppermost level. Down the center of the steps was a dark stain of some kind. It appeared as though someone had deliberately poured ink down the stairs. And there must have been a lot, because the stain spread nearly to the bottom. A strange foreboding crept over me almost as though a ghost had walked by. I shivered.

Smaller temples dotted the land and appeared to be replicas of the central one. They, too, were white. Near the top walls were symbols of some kind in brilliant cobalt blues, terra-cotta reds, and hints of forest green.

I glanced up at Sabirah. She was spellbound and had long forgotten my sad story. I was glad. I didn't know why I'd told her in the first place. I hadn't even told Doctor Bradford what I'd told Sabirah. I hoped she'd forget everything I'd said. What was important right now was the city below and what would happen to us once we were within its walls.

As our procession traveled down the mountain, an uneasy feeling overtook me. The uneasiness could be because we were captives and would soon be thrown to the lions—or whatever they did here—but deep down I didn't think so. It had to do with something else. The uneasiness quickly turned into a feeling of doom so intense my guts felt as though snakes writhed inside me. I ignored it the best I could.

Descending the mountain to the city didn't take nearly as long as climbing up, and soon we were at the city gates. Pushing my anxious thoughts aside, I noticed many men working on the gateway. I heard talking and looked up. Artists worked on sculptures along the large portals. Several men hung from ropes as they painted intricate murals on the massive header that spanned five different entryways.

The mural told a story. One frame was of people on a ship, another had a giant sea monster. The center picture was of a man regally dressed with a jaguar standing beside him. Maybe this mural wasn't a story as much as a history.

Some men on the ground were busily mashing some type of berries, making a green, pasty type paint. Others were grinding blue stones into a fine powder and mixing it with a substance that looked like fat. Still others were busy blending red clay.

Most of them wore breechcloths but were bare-chested. All of the workers had their hair pulled back into ponytails, which probably made it easier for them to work. Several wore different colored bands on their upper arms. I wondered if the different colors declared their status.

A tall, leathery fellow who had been studying a type of blueprint rose to greet Bomani and the princess. On his head, he wore a turban. The cloth was colored with intense blues and reds. Seashells hung from his ears. A crudely cut jade necklace draped his neck. A wraparound skirt of the same blues and reds as his turban finished his getup. He wore bands of gold on his forearms. This guy was obviously the foreman of the artistic crew. I really wanted to talk with them. Despite crude methods, they had created beautiful art.

The foreman raised his arm above his head and fisted his hand. This must have been some type of salute. Bomani did the same, but he didn't stop. Our procession kept marching right through the portals under the giant gateway. The foreman seemed to study Sabirah and me. Weird.

The streets of the city were spotless. Some homes had large potted plants near their doors; others had perches for parrots and other brightly feathered birds, but there were no children playing like in Pagog.

The street led to a market square. Merchants were well dressed and mannered, no yelling at passersby to purchase this or that. They stood quietly by their merchandise, letting the product speak for itself. The patrons casually walked by the vendors, nodding their heads as if to say *"good day."* Unlike the children in the malls of my time, children of these shoppers didn't run wildly about but stood dutifully beside their parents as if afraid. They were immaculately dressed in robes of blues and rust but mainly white. And I noticed something else.

No one smiled.

I was beginning to wonder if I'd walked into a freakish knockoff of *Night of the Zombies*. I wondered if everyone here were clones or puppets. Whatever they were, they certainly weren't real. Except for the frightened children.

I looked at Sabirah, wondering what she thought. She, too, appeared bewildered by these people. Rasha anxiously scanned the market, no doubt searching for her mother. I knew she wanted to leave us, but to do so would only draw the attention of Bomani, and that was the last thing she wanted. Ravid had grown quite somber, as if he were contemplating his fate, which very well could be death. I felt for him. Of course, my fate as well as Sabirah's could be the same. Maybe that had been the creepy someone-walking-over-my-grave feeling tangling up my insides when we neared the city, but I didn't think so.

The princess had said her father would want me. Her words prickled my conscience, making me more than a little nervous. With each step, I wondered what the mighty King Jacob would want with a stupid kid like me.

The palace was skirted by a flight of stairs. As we walked to the top, I saw that six square columns gave access to six entryways. Soldiers stationed there saluted Bomani. He dismissed his footmen. Then he led the men carrying Princess Jamila's litter to the main hall. Soldiers fell in line behind Sabirah, Rasha, Ravid, and me, escorting us as we followed those ahead.

The floor appeared to be made of giant marble slabs. Pillars flanked the hall along with the busts of what looked like fallen leaders. I wondered who they were. Was the evil King Noah's likeness one of them? Or Korihor, the antichrist? My grandmother had told me all their stories.

The thing about the busts was the eyes looked hollow, as if the person had no soul. Of course, the busts didn't have a soul. I thought these likenesses really did represent these men: they had been truly empty inside.

The giant hallway came to double doors gilded with other layers of gold. As we approached, guards bowed and opened the tall, shiny doors. We walked into a cavernous room. At the end, up a few steps, a man sat on a throne.

King Jacob!

I couldn't really see him from here, but I did notice what lay at his feet. Sprawled out before the king was a large jaguar who bore a strong resemblance to the one Princess Jamila had conjured in my mind. The cat's tail swished this way and that. Was this a real cat or a figment of my imagination?

My stomach bunched into knots. My palms became clammy. I looked at the king, who seemed quite content. How could anyone be calm sitting by such an animal? The image was probably Princess Jamila messing with my mind again.

The feline stretched its claws and let out a yowl that echoed off the walls and floors. Fear rippled my skin as fast as a sonic wave. Okay, the cat was real. Which was more frightening, the overgrown hairball or the king?

Definitely the king.

Bomani stopped at the foot of the stairs and bent down on one knee. At the same time, the men carrying Princess Jamila settled her litter on the floor. She got off, favoring her injured leg. Balancing my stone and sketchpad in one hand, and leaning on her cane with the other, she limped up the stairs to her father. Bowing, she handed him the gem, which was my only hope of going home. Placing the stone on the arm of his throne, he then rose and hugged and kissed his daughter.

They looked like a happy family, except I wondered, *Where was the princess's mother?* There had to be a queen somewhere. I gazed around, but there was no other throne. I'd never heard anyone speak of a Mrs. King Jacob. This made me a little curious, though not enough to dwell long on it.

The princess and her father spoke in hushed tones for some time while she showed him Dad's sketchpad. Bomani stayed down on one knee, the soldiers stood at attention, and our little crew of Sabirah, Rasha, Ravid, and I anxiously awaited our fate. At long last, the king sat on his throne, and Princess Jamila turned about.

"Bomani, please bring the prisoners forward and dismiss your men," she said.

The soldiers left in single file. As each passed, I saw pity in their eyes as they glanced our way. Bomani hustled us up the steps. I hung back as much as I could. No sense drawing attention to myself sooner than necessary. Sabirah bravely took the lead, eager for the fight.

I probably would have been, too, if there were hope I'd see my father soon. Brave Sabirah. She was everything I was not. As she neared the throne, Bomani shoved her down on her knees. The rest of us automatically fell to ours, not wanting the same rough treatment.

"Your Majesty." Bomani bowed.

"These are the cretins who dared to kidnap my daughter and kill some of my men and horses?" said King Jacob. His strong voice was deep and filled every corner of the room. I chanced a closer look.

He sat regally on his elaborately carved throne of gold. His robes of deep red carried a trim of even more gold. He was bald, totally bald, shiny-head bald. A wide collar of gold lay around his neck and rested on his chest. No hair there, either, but some kind of tattoo. I immediately thought of my henna tattoo. Much of it had disappeared, but there were still traces. Gave me the creeps to think I'd wanted a real one. What if his tattoo was similar to mine? Would that mean anything? That I had some type of evil streak or something? From here I couldn't tell what it was, but I had a feeling I would learn soon enough, and I was dreading it.

The jaguar-skinned breechcloth and leather sandals the king wore told all who looked upon him that he was important. I expected his fingers to be covered with rings of diamonds, rubies, and emeralds. Surprisingly, they were naked, free from jewelry.

This seemed odd. I stole a look at his face and immediately thought of nobility. Why? I didn't know. This guy was no nobler than Mom's Yorkie, but as I gazed at him a realization befell me. There was something very royal about him. Could be the tilt of his head and the demand of respect that flowed from him. He reminded me of the king in *The King and I,* an old musical that was one of Mom's favorites. If I didn't know the Book of Mormon stories, I would have thought King Jacob was a cool dude.

And even now, I wondered. Maybe the writers of the past had misunderstood him. He appeared to be a great, benevolent leader who was kind and caring. He certainly didn't look evil. He motioned for Sabirah to step forward.

As she rose from her knees, the large jaguar stood and rubbed against the sitting king's leg. The cat nuzzled the man's ringless hand, begging for attention. Never taking his eyes off Sabirah, the king stroked the jaguar. "You *are* a beauty."

Sabirah held her head high as he studied her. She didn't bow when Bomani thought she should and paid for it with a lashing on her back. Bomani grabbed the scruff of Sabirah's neck and bent her over, then let her up. I didn't think the benevolent king would tolerate this abuse. But he said nothing to Bomani.

"I had no idea Samuel's daughter would be so appealing." King Jacob's voice was low, even-toned. He eyed Sabirah, nodding his head as if appreciating her bravery and courage. "Jamila said you think I have your father."

"You do!" A red flush of anger crept up Sabirah's neck, spreading to her cheeks.

The cat hissed at her. King Jacob calmed the feline with a pat. Shaking his head, the king replied, "What a delightful, wild woman you are. But you have been sadly misinformed. How I wish I had the mighty Lamanite prophet."

"You lie!" spat out Sabirah. She stared King Jacob straight in the eyes. I really didn't think that was a good idea. Seems like I read somewhere kings don't like their subjects to look directly at them, and I was pretty certain they didn't like to be called liars. I was waiting for Bomani to crack his whip across her back.

Anger shot from the king's gaze. I could see he could deliver havoc when needed. He rose, jaguar still at his side. "How dare you speak in such a manner to your king. If you wish to see your brother alive, I suggest that you use a measure of discretion with your words."

"You have Asim in your prison?" Sabirah appeared relieved, though wary.

The king slowly nodded. "Arrived a year ago, spouting the same outlandish claims as you."

"You have no reason to keep him!"

"I do not *need* reason. I am the king." A wicked grin spread across his face. "Perhaps you would like to join your brother?"

"Father," Princess Jamila interrupted. "I wanted to keep her, teach her how to serve royalty. Surely she can be taught." Her eyebrow raised as if she had something cruel and horrible in mind for Sabirah. Jamila added, "Besides, what trophies we would have: the daughter of the prophet Samuel seeing to my every whim and his son held in our prison." She smiled at her father, who nodded with appreciation for his daughter's devious mind.

He slowly, regally sat, pondering her suggestion. Placing his fingertips together, he said, "Yes, you may keep her."

The cat began to wander. The creature sauntered to Rasha.

"I would also like the maiden." Jamila took her father's hand, stroking his arm, playing him, manipulating him.

The jaguar sniffed Rasha's leg. I heard her gasp with fright. The king quickly appraised her and then shrugged. "As you wish. What about the man who wounded you? I suppose you want him, as well."

Jamila didn't give Ravid a backward glance. "He is nothing to me."

The king motioned to Bomani to seize Ravid, which he immediately did with great pleasure.

"Now, the boy. What to do with the boy?" The king stood and walked toward me with his feline of terror by his side.

I bowed my head, staring at the floor, trying to ignore the cat that brushed against me and started to purr.

Purr . . . there was no purring with wild predators, was there? What would the king think of his cat purring over me? I didn't want this man to be angry or upset. Besides, what did he and this prowling carpet want with me, Tag Quincy, major screwup and the disappointment of his grandpa's and mother's lives? I swallowed hard as I felt King Jacob's calculating eyes zero in on my head.

I prayed the floor would open up and flying monkeys would take me away. I wanted to be anywhere but here.

A finger came beneath my chin. King Jacob tilted my head so he could see my face. His eyes were not hollow like the busts, nor demonic like Bomani's. They were sky blue and held a soul behind them. A soul who looked at me and made me feel as if I could soar to the moon and back, as if I didn't have a care in the world . . . and as if I belonged.

18

Zouché

Tag

THE FEELING OF EUPHORIA WRAPPED warmly around me followed by a sense of peace and goodwill. "I shall take this one," King Jacob said to Jamila. "These beggar's clothes will need to be replaced." He pointed at my poncho. The princess nodded in agreement. How thoughtful that the king would dress me more appropriately. "Anhanga seems especially fond of him." The jaguar nuzzled my leg, purring up a storm. What a gorgeous, lovely animal.

I glanced to Sabirah and her *what-are-you-doing* expression pulled me out of the king's spell.

That was creepy!

The king had so easily manipulated my mind. The Book of Mormon said this guy was evil. I needed to keep that front and center. The jaguar nudged my hand, demanding attention. I didn't know if the cat was happy because I looked like a Kitty-Kibble meal or what. I cautiously stroked the animal and felt powerful muscles beneath its fur. The purring grew louder.

Looking up, I saw Rasha. Confusion and fear slanted her brows. Her expression told me to watch out, all was not as it seemed.

I knew she was right.

Stepping back from the king and his feline friend, I was certain he was playing a mind game on me, like Jamila had done. Why else would I have this roller-coaster ride of emotions? Maybe what I could do since the king liked me was to become a spy, learn everything I could, and then tell Sabirah about it.

Glancing her way, I gave her an *everything-is-all-right* wink. She kept staring at me as if I'd lost my mind.

"And I can see he has a gifted hand." King Jacob picked up Dad's sketchpad and then gazed at his daughter to confirm what he'd said.

Jamila nodded. "Yes, Father."

He glanced through the etchings. "He has an artist's eye. Very well," said the king, closing the pad. "Tell Malachi he has another pupil until the boy's time of surrender to Zouché." The king walked over and stroked my head as if to give me some type of blessing. As he did, he paused and took a closer look at my hair. He must be studying my red roots and wondering what the deal was, but he didn't say anything, only motioned for Anhanga to follow him back to the throne.

The giant cat did his master's bidding. "I have other business." The king picked up the stone—my stone—from off his throne, along with Dad's sketchpad, and walked away with the jaguar slowly trailing him. They left by a side door.

As soon as the door shut behind him, the warm cozy feeling I'd experienced totally vanished. Wow. The king was powerful. Mind control must be how he tamed a jaguar to be his companion.

With the king gone, Bomani was quick to shove Ravid down the steps toward his new life of slavery. Ravid chanced a glance backward. I could tell he yearned to be with us and deeply regretted his betrayal of Rasha's family. I almost felt sorry for him until I remembered how he'd stormed toward Sabirah, ready to kill her. Only by chance had he wounded the princess instead. As my mother would have said, Ravid had made some bad life choices.

Mom was always lecturing me about being responsible for the choices I made. I missed her so much I felt an ache deep in my heart, the same ache I held in reserve for Dad and Tyler.

Princess Jamila clapped her hands. Scantily clothed handmaidens with chunky jewelry in their ears and feathers braided in their hair swarmed around her. With the princess busy, this gave me a minute to speak with Sabirah. "What are we going to do?"

"Do?"

"Yeah, the king has my stone and sketchpad. We've got to get them back."

"In good time. First, I need to free my brother. If he has been in Jacobugath's prison for over a year, I fear he may be dead or close to it."

"The king didn't say he was dead." I thought Sabirah shouldn't think the worst. "Besides, prisons have standards." I remembered watching a documentary on how wardens rehabilitated inmates. Wait . . . that was back in my time, back where even jailbirds had rights. A different standard ruled here.

"The king does not know who lives and dies in his prisons," Sabirah said. "It's rare for a man to survive even a few months in King Jacob's captivity." Sadness spread over Sabirah's face as she spoke and made me realize more than ever how much she loved her brother.

"I'm sure he's all right," I said, wanting to comfort her.

"I hope so." Sabirah nudged me with her elbow. I nudged her back. My feelings for her had changed since the hike up the mountain on our way to Jacobugath and our talk about Tyler and Dad. She wasn't just the most gorgeous woman I'd ever seen; she was my best friend. Then I remembered I needed to tell Sabirah that the king had used his mind game on me. Leaning close to her, I softly said, "The king manipulates minds, as well. He made me think he was wrongly accused, made me want to be with him."

Sabirah nodded. "I know. Whenever you feel him or the princess trying to manipulate your thoughts, call upon the name of Jesus Christ for them to depart, and they will."

"Is that what you do?"

She nodded. Now I had hope.

Finishing with her servants, Princess Jamila walked toward us. "Rasha, you must go with the others. They will see that you are properly attired to serve." Her handmaidens swooped in and sucked up Rasha in their wake.

Sabirah and I followed the princess down the steps and out the door we'd entered.

"Despite your capturing me, my father has been very kind to both of you," she said over her shoulder as she walked, leaning more heavily on her cane. "Only because I have shown mercy . . . though I have a plan that will make you both pay." Sabirah didn't rise to the bait the princess dangled in front of her. Jamila added, "My father lied."

Sabirah still said nothing.

"Your father did come to us. The king had him flogged and tortured until he died." Jamila grinned.

Sabirah's face paled with deep sorrow.

"That's not true!" I spat out, desperate to ease her torture. The Book of Mormon said nothing about such an action.

Jamila struck me with her cane. Sabirah immediately came to my defense, blocking the blows with her own body. Princess Jamila grabbed Sabirah's arm. I could tell by the way my friend clenched her teeth she barely tolerated Jamila's touch, and it took all her will power not to strike the princess. As though feeding upon Sabirah's emotion, anger sprang red to the princess's cheeks.

"I see you need some gentling," Jamila hissed. She clapped her hands. Two burly guards, one light skinned and one dark skinned, were suddenly beside us. They'd probably been following, but I was so wrapped up in the tension between the women that I hadn't noticed. What were they, bat-people who swooped down from the rafters at Jamila's beck and call? Nothing would surprise me.

"Put her in prison for a day and night. That should break her," Princess Jamila ordered the guards, who strong-armed Sabirah. She fought against them. And I realized that without knowing it, Jamila had given Sabirah what she wanted . . . a chance to find her brother. I watched as Sabirah was dragged away between the guards.

"Tag." The princess now turned her attention on me. "I should have one of my handmaidens take you to Malachi, but my leg is much repaired because of you, so I'll see you get there myself. Besides, I fancy your company." I knew full well what she fancied was more information about Sabirah.

"Concerned about your friend?"

She was doing it again—reading my thoughts. To block her I called upon the name of Jesus Christ like Sabirah had told me to.

"You cannot block me all the time," she said, quirking up an eyebrow as she tried to belittle me.

I didn't want to talk. I wanted to be far away from this woman and her mind games.

She led me to a modest, square adobe house in back of the palace. A guard was on duty outside the door and bowed to the princess before escorting us inside. Entering, I noticed a massive painting of a jaguar on the wall, the focal point of the room. The other walls were emerald green, making the cat appear as if it were prowling through the jungle. There was a table of carved stone on the other side. The man I supposed was Malachi rose from the table where he'd been working and walked around to greet us.

"Princess, I am honored." He bowed, took her hand, and kissed it. "How may I serve you?"

"He is one of the king's blessed." Princess Jamila pushed me ahead of her.

I glanced at the princess, wondering what made her think I was one of the king's blessed. He'd said no such thing.

The man took my hand, and I stared at him. He had been the one who'd greeted Bomani before we passed through the gates of the city, the foreman with the red and blue turban and jade necklace and the one giving the orders to the other artists. He was a Lamanite and had strong cheekbones and a long nose. "What an honor for you, fair one." His voice was kind, gentle, caring.

Not knowing what to say, I answered. "Thanks, I guess."

"Malachi, he is very much like you. He has a gifted hand." The princess headed for the doorway. "Dress him appropriately, and use him as you like. But remember my father has chosen him to surrender to Zouché when the time comes." She turned and left.

King Jacob had said that, as well, and now I wondered who Zouché was and what was meant by "surrender to him." Was Zouché an enemy of the king's?

"Blessed are you?" Malachi asked as he rested his hand on my shoulder.

I scrunched up my face and gave my head a little shake. "Not really."

"Gifted?" he asked.

"A little, maybe." I didn't know what to think of this guy. My discerning ability regarding people had been way off, so now I was taking the wait-and-see approach, especially with this man, who could do what he wanted with me.

"Are you a friend of the woman, Sabirah, who just arrived?" His hand became heavy when I expected him to move, but he didn't. He stood there, grilling me, checking me out, sizing me up.

"Yes. A very good friend," I answered.

"I see." He walked away, going back to his desk and what he'd been working on. I followed, wanting to see what he studied. There, spread out on the stone was some type of papyrus paper with a drawing of another jaguar on it, but instead of the natural animal colors, the image was a cat colored in light serpentine green.

"Nice work," I told him.

He gazed at me. "I do not care for it myself."

"Why?"

"This is the plan for King Jacob's latest god." He carefully rolled up the picture and stored it in a strange tube that looked like the horn of a giant animal. He had several of them near his table.

I'd heard the people had turned to idol worship before Christ was crucified. Malachi's picture confirmed that this was so. And now I was certain King Jacob was evil. He might put on a good show and manipulate a person's mind, but beneath it all, he was as cunning as Satan.

"Actually, my men are busy with the finishing work before the god is unveiled for the people." He motioned for me to have a seat. I sat on the wooden stool, the table between us. Malachi rubbed his chin. Staring at me, he said, "You are not curious about the name of this beautiful god?"

I really wasn't. But I wanted to know what was going on, so I nodded.

"His name is Zouché."

Zouché, that name kept coming up. And it then dawned on me. "That's who the king wants me to surrender to. How can I surrender to an idol?"

"You have yet to be enlightened. Let me say it in simpler terms. To surrender means . . . to die for."

My throat was dry. The room tilted as *die for* sank in. I blinked, trying to keep Malachi in focus and then murmured, "Die?"

He nodded. "You are a stranger; thus, your talent will be given to the new god when you are sacrificed."

19
Well of Darkness

Sabirah

THE GUARDS, DRESSED IN LOINCLOTHS and headdresses, took me into the palace through the back door where the cooks and servants busily worked. Pepper plants lined the windows. Baskets filled with squash, corn, and cucurbits were in abundance. The cooks were plucking quail feathers from several dead birds and gave little notice to a new prisoner being led to the dungeon.

We turned down a dank corridor. At the end were two large iron doors. I hadn't really looked at the guards before, but now as we neared the enclosure, I did. One man had the stern, severe face of a hawk; black paint framed his eyes. The other guard had black skin, like Bomani. His eyes were framed with white paint, his face turtlelike. His movements were even slow. The severe one unlocked the foreboding enclosure and lifted the plank. Swinging the doors open, they waited for me to walk inside. Stone steps spiraled down a deep, dark stairwell. There was no light within. I hesitated. Cavernous blackness reached for me, pulling at me. I have always thought of myself as fearless, able to track and hunt with the best men; yet, I had a grave fear of dark, dank places, especially caves. I had kept my fear to myself, only sharing it with my brother, Asim. And only for my brother would I venture into this well of darkness.

The slow guard noticed my trepidation and took pity. He lit a torch from one already burning and handed it to me. Maybe being a girl did have certain privileges. Taking the flame, I gave him a smile of gratitude, turned, and faced the dark nothingness before me.

I had only taken one step when the iron doors slammed shut. I heard the plank fall into place and the chains locking the doors. Slowly venturing forward, I realized the prison was beneath the palace. How symbolic! King Jacob had literally put himself above the prisoners in mind and in body.

The stairwell soon fed into tunnels and caves and flooded with the scent of mold and damp earth. Soon the scent became heavy with the stench of human waste and the even more pungent scent of moldering bodies. I covered my nose and breathed through my mouth. Eerie silence intensified the smell.

I moved through a tunnel, coming to a man burrowed in a hole. Touching his shoulder, I asked, "Sir?" No answer. Again, "Sir." I shined the light over his face and found him paralyzed in death, his face appearing as though an animal had eaten him. Maggots and bugs infested the wounds. I flinched backward, badly shaken. I had to keep moving, keep searching. Yet, the image remained.

I stumbled from one death hole to another, finding other half-eaten victims. Had carnivorous dogs feasted on the dead? What sort of canines preyed in these tunnels? Panic for my brother spurred me on.

Journeying farther, I thought I heard the footfalls of someone following me. Except, when I stopped, so would the sound. If I hurried, it did, as well. My hand automatically sought the place were I kept my ivory dagger. Gone, of course! Taken from me many days ago.

As I slowly continued down a narrow stretch, the thunderous clap of footsteps rushed toward me from behind. I turned and in that moment saw a creature. Animal or man, I was not certain. He was covered in grime and dirt. Long, tangled hair hung past his shoulders. The glow of my torch caught a crazed gleam of hunger that widened his eyes. As he leaped, he bared his yellowed teeth and clawed at me with his hands. Dropping the torch, I stepped toward him, grabbed his outstretched arm, and flung him over my shoulder. He yelped like a dog when he landed and skulked off, melting into the shadows.

Shaken and yet inspired with more urgency to find Asim, I snatched the still-burning torch from the ground and continued my search, more frantic than before.

I came upon a few lost souls still alive, yet harrowed of spirit. Their eyes were devoid of hope. Some growled at my intrusion. A man dressed in soiled rags, his head one mass of hair and beard, begged, "Food?" His mouth opened like a baby bird waiting for me to toss him a morsel.

"No." I showed him both my hands.

Stumbling, he mumbled, "Liar like the new."

I quickly grabbed his arm. "New?"

He violently shoved me back so hard that I slammed against the stone wall and fell to the ground, nearly dousing my torch. By the time I rose to my feet, he'd fled.

Then out of the darkness, I heard, "Sabirah?"

I turned to find Ravid. He'd been stripped of clothes, only wearing a loincloth. His back was bloodied, probably from Bomani's whipping cords. "Ravid! You are hurt."

"Yes, but I am much better now that I have found you," he said with relief in his voice.

I could hardly believe a man who had tried to run me through with a sword only a few days ago was happy to see me. Could I trust him? His alliance was as fickle as a spring wind.

"Sabirah, I know my betrayal was wrong. Like Esau of old, I allowed my hunger to betray my heritage." In the glow of the torchlight, I saw tears pool his eyes. He seemed sincere.

I asked him the question uppermost in my mind, "Have you seen my brother?"

"Not long here myself, I haven't." He shook his head.

"Help me search?" I asked.

"Of course." He bowed as if he were my servant.

We set to work, with Ravid filling the role of the daring one, turning bodies over only to find them half eaten and dead. We would then move on, questioning souls who muttered in the darkness, talking to ghosts.

Hours passed as we traveled deeper into hell's pit. How could anyone survive for long down here? Fear prickled my spine and whispered in my ear that I'd never find Asim alive. Tired, hungry, and full of grief, I stopped and slid to the ground.

"I shall go on. You rest," Ravid said, taking the torch from my grasp. I didn't want to let go, yet as I thought of my sorry state, my hope vanishing, I gave the torch to his charge. My journey had been useless. I would never find Asim . . . or my father. Tag, the wayfarer, was at the mercy of Jamila and her father. Rasha served as a handmaiden. How could I have led them into this trap? I'd been selfish in my quest, and now all was lost. I'd never been a woman who gave into frail emotions, but at this moment an overwhelming yearning to cry came upon me.

"Lord, why?" I bit my lips together, fighting the urge to give in.

"Sabirah!" Ravid's voice echoed through the tunnel.

The glow of the returning torch reflected off rock walls. He was coming back. I could not let him find me in such a state. Swiping a hand over my face, I rubbed any trace of moisture away.

"Sabirah—" As he came into view I saw he was helping someone walk. The man beside Ravid looked as though he had tussled with a great cat and had lost: hair matted, eyes dark and sunken, dirt caked on his body in layers, his clothing tattered rags. As his eyes found me, he managed to stand on his own, gazing in my direction as though I were a ghost.

I leaped to my feet. Pounding the ground to get to him, I raced like a cumom. As I neared, my heart thrummed as though hummingbird wings were in my chest. A flicker of joy showed in his bleak eyes. "Sabirah," he muttered as if to convince himself.

"Asim!" I dashed to my brother's open arms. He fell on me, sobbing. I wrapped him in my embrace, tight as a boa constrictor, unable to believe that at last he was with me.

☙

Tag

A CHILL WASHED OVER ME like a tidal wave. Numbness fizzed around my lips. I couldn't stop blinking as the room whirled around. "Sacrifice!" Crazy, barbaric. "What the . . ." Dazed, I managed to finally focus on Malachi. "Why me?"

"You are a young, talented stranger, the perfect candidate. King Jacob thinks such a gift to Zouché would please the new god." Malachi rose and motioned for me to follow him.

At first my legs would not obey. Sheer willpower brought me to my feet. It wasn't every day I was told I was to be a human sacrifice.

Malachi stood waiting while I walked up to him. As we left the building through the back door, I noticed no one guarded this entryway. Maybe I could escape through here. As fast as the thought ballooned in my mind, it deflated with a question.

Where would I go? The answer: anywhere but here. At least I'd be alive. I could hide in the mountains, but for how long? Immediately, I thought of Dad's sketchpad and the stone, which Princess Jamila had given to her father. I wouldn't escape without the pad, and I couldn't go home without the stone. I had to get them back. I had to be as fearless and strong as Sabirah.

We stepped out into the courtyard. On a grassy patch, guys were playing some type of game with a black ball, which was bigger than a baseball but not as large as a volleyball. As they played, they hit the ball with a leg, arm, body, or head, but no hands or feet. They wore some type of padding around their chest. I recognized the players as some of the artists who had been working on the gateway.

"Come, I will show you to your living quarters." Malachi had been watching me assess my new surroundings, his thoughts hidden from my gaze. He waved to the guys as we walked to another section of the building.

I'd just been told I was to be a sacrifice and was then led out into a courtyard where people went on with their lives as if nothing out of the ordinary were about to happen.

And it wasn't—to them.

Stepping inside the living quarters, I was surprised to see the walls splashed with bold, brilliant colors of sienna yellow, violet blue, and cranberry red, all artistically painted with the colors spiraling the room. There were several cots against one wall and a large table against the other, tucked beneath a huge window hole overlooking the courtyard. An array of crude art supplies lay on the table. Several charcoal sketches in various stages waited for the artists. This was an artist's haven, a true art colony—a place where I'd always wanted to be but not under these circumstances. Now I had this cloud of impending doom hanging over me, the worry of what was happening to Sabirah and Rasha shadowing my steps, and the little problem of being misplaced in time constantly creeping into my mind.

That's all—little life and death things that seemed of no concern to everyone else. No longer able to ignore my fear, I asked Malachi, "When will my sacrifice take place?"

"As I stated, when my men finish their work." He acted as though he'd grown weary of the subject.

"Are they close?"

"Closer every day."

"But . . ." I couldn't finish my thought. I had to keep control of my emotions and not let this guy know I was in full-out panic mode. I had to appear strong. Maybe I'd gain Malachi's respect, and then maybe he'd tell me more, though I wondered if I really wanted to know.

"What is your name?" Malachi swiped his hand over his face as if this was the end of a very long day and he wanted the formalities over with.

"Tag."

"Tag, your cot is at the end. Your roommates are Habib—" Malachi looked out the window with no glass, pointing to a muscular fellow. Though his chest and legs were covered with ball gear, I could see colorful tattoos on much of his exposed skin. I once again thought of my fake one, wishing it were gone. "—and Josu." He singled out the thin, willowy guy taking a breather on the sidelines. "Clothes more befitting an artist are in the cupboard. Change, then join me in my office." With those words, Malachi left.

Feeling sorry for myself and the strange predicament I was in, I slowly made my way to the hutch Malachi had called a cupboard. I opened the wooden doors, expecting to see tunics, ponchos, and such. Instead, I only found small patches of material: loincloths.

No way! I stood there for the longest time, trying to figure out what to do when the guy named Josu entered.

"Tag?" He looked at me, waiting for confirmation that he'd pronounced my name correctly. I nodded. "Malachi wanted me to help you." His face was sprinkled with freckles, much like mine. He'd taken off his ball gear. His bare chest and legs were freckled so much they appeared tanned. His loincloth looked natural on him.

"I can't wear this," I said.

"Why?"

"I don't know how to put it on." I thought that was a good answer until the guy started to laugh. It really wasn't funny. I was dead serious. My other bunky strolled into the room, the one Malachi called Habib. He, too, had taken off his game gear, and I could clearly see his brilliant tattoos: one of a red and blue parrot covered his right shoulder. On the other shoulder was a wicked looking spider. Giving Josu a curious look, he turned to me. "Why is he laughing?"

"No reason." My answer made Josu laugh even harder. Humiliation had now migrated to my neck and was fast approaching my chin, ready to drown me.

Catching his breath in between gasps, Josu said, "He does not know how—" A fit of laughter threatened him. He quickly calmed himself and finished, "—how to put it on." He held up a loincloth and caved into another round of laughter.

Habib tried to maintain a straight face and looked seriously at me. "What is so difficult?" He took the material from Josu and held it up. I felt like the country hick who had come to the big city, but I didn't care. I was tired of the non-joke Josu found so funny.

"It's more like I don't want to put it on." I stepped away from Habib. He gazed at me, thinking . . . I didn't know what he was thinking, and at this very moment I didn't care if he thought I was a swamp creature. I was not going to wear a little strip of cloth.

No way. No how.

And since I was already marked as a sacrifice, I had nothing to lose with my rebellion.

Habib tossed the cloth back into the cupboard. "Come." He headed out the door. I gladly left Josu and his mockery behind, following Habib into a hallway. He led me to another room. Once we were inside, he closed the door. "Rumor has it you are the chosen one for Zouché. Is that true?"

I wasn't about to confide in this guy. For all I knew, he was a spy for the king. "What's it to you?"

"If you are, you can wear something other than artist's clothes." He smiled a genuine *I-want-to-be-your-friend* smile, turned, and opened a closet. Inside were tunics and breechcloths of brilliant purples, reds, blues, and greens.

"What, no stylish underwear?" I chuckled a little.

"No." He appeared all serious, my joke wasted. "They save the stylish undergarments for the women." He wiggled his eyebrows and smiled like he was proud he'd thought of a comeback. Great! For my last days on earth, I was surrounded by a troupe of comedy players with dry senses of humor. It could be worse, I supposed.

Habib became serious again. "Change, and I will take you to Malachi. He is waiting." He then left.

I quickly picked out a red tunic with gold trim and put it on, leaving my dirty poncho and tattered tunic I'd traveled in on a stool. As I stepped from the room, Habib was waiting. He took the lead, assuming I'd follow, which I did. We crossed the courtyard. The game the others had been playing was over, and no one was in sight. We reached Malachi's quarters, and Habib knocked.

"Enter," came the voice from inside.

"Go with luck, Tag." Habib turned and walked away. Why did I feel as though I'd been delivered up for punishment? I thought about the sacrifice issue, and once again my heart raced, my palms became clammy, and I wanted to throw up.

As I reached for the door, it opened. There stood Malachi. He did a double take, staring at the red and gold trimmed outfit I wore. I realized I'd picked the same colors as the king's robes. Malachi must have seen the king earlier, and now seeing me, he could have done a rapid assessment of my choice and wonder if I was some kind of suck up.

What could I say? Nothing. I needed to act normal, like I had no idea what he might be thinking. And I didn't. But . . . was there something seriously wrong with me? Had the king left some mind manipulation in my brain that at some deep level controlled my subconscious, making me pick the same colors? And what else would I end up doing? I chewed at my bottom lip.

Malachi smiled. "I said enter."

"I'm coming." This guy was like Mom, checking out what I wore, not particularly happy with what I chose, and angry. All at once I missed her more than ever.

He motioned for me to sit in the same chair I'd only vacated a short time ago. Malachi leaned against the stone table, folding his arms. "Tag, I want you to be comfortable while you stay with us. Are you still upset?"

"I'm plenty upset. How would you feel if someone told you that you were going to be killed for an idol?" Here I was talking about my death with this guy, this stranger, and tears pricked at the back of my eyelids. I was sixteen, and I had to get a grip. Crying would only make matters worse, just like panic. And right now, matters were bad enough without those two old enemies.

"Plenty upset, huh?" Malachi folded his arms. "Though, I thought you were smarter than that."

I stared at him. What was he up to?

He continued, "I thought you might try to escape while under my charge."

I kept eye contact with the guy. He wasn't going to crack me.

He leaned closer. "You may be a blessed boy. More blessed than even King Jacob knows."

I swallowed. What was this guy's angle? What did he want?

"I know who you are, Tag." He straightened. "Samuel told me you would come. And when you did, our Lord's Crucifixion would only be days away. It is time to leave Jacobugath."

20

Rippers

Sabirah

Joy filled me!

My brother was alive!

"Sabirah, beautiful sister, you shouldn't be here." His body trembled; his voice grew raspy, but his eyes were still lit with happiness. Worried for him, I helped Asim sit. Ravid assisted as best he could and sat on his other side, holding the torch.

"I am where I am needed." I leaned his head on my shoulder, marveling at our good fortune yet concerned by his fragile state. My brother had lost a lot of weight. No longer was he the strapping man who had left in search of our father. He seemed old and withered. "Where did you find him?" I asked Ravid.

"Hiding in a crease in the wall. I almost passed him." Ravid smiled, pleased he had been successful.

I wished I had food to give Asim. "When was the last time you ate?" I asked.

"Don't worry about me," Asim said. Always thinking of others and not himself.

I turned to Ravid. "We have to find food and water."

"There is an underground stream down the tunnel a short distance." Asim pointed. "Although the Rippers may still be there." He trembled and quaked as though upset by the mere mention of them.

"Rippers?"

He glanced up and down the tunnel as if afraid of being overheard. "Men who roam the caves, searching for the weak and feeble so they can feast on them."

I thought of the creature who had jumped at me not long after I had arrived in the tunnels. He'd looked crazed and wild-eyed, almost animal-like, a man turned wild from starvation. I tried to calm my brother. "Ravid will keep us safe." I looked at my friend. Though in pain himself from his beating, I knew he wouldn't let me down. He nodded as if he'd be honored to perform his new assignment.

Asim began wringing his hands together and then wiping his worried brow, shaking his head. "Too many. Promise me we'll not go to the water until they leave the stream to hunt."

Realizing my brother wouldn't relax until I agreed, I nodded.

Asim immediately calmed. Wanting to talk of something else, I asked, "Have you seen Father?"

He gazed at me as though wishing he had a different answer. He eventually shook his head. "Though I believe he visited near the city a few years ago."

"Why do you think so?" I helped Asim to his feet, thinking it might be best if he kept moving in case one of those Ripper people came upon us. I guided him around a rock, for a moment stealing his thoughts away from the most important topic.

Walking on a smooth path once again, Asim said, "Many tunnel dwellers are believers of the gospel. They were imprisoned for their belief. Sabirah, they are people father taught."

∽

Tag

I DARED NOT MOVE, AFRAID I'd wake up from this dream of Malachi being a good guy—at least he sounded like he was, but since arriving in Jacobugath nothing was like it seemed.

"Tag, are you well?" Malachi leaned toward me and felt my forehead.

"I'm fine." I needed him to talk about his meeting with the prophet. Then maybe I could tell if he were truly on my side. "You said Samuel the Lamanite was here?"

"Not here in the city." Malachi drew back. His voice calmed, and his face was framed in fond remembrance. "My crew and I traveled to the wilderness of Akish, far north from here, for the precious mountain clay that makes our red colors so brilliant. That is where we met our friend, Samuel.

"He stayed amongst us for several days and converted all of the artists as well as others. He had such a force of goodness about him we couldn't turn away from his teachings. His words cut to our hearts, to our very souls. We couldn't deny that what he said was true."

A warm, comforting feeling came over me, and I knew Malachi was the real deal. Most importantly, I could hardly wait to tell Sabirah that we might actually find her father. "How long ago was this?"

"Several years."

Hope vanished. But at least I could tell Sabirah her father was too far north to be under King Jacob's rule. That should give her some comfort, small though it was.

Malachi continued, "We wanted to follow him, but Samuel insisted we return to the city. We wanted him to come with us, but he said the Lord needed him elsewhere. He was worried about his son and feared for his life. But the Lord had confirmed to him that his son would be all right. Samuel told me his daughter, Sabirah, and a stranger would arrive in Jacobugath, and when they did, they would need my help. When you mentioned that you had arrived with her, I decided that you were the stranger because your speaking pattern doesn't match ours. You're not from here."

Brother, was he right. I wasn't from here. I thought of what Samuel had told him, that when I came Christ would soon be crucified. Possibly at this very moment in Jerusalem, a half a world away, Jesus Christ was on trial.

A shiver covered my skin. My mind could hardly comprehend that I was living in an era when the Savior lived and walked upon the earth. True, He was half a world away, but He was alive—right now. "I remember my grandma telling me that after Christ was crucified, there were terrible earthquakes and volcanoes erupting. The entire world changed. Oceans rose and mountains fell. Whole cities were destroyed. And then there were three days of darkness. Not dark like night but a darkness so intense you couldn't see a candle flicker before your face." I looked at the expression on Malachi's face. His Lamanite complexion had paled. His eyes were wide. And I knew I'd once again said too much about the fate of this people.

"Please, Tag, continue."

I seriously didn't think he wanted to know his future. I mean if someone had told me I was going to go back in time the day before I did, I don't think I would have believed it. And here I was telling Malachi the world was going to go through a major overhaul.

"Please," he asked, sincerity creasing his brow.

"Here's a good thing. Grandma said after His death, Christ would appear in America. But before that, Jacobugath would be destroyed and Zarahemla as well as many other cities." I paused, letting him digest this information.

"Was your grandmother a great shaman?"

I couldn't help but smile. "Oh no. She studied the Book of Mormon a lot."

"Samuel told me about the same occurrences. You are truly the wayfarer he told me to watch for." A sure knowledge gentled Malachi's brow because he had realized who I was. "Your grandmother was a wise person."

"Yes, she was." The thought of her brought a rush of memories to me: Grandma holding me on her lap and telling me stories; Grandma taking me fishing and putting the worm on my hook;

and Grandma as I'd last seen her, happy and alive, sitting next to the fireplace looking up at the picture of Christ my father had painted.

Yes, she was a very wise person. And she would be the first to say I needed to do all I could to help Malachi and my friends. "We need to discuss leaving." I looked at Malachi. "But I can't leave without the friends I arrived with."

He rubbed his chin. "Sabirah and the others who were with you when you entered the city?"

I continued, "Yes. Her brother is in King Jacob's prison. His name is Asim." I wondered why Malachi didn't know Asim was Samuel's son. But Samuel had only said his son was in danger and to watch for Sabirah and a wayfarer, so maybe that was why he didn't know. Also, Asim had arrived alone. I continued, "And then there's Rasha. We can't leave her." How were we going to save all of them? Panic stirred once again to let me know it was still alive and well within me. "And there's my father's sketchpad the princess stole from me and the thing that's most important, the stone. It's very powerful and shouldn't be in the hands of King Jacob."

"You have a long list. We shall take care of the people first, and then we shall see about things."

Malachi was right. People first. Even if it did mean I may never see my father's sketchpad again. I had to let it go. Maybe I could sketch the pictures in it on something else. Though it would never be the same. He had created those pictures with his own hand. The stone, however, I had to get back. For the first time, I wondered if the king could use the stone to travel through time as I had.

Great! What if he did? I didn't want to think of the harm that could happen to my family or even the world if such a wicked man turned up in the wrong era. "We have to get the stone. I can't explain, but it's very important that we take it away from the king as soon as possible."

Malachi probably noticed my stress level had kicked up a notch. He went to the large animal horns where he'd stored his drawing. Carefully looking them over, he chose one and pulled it out. Malachi smoothed flat a map on his table and placed rock weights on the ends to hold down the curling papyrus. It was of the palace and the prison beneath. He motioned for me to come to his side. "Where did you last see your friends and the stone?"

I explained Rasha had been taken away with the princess's handmaidens. Malachi pointed to a room. "She would be near Jamila. Go on."

"Sabirah was sent to the prison for the night. She would be there and hopefully her brother, as well."

Malachi traced a line beneath the palace. By the blueprints, the prison was more like a dungeon deep underground. Getting them out was going to be an enormous challenge.

"You said Sabirah would only be there overnight, correct?"

"Yeah."

Malachi rose and paced back and forth. Every once in a while he'd rub his chin. He tugged off his turban. His hair was drawn up in a bun on his head. It looked so odd and yet, it didn't. Malachi fidgeted with his turban, set it down, and pulled at his eyebrow hairs, deep in thought.

Finally, he said, "I have decided on a plan, but *you* will need to be very brave." He shot a challenging stare my way.

"I'm listening." Before I became too concerned with how brave I'd need to be, I wanted to hear what he had to say.

"Zouché is nearly complete. We shall speed up the work."

"What?" This guy was crazy. "When you finish the idol, King Jacob wants to sacrifice me. I plan to be long gone before then." Malachi was crazy if he thought I was hanging around.

"Exactly!"

Now I really wondered whose side Malachi was on. I mean, just how much did I know about him? He said he had converted to the gospel, though now he was talking like a king-man, a true follower of King Jacob. I swallowed hard, wondering what to do.

He placed his hand on my shoulder. "Tag, do you not see? At the ceremony for the sacrifice, most of the guards will attend. King Jacob will be there, the princess will be there, and no one will be concerned about the prison. With Sabirah's help, she will show us how to enter the prison, and we can free her brother, snatch Rasha from Princess Jamila, and perhaps find this stone you say the king has."

"Yeah, but aren't you forgetting something?"

Malachi paused a moment. "No, I am very thorough."

"I'm to be *sacrificed*. You know, *killed?*"

"Oh, did I not mention we would slip you away?" He waited for me to confirm he'd said what he hadn't. I shook my head. He continued, "Well, we shall. With the help of the other artists, everything will work out. We may need to refine the plan a little."

His eyebrows jackknifed as his entire face lit up. "I know what to do. The king will naturally want a ball game before the sacrifice. We can set forth on our plan of escape then. The king likes to watch a good game and will want everyone there, as well. This time, I shall make a bargain. If the artists' team wins, you will not be killed, and we will sneak you out of the city unharmed." A cloud overcame his face. "Though, King Jacob may still want to bleed you. He thinks fresh blood on the temple stairs appeases his gods."

I thought of the first time I'd looked at the temple from the mountain and the stains I'd seen on the stairs. So it was blood.

"But—" Malachi continued to think out loud. "—at least he won't cut out your heart and place it in the chac-mool."

"What?"

"The chac-mool. A stone vessel carved in the shape of a dying king who carries a dish in his arms. Actually, the chac-mool is quite an impressive little sculpture. Josu reluctantly made the new one. The king hasn't had a sacrifice in Jacobugath for many years, waiting for Zouché to be completed. You are the first since the artists and I met Samuel and converted. We've stayed in Jacobugath waiting for you."

"I'm glad you did, but I don't give a flying leap what a chac-mool is. Explain the part about cutting out my heart."

"I should have left those words unspoken." Malachi shook his head.

I agreed with that.

"At least if we win the game, your head shall not be added to the skull rack on top of the temple, nor will your arms and legs be eaten at the feast." Malachi smiled at me as though what he now said should give me great comfort.

However, his words had the opposite effect. Trying to calm myself with a few deep breaths, I finally controlled the hysteria I felt and asked, "Maybe we need to run this plan past Sabirah?"

"Sabirah can help." Malachi nodded. "The plan can be adjusted if need be."

I wanted the plan adjusted. I wanted it ironclad—especially the part where the artists' team won the game and I slipped away alive and unharmed.

21

Summoned

Sabirah

As we walked closer to the stream, Asim grew overly anxious and kept looking behind us. "You have to douse the light," he demanded.

"But we won't be able to see where we are going," I reasoned.

Without another word, Asim grabbed the torch from Ravid's hand, threw it to the ground, and stomped it out. "The Rippers won't find us now."

We stood in the dark, the sound of our breathing our only comfort. I knew Asim was driven by fear, yet his fear had kept him alive in this pit for over a year. Ravid took ahold of my arm and Asim's, guiding us in the inky blackness to a boulder. "My eyes have adjusted quickly," he said. "Stay here while I check near the water and see if the Rippers have left." Ravid disappeared.

We sat in silence, my brother and me. I had waited for so long to be with him, and here I sat unable to think of something to say. I should tell him about home. "Mother has fallen ill. Seeing you again will definitely make her better."

"My heart grieves that I left you alone to take care of our family," Asim replied, his voice a mere whisper. "What of Grandfather?"

As I was about to reply, a feeling of being watched overcame me so powerful I searched through the darkness. My eyes had adjusted to the point that I could see darker shadows that dodged into pools of black. In that instant a loud yowl, like that of a tortured beast, echoed off stone walls as three creatures leaped at us.

℀

Tag

When I awoke the next morning, I found Josu and Habib sitting on their cots, staring at me. I immediately sat up; my blanket fell to my lap.

"What is it?" I was certain something bad had happened.

"Oooh!" Josu stared at my chest. "You are right, Habib. He is white as alabaster, but his face and arms are red as Akish clay. And the strange white ring around his neck. Are those faint markings like the king's?" He pointed to my chest.

"What?" I then realized his last comment was about my henna tattoo. It had nearly disappeared, leaving only the murky image of the skull. I was a bit creeped out that he thought it looked like the king's tattoo, but I was not about to let this dude know that. Plus, I was a bit annoyed that they were making fun of me. "No, they're not like the king's! And you've never seen somebody with a sunburn?" Even though my skin had peeled, it was still red. I knew I looked like an idiot, especially my neck where my dog collar had been, but that was the way of it. Not much I could do.

Josu sighed and said, "You make funny noises in your sleep."

I stared at the guy dressed in his loincloth ready for the day: hair pulled back in a ponytail, bands on his arms, and all bright eyed. "Yeah, well, you have the face of a skunk," I countered.

Habib chuckled at my words. Josu looked at his friend as if he were a traitor. Habib quickly grew solemn. He was dressed and ready for work, as well. I didn't want Josu, the giggling jokester, to start on me already, but it was too late for that. This day would be one dry joke a minute with these two. I rubbed sleep from my eyes and reached for my clothes at the foot of the bed.

Standing, I stretched, forgetting I wore only my briefs. Both Josu and Habib stared at my underwear. When I had gone to bed last night, they'd both been asleep, so they hadn't seen.

"What manner of clothing do you wear?" Habib asked studying the elastic band at the waist. He pulled at it.

I hit his hand away.

Josu stared at the material layered in front of my underwear. I turned my back to him, but he followed.

"What? You've never seen briefs before?" I quickly pulled on my tunic.

"Briefs?" Habib rolled the word over his tongue. "You use strange words. You truly are the wayfarer our prophet Samuel foretold would come."

"Yeah, well . . . maybe."

"Where are you from?" asked Josu.

"Idaho Falls." I wasn't offering any more explanation. The two looked at one another. Confusion shone through their eyes and flushed their cheeks.

"Have you eaten yet?" My stomach was as empty as the land of Desolation.

"Ah, I forgot." Habib handed me a piece of cornbread. I gratefully took the food and chomped it down in three bites.

Lacing up my sandals, I asked, "Is Malachi in his office?"

"No. He said he had business with the princess, but we were to take you with us to complete the work on the gateway." Habib started for the door. Josu stood beside me. It looked like I was stuck with these two for the duration.

ço

Sabirah

THE RIPPERS WERE ON US as fast as starving wolves, foaming at the mouth and issuing growls. I leaped to my feet. Two came at me, one at Asim. I jabbed at the eyes of the attacker in front of me, making him stagger away. The other attacker jumped me from behind, wrapping his arms about my chest. Clutching my forearms over his, I lunged backward with as much force as I could, ramming him into the wall. He groaned. Thrusting my arms out, I broke his hold. Grabbing his hands, I flipped him over my shoulders, throwing him into the attacker I had blinded. They both fell to the ground, the blind one hitting his head, making him unconscious. The other one came at me again, undaunted.

I stepped back with my left foot, turning my side to him as he leaped with both arms reaching for me. As I turned my hip, I thrust my right arm up, smashing my fist into his throat and collapsing his wind passage. At once, he grabbed his throat, choking and spewing up blood. He scurried away into the shadows.

Turning about, desperate to see to my brother, I found a Ripper still on Asim. As the Ripper raised his arm to strike my brother, I latched hold of him, twisting his arm as hard as I could and bringing him to his knees, yelping in pain. With him down, I kicked him in the face as hard as I could. He slumped to the ground and moved no more. I tried to see what had happened to Asim.

"Are you all right?" I asked as I helped him to his feet.

"I think so." He slowly rose to stand by me. "I had forgotten how well you could fight," Asim said with pride in his voice. "Do you still carry the dagger I made for you?"

"Princess Jamila's men took it." I hated telling him.

"I shall make you a new one." I was grateful to hear him talk about the future because it meant he had hope of getting out.

Someone rushed toward us. Asim and I braced for another fight.

"I heard a commotion and came as fast as I could," Ravid said, out of breath.

"We were attacked by Rippers," I told him.

"But you're all right?"

"Yes. Can we go to the stream?" I didn't know if my brother could tolerate more fighting.

"There are people there, but I spoke with them. They are friendly." Ravid tried to reassure me.

"Must be the followers," Asim said. "Come, sister, meet the people who love our father almost as much as we do."

ℰↃ

Tag

WHEN WE ARRIVED AT THE gateway portals, we found we were the only ones working there. Malachi had reassigned the other artists to work on Zouché.

The header over the entry was almost finished, but the accent color needed to be applied. Josu set me to mashing berries into a mixture to make green coloring. His fingers were stained, so I suspected this had been his job before. I busied myself with the tedious task while Habib and Josu laid out the knives and rags they would use to apply the color. When they finished, Habib fastened a harness to Josu. I gave a pallet of freshly made color to him, and together Habib and I hoisted him up.

"I see you are nearly finished." Malachi walked toward us, and at his side was Sabirah! She was dressed in flowing robes and handmaiden clothes that exposed her midriff and much of her legs. I was dumbstruck by her beauty: long, shiny, black hair hanging loosely about her shoulders, dark all-seeing eyes that could reach into my soul. The word *goddess* came again to my mind as it had when I'd first seen her in the jungle. And though her clothing had changed, something else was different. A sadness wrapped around her.

I let go of the rope.

Habib grunted a little as he took up the unexpected slack.

Embracing Sabirah, I said, "You look well. The last time I saw you, two of the king's thugs were carting you off to prison. I'm

glad the princess kept her word and only left you there overnight."
I noticed a little green from my hand had rubbed off on her arm.

Sabirah glanced at the spot and smiled. "Jamila merely wanted
me to taste prison life. Her guards retrieved me this morning. She
demanded I dress in this clothing."

"Looks good." I glanced at her body again but didn't stare,
though I wanted to.

She shrugged and then continued, "Malachi has great sway
over the princess because when he told her that he would paint her
likeness on the city's portal if she allowed me to go with him, she
gave in. Although she threatened that if I tried to escape or made
trouble, she'd kill my brother."

"You found him?"

She nodded. "Indeed, I did."

I was happy for her. "Did Malachi tell you of your father?" I
hoped that would cast away the sadness in her eyes.

"I only had time to tell her of my meeting Samuel years ago.
She recognized her father's work on the necklace I wear," Malachi
said as he showed me the fish-shaped talisman. A group of people
walked past, giving us a wary once-over. Malachi motioned for
Sabirah and me to follow him from the main byway. "Let us go to
my workplace where our words won't be overheard." He waved at
Habib and Josu and then hurried us back to the artists' sanctuary.

Once we were safely within Malachi's walls and seated about
the stone table, Sabirah told us what had happened to her since
we'd parted. When she finished the remarkable tale of finding
Asim, fighting the Rippers, and meeting the followers, Malachi
rose and shook his head. "You are as brave as your father said." He
turned to me. "Tag, we need to hurry and inform Sabirah of our
plans. Princess Jamila wants Sabirah to return quickly or she shall
make good on her threat to kill Asim."

I gave Sabirah a quick recap of what we would do at the game.
Malachi then told her that if the artists lost, I would be presented
as an assumed sacrifice, and even though he tried to reassure her

I would be safe, she was more than a little upset. She said, "We cannot risk harm coming to Tag."

"No harm will come to him," Malachi said. "As players of the game, all the artists will be near. And they will win. But in case they lose, we will protect him, though we may have to let the king think Tag will be sacrificed. We could make a fight break out that will take the king's attention away, and that is when I will free Tag. The artists will give us cover. But if this doesn't work to our advantage, I will store weapons behind the wall of skulls at the top of the temple. If they bring Tag to the temple to sacrifice him, the artists and I will be prepared to set him free and to fight." Malachi pointed to Sabirah. "While the game is going on, you will need to free your brother from the prison."

Using the map on the table, Sabirah showed us the passageways of the prison as best she could. "We have to save the followers, as well."

Though I had the same nervousness I had last night as we came up with this plan, a feeling of warmth came over me accompanied by the comforting thought that I'd be all right and that Malachi's plan would work. I opened my mouth to speak, but for a moment I couldn't form words; the reassuring knowledge was still so strong. As it ebbed, I said, "Sabirah, the plan will work. We don't have time to think of another one. The promised Messiah will soon be crucified, and we'll need to be long gone from here."

She stood, reached down, and pulled me to my feet, hugging me like I'd always dreamed she would. Then leaning her forehead against mine, she smiled. "My father said the wayfarer would aid me when all seemed lost. I didn't know such actions would also put your life in danger."

Malachi patted us both on our backs. "Worry not. All will be well. Zouché should be completed by tomorrow. I have sent word to the king. The game and ceremony will be in two days because the cooks need time to prepare the banquet, and the ceremonial decorations shall need to be put in place. On the sacrificial day much excitement will fill the air. People won't be watchful, and this shall allow us to set forth our plan. With the help of the Almighty, we shall escape danger."

Sabirah returned to the map on the table. "And where is the sacrificial altar?"

Malachi pointed to the central temple. "On top."

It was wrong to use a temple as a place to kill someone. But many things in Jacobugath were wrong.

At that moment, Josu and Habib rushed in, gasping for breath.

"What is it?" Malachi asked.

"King Jacob!" Josu said between breaths.

"Yes . . ." Malachi coaxed more information from them.

"Sent a messenger," Habib said, catching his breath more rapidly than Josu. "He has summoned Tag to the throne."

I looked at Sabirah. The doomed and wary expression on her face made me feel as though I'd swallowed a big, jagged stone that sank to my gut.

Malachi heaved a great sigh before saying, "I was afraid of this. I shall go with you. This will be the perfect opportunity to propose the game."

22

Tip of the Knife

Tag

SABIRAH WALKED WITH MALACHI AND me to the palace. The place was alive with preparations for the ceremony that was still two days away. Servants hustled about the halls, maidens talked of what to wear, how to style their hair, and every other girly thing. Sabirah had to leave and report to Jamila. As she disappeared down the marbled corridor, I wished I could have followed her.

Malachi and I soon came to the hallway leading to the throne. The guards even smiled as we passed. Gone were the dronelike faces that had welcomed us before. They must be glad I was the sacrifice and not one of them. Or perhaps they'd decided I wasn't a bad guy after all because I was supposedly giving my life for their new god.

We walked down the great hall of past leaders. Again, I felt their hollow eyes on me, mocking me. I was more frightened than I could ever remember.

The guards opened the huge doors to the king's chamber. There, he sat on the throne with his pet jaguar at his feet. Did the guy sit there all day waiting for people?

As we approached, the mighty cat Princess Jamila had called Anhanga stretched and started toward me. I glanced up at Malachi, whose sole attention was on the king. I wished I had the confidence of Malachi. I mean, I knew everything would be all right because

I was sure that comforting feeling I felt as we told Sabirah of the plan was the Holy Ghost. Still, fear crept into my being, nibbling away and creating doubt. I watched Malachi and saw a sliver, just a sliver, of wariness directed toward the king.

We stopped at the bottom steps leading to the throne about the same time the jaguar reached us. The feline rubbed its head against my leg. A false feeling of warmth and goodwill flushed through my body. This was different from the comfort of the Holy Ghost, and I knew the king was once again casting his spell.

Malachi bent to one knee and pulled me down to mine, as well. The beast beside me purred. The calming sensation grew stronger.

"Rise," the king ordered. He motioned for us to climb the stairs to him. Anhanga stayed close to my side as we went up to the king. Drawing nearer to him, I saw he was dressed in robes of red and gold. Plus, he held the stone in his hand. This was why he had summoned me.

"Malachi, I did not request your presence." His voice rang through the room. His eyes bore down on my friend. I wondered if King Jacob was mind-reading Malachi. But I really didn't think so. No, I was the victim here. The king was a spider mesmerizing me before the kill. The jaguar purred louder, as if reinforcing my thoughts.

"My lord," Malachi began, "I thought it best to come with the boy. He is unfamiliar with the city."

"He is safe. You may go." King Jacob was sending away my lifeline. If Malachi walked out the door, I knew I would be trapped in the king's web of false comfort.

"Your Majesty, I beg to stay. My charge will never find his way back, and I sorely need him to help complete the work on Zouché." Malachi's focus did not waver from the king.

"Your messenger said the job was complete." King Jacob rose, stone in hand. He stepped away from the throne. Concern creased his brows; his bald, leathery head shone as if polished.

"Be assured, it will be accomplished by the ceremony, but it must be perfect. Tag should be the one to apply the finishing touches. It is only fitting the sacrifice complete the work." Malachi was so smart. I knew the finishing work he was thinking of was collecting weapons and preparing our escape, not working on the idol.

King Jacob mulled over Malachi's words. "Perhaps you are right. Instead of treating him like the other lambs I have prepared for other sacrifices, he shall be different." His dark eyes settled on me, and I felt as though he were reaching for my soul.

I gulped. My knees shook. Anhanga rubbed against me. I wished the cat would go away. A quivering rumbled through my stomach. The king walked to stand directly in front of me, almost toe to toe. He liked to play games and wanted me frightened. He cupped his hand to my cheek, as if he regretted something. Pulling his hand back, he said, "Yes. Instead of my testing him, you may take him back, but return the boy early tomorrow so my daughter can properly prepare him." King Jacob returned to his throne and sat. I hoped Anhanga would follow him, but he stayed by me.

"As you wish, Your Majesty. However, there is also the matter of the game." Malachi tossed out the bait. I hoped the king was biting.

"Game?"

"Yes." Malachi acted all concerned. "The ball game played before every sacrifice?"

"Games are for the gods of seasons, not Zouché. A silly game will not appease him." King Jacob looked at his nails as if checking to see if they were evenly trimmed.

"But, lord," Malachi pressed. "Would not Zouché be jealous if you played the game for your other gods and excluded him?"

King Jacob readjusted in his seat. Folding his arms, he said, "Perhaps you are right. Why not play the game? The artists against my team."

"And if the artists win?" Malachi was leading him on.

"The artists have never scored against my military."

I instantly thought of the burly guys who had captured and dragged us across the desert. Those fellows were gigantic compared to the scrawny artists. This plan would never work.

"Even so, my lord." Malachi was sticking to the plan. "Why not make a wager?"

"A wager? You want to wager with me, the king?" He chuckled; a throaty gurgle escaped his lips.

"Though it is impossible . . . let us say if the artists win, our new talent, Tag, is spared from sacrifice. I could use his talent to help bring more beauty to the city." There, Malachi had said it.

King Jacob cocked his head, much like a hawk trying to focus on a moving mouse. Then uproarious laughter erupted from him. He waved off Malachi. "In fact, let us say the first team to score wins, and if your puny artists are the winners, he is saved. Yet, there must be a sacrifice of talent for Zouché." He thought a moment. "You, Malachi, will take his place."

"No!" I yelled.

Malachi bowed to the king and took my hand, trying to lead me away.

I jerked from his grasp. "This is not right! I don't want you to die for me."

"The king is just." Malachi glared as if to say, *"shut up."*

I glanced up at the king, who glowered down at us, watching our every move. Then I realized Malachi knew this would happen all along. He must have a lot of confidence in our plan of escape. Still, I was in shock and backed away from the king with my friend. The giant cat followed, but I ignored him. We'd made it. And though there had been an unexpected kink in our plan, the king had taken the bait. We'd somehow pulled it off. I couldn't wait to get outside and talk with Malachi.

The king cleared his throat. "I would like to speak with the boy alone. Malachi, if you fear the boy cannot find his way back to your sanctuary, you may wait outside."

Anhanga blocked my path.

The world stopped.

My escape had been delayed. Malachi squeezed my hand. His message: hang in there, be strong, and don't give up. It was amazing how much communication could come from a hand squeeze.

Without looking at me, Malachi nodded to the king, descended the first few steps backward, and then turned and walked away. I had to will myself to stay put, not to chase after my friend and ally. I knew I had to face whatever was coming . . . alone. I must be strong like Malachi and fight any false feelings of comfort.

The jaguar left me and slowly walked to King Jacob, paid his respects, and lay on the floor.

I heard the large doors to the room shut as Malachi left. Now I really was alone with this man, this crazy man who had sentenced me or Malachi to death for an idol.

The king sat on his throne. "Tag—" He raised the stone. "—where did you get this?"

I wasn't prepared for his question. Actually, I wasn't prepared for anything, but I knew in the bottom of my heart that even if I told him, it wouldn't do any good. But I had to answer.

"I found it."

"Where?"

"On the way here." In a round about way, I had.

"Father, he does not speak the truth." Princess Jamila stepped from behind a pillar near the throne. Atop her silky blond hair rested her feathered crown of brilliant blues and greens. I was surprised because I thought she would be with Sabirah. Maybe she was. Gazing behind the princess, I couldn't see my friend. Disappointed, I realized the princess could have been listening to everything. Had she been reading my mind through it all? I should have known she'd make an appearance. Just what I needed—her picking my brain.

Robes of azure billowed behind Jamila as she walked with only a slight limp now. She stopped at her father's side. She bowed and kissed his hand. Turning to me, she said, "It seems my arrival is most timely. Tag, admit you had this stone when Sabirah's men captured me."

I had to be careful with my thoughts. "Yes, but I've been on a journey to this place for a very long time." I raised my eyebrows and smiled.

"Come, come." She walked closer and trailed her finger around my neck as she did her circling thing. Leaning next to my ear, she whispered, "Let go; think about where the stone came from. Relax. We mean you no harm."

Her breath was warm against my skin. I flinched. Panicked that I might actually think of who gave the stone to me and the princess would learn the truth, I remembered what Sabirah had said. She had told me to think of Christ to block Jamila's mind probing.

Closing my eyes, I spoke in my mind. *In the name of Jesus Christ, my Savior, I command thee from my mind.*

Opening my eyes, I looked at the princess. She had a perplexed expression on her face, like a child who'd had candy taken away.

"Daughter, are you well?" The king rose and reached for her hand. "Jamila?"

Upon his touch, she shook her head as if awakened from a trance and looked to her father. "I am fine." She turned her tantalizing eyes on me; a sly smile upturned the corners of her thick lips. "I cannot be stopped."

Princess Jamila pulled her robe sleeves up her arms and clapped her hands. In rushed her handmaidens, including Rasha. They were dressed in what looked like bikinis, though sheer long robes covered them. Unable to meet my gaze, Rasha hung her head in shame.

I wanted to go to her but didn't dare. The king and princess would pick up on my affections for Rasha and use it to their advantage.

"Come forth, Rasha." Princess Jamila's sensual voice coiled the command through the air as hypnotic as a snake charmer's music.

Rasha slowly walked to her. The princess pulled a dagger from beneath her robes and grabbed Rasha's arm. Jerking my friend to her knees, Princess Jamila placed the tip of the knife under Rasha's right eye. "Tell me where you found the stone, Tag, or I promise I shall take first one eye and then the other." The handmaidens gasped.

I knew she meant every word, and I was helpless to come to Rasha's aid. If I told them I had stolen the stone from John Doe and his friends in the twenty-first century, they wouldn't believe me.

I had to think of something—and fast.

23

The King's Decree

Sabirah

I HAD TO GET WORD to Asim and Ravid of the escape plan. Upon returning to the princess's quarters, I found she and her handmaidens weren't there, which was very fortunate. Grateful for this chance, I quickly stole away, returning to the big iron doors of the prison. The same guards, dressed in loincloths and headdresses who had escorted me here yesterday and who had delivered me from the prison this morning, were still standing watch. The dark turtlelike one who had shown me mercy by giving me the torch had a look of concern as I approached. But his eyes grew wide as he took in my new apparel. The princess had me dress in this new clothing after I'd been released earlier in the day. He obviously found me appealing. I would use him to serve my purpose.

"Have mercy, sir," I said. "Please, could I check on my brother?" The hawkish one with the stern face shook his head severely, but the kind one thought it over. I coyly smiled at him, and he inhaled deeply as though I'd promised him my hand. I could tell I only needed a little more begging. "I bring no weapons. I shall take nothing in and take nothing out. You can search me, if you'd like." The slow one was thinking it over. I added, "I merely want to see how my brother is. He wasn't well when I left him." I tried to appear meek and mild, which wasn't my nature.

The merciful one looked to his partner. "Hod, she is no threat. What does it matter if she comes and goes? None will escape."

His partner shook his head but did nothing as his friend unlocked the doors and pulled up the plank. I expected the kind guard to search my person. Gazing at my body clad in the outlandish clothes, he gulped, focusing on my chest. He began to reach for me, and then, as though embarrassed, he stopped.

"Mooda, the least you can do is find a little pleasure since you have put both our lives in danger." Hod scoffed.

"I can see she hides no weapons." He cast his gaze to the floor.

Hod said, "We might let you in, but you've no promise from me that I'll let you out." He had stepped in front of his partner, Mooda, making sure I understood.

Ignoring the threatening words, the gentle one named Mooda handed me a torch. "Be quick. We shall be replaced soon," he warned.

I nodded thank you, took the torch, and fled into the prison.

თ

Tag

"OKAY, I STOLE THE STONE." I didn't know if the king and princess would buy my story, but I prayed they would.

"Is he telling the truth?" King Jacob asked his daughter. Princess Jamila nodded, even though at this moment she couldn't read my thoughts. She didn't release her hold on Rasha. I'd do near anything to make the princess let go.

"Where? Where did this happen?" The princess grabbed a handful of Rasha's raven hair while keeping the sharp point of the knife pressed to her cheek below her eye.

"Please, don't hurt her!" I begged. If the princess slipped or even coughed, Rasha would be permanently blind. I spat out, "Release her, and I'll tell you. I swear . . . I swear as God is my witness, I'll tell you where I stole the stone and anything else you want to know if you'll first let her go."

The king shot to his feet. Anger seemed to churn within him like a twister as he walked toward me.

Why? Then I remembered saying "as God is my witness." The words had fallen out of my mouth without thought. Before coming to this time, I never would have said such a thing. For so long, I'd been mad at God. He'd turned His back on my mother and me at a time when we needed Him most. But the last few days of watching Sabirah, listening to Malachi, and learning of the bravery of Samuel the Lamanite, I knew that deep down I believed, and I had to stand tall. Cowering would only incite the king more. Leaning on God for courage, I stared up at the man, never diverting my attention nor flinching away.

He studied me as though expecting at any moment I'd crumble, yet I remained strong. Suddenly, a slight smile flickered to the king's mouth. A smile I didn't trust. He said, "Let go of the girl."

"But father . . ." The princess glared at him, trying to understand.

"Release her!"

Princess Jamila let go. Rasha looked up at me, and, amazingly, I saw admiration in her gaze. My words had put her life in danger but saved her at the same time.

"Leave us," King Jacob spat out.

Princess Jamila hustled Rasha and her other maidens from the room. The princess turned to come back.

"I said leave us!" yelled the king.

Princess Jamila bowed and left.

My courage rapidly decreased. *Please, God, stay with me.* My eyes locked onto the king's.

He stepped toward me, stone in hand. "How dare you speak His name in front of my people? I should have the ceremony today. I should sacrifice you now, myself." Hot rage strained the creases on his face. The blood vessels in his neck visibly pulsed.

I stood perfectly still. Not hanging my head, not backing down. I really didn't think the king would soil his hands with my blood. He was more the type who would have someone else do his dirty work. Still, what did I know?

"Zouché will witness your death. Your God will not help you. Never say His name again in my presence!" He walked up to me and tapped my chest hard. How was I to reply? Despite my weak knees and cowardly soul, I said, "I understand."

The king's mood instantly became lighter. "Tag, tell me who you stole the stone from. No more games." He had accepted what I'd said and was now turning to the real business on his mind.

"I was in Palisades. This guy kept the stone in a box. I took it in the middle of the night and ran away. That's the truth."

King Jacob tossed the stone between his hands as if it were a baseball. "I know a story about such stones. Do you know of the myth about the brother of Jared?"

He waited for me to reply. I was speechless.

"You think I don't know of the lies my people have told? Such foolishness to believe miracle stones were touched by, who was it now—" He tapped the stone to his chin as if deep in thought, then grinned at me, and said, "—God?"

I swallowed, trying to get rid of the boulder blocking my throat. Since he knew the story behind the stone, did he know of the time-traveling powers it possessed?

The king stared down at the gem in his hand. "I have gone to great lengths to stop the spreading of such fables. It is my desire to create a new history, one where those precious stones were given to me. So far you have helped a great deal. But I need *all* of the stones, and you are going to help me find them. Where is the land of Palisades?"

I had sorely misjudged King Jacob. My hope had been he would only see wealth in the possession of the stone and never learn of its powers. If God had the power to make the stone work, He had the power to stop it, didn't He? Of course, what did I know of the power of God? On the off chance the king might stumble upon the stone's time-traveling ability and if for some reason far beyond my understanding Heavenly Father didn't control it, I needed to choose my words wisely. I didn't think John Doe and his friends had the other fifteen stones in their possession, but I didn't want to take any chances of King Jacob traveling through time and demanding the stones from them. I dared not move a muscle, afraid the slightest twitch would make the king feel that I was lying. I replied, "It is a land far, *far* north of here."

"Can you find it on a map?"

I was pretty certain Palisades, Idaho, wasn't on a map he would have. I had to think of something. "Your Highness, I really doubt there are more stones with the gentleman I took this one from. He travels a lot to make his living, and I really don't think he's still there."

"But he would know where this one came from. He sounds like a merchant." The king jumped to his own conclusion, and I wasn't going to correct him. I didn't know who Bob Jones, Steve Smith, and John Doe were or what they did for a living, but I knew they weren't traveling salesmen.

As I thought back on my brief encounter with the three, I knew they were special. I wasn't sure how, but they were. If I ever made it out of here and back to my own time, those guys had some explaining to do. And I had some confessing to do about taking—no, borrowing—the stone. Anyway, I needed to set things right. I only wished I could do it sooner than later.

"I want you to draw a picture of the merchant so that after the ceremony I can send my men to find him." The king waited for my response.

"Well, maybe you should postpone the ceremony, and I could go with your men. Lead the way, so to speak. Nothing like having the guy with firsthand knowledge." Okay, I'd taken a slim chance that he'd postpone the sacrifice and fall for this.

King Jacob grinned. "Oh no! Once you are sacrificed, Zouché will aid my men and me in stopping the spread of lies. We will find the merchant; of that, I am certain." He settled back on his throne. "You may go now. Tell Malachi of your drawing assignment. I want it by tomorrow."

I'd been dismissed.

☙

Sabirah

Asim and Ravid weren't hard to find. Before I'd left them this morning, they'd told me that in case I returned, I should look for them near the crease in the wall where Ravid had first found my brother. The crease was a portal to other tunnels and a safe hiding place. Running fast to avoid being attacked by the Rippers, I quickly found my way to safety. Asim and Ravid were there along with some of the followers.

Asim seemed embarrassed to look upon the new clothing the princess made me wear. I could do nothing to cover up, so I ignored him, focusing on the message I'd brought. I told them of the plan of escape. At first the followers were fearful, sure that Malachi and the artists were devising a trap. As soon as I explained how my father had converted them in the land of Akish, the followers calmed down.

I continued to inform them of the plan and that in two days' time they were to meet me at the prison doors. Hope shone in their eyes. They didn't know that my challenge was to devise a way to get them out. Ravid had grown quiet until I started to leave. He followed me and Asim to the stairwell.

"Sabirah," Ravid said. I stopped and looked at him. "Princess Jamila will find a way to stop you. She is as cunning as a puma. Be wary. When the time is near, I'll move everyone near the doors."

"I'll be careful. Don't worry," I said. Ravid had changed. I knew I could trust him with my life and with my brother's and the followers', as well. He would do everything in his power to meet the demands I placed upon his shoulders . . . his scarred and bloodied shoulders. Sadly, he had learned the lesson well of what happened to those who followed Jamila.

While embracing Asim, he slipped me a crude weapon, a dagger shaped from stone. Taking it, I said, "How did you . . . ?"

"The followers helped me. With this sharpened rock, you can sling the weapon or stab your enemy."

"Thank you." I quickly slid it under my waistband. "In two days, I'll return. I've found a friend in one of the guards." I hugged Asim once again. Then pretending confidence and courage, I left.

ero

Tag

MALACHI HAD WAITED FOR ME just outside the throne room. I didn't speak until we were out of the palace. On our way to the artists' compound, I explained how King Jacob had grilled me over the stone.

Patting me on the back, Malachi told me not to worry. Of course, I didn't tell him of the stone's time-traveling ability. I thought it best to keep that knowledge between Sabirah and me. Then I remembered that if I were saved from sacrifice, Malachi would die. Gratitude filled me, but I couldn't let him go through with this. "We have to change our plans. You can't be killed for me."

"Not to worry. I'll be long gone before King Jacob knows what has happened. While you were with the king, I sent word to Sabirah to meet with us tonight. We shall finalize our plan."

Things were looking up, I guess. Strange that I could think such a thing, especially with our impending deaths looming before us. But I had faith. Somehow Malachi, Sabirah, and I would figure a way that we could beat King Jacob and Princess Jamila and save us all.

The artists had finished Zouché and were at the artist compound waiting for us. Malachi set them to practicing their ball game, while I tried to draw a picture of John Doe. All I could remember was he had dark hair, a nice smile, and a dimple in his cheek. Oh, and the blue color of his eyes, though I painted them brown. Besides, it really didn't matter. John Doe wasn't here; he was comfortable in the twenty-first century. I wondered if he'd discovered the stone missing. Did he use the stone to go back in time himself? What if Steve Smith, Bob Jones, and John Doe were some type of time travelers?

If they were, would my drawing of John put him in danger if he happened to come to this time? Of course, he couldn't now because King Jacob had the stone . . . unless John had the other stones. I really didn't think he did, but just in case, I decided to shorten his nose on the portrait and do away with the dimple.

Then the troubling thought of King Jacob using the stone to time travel surfaced in my mind again. I could do nothing to stop him. I prayed he wouldn't and tried to remain focused on taking the stone back and not worrying about what-ifs. I planned to speak with Sabirah about this concern tonight.

જ

Sabirah

I rapped on the prison door as I tried to leave.

No one came.

I pounded harder.

Still no one. Had the guards changed so soon? I didn't think I'd been that long. Again, I beat on the door.

I heard faint sounds of chains moving against it. Relief flushed my skin as I eagerly anticipated the doors opening. The plank scraped the metal. When the doors swung open, I was grateful to see Mooda and Hod. I started to walk out as they stepped back to reveal Princess Jamila.

"So, you've found your brother." The princess stared at me with a wicked gaze.

"You knew I would," I replied, not cowering.

"Perhaps you should stay with him permanently." She folded her arms; her fingers dug into her bare skin below her gold armbands. Her eyes became mere slits as she called upon her powers to read my mind.

My faith was stronger than her power. I remained calm. "As you wish." I turned to go down the stairs.

She grabbed the torch from my hold. "I could push you down the stairs to your death," she said, a crazed gleam in her eyes.

I felt her free hand on my back. I didn't fear. If she pressed I'd flip her over as fast as a striking snake and send her to her death.

"Or—" She looked at each guard beside her. "—I could let my men have their fun with you."

This didn't frighten me, either.

As though frustrated with my lack of reaction, she grabbed a fistful of my hair. "I shall think of something more appropriate." She pulled out my hair. Tempted to strike her, I controlled my reaction. Jamila dropped the hair strands on the floor and motioned for Mooda to take hold of me. In one fell swoop, he slung me over his shoulder, and I let him. I had to remain on the outside of the prison where I could best help Asim.

Mooda carried me to the princess's quarters where he plopped me down on the hard floor as if I were a bundle of kindling wood. Surprised by his harshness, I glanced up at him. His turtle face had turned to stone as the princess watched him. When she ordered him to leave, he signaled me with his index finger, out of Jamila's view. And I understood that he, too, was forced to do things he didn't want to do.

Turning her entire attention on me, Jamila circled about, glaring as though she were to wear me down. Patience spent, she said, "What did you learn down there?" She was talking of the prison.

"The prisoners are starving." I found it odd that she would ask.

"They are given food once a day," she scoffed.

"Some are so hungry that they attack the weak to eat them." I waited for her reaction, wondering what she'd say.

Jamila paused a moment and then smiled. "You lie. Though my father is a firm ruler, he has a heart of gold. He'd never allow such atrocious behavior, even in his prisoners."

"Your father has the heart of a peccary."

She stopped in back of me. I wouldn't turn around. I meant what I said. Instantly, she was at my side. "Say it again." She reached up and with the ivory dagger my brother had made years ago—the dagger she'd stolen—cut the necklace my father had given me from my neck. How dare she use precious items made for me by family to torment me? I swung around, ready to strike.

She held my beloved talisman, teasing me. "While in your village, Ravid told me that your father gave this to you. It is not my father who has the heart of a peccary but yours. Why else would he burden you with such a momento when he had no intention of returning to his family?"

I yearned to wrestle the last gift my father had given me away from her and wrench the dagger from her hand, yet I knew that was what she wanted.

She laughed, relishing my inner conflict, and then said, "My father has the heart of a jaguar. And though he is strong, I am stronger. If anything goes adrift with the games or the sacrifice, you shall pay." She went to the balcony and tossed my necklace into the night. My hand went to my waistband where the new weapon Asim had given me was hidden, yet I restrained myself. Now was not the time. I knew my father would want me to use the good reason he'd taught me and wait.

"The king has decided to have more sacrifices to Zouché." Princess Jamila's eyes sparkled with delight. And I knew she was about to tell me something I didn't want to hear.

✼

Tag

As the artists were about to go to bed, Sabirah arrived, visibly shaken. I noticed right away the wing-spread eagle that had hung from her neck was missing. Malachi showed her to a chair. "What has upset you, my friend?"

I was certain something dreadful had happened. "Did they hurt you? Is Asim all right?"

"I am well." Sabirah smiled at me. "Asim and the others are anxiously waiting to hear more of our escape plan. I had to wait until the princess was asleep before I sneaked past the guards."

"Then what's wrong?" I asked.

Sabirah seemed reluctant to speak. Malachi glanced around the room. All the artists were waiting, as well. Some had never seen Sabirah before and were overwhelmed by her beauty. Malachi shooed them out to the courtyard. A few mumbled under their breath, but most of them obediently left. Before leaving, Josu and Habib asked if they could be of any help. Malachi told them to get some rest. They would need it for the game. They reluctantly followed the others, but as they walked through the door, I noticed the way they looked at Sabirah as though in their minds they were saying, "hubba hubba." I couldn't blame them. She was drop-dead gorgeous, even with her hair tangled and her face creased with worry.

After the door closed, Malachi said, "I have bad news of my own." This was a surprise. He looked to me as if to apologize for keeping something from me and then continued, "I learned this afternoon that one of my artists has the ear of the king. I have always known King Jacob has spies everywhere, but learning that he has turned one of my artists against me is most troubling. I was hopeful to catch the person before telling you, Tag, but now I fear our mission may be in jeopardy. We must trust no one."

Yep, that was bad, though I had an even worse feeling about the news Sabirah was going to share.

"Sabirah," Malachi placed his hand on her shoulder like a caring parent, "tell us what you've learned."

With a deep sigh, she said, "Princess Jamila told me the king wants more sacrifices for Zouché."

I breathed a sigh. "Yeah, if the artists win the game he's going to kill Malachi instead, but Malachi has another plan."

Sabirah appeared confused. Malachi ignored what I said. "There is something more?"

She nodded. "Because Tag seemed reluctant to draw the likeness of the man who gave him the stone, the king has decreed that if the man is not found to match the drawing—" She bit her lips together.

"Tell us!" A chill skittered over my skin.

Sabirah turned to me and with a crestfallen expression and said, "If your drawing doesn't help find the man, the king will sacrifice all of the followers in the prison, my brother, and me."

24
Blood Flowers

Tag

"HAVE NO FEAR. WE'LL REWORK our plans so we'll be gone before the king's words can be fulfilled," Malachi said. Though he seemed sure of himself, I detected a hint of fear by the sudden twitch of his hand. Not the all-out we're-doomed fear, but the slight this-better-work-or-we're-toast fear.

"Okay. What are we going to do?" I asked.

We talked long into the night and finally hashed out two plans in case the first one didn't work.

Plan A: We refined our first plan. With the king and his minions involved in watching the game, Malachi, Sabirah, and I would sneak away. Malachi and Sabirah would distract the guards at the king's quarters while I slipped in and grabbed the stone. We would meet up at the kitchen and free the prisoners. We were most hopeful that this plan would work, but just in case we couldn't sneak away, we worked out a second idea.

Plan B: While the king and his people celebrated their win by placing me on the sacrificial altar, Malachi and the artists would overpower the king and his men with the clubs and swords they would stash behind the wall of skulls. While that was going on, Sabirah and the guard she believed she could trust would free the prisoners. If time allowed after saving me, Malachi would help me find the stone.

"From the top of the temple, Tag, we shall escape the back way." Malachi was looking at me.

"The back way?"

"Yes. On the north side of the temple is another set of stairs. No one should be on them since the celebration is on the south stairs, and in the confusion, it will be the safest route. We will meet Sabirah, her brother, and the followers at the gateway," Malachi explained.

Sabirah nodded. I could tell she was deep in thought and probably worried about what would happen should we fail. My thoughts were focused on who among the artists was the traitor. I wished I could grill them and make the spy talk, but that would only alert the king that we knew. I had to stop worrying about things I could do nothing about. It was better to be positive. With renewed hope, I prayed that somehow our plans would work.

A knock came at the door from the inner compound. Malachi opened it to find Josu. The artists were having a hard time sleeping, with questions over the game. Malachi excused himself and went with Josu. Now was the perfect time for me to speak with Sabirah about King Jacob and the stone.

She'd risen, ready to leave.

"Here's the deal," I said. "Remember the stone?"

She nodded slowly, waiting for me to continue.

"Do you think King Jacob could use it to travel to the future?"

Sabirah frowned and said, "That's a disturbing thought." She smiled and brushed the fringe of my hair away from my eyes. "But remember, the stone is the Lord's. I believe it will only work with time-traveling powers when He wants it to and when the right person has it. Take heart. All will be well." And then she left.

I stood staring at the closed door, praying she was right.

❧

Sabirah

Dodging through the streets of Jacobugath and hiding in shadows as people passed me by, I overheard their chatter. Many were excited about the game, but most were looking forward to the sacrifice. As I walked, I was glad Father had not traveled these streets. If he had seen how corrupt these people had become, great sorrow would have lodged in his heart.

Nearing the palace, I decided to take a chance and skirt around back to look beneath the princess's window for my necklace. As I neared the area, light from the palace shone down on a garden thick with Blood Flower and Lion Ear plants. If the necklace fell among them, I might never find it. Still, I had to look, though the faint light would make it near impossible to see something so small.

Crouched on hands and knees, I crawled across the ground. My fingers found something long and round. As I held it up, I found it squishy and light. A fat worm! Searching on, I felt the many feet of a centipede crawl up my leg. I quickly brushed it off and kept looking, patting the ground, hoping to find the only piece of jewelry I'd ever had in my life. The fact that my father created it with his own hands made me desperate to find it.

"You have taken a great risk slipping past the guards to prowl around in the garden. What is it you search for?" The voice came from the shadows.

I didn't answer, not knowing who it was. My hand went immediately to the waistband where I had hidden the crude weapon my brother had given me.

"Do you seek help?" Out stepped Hod, the stern-faced guard.

Though he was a threat, I pretended I was at ease. "A necklace. I dropped a necklace." I rose, wiping my palms together to get rid of the dirt that clung to them.

"Your necklace?" he questioned.

If he knew it was mine, would he help? If he knew the princess had stolen it from me and thrown it away, would he tell her I searched for it? I hesitated to reply.

"Princess Jamila told the guards that if we should chance upon a jade talisman of a wing-spread eagle we were to give it to her immediately." He paused. "Is that the necklace you seek?"

I still refrained from speaking, sensing trouble.

"You don't trust me, do you, daughter of Samuel?" At first, I was surprised he knew who my father was, but I realized everyone in Jacobugath had probably heard my story. I remained silent.

"Have no fear. I met your father and converted."

I wished I could plainly see his face so I could tell if he lied or was playing me for a fool.

"Please tell no one of my conversion. I tell you at the risk of my life, but I had to. I must warn you that Mooda isn't what he seems. I know he has shown you kindness, but he is Jamila's favorite. He'd never do anything to upset her or cause her to think poorly of him."

How could this be? I'd always relied on my instinct and the Holy Spirit to tell me where to place my trust. My trust had been with Mooda. He'd shown me kindness in giving me the torch to take into the prison. Hod had not. Mooda had allowed me to go in the second time. Hod had not. Though Mooda had thrown me to the floor in Princess Jamila's quarters, I knew he'd done it to show his allegiance to the princess, not to hurt me.

"I tell you this now to let you know where your trust should be placed." Hod began to walk away and then stopped. "Sabirah, know if you need help, come to me first." Then he walked away, leaving me standing in the garden of Blood Flowers wondering whom I should trust.

కొ

Tag

THE NEXT DAY, I ONCE again worked on the portrait of John Doe. As soon as I'd finished, a messenger delivered it to King Jacob. Then I was fitted for my ceremonial attire.

My death clothes.

They were really quite simple: plain white tunic, gold bandlets for my wrists and ankles, and a really dorky headdress. I looked like I had a roof of magpie feathers on my head. Fortunately, my fading temporary tattoo had vanished. I was very grateful.

Night came too quickly. I lay in my bed and thought of all that would take place tomorrow. In the morning, the artists—including the traitor among them, whoever he was—were going to have one final practice. I was to leave Malachi's and go to the palace. Princess Jamila would anoint me for sacrifice. This worried me. King Jacob obviously thought the artists would lose, anointing me before the game had even been played. No doubt this was thanks to the traitor among the artists. He probably promised to throw the match. The ball game would take place in early afternoon. If the artists lost, I'd be dressed in those ridiculous clothes for sacrifice.

After the game was a special feast, a type of celebration for their new god, Zouché. Tomorrow afternoon or tomorrow night my life would change. I prayed with all my heart that despite my giving my mother grief and running away from Grandpa, God would help me through what lay ahead.

Again, my thoughts turned to my mom. I missed her, missed her a lot. When Dad and Tyler had first left us, we had gone through life like zombies—not really looking at each other, not really caring, just hurting so bad that to talk with one another would only make our wounds deeper. But I loved my mom. I did, and I wished I could make up to her all the trouble I'd caused.

I pictured her in my mind. Her dark hair cut short made her eyes sparkle like sapphires, and when she smiled, the whole room brightened. Smiling wasn't much on her agenda lately. And that was because of me. But Lily Quincy, my mother, had been through a great deal. To keep life moving, she made lists of things to do. She wrote one for everything: a list for chores, a list for groceries, a list for things to pack, a list for a good life. I wondered if she'd really written that one. Well, I was certain her being left alone with one son for the rest of her life was not something she'd written down. Nor was dating again.

This made me think about Doctor Bradford. He wasn't a bad guy. In fact, I had to admit, I kind of liked him. In the last while, I felt as if he were the only person who really listened to me; that is, when I chose to talk. Most of my therapy sessions were questions from him and one-word answers from me. Once in a while he could get me to open up. But afterward, I felt as if I'd betrayed myself by spilling my guts about how life sucked and wasn't fair, and I was going to do something about it.

My big idea of doing something was painting graffiti. Then that got me mixed up with the dumb Prime gang, and after they threatened Ethan to make me do what they'd wanted, I knew joining with them was not what I wanted to do. I was glad I had gotten away from them when I went to Grandpa's cabin, but I had just run away from that, too, which solved nothing. Look where it landed me—in a Book of Mormon drama where I was about to be sacrificed by a wicked king.

But here in Book of Mormon times, I'd discovered life should be something more. Becoming involved in other peoples' lives and truly caring about their welfare over my own had made me think that maybe my life had some type of meaning. Watching Sabirah and how she valued her family had made me realize just how important *my* family was to me. If I ever went back to my time I'd make sure my mom was happy. She was going to be number one on my list. Two would be Grandpa. Three would be Ethan. Yes, even Ethan deserved to be on someone's list.

Life! How I wanted to live.

I couldn't help but think of tomorrow and the possibility that something could go wrong, and I'd end up on the altar. There was a chance that I could die tomorrow . . . or Malachi could die . . . or . . . stop! I couldn't think this way. Malachi believed we'd be out of the city before the king could capture us. I had to believe it, too.

Still, my mind went back to questioning. What if the artists lost the game and we had to do Plan B? Malachi and the artists would be on top of the temple with me. They'd never let King

Jacob actually kill me. I was sure they'd keep me safe. And Malachi could sway the king. I'd seen him do it before.

But there was the traitor factor mucking up the works.

No buts! I turned over on my cot. I couldn't keep thinking like this. I had to sleep because I would need all my strength tomorrow.

Closing my eyes, I tried to clear my mind and think of something totally different. I remembered something Grandma had told me she would do when she had trouble sleeping. She'd sing a song. I tried several of my favorite tunes. Nothing worked. Then all of a sudden, I started singing "I Am a Child of God." And that was all I remembered until morning.

☙

"Tag, you need to wake up. They are here."

I cracked open an eye and saw Malachi's worried face. Sitting up, I asked, "Who is here?"

"The king's men. They are here to deliver you to the palace." Malachi gave me a sympathetic smile. "I had hoped to give you breakfast, but . . ." He handed me my tunic. "Everything will go as we planned. Don't worry, Tag." Malachi placed his comforting hand on my shoulder and then nudged me to get going.

I quickly dressed, and then Malachi walked with me to the sober-faced guards. I could say nothing, afraid that once I started to speak, I'd have diarrhea of the mouth and beg him to hide me.

With people bustling through the streets busily preparing for the sacrifice, I couldn't help but think of Christ. I remembered that Malachi had said His Crucifixion was near. Were the people of Jerusalem crowding the streets to catch a glimpse of the man they had betrayed?

I had spent the night before my supposed sacrifice on a cot sleeping. If this was the day of the Crucifixion, Jesus had spent part of His night in the Garden of Gethsemane in pain so intense He bled from every pore. He was then paraded before Pilate and flogged. Maybe at this very moment, all those things were happening.

Or maybe not.

I remembered Mom telling me that thoughts come to us for a reason. Well, for some reason, I believed Jesus was at this moment suffering through His sacrifice for mankind. This made me really think about what would happen to me and why I was here.

Today I would be dressed and prepared for sacrifice, my body cleansed, and fine clothes placed upon me. I wondered what the Romans would make Jesus wear, and then I remembered a crown of thorns. My magpie headdress didn't seem so bad. If the artists lost the game, I would be carried on a litter to the altar. Jesus would drag His cross through city streets. I would supposedly be strapped onto the altar. Christ would be nailed to the cross. I would hopefully be rescued. Jesus Christ would . . .

Sorrow mixed with gratitude took root in my heart because I knew Christ would give up His mortal body and die. I could hardly imagine the courage that would take.

We had arrived at the palace steps. As we walked up, I thought of Sabirah's words: *Remember to think of Christ.* I had been and would continue to.

With more courage than I felt, I stepped over the threshold of the palace.

25

Floating Logs

Sabirah

I STOOD WITH THE TRAY of breakfast in my hands for the princess and watched as Tag entered the palace. Two guards escorted the brave wayfarer, taking him to be dressed for his supposed last day on earth. With a heavy heart, I turned away. Even though I feared the worst for Tag, I had to devote my concentration to Asim and getting him and the followers out of prison.

The only way I could save Asim and the others was to enlist the help of Hod or Mooda. Since my strange encounter with Hod, I didn't know whom to trust. Hod had said all the right things, yet I still felt uneasy about him. And Mooda? I thought of how he had so willingly followed what Jamila commanded without so much as a hesitation of any kind, though that could be a performance. I wanted to trust the guard with the face of a turtle and slow thoughtful movements, yet Hod's words made me doubt my instincts.

I thought of something my father had told me years ago while we fished on the River Sidon. *Trust no floating log in the water, for it could be a caiman and bite you.* Both Hod and Mooda were floating logs. How was I to know the true caiman?

A cluster of handmaidens passed by. I saw Rasha in their midst. She smiled weakly. The leader of the girls came quickly to me. "Tarry not. The princess searches for you. She is angry that you have taken so long to bring her food." The girl was beautiful, with long, straw-colored hair and straight, white teeth.

"Thank you. I'll hurry." I left them, looking back at the only maiden who concerned me, my cousin, Rasha. Should I tell her of the plans so she would be ready to flee when the time came? Or would it be best that she not know in case something went wrong? I decided to wait.

Approaching Princess Jamila's quarters, I found Mooda standing guard. He smiled and quickly checked the hallway to see if I'd been followed. When certain we were alone, he leaned over close to my ear and said, "I found something that is yours." He pulled my talisman from the band of his loincloth.

I wanted to snatch it from his hand right away, yet hesitated. Staring at him, I tried to make note of any telling movement, any sign that he could be deceitful. No twitch, no regret. Here before me stood a simple man, a man who looked as though he would rather injure himself than cause harm to me.

Deciding to take a chance, I smiled. He did, too. Taking the necklace from him, I said, "Thank you, Mooda."

"Don't tell and whatever you do, don't show the princess." He peered down the hallway again.

"I shall keep it safe." I wanted to ask him about what Hod had told me, but creeping doubt of his loyalty stopped me. Instead, I made ready to go to the princess with her breakfast.

"I have something else, as well," he added.

I stared at Mooda, perplexed. What else could he have?

He reached down to the strap on his leg and pulled out my ivory dagger. How did he know it was mine?

"I hoped it was yours, and by the look on your face, I was right." He smiled, handing it to me, proud of himself.

I said nothing and cautiously took it from him. "Again, thank you."

Before I could speak, Mooda said, "Be wary of Hod. He is most cunning and will stop at nothing to see that your father's people and followers are killed."

Returning my necklace and dagger could be his way of making me trust him. And I wanted to trust Mooda. Was he a log sent to help or a caiman here to kill? There was no time to think it through. I had to hide my necklace and weapon and take the princess her food.

I nodded my gratitude and quickly left him.

☙

Tag

THE STANDS, MADE OF STONE, were full of people who had come to watch the game. King Jacob had me sit in his viewing box. Princess Jamila sat on his right side. Sabirah stood behind her as though waiting to do as the princess commanded. Anhanga, the jaguar, was between the king and princess. The feline kept a close eye on me, the mouse. I shut the cat out of my mind and looked to Malachi, who had been allowed to sit with me. He patted my knee as if to say, *"hang on, we'll get through this."*

The game was to be played between two parallel walls. A stone hoop was near the top in the middle of each. It reminded me of a basketball hoop, except the hole was smaller and perpendicular instead of parallel. How on earth could anyone knock a ball through the hole without touching it with their hands? I supposed rules were rules, and I was about to find out how the game worked.

Drums rolled as the teams jogged into the courtyard. The crowd gave a tumultuous roar of applause. Bomani and his guys were dressed in red tunics. Their waists were wrapped with several layers of wide cording. On their left legs, they wore some type of shin guard that covered the leg from the foot to above the knee. They wore various odd-looking headgear. One had the head of a deer; another looked as though a rooster had perched on his noggin. Bomani's headgear was a tangle of feathers and replicas of snakes.

The artists entered. Malachi and I stood and cheered. Their team wore their everyday attire and not the garb I'd seen them practice in. Loincloths, sandals, no shin guards, no cords about their waists, no headgear. Were they crazy? The king's men were going to steamroll right over them. As I stared at the artists, I couldn't help but wonder which one was the traitor.

A loud gong sounded, and the captains of each team met in the center. Habib and Josu were co-captains, so they both went. Bomani was the captain of the other team. Some guy with the headdress of a skunk stood between them. I knew something about this game stank.

I guess they did the equivalent of a coin toss by using a dagger, throwing it near their opponent's foot. Bomani won, nearly wounding Habib. The king-man almost skipped to his team. Habib and Josu looked up at me. Habib nodded and smiled. Maybe losing the toss was part of the artists' plan, and maybe they'd dressed as they had so they could move faster.

King Jacob rose. A servant handed him the black game ball. He walked to the edge of the viewing box and held it high in the air for everyone to see. The crowd cheered and whistled. They grew louder and louder until, finally, the king tossed the ball down into the playing field at his team.

Bomani and his men sprang to action. One guy hit the ball with his arm, sending it to another, who kicked it with his guarded shin. The ball flew up, touching the hoop's rim. The artists were right in the fray, jockeying for position, ready for the ball to fall to them.

Habib was the first to make contact, knocking the ball forward with his head toward Josu. As Josu reared back to knock it with his shoulder Bomani body-slammed him to the ground, sitting on him. To add insult to injury Bomani bounced as if Josu were a cushion. The crowd cheered.

"That's a foul!" I shot to my feet. King Jacob glared at me as if to say, *"shut up."*

I realized I had no idea what the rules were, but I had nothing to lose. "Come on, that isn't fair!"

The king ignored me. I turned to the princess. "Bomani is twice the size of Josu. He's going to kill him."

"They know the risk of the game." She turned her steely eyes back to the action.

Sabirah slightly shook her head, as if to say, *"Make nothing of this."* I turned to Malachi. He, too, cautioned me with the look in his eyes. I wondered when we were going to slip away.

Turning my attention back to the game, I saw that Josu had managed to break free. The artists had regrouped and positioned themselves in key spots on the court. The ball bounced off the wall and down the courtyard, from one king-man to another. The artists tried everything, but the other team was too tall, too strong.

Despite the odds, in a stolen instant, Josu hit the ball, sending it forward to Habib.

Good! Now we were getting somewhere. The artists had a chance. I searched the field for Bomani. He was at the other end of the court, too far away to be a threat. All the artists had to do was keep their cool and score. Habib juggled the ball back and forth on his knees. What was he doing? He was wasting time. Habib motioned for some of the other guys to block Bomani, who was now on the charge. They couldn't hold him back. He plowed through them, coming full steam ahead at Habib.

Bomani put his head down like a bull ready to flatten his opponent. Habib knee-kicked the ball. It soared up in the air, and, suddenly, everything and everybody moved in slow-motion.

The ball glided straight for the hoop as if carried by angels. Time stood still. I hardly dared breathe.

And then the time bubble popped.

The brawny king-man with the deer's head jumped up against the wall. The antler of his headgear caught the ball and deflected it. As he came down, his headdress rammed Habib. An antler stabbed into my friend's arm. He fell to the ground, bleeding, but play still continued.

A guy was down. There should be a timeout or something! But they kept playing, ignoring the blood, ignoring Habib's pain. Malachi and I rose to go to him, but King Jacob's guard blocked our path, forcing us to stay. And that's when I realized there was no way we could sneak off because there were guards blocking all the exits. The traitor had to have clued the king in on our Plan A.

I numbly turned my attention back to the field. Time spun fast-forward with no way of pulling it back, slowing it down, or taking a breather. The dude with the rooster top kicked the ball with his foot through their hoop.

Feet could not make contact with the ball! Foot contact was a definite foul, I knew that. But the crowd cheered anyway, and drums rolled, proclaiming that King Jacob's team had won.

Won by cheating! But what could one expect?

As soon as the game ended, Josu went to Habib to wrap his arm. They stared up at me. I knew they'd tried their best and were flustered; I could tell by their slumped shoulders and sorry expressions. I waved to them. It was all right. We still had Plan B.

I guess, deep down, I'd always known it would play out this way—with me walking up to the sacrificial altar.

☙

Sabirah

UNABLE TO MAKE CONTACT WITH Malachi or Tag, I slipped away from Jamila's sight as the celebration of the king-men's victory began in earnest. Obviously, we had to use the second plan, which meant I had to find either Hod or Mooda and plead for mercy, hoping one of them would give me the key to free the prisoners. I couldn't debate over which one was good and which one was evil. The time had come for the real hero to step forward. I had to trust the first one I came to. No more time for hesitation! No more time for second thoughts!

I nearly flew down the hallway to the cooking area. More cooks than ever before were busy plucking birds, stirring soups, mixing bread, and chopping vegetables. I noted that instead of the usual somber mood, the kitchen was alive with chatter. Though I gained a few looks, they turned their attention to the work at hand.

I sprinted to the hall leading to the prison. Turning to enter, I suddenly came to a stop. No one stood guard. How could I possibly open the lock without a key? Panicked, I went back to the cooking area.

"Has anyone seen the guards usually stationed at the prison doors?"

As if answering my summons, Mooda appeared, and I realized he had been in back of a stack of baskets. His headdress was askew. A maiden giggled and escaped from him, straightening her tangled hair.

Once he realized I was the one who had asked, he moved faster, coming to me as though eager to hear what I had to say. I pulled him away from the cooks' gawking eyes and down the hallway leading to the prison. "I need you to unlock the doors."

"The king ordered that under no circumstances were we to open them."

Hod suddenly charged toward us. "Mooda, what are you doing?" His stern face twitched near his eye.

Was Hod concerned for my safety or merely doing his duty?

I stared up at Mooda and made my choice. He was my log, not a caiman. "You have to open it."

"Mooda, don't listen to her. She is the daughter of a liar." Hod pulled out his double-edged sword. Glaring at me, he added, "I spoke the truth to you in the garden, but I left out that my mother was tortured and killed because she believed your father."

"I'm sorry for your loss, but please have mercy in your heart and release the prisoners," I begged, hoping he would understand.

"Fortunately," Hod said, "I pledged to kill the offspring of the false prophet whose words led to my mother's death. And here you are." He jabbed his sword at me.

As I whirled around avoiding his blade, I pulled the ivory dagger from its position on my thigh and stuck Hod in the arm, slicing through to the bone. Blood splattered him and dripped to the floor as he dropped his sword.

Before I could pull back, he latched onto my arm, wrenching it behind me and pulling hard until I dropped the dagger. He kicked it down the hall. I pushed off the wall with my foot, lunging backward with my head and ramming him in the nose. He let go of me, his nose bleeding profusely. He ignored his wounds and scooped up his sword. Unarmed and trapped, I hesitated to think of what to do next.

Hod charged. Just as he lunged to thrust the long, sharp blade through me, Mooda jumped him from behind. Hod fought back like a foaming dog sick with fever and easily regained his feet. Mooda's slow reactions were his downfall because Hod stuck him with his blade in the stomach. My friend gasped and then slumped to the floor. Hod withdrew the bloody sword and turned to me.

The only weapon I had left was the crude one Asim had made in the prison, the one carved of stone and hidden in my waistband. Hod was too close to throw it. Instead, I slipped the weapon into my hand, knowing the only way to deliver a lethal blow was to stab him in the neck in his life vein.

Feigning fear, I pleaded, "Hod, you knew my father. You listened to his words."

He walked toward me, hateful determination on his face.

I stood my ground, calling upon courage from the Holy Spirit. I added, "He spoke God's words."

Hod dropped his sword, cackling like a jackal. He came at me as though he relished killing me with his bare hands. Stepping close enough that I could bite his nose, he said, "There is no God."

Like a jaguar, I clawed his face and at the same time stuck my crude weapon in his neck. Shocked, he fell to the floor, blood quickly pooling around him. I searched his body for the key and could find nothing. I had to be fast. At any moment, the cooks could come to investigate the commotion.

"I have them."

I glanced down the corridor and saw Mooda. Though slumped over, he held the key out for me to take.

Running to him, I pulled his head up. He struggled for breath, his eyes glassy. I said, "Thank you, Mooda. My brother waits on the other side of the doors. He and Ravid will take you to safety."

Mooda only stared, not blinking or saying anything, and I realized he was gone. His dying act was to help me.

I heard the rush of footsteps coming. No time for grief or gratitude.

Sprinting down the corridor, I quickly unlocked the chains, dropping them to the ground. With all my strength, I raised the plank.

Swinging the doors open, I was terrified to find Rippers waiting on the other side.

꿍

Tag

BY DUSK, WAR DRUMS POUNDED as if in attack. Fires burned brightly around the city. Streets bulged with crowds of gaily dressed people, who were full of food and wine and ready to feed their new god, Zouché.

Sitting on the litter that made its way through the city, I felt every eye on me. I kept my mind on the plan. Soon this would be over, and my friends and I would be away from this wicked place.

We came to the temple. More men were enlisted to escort me up the steep stairs. As I started up, I felt as though at any moment, I'd topple over backward. I leaned forward. Flanked by guards, I slowly made my way toward the top.

I hoped Sabirah had made it to the prison and was now helping the prisoners break free. The followers were good people, only guilty of believing in Christ and following the counsel of the prophet Samuel.

I thought of Ravid. Sabirah had said he was there and that he'd helped find her brother. I was glad that the man who once tried to kill her was now helping her brother and others escape.

People crowded the steps, gawking at me. Some cheered as I passed, as if I were some hero. Many threw flower petals. The drums grew louder, their beat pounding in my brain. The air was heavy with the scent of burning wood.

As I reached the top, I saw the alabaster altar stained with blood that I was to lie upon. The guards guided me, and we circled the place of sacrifice, passing Princess Jamila and her handmaidens. They bowed.

I eagerly searched for Rasha. At first I couldn't see her. I had to know exactly where she was so when Malachi and his men made their move I could find her. Finally, I caught sight of her shiny hair and sober face. She was in the back, kind of standing away from the rest of them. There was an older woman by her side, and they were talking in earnest.

We passed Malachi and the artists. They stood in front of the wall of skulls. Bleached white bones shone in the firelight. Behind this wall should be the weapons Malachi had hidden.

Moving on, I came to the artists. They bowed. I felt a great gratitude for them. I'd learned they had not dressed as the king's men for the ball game because the king had ordered them not to. What brave men these artists were. I hoped the traitor in their midst, who had the ear of the king, had not learned of Plan B.

The guards and I stopped in front of King Jacob. Behind him was the mighty statue of Zouché, a twenty-foot tall jaguar carved of green serpentine stone. This had been what the scaffolding had concealed. The figure's eyes were huge blue topazes that caught the firelight and made the idol look as though he delighted in the ceremony and couldn't wait for my blood to run free and join the stains on the altar steps.

King Jacob and the idol were surrounded by his henchmen, who were all armed with spears and swords. A few in special costumes stood beside the king. The man who wore a deer's head during the game had added a deer hide as his cape. Another fellow wore the likeness of a parrot. Bright feathers of red, blue, and green decorated his headpiece. He wore a small shoulder cape of the same colors.

Another man wore what looked like a vulture's head. White paint covered his face. His cape was made of black panther skin. In his hand, he shook a club, making a sound like thousands of rustling leaves in a windstorm. This guy stepped forward and held out his free hand to me. A stench of soot, smoke, stale incense, rotten flesh, and dried blood—the scent of death— flowed from him.

Knowing what was expected, I placed my hand on his. The guards beside me quickly scurried away, melting into the crowd. I looked around. People swayed with the beat of the drums and moaned as if in a trance.

Vulture-head man guided me to King Jacob, who sat on his throne at the top of several steps. The king rose. He wore black eye makeup, his nails were painted black, and a choker with teeth dangling from it was strapped to his throat.

For a millisecond, I saw myself as I had been in my own time. The image churned my stomach. How could I have ever thought the look appealing?

Upon King Jacob's head was a huge feathered crown of gold, orange, and green made of hummingbird and the precious quetzal feathers I'd heard the artists talk about. His shoulders were covered in a feathered cape the same colors as the crown. The cape flowed down his back, draping to the floor. Many birds had given their lives for this beautiful mantle. King Jacob also wore a necklace that dangled to his chest, and from it hung the stone.

My stone.

John Doe's stone.

The Lord's stone.

How would I ever be able to take it away from him? A charge of panic riffled through me. Anhanga, the jaguar, stood beside the king. The animal seemed to know what was going down and stood regally by his master. The drums abruptly stopped. The king motioned to Zouché and back to me. He shouted something unintelligible.

Then the drums pounded in a wild frenzy. Vulture-head guy started screaming and dancing. He circled me, waving his club and making strange rustling noises. With his arms up, I caught a stronger whiff of burning bones. He danced in front of the crowd and gave the scream of a tortured animal. Flickering flames crackled from pots stationed around the ceremonial area. Sparks swooshed into the night.

I stole a glance at Malachi. He was intently staring at someone, visibly upset. I followed his gaze to Josu. He must have done something to upset Malachi, but I couldn't figure out what. The dancer stole my attention as he pranced in front of the princess. She giggled and clapped as if this were her birthday and she were about to receive a big present.

I, once again, looked for Rasha. She was not in the back anymore with the woman. In fact, I couldn't see her at all.

Drums pounded louder and louder. With each thud, I knew something was wrong—very, very wrong—so wrong I wasn't certain what to expect next.

Vulture-head man danced toward me, shaking his club, screaming and shouting. He circled me and took my hand, leading me to the altar.

Now would be a good time for Malachi and the artists to make their move.

I tried to crane my head around, searching for my rescuers, but was pushed on. I walked closer and closer to the altar. King Jacob followed, chanting loudly.

Reaching the stone slab stained with blood, the dancer madly shook his club over it, danced completely around the small platform, and then stopped. Wrenching my arm, he pulled me toward the altar.

I quickly glanced around, desperate to see Malachi and his men.

They had vanished!

Where they had stood before, King Jacob's army was in their place. What had happened?

Vulture Head pulled me onto the altar. I tried to get away, but another man on the other side took ahold of me and held me down while Vulture Head tied me to the slab with thick, rough ropes.

Wild fear shot through me.

Prickly heat spread through my limbs.

And all at once, there stood King Jacob. His robe was solemnly lifted off his shoulders. A lather of sweat coated him, making his body shine in the firelight.

Again he shouted something unintelligible and raised his arms high above his head as if pleading to the heavens. He picked up a knife. Carved in its handle was the image of a jaguar. He raised it high above his head, the sharp obsidian blade pointed directly at my chest. Josu stepped forward carrying a small figurine carved of stone. The figure held a bowl.

The chac-mool!

Malachi had told me about this object, the container for my heart. Josu was here to save me! What quick thinking on his part to pretend to help the king. Where was Malachi?

The earth suddenly rumbled.

I stared beyond the king into the heavens and saw billowing thunderclouds in the night sky. Shards of thick lightning cut through the darkness like long, striking tentacles reaching down to the earth, searching for victims. Thunder split the air and shook the ground.

Sheets of rain burst over the crowd. King Jacob kept on with his screaming tirade.

The stone hanging from his neck began to glow. The light grew and grew. King Jacob hadn't noticed, he was so intent on the ritual, with the dagger clasped in his hands and a satanic glaze in his eyes.

An odd high, then low hum, like the surging of angry bees in a hive, electrified the air. A tremendous boom sounded, shaking the earth. At the same time, a single, gigantic bolt of lightning ripped the night sky and came straight down at King Jacob.

In a split second, time stood still. The bolt hit him dead on, and King Jacob's entire body glowed as bright as the stone. Through the glow, I saw him accusingly look down at me as if I had done this. Pure hatred filled his gaze and then fear overcame him as he began to fall. The light vanished. He dropped the sacrificial knife, and the blade clanged on the altar as it glanced off the side. King Jacob crumpled to the ground like a limp marionette.

Smoke filled the air as the earth shuddered and pitched. People screamed and ran, and I tried to get up but was bound in place. My arms and legs strained against the ropes that held me captive.

I frantically looked for Josu. He had disappeared.

"Help! Somebody help me!"

"I will help you." Princess Jamila held her father's knife. With both hands grasping the hilt, she raised it high in the air. "You killed my father, and now I will kill you!"

Once again, I knew death was but a breath away. This time Jamila would finish what her father had started. My flesh tingled as if stung by hundreds of scorpions.

As the princess thrust her arms downward, she suddenly slumped, dropping the knife from her hands. Malachi pulled a sword from her back and then cut the cords binding me.

"Where were you?" I yelled over the roar of thunder

Bracing himself as the earth shook and pulling me from the altar at the same time, he said, "I was detained!"

Greatly relieved, I tore off the magpie hat. I had little time to retrieve the stone and find Rasha. Because of the earth's revolting, the king's body had been thrown at the feet of Zouché. As I started toward him to retrieve the stone, the earth pitched again. Fear for my friend made me yell, "Where's Rasha?"

"Lost!" Malachi tugged on my arm.

Panicked, I said, "We can't leave without her!" Scanning the area where I'd last seen her, I noticed the maidens running for their lives along with everyone else in the crowd. Through the flashes of lightning, I caught a glimpse of Rasha struggling with the older woman she had been talking to. I had to get to them before they were both killed.

Tripping over skulls tumbling from the wall and dodging fallen debris, I raced to Rasha. Grabbing her arm, I yelled, "Come now!"

"This is my mother. I cannot leave her!"

The older woman jerked from her daughter's hold and disappeared in the crowd. Rasha tried to give chase, but I held her back. "She can't be helped. You must leave or die."

Rasha, still fighting, shouted, "She's my mother!"

Without saying another word, I latched my arm about her waist and dragged her away, and in that moment, I remembered Grandpa grabbing me, pulling me away, but my mind blocked me from seeing what we fled from. The old ache I carried in my heart burned fresh, though I could not tend to it now.

I held onto Rasha, fighting her need to chase after someone she'd never see again. For a crazy moment, Dad and Tyler came to mind and scenes of a frozen lake.

Not now! No, I had to push on. Run away!

As I dragged Rasha past Zouché, I saw King Jacob. His lips and throat were blackened and charred as well as his head. Blood leaked from his ears.

Then I saw it, the stone around his neck shone brightly. Hope breathed within me. I needed the stone. Had to have it to return home . . . and there it was.

At that moment, Rasha escaped my grasp.

The ground shuddered. Stones crumbled beneath my feet.

I only had time to catch her . . . or grab the stone.

26

Wo unto This People

Sabirah

A LOUD ROAR LIKE THAT of an angry panther billowed from the prison as the Rippers burst into the hallway.

Not knowing what else to do, I turned and ran like a fleeing deer, Rippers fast on my tail. I leaped over Hod and Mooda, hoping beyond hope that the Rippers would stop. I chanced a look back. A few stopped, but most of them charged at me, teeth bared.

Where were Asim, Ravid, and the followers? Had the Rippers killed them all? I arrived at the cooking area and yelled, "Run!"

Baskets full of vegetables toppled over and feathers burst into the air. I rushed toward the fire, seeking the only weapon I could find. With the long tool they used to move the coals, I scooped fire into the bowl-like end and flung hot coals at my attackers.

Cooks and Rippers screamed as embers sprayed across the room. Again, I shoved the end into the flames, filling it for another throw. As I turned, I saw that the Rippers had run away, licking their wounds. Several cooks who had not fled hugged one another, staring at me as though I'd gone mad.

Suddenly, a rumbling shook the floor so violently it knocked me to my knees. The room swayed as though tossed on the sea. A terrific boom of thunder cracked the air. The cooks screamed even louder and looked at me as though I were a sorcerer. Trying to run across the pitching floor, they attempted to escape.

Through the frenzied madness, I heard a familiar voice. "Sabirah!" Asim raced from the corridor, followed by Ravid and the followers. They fought to stay on their feet as they made their way to me. I dropped the fire tool into the pit and embraced my brother. We hugged for only a moment, as once again the earth lunged. Parts of the ceiling fell to the ground, narrowly missing us.

Grabbing Asim, I yelled, "We've got to get out of here!"

⌘

Tag

Ear-splitting thunder cracked and rumbled. The earth pitched and shook as though turning inside out. My eyes focused on the stone, blacking out everything else. There seemed to be no air, no time, no nothing. If I grabbed the stone now, while it glowed, I might be sent back home.

I had to have it, or I'd be stuck here forever—doomed to live in a place I didn't belong, where everyone and everything was foreign to me. I had to reach for my future, for my life. Bits of serpentine crumbled to the ground. Zouché was falling apart. I only had a second to decide.

In a flash, I thought of Sabirah fighting for her brother. I thought of Rasha desperate for her mother. And I thought of Malachi willingly putting his life in danger for me. Sabirah's words of her father's prophesy played in my mind . . . *He would send a young wayfarer to aid when all seemed lost.* Deep in my heart, I knew what I had to do. Finding strength I didn't know I had, I willed myself to turn my back on the stone and give chase to Rasha.

A split second later, the head of Zouché fell down on the king; flicks of green rocks shot through the air like bullets chasing me as I ran. I came upon Rasha as she stood at the top of the crumbling stairs. Disks where the fires had burned had fallen to the ground. Fire dripped and rolled down the temple despite the rain. I didn't know how it stayed aflame, but it did.

People scattered like squirrels, hopping over flames and chunks of tumbling earth. Giant bolts of lightning charged through the night sky. Rasha's mother had disappeared in the fray.

I grabbed ahold of Rasha's thin arm and jerked her away from the horrific scene. "Come on! There are stairs on the other side."

We raced to the back of the temple, jumping over rubble as if leaping over hurdles. Malachi and Habib waited, motioning us to go before them. Habib's arm had been wrapped from the wound he'd sustained during the game, but he paid it no mind, encouraging us to hurry. We sprinted past and started down the stones that pitched precariously back and forth. I maintained a viselike grip on Rasha's arm, afraid if I let go she would vanish.

Frantic to get down from this rapidly deteriorating man-made mountain, my legs seemed manipulated by a higher power. My feet found ground that was never stable but somehow supported me. Descending those steepled stairs took forever, but at long last, we were down.

Malachi led us toward the gateway where we'd agreed to meet Sabirah and the others. Buildings toppled before us. Rain fell in torrents. Fires burned out of control as if fueled by Satan himself. People's terrified screams pierced the night; people were frantic— some trapped beneath the rubble, some on fire, some walking aimlessly in a state of shock.

We pushed onward, jumping cracks that appeared out of nowhere in the earth. We fell several times. Still, we pressed on, wiping rain from our eyes and knowing if we stayed in the city, certain death would find us.

At long last, we reached the beautiful gateway where a few days ago I had helped Habib and Josu add the finishing touches. It had crashed to the ground and had broken into large chunks. I frantically scanned our surroundings, panicked that someone might be trapped beneath, but I saw no one. Then I looked around, anxious for a glimpse of Sabirah. She was nowhere to be seen.

Malachi yelled, "We cannot wait!"

I took one last look, hoping that Sabirah, my Amazon Warrior, would appear. I couldn't leave without her. She was the reason I was here—to give her aid when all seemed lost. I had to stay, but not where more pillars could fall at any second. I could wait a little ways from here for a while and make Malachi and the others leave without me.

I remembered Grandma saying that when Christ was crucified, the earth revolted for three hours and then darkness came. We had to get away from Jacobugath because soon the entire city would be destroyed.

Climbing over the collapsed entry portals and leaping over rubble, I gashed my leg on a jagged piece of stone. I didn't stop to check it. Adrenaline pulsed within my veins, pushing past pain, spiriting me forward.

Once we were outside the city walls, I heard someone shout my name. Searching the darkness, I caught sight of a torch.

"Over there!" I yelled to Malachi and his men.

We raced to the light. As I drew near, I saw Sabirah. Her clothes were torn, her face bloodied from a good-sized gash on her forehead, but she was here!

The earth paused for a moment, as if to catch its breath. Rain continued to pour.

Behind Sabirah stood Ravid and another man. He had to be Sabirah's brother, Asim. Behind them were others, and I knew they were the followers. Ravid smiled at Rasha. She ran to her old friend, all past wrongs forgotten, and hugged him, genuinely glad to see he was safe.

"You are not dead," Sabirah said as she embraced me. Another rumbling started beneath our feet. We were in for another good shaking.

"No, not yet," I shouted. "But we're going to be swallowed by the earth if we don't find a safe place."

"Where?" Sabirah shouted against the wind and rain.

"Follow me." Malachi took the torch that fought to stay aflame.

Sprinting through the tropical forest, dodging tree limbs falling from somewhere above and praying trees would not smash us to the ground, we pressed forward the best we could.

The trail turned and went up the side of the mountain. The mountain seemed bent on tossing rocks on us from high cliffs overhead. I couldn't figure out where Malachi was taking us.

We scaled wet boulders and tramped on thorny bushes while trying to stay upright. About forty feet up the mountain, we came to a section of shale rock crossing the steep path. As soon as Malachi stepped on it, he fell, dropping the torch down the mountainside. Through strobes of lightning, I saw him slide and frantically reach for something to hold on to.

I grabbed for him, clutching a piece of his robe. It was enough to hold on to and stop him from crashing to the rocks below. The earth pitched forward, and I was thrown onto the shale, fast falling toward Malachi.

Sabirah latched onto me, digging her feet into the mud that was somehow more secure than the sliding rocks. I felt as though I would be torn apart, being pulled by Sabirah on one side and trying to hang on to Malachi on the other.

Pebbles pinged over us like hailstones.

As the thunderclouds rumbled and the earth groaned, Asim and Ravid sprang into action. They took ahold of Sabirah's waist. The followers grabbed the two men and pulled. Slowly, they eased both of us to safety. Rasha hugged me tight.

The earth shuddered in torment. No time to rejoice. I quickly scanned our position. In the distance, a volcano spewed red-hot lava into the night sky. Though the monster mountain was distant, we were still very vulnerable. We had to move on and face the slippery shale rocks up ahead.

Malachi regained his breath and started up the hill, and then I understood that we had to go around. We followed and continued to climb up the mountain. Finally, at the top, we found the mouth of a cave.

Malachi motioned for us to go in. Oh, yeah, go inside a cave during an earthquake. That made a lot of sense. But what else could we do? Where else could we go?

Rasha and I entered. Dust filled the air, though nothing fell from above. I leaned against a wall, pulling Rasha with me. We needed to move back so the others could enter. Sabirah stepped beside me along with Asim and Ravid. The followers scurried past, and then Malachi came in last.

Safely in the cave's shelter, Malachi, Sabirah, Rasha, and I stood at the entrance, looking at one another tentatively as if waiting for the other foot of the mighty earth to fall with its continued revolts.

Yet, in this chaos, peace settled upon me, and I knew the devastation going on outside would not reach us. We were safe inside this cavern.

Lightning again lit the night sky, but I knew it would only be temporary. I leaned over to Rasha, who looked out on the devastation. I knew she was thinking of her mother. "You did everything you could to save her."

Rasha gazed at me. In a deadpan voice, she said, "No, I didn't."

She was torturing herself for something that was out of her hands. For some reason beyond my own understanding, I felt her pain and wanted to help. "I'm glad you are safe here with me." I put my arm around her, drawing her to me.

Leaning her head on my shoulder, she said nothing. We couldn't stand here and dwell on what we should have done. We'd done the best we could under the circumstances, and if my memory served me well, our circumstances were going to become worse still. I looked at Sabirah. "Soon the darkness will come. It will last for three days. We'll need water and food."

"Fortunately," said Malachi, who had overheard me, "I had the artists pack supplies for our escape and journey."

I couldn't believe our good fortune. Several of the artists stepped forward; some had goats' bladders and gourds filled with water, and many had packed cornbread, fruit, and dried meat.

One even had my old poncho and tunic. Another had clothes for Sabirah, Rasha, Asim, and even Ravid.

"I tried to think of everything, though I misjudged how many followers would be with us." Malachi turned, peering into the cave. I had, as well, and though I could not see them, I knew many of them were watching us.

"We'll share. They're just grateful to be alive." I hoped my words would soothe Malachi's worries.

"During the ceremony, some of the king's men found our weapons and supplies hidden behind the wall of skulls. We had to distract them. That is why I was delayed in coming to your rescue. I was trying to get Josu's notice to delay." Malachi looked at me all apologetic-like.

"It worked out." I marveled at our situation. Despite great obstacles, Father in Heaven had watched over us, even while His Son hung on a cross. I suddenly realized that because Christ had willingly given up His mortal life, I had been saved by the bolt of lightning, saved by His Atonement . . . saved in so many ways. I marveled at my Savior's love.

With a whimper, the earth fell silent. Peering from the cave's opening, I saw darkness snuff out the stars and moon. Darkness, thick and frightening, filtered around us. Keeping hold of Rasha with one hand, I reached out until I felt the cave wall. Using it for a guide, I sat, taking Rasha with me. Where the others were I had no idea, but I did know that Malachi, Sabirah, Asim, and Ravid could take care of themselves.

Out of the black nothingness came a voice, saying, "Wo, wo, wo unto this people; wo unto the inhabitants of the whole earth except they shall repent; for the devil laugheth, and his angels rejoice, because of the slain of the fair sons and daughters of my people; and it is because of their iniquity and abominations that they are fallen! . . .

"O all ye that are spared . . . will ye not now return unto me . . . that I may heal you? Behold, I am Jesus Christ the Son of God . . . I am the light and the life of the world."

After the voice stopped, no one spoke, as if we were questioning our own sanity, as if we were afraid to breathe.

I can't explain it, but I felt as if someone had poured warm water into my soul. Grandma had read those very words from the Book of Mormon. I had had no idea how powerful they were or how they'd resonate inside me.

And the voice—

I had heard the Savior's voice, and I would never forget it.

"Your father was right, Sabirah." Malachi spoke reverently. "The Savior lives!"

I thought about Sabirah's father, Samuel the Lamanite, and wondered if he were still alive. Surely, if anyone deserved to be saved, he did.

Rasha snuggled up to me. "The prophet is safe."

"What?" How could she possible know who I was thinking about?

"Sabirah's father. I know you think of him. Just as I know wherever he is, my uncle Samuel is safe." She brushed my hurt leg, and I flinched back in pain.

"You're injured." I felt her hand search for my wound.

"It's nothing. Believe me." And though I knew it was bad, it wasn't like we had Neosporin or any type of first aid with us.

I heard material tearing. "What are you doing?"

"Be still." She wrapped my leg with something, and then she cuddled up to my side. She relaxed against me, and I knew she'd fallen asleep.

I, however, was far from sleep. The rock against my back was hard, my arms and legs ached, and I had the worst pounding migraine. But I was alive. We'd all survived. That was a miracle. And though I was stuck in this era with no hope of ever going home, somehow I knew I'd be all right; we'd be all right. God was with us.

27
The Traitor among Us

Sabirah

THOUGH I FEARED THE CLOSE confines of the cave Malachi had led us to, I was grateful for the shelter. Many people fleeing the city had not been as fortunate to find a safe haven. Though the cave was cold, dank, and unnerving, and I found myself wanting to cry or scream, I calmed my fears with the knowledge that I was surrounded by good friends and had the comfort of my brother, which helped to ease my childish torment of close spaces. Drawing courage from my friends' voices, I managed to change into a tunic that covered my body as I was accustomed, grateful to be shed of the sheer material Jamila had forced me to wear. I could hear others changing, as well. Before this day had started, I'd hidden my father's necklace under the waistband of my clothes. Though it was dark and I couldn't see, my fingers tied it about my neck. I felt the wing-spread eagle on my chest and felt my father near.

As grueling time dragged by, we slept and managed to pass each other morsels of food and skins of water that Malachi had packed. The heavy darkness was endless . . . suffocating. Yet, I clung to hope.

After what seemed an eternity, a ray of light shone at the mouth of the cave. Dawn! Three days of darkness had been endless torment. I quickly rose and went to the entrance. Gazing down the mountainside, I saw a sad, dismal sight—the rubble of Jacobugath. Ashen soot covered the land. The temple had disappeared from view, swallowed by the earth. Other buildings had been burnt away. Only ragged scars remained in a desolate wasteland. Where once a bustling city stood, death now lay. Had it only been three days ago when I had helped my brother and the followers escape King Jacob's hellish prison? I thought of the king's guard, the turtle-faced man who had died before my eyes so that I might live. The events were a horrible nightmare and yet true.

Today was the new beginning my father had long preached about. The fresh start for the world and the promise of eternal life had begun. The Resurrection of Christ had finally come to pass.

I rushed back to Asim and shook him. Rubbing his eyes, he stared at me. "I can see you! There is light!" So long he had lived in darkness, and now he could behold a world he had nearly forgotten.

The others began to awaken. Tag, Rasha, Malachi and his artists, even the followers trailed out of the cave, eager to feel the sun's rays warm their skin. Asim and I joined them. I could actually take a good look at my brother. He stood taller than he had in the prison, taller than me. And I could see traces of Mother's features: the kindness in his brown eyes that assessed a person in a glance, a mouth that turned up in a grateful smile, and the countenance of someone who had suffered much yet had strength enough to endure. Like me, he had the black hair of a raven—though a few white streaks had appeared—and brown skin. A wide smile creased his face as he basked in the sun.

Malachi and his artists joined us. "Ah, a new day, as your father promised there would be." Malachi stretched and took a deep breath. He glanced down at the city—his home. Shaking his head, he said, "Such waste." He turned his back to the scene.

Knowing we had to organize quickly, I said, "There is much to do, my friends." I looked at Malachi and Tag. "Our supplies are low, and we have a long journey." I had stepped back into my role of leader. I glanced at Malachi, who had led us out of danger three nights ago and wondered how he would react to my taking charge. He nodded as though he knew I was doing what came naturally.

We ate a breakfast of dried meat and corn tortillas as we strategized the best way to return to Pagog. Malachi thought we should head east toward the sea. I wanted to return by way of the land of Desolation.

"But what about the shifting sands?" Tag asked. I knew he remembered how Rasha had nearly died. "We no longer have Bomani to guide us through."

Asim spoke up. "He's not the only one to know the way. I traveled it alone." My brother appeared sure of himself and much stronger. By the time we'd reach the edge of the desert, he would be in good enough health to guide us through.

"But with the quakes, the land will have changed," Malachi pointed out. "At least we know if we reach the sea, all we need do is follow it south and eventually we will come to the land Bountiful."

"Returning by sea would take too long, and it does not lead us straight home," I countered. "When we left, my mother was gravely ill. I fear what has happened to her during my absence."

"I'm sure Hashim has taken good care of her." Tag tried to quiet my fears.

"Tag, though he appears as strong as a burro, my grandfather is very old. There is no telling what has happened to them."

"And my father," Rasha joined the conversation. "I have great concern for him, as well."

I looked at the followers. "I know many of you have loved ones you are concerned about. The land to the seashore is unfamiliar. Desolation is not. We have traveled through it once before. Even though the trail may have changed from the quake, there should still be some familiar landmarks. You are welcome to join us."

One tall, thin man who seemed to be their leader spoke up. "We are most grateful to you, but we shall go by way of the sea. We wish to settle in the land Bountiful."

Teetering on going with them, I held firm to my conviction. "We shall miss you. Go with God."

Then the rest of us began our journey toward Pagog.

∽

Tag

FOR MOST OF THE MORNING, our travels took us over ground covered with soft ash that kicked up in the air with each step. Coughing and hacking like the others, I found myself covering my nose and mouth with my hand much of the time, wishing we had the scarves we'd used when we'd crossed the desert.

By afternoon our path left the ash behind. The land looked familiar, though I wasn't sure. I glanced at Sabirah. "Do you know where we are?"

She shrugged. "Mountains stand where valleys used to be. My prayer is that the land of shifting sand has not been too altered, or Asim may have difficulty guiding us through."

Didn't Malachi say the same thing before we started? Great! *Now* Sabirah was doubting. We should have gone with the followers. Still, we were into it now; no sense stating the obvious. I knew I needed to hang tough and support the leader.

As we continued our endless journey, I found myself walking with Rasha. "So when we reach the village, do you plan to tell your father that you found your mother?"

"No. And please don't tell him." She stopped and looked up at me with worried eyes. "He grieved her disappearance for months. What good would come by his knowing she betrayed her faith and family? We have to keep this from him for his own good. I know Sabirah will not tell him. Will you?" She stood there waiting for me to answer. Her fine brows bunched together, forehead wrinkled in concern. I didn't want to upset her, but I also didn't know how she could keep something so important from her own father. I just didn't know if Rasha was right. Would telling him only cause him more pain and sorrow? For some odd reason, I thought of my mother. Would she keep something from me if she thought it would hurt me? I didn't know.

"Tag, please." Her bottom lip quivered, and my heart melted.

"I won't tell him," I said. Immediately a relieved smile softened her face.

At that moment, Habib and Josu joined us. "How much farther must we travel before we come to the shifting sands?" Josu asked.

Irritated that they would pick this minute to complain, I said, "Everything has changed. It's anyone's guess."

Rasha waved and hurried off to walk with Sabirah. Rasha had a strength in her that most people didn't see—a strength I greatly admired.

"You like her?" Habib nudged me with his shoulder.

"What?" I didn't know I'd been that obvious.

Josu chimed in. "Your eyes get all sparkly, and you show her favor."

I kept walking. They trailed after me.

"Admit your feelings," Habib taunted.

I stopped. "I never told you, but you played a great ball game against the king's men." I hoped that would focus their minds on something else.

"Not great. We lost." Habib hung his head as if he were ashamed.

"Yeah, but they cheated." I patted his arm. He winced. I'd forgotten his injury. "Sorry. How's the arm?"

"Good." He tried to flex it but winced again. "Still healing, and we would have won." We started walking again.

I knew he didn't want to dwell on his pain. "You know, that game was rigged. Someone must have given Bomani your playbook or something. In fact, before all that went down, Malachi told me he feared there was a spy among the artists."

"Spy?" Josu asked.

I'd almost forgotten he was with us, he'd been so quiet. "Yeah, you know. A spy is someone who pretends he is on your side, but he is really your enemy." As I looked at Josu, he seemed to squirm.

And then I remembered him on top of the temple, carrying the chac-mool to the king. He had looked as though he was more than playing a part, as though he were on the king's side.

"Do you know something, Josu?" I asked. That got his attention, and he stared up at me as innocent as a child caught playing video games when he should be in bed.

"Know something?" he repeated.

Habib nudged his friend. "Tell him."

"Tell me what?"

Habib chuckled. "He thinks Rasha is beautiful."

Josu punched Habib in his weak arm. Josu said, "You lie!" He took off, catching up with the others.

Habib rubbed his smarting arm. "You might warn Rasha. Josu is a man who hides his feelings. And he doesn't like to be made fun of. I better catch up with him and make amends."

As Habib joined Josu, I thought about the two of them. They'd been friends for a long time. Malachi trusted them, but there was something not quite right with Josu. And this nagging doubt had nothing to do with Rasha. I'd keep my eye on him, and when the time was right, I planned to ask him more about his relationship with the king.

We tromped through the jungle up one mountain and down another for more than five long days. Our food supply was low, along with our water. Tired feet, aching legs, and empty stomachs made the time creep by. This journey had only taken two days before.

Habib and Josu helped keep everyone's spirits up, cracking jokes and telling stories. Malachi grew more somber with each passing day. He was not one to argue, but I knew he was wishing we'd decided to go by way of sea as he had proposed.

We finally came to the edge of the desert where Princess Jamila had enchanted my mind by fabricating a jaguar. The place was untouched by the quakes and still had water. This cheered everyone and gave us hope.

The artists killed some buzzards and roasted them over a fire. We were finally going to have some fresh meat. When the birds were fully cooked and everyone started to eat, I couldn't see Sabirah or Asim. I thought they would be as hungry as the rest of us.

I went in search of them, finding them overlooking the land of Desolation. Brother and sister stood side by side, arms folded, a wrinkle on each brow.

"Hey, you two, dinner's ready."

"Thank you," Sabirah murmured, still staring out at the desert.

"Aren't you hungry?" I couldn't believe they were merely standing there. Were they worried about our journey tomorrow? It didn't look as though anything had changed.

"Yes, we're hungry," Sabirah answered.

"So . . ." I motioned toward camp. If they didn't hurry, there might not be food left, especially since Habib was eating with both hands now that his arm had healed.

"So . . ." Asim turned to me and put his arm around my shoulders. "We shall eat."

The three of us walked back to camp. I couldn't shake the feeling that all was not well and that Sabirah and Asim knew of a danger they weren't sharing. Maybe keeping silent was good. Why worry everyone else?

After Sabirah, Asim, and I had eaten our fill and everyone had bedded down for the night, I noticed Sabirah had left camp, going back in the direction where I'd found her and Asim. I had to know what was going on, so I followed.

She didn't turn around as I walked up behind her but said, "Tag, aren't you tired?"

"Eyes in the back of your head?"

"No, I know your step."

"Ah, I could ask the same of you. Not tired?"

"No."

I followed Sabirah's gaze over the desert tipped with a silver glow from the full moon. "It's quiet," I said.

"The desert usually is."

"Yep." Okay, I'd had enough. Time for answers. "Is something bothering you?"

"Yes."

A direct answer meant I was getting somewhere. "What is it?"

"You lost the stone." Sabirah turned to me.

I hadn't seen that coming. After thinking about it for a while, I replied, "It's not lost. I know exactly where it is."

Sabirah gave me a rather quizzical look.

"It's buried with King Jacob and Princess Jamila in their temple."

She chuckled and then sobered. "Tag, you can never return to your time."

I couldn't believe she was worried about me. "Is that what you and Asim were talking about earlier?"

"Yes. It concerns us both. Malachi told us how bravely you faced the sacrificial altar, how you courageously lay before the king. Your actions gave me and the others time to escape. Now, your chance to return to your own time is lost."

"I chose life over the stone. I don't think that's wrong, do you?"

"No." The voice came from behind. Rasha stepped forward. "Especially since it was my life you saved." She came to stand beside me and linked her arm with mine. It felt so natural for her to be by my side, as if she'd always been there and as if she would always be. I wondered how much she'd overheard. I asked her, "Do you know about me?"

"I told her." Sabirah answered. "As we have journeyed the last few days, my heart told me she needed to know you are from another place and time." Sabirah often talked about her heart telling her to do something. Since my arrival in her era, I'd learned to listen to my heart tell me many things, as well.

Maybe Sabirah was right in sharing my story. Though I still had concerns. "So you've told Asim and Rasha. How many other people have you told?" I needed to know.

"No one else." Sabirah placed a hand on my shoulder and a hand on Rasha's. "We have been through a lot, the three of us. We are family. And family has no secrets."

With more people knowing, the chance grew that something bad, really bad, could happen. I knew I was being paranoid, but I couldn't help it. "That I'm here is a mistake. I could interrupt history because I stopped someone from dying or caused someone to die who shouldn't." Then I thought of Mom. With me gone, she was the only one left at home. I'd give anything to hear her voice, even if she were nagging.

"Tag," Sabirah said. "You are the wayfarer. You were meant to travel. My father foretold of your coming, but that was all. We don't know your future, but you are welcome in our family."

They were my family now. I didn't know how I could ever get back to my mom, and if there wasn't a way, I needed to get on with my life. I had a terrible feeling that my life had stopped progressing once before, and I didn't want that to happen again. I needed to trust in my new faith in the Lord and hope He would help me move forward in whichever time period I was supposed to be in."Thanks, but could we keep my coming from a different time among the three of us for a while?" I looked from Sabirah to Rasha.

"And Asim?" Sabirah asked.

I nodded.

"Let's return to camp and rest. When the sun rises, we'll have a hard day before us." Sabirah started to leave. As I followed, I heard a rustling in the brush ahead.

I became anxious, expecting a jaguar to appear. Then I remembered the one I'd seen here before was an illusion. Nothing was there. The wind must have rustled the leaves.

Sabirah and Rasha went to their side of camp to sleep. As I was about to lie down near Malachi, I saw Josu looking at me. He'd been watching. Had he been listening to us? Did he now know my secret? Or had he just awakened as we'd come back?

Then I remembered walking with Habib and Josu the other day and how Josu had asked me what a spy was. The look on his guilty face came back to me, and I couldn't help but wonder if Josu was the traitor. Had he been the one who had the king's ear?

I crept closer for a better view. His eyes were closed. Maybe I had been seeing things.

28

Let Him Go

Tag

I STOOD THERE WONDERING WHAT to do. With King Jacob dead and the entire city of Jacobugath destroyed, I didn't know if there was a need to awaken Malachi and tell him my concerns over Josu. Malachi would think I was nuts. And besides, Sabirah and Rasha hadn't noticed the bush moving, nor did they see he was awake when we'd returned to camp. I was just being paranoid. I guess nearly being sacrificed would do that to a person.

I settled down on my mat and gazed up at the stars, wishing I could see the Big Dipper and the Little Dipper, thinking of Grandpa and how he had said Dad kept forgetting where it was. I thought about how Grandpa talked with Grandma even though she was dead. I couldn't help but wonder if he truly believed she was with him and if he really saw her. It sure seemed like he thought she was right there, and it didn't bother him that the rest of us believed he was crazy or had Alzheimer's.

Looking over at Rasha sleeping so soundly, I thought how beautiful she was with her hair webbed over her shoulders and her childlike face relaxed in dreams. I could understand how Grandpa felt about Grandma and how he wanted to keep her with him. Though I'd only known Rasha a short time, I felt like I was really falling in love with her. But deep in my heart, I knew my being here was wrong, and another guy was destined to be with her, a guy who would make her far happier than I ever could.

I was confused about my feelings. Hadn't Sabirah said I was family? I didn't have the stone, so I could never go home. Why couldn't I dream of Rasha and me being together?

More of Sabirah's words came to me. *Tag, you are the wayfarer. You were meant to travel.*

I turned over, trying to quiet my mind. I had traveled a lot since I'd arrived in this time era. Would that stop once we arrived at Pagog? Or would something else happen that would send me to another place? So many questions and so few answers. I could see Rasha sleeping. The sight of her made me feel better. I would look at her and think of nothing else except how beautiful she was and how lucky I was to know her.

℘

Sabirah

WE MADE A HUMAN CHAIN as we started our journey over the desert, tying ourselves to the person in front of us. Asim was well acquainted with the shifting sands of this desert and knew how fast we could find ourselves in danger.

Asim led, and I followed him, with Rasha, Tag, Ravid, Malachi and his artists after. The sun became unrelenting. By midmorning, the desert wind was as hot as red coals. I remembered how Tag's skin had burned before. I looked back at him. Where once a brilliant sunburn had been, tanned skin had taken its place. He should fare better on this trip.

Asim never hesitated, always leading and pushing forward while making certain we stayed close together. I was proud of my big brother's skills and knew as he grew stronger, the days of my leading our people were numbered. And for that I was grateful.

I thought of Mahir and wondered what he'd done in my absence. Had he survived the earthquakes? I hoped the quakes weren't as severe in Pagog. Had Mahir found favor with another woman in the village? Perhaps the shy Ruth had caught his eye. She was strong and sturdy and would stay home birthing the many babies he dreamed of. I should be happy if he had. I wanted Mahir to find peace, yet if I were truthful with myself, I wanted his happiness to include me.

By noon we stopped for a brief lunch. The corn tortillas Malachi had supplied were gone, so we chewed on pieces of dried meat and had but a sip of water. Before long we were once again on the trail. Toward nightfall the jungle had not appeared on the horizon. I didn't want to raise concern. But as the sun set and we still walked, I fell into step beside my brother. "Aren't we stopping for the night?"

"Not here," Asim said. "Too dangerous without shelter. The moon is full and will light our way. When we reach the jungle, we shall rest."

He was right. The dangers of stopping were numerous. Scorpions, tapirs, and muan searched for food by moonlight, but worse still were the poisonous vipers. Knowing Tag's fear of snakes, I also thought it wise to continue our journey.

We walked until the dark shadows far ahead became an outline of the jungle. At last! Only a few miles over rocky terrain and then we would be able to rest under cool, soothing ferns. On our way to the shelter of trees, we passed a ledge of overhanging rocks. Some of the artists, anxious to reach the jungle, cut their ties and broke the line. At once I heard the rattle of warning that could freeze a person with fear.

A scream tore through the night's silence.

The thin, awkward Josu lay writhing on the ground, grabbing a viper hanging from his neck. Tag cut the tie that bound him to us and ran to his friend. He wouldn't know the danger still around us. He courageously grabbed the tail of the snake and flung it onto the rocky ledge above.

I glanced at the ledge. Asim was by my side. "The rocks move." We both knew they were not rocks.

"Pit vipers!" I pulled at Tag, coaxing him away, yet he remained by Josu. I motioned for Asim to grab the artist's legs while I took ahold of his upper body. We dragged him from immediate danger. Everyone gathered around.

Josu desperately reached up to Malachi, grabbing hold of his tunic. "I shall die, I know. This is my punishment. I was the one who told the king of your plans. I listened at the door the night you made them. I told the guards where our weapons and supplies were on the temple. But when the lightning hit King Jacob, I knew the prophet Samuel spoke the truth. Forgive me for not believing. Please!"

Malachi reached out a fatherly hand and smoothed Josu's hair from his eyes. "Calm yourself, son."

Josu shook his head. "You cannot prevent my fate." His eyes searched the crowd as if he were looking for someone. When he found Tag, he said, "I know your truth." With those words, Josu's body went limp. Malachi closed the artist's lifeless eyes. Habib dove to the side of his longtime friend. "No! It was but a single bite. You will be fine. Come on."

Malachi pulled Habib to his feet. "The bite was in the life vein. He had no chance. Josu no longer feels pain. Let him go."

My heart sorrowed for Habib. I knew the torment of losing a loved one, of not being able to see that person who means the world to you. I thought of my father. Even though I hadn't seen him in many years, could I let him go as Habib must Josu? The comparison was different and yet the same. At least Habib knew his friend was now in heaven. I had no idea where my father was. I'd have no peace in my life without knowing what had happened to him.

29
Unfinished Business

JOSU HAD TO HAVE HEARD Sabirah, Rasha, and I talking the night before. He'd wanted me to know that he knew my secret before he died. Maybe he thought he would rest in peace confessing all. And even though he'd been the one who betrayed us to the king, I hoped he did find peace. I grieved his passing. Malachi took great care as he bundled up Josu's body. I watched him lovingly caress the young man's head before pulling the cloth over his face. The loss of Josu was heavy on all of us, but mostly on Malachi, who had been like a father to him.

Despite not wanting to bury him in the land of Desolation, we knew we had to. We didn't know how many more days we had until we reached Pagog, and by then Josu's decomposing body would really stink. We had no choice. I helped the artists dig his grave, using crude sticks and even our hands. When the hole was dug deep enough for Malachi's satisfaction, he stood at the head of the grave. Asim and I lowered the body into the ground. Crawling up out of the hole, I stood beside Rasha and Sabirah. Rasha trembled. I put my arm around her shoulders as she cried.

"Rest in peace, my son." Malachi took a handful of sand and dropped it on the body. Then all the artists one by one did the same. The last was Habib. He paused, and I thought he was going to say something. He stood there for a while, and though I couldn't clearly see his face, I knew he struggled. Josu had been his buddy. But Josu had also betrayed him. So many emotions must have Habib tongue-tied. Malachi went to him and whispered something in his ear. Habib nodded and tossed his handful of sand on the body. Malachi then led Habib away, probably to help him come to grips with all that had happened.

The rest of us filled the grave, making a mound. Asim and Sabirah placed a large rock over it as a marker, though the likelihood of any of us coming back here was very remote. It seemed the right thing to do. We slowly journeyed forward until we left the desert behind and came to the jungle where we could spend the night.

The constant strumming of crickets and chirps and cheeps of other jungle creatures seemed louder in this jungle. In the distance, I could hear the shrieks of spider monkeys high in the trees as a light tropical rain fell. I bedded down under a tall ceiba tree near the others. Everyone was asleep except for Sabirah and me. I could see her tossing and turning. I knew she was anxious to reach Pagog. The worry over the fate of her mother and grandfather followed her like the worry I felt over my mom and grandpa. I'd been gone for such a long time. Maybe they'd already given up hope of ever seeing me again.

And that would be all right . . . I guess. Maybe. A chunk of my heart hoped they hadn't and that they would always wait for me, like I would always wait for Dad and Tyler to return.

Dad and Tyler.

Though they were gone, they were always in the shadows. I couldn't think this way. I forced myself to close my eyes and tried to tune out the jungle music of nature and the stinging gnats.

જી

At first light, as we ate guava for breakfast, I found Sabirah and Asim studying the jungle.

"Soooo, what's up?" I asked, biting down on the fruit.

"This jungle is unfamiliar. We have taken a wrong turn."

My appetite was gone. "Do you have any idea where we are?"

They both shook their heads. Malachi joined us. "What troubles you?"

"The land has changed," Asim said. "I am uncertain where we are." Frustrated, he grabbed a plant and pulled it up by its roots. As he was about to toss it, he stopped and examined the dark, green leathery leaves. He studied the white blossoms and then smiled. "This is Tail Flower."

"And that's important because . . ." I didn't give a hoot about what flower it was. We were lost in the middle of who-knows-where, and our guide was looking at flowers.

Sabirah took it from him. "Are you certain?" She sniffed and smiled. "Yes, you are right."

"What's the big deal?" This had better be good. We were in the middle of a crisis, and they were excited about a stupid plant.

Malachi patted my shoulder. "The big deal is that Tail Flower grows in the mountains of Bountiful."

I stopped. "The land Bountiful?"

All three nodded their heads.

Rasha joined us. At first she looked concerned that we were arguing, but then seeing the smiles on the others' faces, she appeared relieved but confused. I took her hands. "We're lost, but we know where we are." I laughed, knowing how ridiculous I sounded.

Sabirah helped me out. "We are near the land of Bountiful. Over this mountain will be others who can help us. We can eat and rest for a while."

"But aren't we going to Pagog?" Rasha nervously wrung her hands.

"Yes, my cousin. From there, we shall go home. And there is a chance the people of Bountiful will have heard what has happened to Pagog."

That brightened Rasha's worried face. Our path had been detoured, but if Sabirah, Asim, and Malachi were all right with it, so was I.

Asim took the lead as we started out again. He had journeyed to Bountiful many times, though from a different direction, but he still seemed to know where he was going. In the air was the scent of Tail Flower, wood, and damp earth. Trees clustered together in thick barricades as we climbed farther up the mountain. The biting gnats were especially hungry in the dense foliage. No one had the wonderful ointment that Gian had shared with me so long ago. As we traveled, I found that even here there were deep cracks in the ground and uprooted trees from the quake.

As I looked at the effects of the quake, my thoughts turned to the incredible events yet to happen in this world. Suddenly, I remembered that when Grandma had told me about the destruction that happened in America after Christ was crucified, she had also said Christ appeared in America. The destruction happened at the first of the year and Christ visited toward the end of the year.

I really hadn't prepared myself for the possibility of actually meeting the Savior. Whoa! I could possibly see Him face to face. We were headed straight into the land Bountiful—the land where He appeared. No actor would play the part of Jesus. I, Tag Quincy, had a good chance of shaking the Lord's hand, of looking Him right in the eyes.

A shudder glanced through me. Would He be able to see into my soul? Yes, and more. I knew He could read my mind and know my thoughts far better than Princess Jamila ever could. He would know I was from a different time. He would know what my mind had hidden, the blank spaces I'd been unable to fill in. Fear as hot as the desert wind swept over me. And I knew I couldn't meet Him. No way could I let Him look into my soul and see me for what I truly was. Incredible sadness blanketed me. I wanted to disappear into the ground. Where was an earthquake when a person really needed one? I should have stayed at Jacobugath; King Jacob or Princess Jamila should have killed me, and then I wouldn't have to be thinking of all the things I had tried so hard to block from my mind. Instead I concentrated on the trail.

We'd cleared the summit and were starting down the mountain. By afternoon the midday rain had stopped, and we were nearly down the mountain when I saw children playing near the base of the trail. Asim, Sabirah, and the others saw them, as well. The children waved at us. Some took off yelling to the camp below; others ran toward us, which struck me as odd. Wouldn't they be frightened of strangers? But then I recognized a few of the kids who ran up to Sabirah and Asim. Asim scooped a small boy up in his arms. These were some of the children who had greeted us when we had entered Pagog. Before we knew it, we came to a campsite and were surrounded with familiar faces and some not so familiar, but all were happy to see us.

And then the crowd parted, allowing Hashim and Ashraf through. Where in the world had they come from? Asim had been certain we were far from Pagog.

Rasha fled to her father's waiting arms.

"Heavenly angels have guided us to each other!" Hashim was all smiles; joy radiated from his eyes as he hugged a joyful Sabirah. Savoring his granddaughter's hug, he buried his face in her neck. When he looked up, Hashim spied Asim. "Bless the heavens. Do my eyes tell the truth? Is this our most precious Asim, my beloved grandson, returned to the bosom of his family?" Tears rolled down the old man's round cheeks as he gave his long-lost grandson an elephant-sized hug. Composing himself, the old man asked Sabirah, "What of your father?"

Sabirah inhaled a deep breath before saying, "We heard that he was far north of Jacobugath. We would have set out to search for him again, but after the quake, we were worried about you and Mother."

"I see," Hashim said, his voice shadowed with disappointment.

"I can tell you—" said Malachi, who stood on the outskirts of this joyful reunion with his artists, "—Samuel was in the wilderness of Akish a few years ago. He was in good health and preaching the Lord's gospel. He converted me, my men, and many followers."

"Ah, a great and marvelous work he has done, too." Hashim shook Malachi's hand. "Welcome! Welcome!"

"Grandfather, how did you get here?" Sabirah had calmed down enough to remember her worry once again.

"The quake destroyed Pagog."

"My mother?" Sabirah clutched her grandfather's hand.

"See for yourself, my dear." Hashim motioned to a humble lean-to across the campsite. Standing with the help of a cane was the thin, frail figure of Lena, Sabirah and Asim's mother.

Asim raced to her, grabbing her in a long-overdue hug. Sabirah was right behind him. The heartwarming reunion was enough to make even me teary eyed. One villager brought a chair covered with soft animal hide for Lena to sit on. Sabirah knelt by her mother's side. Asim stood behind her, his hands on her shoulders. Lena put a hand over his, and with her other hand, she cupped Sabirah's face.

Hashim put his arm around my shoulders. "Wayfarer, you have served my family well! Come, I shall make a feast to amaze you, and we can share our stories!"

I could imagine a feast prepared by Hashim filled with peppers, hot peppers, burn-your-tongue-like-fire peppers. But at this moment, even Hashim's food sounded great.

In the commotion, I had lost track of Rasha. But I found her arm in arm with Ashraf. His relieved and loving expression said it all. He looked as though he never intended to let his daughter go again. I couldn't blame him. I felt the same way.

As all the merry greetings took place, I noticed Mahir standing behind Hashim's lean-to, trying to stay out of sight. He was watching Sabirah, smiling at her joy but reluctant to make himself known. Why didn't he come and greet her along with everyone else?

I noticed that Sabirah saw him at about the same time. Their eyes locked, and for a moment, I thought they were going to go to each other because they looked so happy and relieved, but then as if thinking better of it, Sabirah turned away. Instead of going to her, Mahir walked off. Obviously, there was something going on between those two. I hoped at some time they would meet up and settle things.

Hashim was in his element, cooking in the campfire outside his shelter and telling us of how they had to leave Pagog. They had heard there was food in Bountiful, though the city was in ruins, so they decided to come, praying that the Lord would somehow guide Sabirah to them.

Once the stew pots were filled and bubbling, Hashim had Malachi give a blessing on the food. Then Hashim passed out corn cakes as Sabirah, Malachi, and Asim took turns telling about our escape from Jacobugath, my close shave with sacrifice, and the earthquakes.

"Did you hear the voice?" Hashim asked as he chopped a good supply of sweet potatoes and dropped them into another huge pot of boiling water.

"Yes, we all heard it." Sabirah nodded. "Father was right about a good many things."

"Indeed he was." Ashraf added more wood to the cooking fire. "I wish I would have gone with him."

"He told you to stay," Hashim said. "He knew what his mission was, and it gave him great comfort that his brother would be here for his family."

Sitting between Sabirah and Asim, Lena added, "Ashraf, you and Hashim have made me well. You have honored your brother."

Ashraf smiled and settled down beside Rasha and me. Hashim passed around mugs of cherished chichi, the milk of corn. Soon a gruel of pigweed followed, along with a stew of ox meat, squash, peppers, and sweet potatoes. We drank and ate to our hearts' content.

Hashim asked everyone if they liked his cooking. We nodded yes. Surprisingly, his food was genuinely good. Ashraf must have convinced his father to tone down on the spice.

I wandered away from the camp, needing to be by myself for a moment. This was my home now. Could I really become used to no cell phone, no TV, no hamburgers, and no comfortable bed to sleep on?

Yes.

Life was full of living here. Everyone appreciated each other, talked with each other, and actually enjoyed being together. I could do without the comforts of my century, though I knew I would always miss my real family, especially Mom.

I wondered if in the time I'd been gone, she had married Doctor Bradford. My thoughts tumbled to if she would have children with him. That was a bit unsettling. My mother with a different family—without me, Tyler, and Dad. The last two years she'd made do without Dad and Tyler. I took a deep breath and slowly let it out. So she could certainly survive without me. I had only been a constant worry to her. Without me around, she had a chance at true happiness.

My thoughts turned to other people I'd left behind, namely the Primes. I didn't really know them. For instance, what were Gordo's parents like? Where did Dino live? Did they have brothers or sisters? I never knew them as people. I only knew them as weird dudes trying to appear cool.

What was cool? The word had an entirely new meaning for me now. Cool meant family, loving relationships, helping one another, being there when times were tough. That was cool.

"You want to be alone?" Sabirah stepped beside me. I should have known my good friend would notice my absence and seek me out.

"No. I've just been thinking."

"Remember, you are part of my family now." She looked at the night sky and then at me. "Your home is with us."

"I'm counting on that." I smiled, nudging her with my elbow.

"Good, because tomorrow we are going to find land to build permanent dwellings."

That surprised me but, at the same time, it didn't. "I guess you might as well."

"*We* might as well. *You* are going to build one, too." She smiled at me.

My own home. I smiled. "Yeah, I guess so."

"Here, I find you two off talking again." Rasha walked up to us. "Father wants to turn in, but I wanted to say good night." She gazed at me. "Has my cousin told you where we are going tomorrow?"

"Yep. To find land."

"We will be here early." She leaned over and gave me a kiss on the cheek, and then she hugged Sabirah. "Sleep well."

I couldn't help but wonder . . . would Rasha share my home someday? I certainly wouldn't be thinking like this if I were back home in my own time, but here? Well, it wasn't a bad idea at all.

Ashraf waited for her to join him, and then, arm in arm, father and daughter walked away.

"She told me she wasn't going to tell him about her mother," I said.

Sabirah watched them disappear into the night. "No. She would not burden him with such a memory. I think she has closed her mind to it, as well."

"I wish I could close my mind to some things." I wished I hadn't said that out loud.

"Some things need to be remembered before we can put them to rest." Sabirah looked wise beyond her years, and I imagined she probably resembled her father right then. She continued, "A shadow of your past has long followed you. I've seen it since the day of your arrival. I thought your helping me, as Father foretold, would make it disappear. But it still remains. There's more for you to do, Tag. I think your answer is at the temple in Bountiful."

Uncomfortable, I turned to go but caught a glimpse of Mahir near Hashim's lean-to. "Speaking of things yet to do. You need to go talk with Mahir. He's been waiting since we arrived."

Sabirah looked at me, shocked, and then followed my gaze. Her face brightened at first but saddened as she nodded. "I thought he'd left. You're right. I can no longer put this aside. Please keep the others away if you can."

I nodded, and then Sabirah left to settle unfinished business.

30
Nephi—The Prophet

Sabirah

I WAS SURPRISED THAT MAHIR had returned. As I walked toward
him, I wondered what I'd say. When we'd first entered camp, I'd
wanted to go to him, but there was Grandfather, Mother, and
Asim who needed me. I also knew Mahir would want an answer
from me—an answer I was most reluctant to give.

So much had happened since we'd parted, and, yet, I felt as
awkward as the night I'd left him to chase after Jamila. Approaching
him, I said, "I see you survived the earth's great upheaval."

"Yes," he said, his coal-black eyes staring at me like a mighty
cat ready to pounce. He folded his large, muscular arms that I'd
seen lift timber from the trail with little effort and continued,
"During the earth's quaking, I helped Ashraf and Hashim gather
the villagers to the granite cave above Pagog. I hope you approve."
Bitterness dripped from his words like rancid oil from a cup.

"I left knowing the village would be safe in your hands. We hid
in a cave, as well." This conversation wasn't the purpose of his visit.
I thought of what Princess Jamila had said. *Your man needs a real
woman to make him happy, not a horsewoman who roams the hills.*
She'd spoken the truth. Mahir deserved a real woman.

His arms remained folded in front of him as if they'd become a
shield.

I couldn't risk leading him to think we had a future. Though
we had feelings for one another, Mahir wanted me to be someone

I wasn't and never could become. I couldn't step down from the role my father had trained me for, nor did I want to. How could I make Mahir understand that though I cared for him deeply, I'd never follow the traditional path of other women?

"I brought them safely here," he said.

I'd been so wrapped up in my thoughts that I'd forgotten we were talking about him fulfilling his duties to our people. "Good." I yearned to have him take me in those big arms of his and hold me tight but knew such a fantasy would never happen. Plainly, he didn't seek it. "Is there anything else you need to tell me? Grandfather awaits."

"Your grandfather is busy with his guests."

By the tone in his voice, he wanted to argue. Our conversation was fruitless. "Still, I should go." I turned to leave.

"Wait . . ." His arms dropped to his side. "I . . . ah . . . missed you."

"I missed you, too." Again, I started to leave.

"Wait . . ." He rubbed his chin as he stared at me. "I have thought of you long and hard and of your ability to lead. I know you think that if we became man and wife, I'd expect you to do as the other women in the village and that I might even want to take your position as leader, but that's not so."

I'd not thought about him becoming the leader, but because he'd stated such a concern, it now became mine. He was right. If we married, he would assume my role. Yet, with my brother here, he was now the leader. "Asim has returned to lead."

"True. Even with the return of your brother, the village needs you and your skills as a tracker and fighter. Thus, you believe you could never find love because you're different." He paused, staring at me as though waiting for me to confirm his words.

I reluctantly nodded. I wanted to hear more because I wasn't sure if my ears were deceiving me. I had had this conversation in my own mind so many times that I didn't know if it was actually coming from his mouth.

"Though you are different from the other women, I believe your heart still beats for love. Your arms still yearn to hold another." He took my hand and looked into my eyes. "Sabirah, I shall carry you forever in my heart. We're meant to be together. Ours is a different course. With the men, you will always be the leader, but in our home, we shall be as one."

"What do you mean?"

"We shall hunt together, cook together, have our children . . . together."

Though shadowed in moonlight, I gazed into his dark eyes and saw my future. I leaned closer. He leaned closer, too. And then our lips met. His arms drew me to him as mine drew him to me. The kiss deepened as a spiral of fire twisted within me and seemed to light my body aflame. I'd never known such pleasure . . . and I never wanted to be without it again.

 es

Tag

Sabirah and Mahir were married by a small waterfall that fed into a stream framed with large tropical flowers and lush green plants. I'd never seen people get married in real life. I'd seen it plenty of times on TV and in the movies. But this was different. Mahir and Sabirah had love in their eyes, which made the simple ceremony Ashraf performed profound. They didn't have a honeymoon, though, because shortly after the ceremony, we loaded up camp to move closer to the city Bountiful where we planned to build our new village.

A light, misty rain turned off and on throughout our travel. But soon we came upon the rubble of Bountiful. Many buildings had experienced severe damage. Pillars had toppled, walls had caved in, and homes were flattened.

It needed a lot of work. We set up a makeshift camp in a glade canopied by trees near a stream of fresh water. The first few days, we slept under the stars as we had for so many nights. Sabirah and Mahir went off on their own. During the day, we were busy building small huts with thatch roofs just as they had in Pagog. Sabirah tutored me as I built mine, but I was quite proud of my home when I'd finished.

My first home built with my own two hands.

Soon our village was complete, and we turned our attention to helping the people of the city. Days turned into months filled with hard work, laughter, and the joy of knowing we'd helped to make someone's life more bearable.

I fell easily into the routine of eating dinner with Hashim, Asim, and Lena and, of course, the lovebirds, Sabirah and Mahir. Rasha and Ashraf were also with us most nights.

One evening after Rasha and Ashrif went to their hut and I'd retired to mine, Sabirah came for me. "We have a visitor."

"What do you mean, 'we have a visitor?'" I grabbed the poncho I'd just pulled off and slipped it back on.

"Nephi, the prophet. He has come to thank us for our help. Hurry." Sabirah left as I laced up my sandals. Just as I was about to go out the door, I stopped. The prophet Nephi? I remembered Grandma telling me angels were with Nephi daily just before Christ was crucified, and that Nephi had raised his brother, Timothy, from the dead.

I sat down, hesitant to leave my hut. All those stories my grandma had told me had turned out to be true, and I was about to meet a prophet who had the courage to foretell of a chief judge's death before anyone knew. Maybe, just maybe, Nephi could send me back to my own time. Then, as quickly as the thought came to my mind, I realized prophets didn't send people through time. A prophet was a seer and revelator, not a wizard. Besides, I was being totally selfish. Feeling unworthy to meet such a man, I decided to stay in my hut.

"Are you coming?" Sabirah stepped inside; aggravation creased her brow.

"I thought you had left."

"Come." She motioned.

"Nah. I'll pass. I'm sure he'd much rather talk with your family." I couldn't look her in the eyes.

"He has asked for you." Sabirah stood there all serious and with no intention of leaving me alone.

"Me?" Why would he ask for me? How did he even know about me?

Then I remembered. Angels spoke with him daily. Of course he knew. He knew all about me. Great. I had to go.

I rose and followed Sabirah outside. There, by our community fire pit, stood a tall man. People surrounded him: Ashraf and Rasha had returned. Mahir, Lena, Hashim, Asim, Malachi, and the artists were there, too.

Nephi's hair was pure white and combed away from his narrow face. Even though he was busy conversing with the others, I felt his eyes on me, and the urge to run was nearly overpowering.

Sabirah patted my shoulder as if to let me know she wouldn't allow me to turn tail and run. As we drew closer to the small gathering, I noticed Nephi was dressed in a knee-length, royal blue, poncho-type robe. He was quite tall, looking to be about six foot four. Gazing up to his face, I saw that his eyes were a rich cobalt blue.

My hand trembled as I reached out to shake his. He took mine between both his hands and drew me to him, hugging me tight.

"Tag." His voice was low but melodic. "You have been of great service to our beloved Samuel's family. When his son and daughter told me of your bravery and that you were now helping us repair our fair city, I had to meet you. It is an honor."

I was speechless. What do you say to a prophet who says it's an honor to meet you? I opened my mouth to speak, and only a gurgle escaped my lips. But words finally came. "Sir, the honor is mine."

He smiled.

And then Ashraf stepped in. "When does the work begin on the temple?"

"Tomorrow it shall begin in earnest." Nephi cast his gaze between Ashraf and me, as if he were torn as to whom he wanted to speak with. Then, taking a deep breath, he addressed everyone. "We will need many hands to right the pillars that have fallen. The city still needs more work, but it is of utmost importance that we begin on the temple site tomorrow."

I knew why.

Nephi knew why.

Jesus Christ was coming.

He would appear at the temple as they were working. My heart raced at the thought of actually meeting the Savior. As if reading my thoughts, Nephi turned, his gaze catching mine. He smiled and nodded, and I knew what I'd thought was true.

Nephi said, "You'll come and help us in the morning, won't you, Tag?"

This wise prophet, who knew everything, wanted *me* to be there. I nodded, not saying a word. I didn't want to lie, not to Nephi. But I certainly didn't plan on being at the place where Christ would appear. I wasn't worthy to witness such a miracle.

"Nephi!" A tall, slender man came running down the pathway from the city. "You must come. There is a disagreement over which building you'll use to conduct the Church's business. I told them it needs to be big enough for you to preach your sermons to everyone." He wiped perspiration from his brow. This fellow looked an awful lot like Nephi.

"I must go. Timothy needs my help." Before he left, Nephi stopped in front of me. "See you on the morrow, Tag?"

I nodded again, unable to look up at him. Was a nod a lie? I hoped not. I watched the two men walk up the path and felt ashamed that I would disappoint Nephi.

"We have a lot to do tonight if we're to help with the temple." Sabirah spoke to Mahir and Asim as they walked with Lena back to their huts.

"I want to help at the temple, too." Lena's voice was soft but determined.

Oh no! If she went to the temple, I'd have no excuse to stay behind. I hoped Sabirah and Asim would talk her out of this.

"Are you certain, Mother?" Asim asked, stopping in front of her.

"Yes." She sounded determined. I quickly sought Sabirah's gaze. I shook my head, hoping she would understand I thought it would be too dangerous for her mother. Though, if I really thought about it and quit being selfish, I knew Lena should be there to see the miracle that would happen.

Sabirah ignored me and said, "Your help will be welcome. Mahir, Asim, and I will see that you arrive safely, and Tag can find a place for you to rest while you're there."

I knew Sabirah was pretty savvy, and she probably knew if a prophet wanted all of us at the temple, there must be a good reason. Plus, she was making it nearly impossible for me to chicken out.

I had to think of a reason not to go. I just had to.

31

Immaculate White Robes

Tag

I FOLLOWED OUR VILLAGE'S PROCESSION to the Bountiful temple grounds. There were a lot of people there already, milling around the great pillars, worried about how they would pull the structures back into position at the top of the temple.

The small journey had tired Lena. I made sure she had a place to rest in the shelter of large red-barked trees with a nice comfy mat and water to drink.

Everyone set to work. Some of the followers who had journeyed here after we parted ways at Jacobugath were there, as well, helping to sweep and clear rubble. They seemed to have adapted well to their new surroundings. Malachi and the artists studied the pillars' fine carvings, seeing where they could repair the damage. I knew Malachi probably expected me to join them.

Sabirah and Mahir quickly set to work helping to move fallen trees. Asim, Hashim, and Ashrif helped them. Rasha helped a young man move debris from the temple steps and then came to sit with Lena and me. I knew I had to hightail it out of here and fast. I thought of the perfect alibi. "We forgot something to eat to keep up our strength. I'll go back and fix something."

"No need," Rasha said as she revealed a large basket filled with cornbread and fruit.

"But there's something else I need. I'll be right back." I took off. If I had to, I'd lose myself in the jungle for the rest of the day, but I wasn't sticking around the temple grounds.

When I reached our small village, I felt empty—hollow like the statues in King Jacob's palace. What a chicken I'd become. In the back of my mind, I could hear Gordo yelling at me from the back door of the funeral home, "There goes Quivering Quincy, the spineless wonder." What had happened to the brave wayfarer who had helped the righteous escape the wicked city Jacobugath? I was brave when it had to do with others but not when it was something personal and had to do with feelings deep inside.

I couldn't sulk around waiting all day. I looked around the village and wondered what I could do to pass the time. I was sure everyone would stay at the temple most of the day. Staring at the roofs of our huts, I thought of the perfect project. I decided to add thatch to them. The rainy season was coming, and we needed strong roofs over our heads.

The work was hard. Swinging my sword and cutting the long grass, I gathered and hauled it to the village. As midday approached, I'd collected enough to do one hut. I needed the ladder Asim had fashioned by tying poles together, but I couldn't find it. I could use one of my own, so I spent the remainder of the day making a new one.

Finally at dusk, people began to return. A golden aura seemed to illuminate each person's being. Lena walked as though a new energy coursed through her legs. Hashim, Ashraf, Sabirah, Mahir, and Rasha came behind her, faces radiating joy and peace.

"What's with your mother?" I asked Sabirah as she and Mahir approached.

"Tag, you missed the most remarkable event. I am so sorry. I should have searched for you when He first arrived, but I couldn't pull myself away."

I'd succeeded. I'd missed the miracle. Missed seeing Him heal the sick, missed seeing the angels bless the children—missed it all.

Sabirah placed her hand on my shoulder, and I felt a small charge pass from her. Being in Christ's presence had filled her with a wondrous force.

"While we worked, a voice came out of the heavens." Sabirah's face glowed with remembrance. "At first, I didn't understand what the voice said. It came again and again, and, suddenly, I understood. It was Heavenly Father's voice, and He said: 'Behold my Beloved Son, in whom I am well pleased, in whom I have glorified my name—hear ye him.'"

The others had gathered around us. Asim picked up the story. "We saw a man descending from the heavens. He was dressed in an immaculate white robe, and He came and stood amongst us."

Hashim seemed to relive the scene as he spoke, "My son's prophesy came to pass before my very eyes. I dared not move. He put forth His hand and said, 'Behold, I am Jesus Christ, whom the prophets testified shall come into the world. And behold, I am the light and life of the world; and I have drunk out of that bitter cup which the Father hath given me, and have glorified the Father in taking upon me the sins of the world in the which I have suffered the will of the Father in all things from the beginning.' After His words, I fell to my knees and bowed to Him."

I felt a great sorrow settle on me. Because of my fear and stubbornness, I'd deliberately avoided the Savior Himself. I'd done it again, made the wrong choice. Goosebumps rippled over my skin. I bit my bottom lip, forcing back regret so strong I thought I'd burst into tears at any second.

Mahir continued, "He asked us to step forward and touch His hands and side where the nails and sword had pierced His body. He wanted us to be a witness that He was Jesus Christ." Mahir stopped and gazed at Sabirah as though he could hardly believe what they'd witnessed.

"Did you touch Him?" I knew before asking he had, but I wanted someone to keep talking.

Rasha said, "Yes. We all did. I can't explain how I felt, standing in His presence, touching Him, and knowing the man before me was the living Savior."

"The Savior of the world," I added.

Sabirah gazed at me. "Oh, Tag, I'm so sorry you missed seeing Him. He gave Nephi the power to baptize. He also called eleven others to help Nephi with his many duties. He taught us how to pray and gave us guidelines to live by. He told us there's to be no more sacrifices to our Father. He healed the sick. He even put His hands on Mother's head and blessed her with renewed energy.

"Then the most miraculous thing happened." She stopped, caught up in the story.

"What?" I had to know.

Lena continued where her daughter had left off. "Angels, radiant with heavenly light, descended from the sky and helped Him administer to the children. A ring of fire encircled them. I think I saw—" She bit her trembling bottom lip; tears pooled in her eyes. "—my Samuel with the angels. He looked happy, even smiled at me. I don't know if he was alive or dead, but I shall never forget this day for the rest of my life."

What had I done? I felt as though my life source drained from my body. I became paralyzed by my stupidity. Rasha took my hand, drawing my attention. Sweet Rasha didn't know the real me.

Asim motioned for us to join him and Lena. I told Rasha to go on and I would follow. They were going to her father's hut for dinner. Reluctantly, she left. Sabirah began to follow everyone but stopped when she noticed I hadn't moved.

"Tag, the Savior will come again on the morrow. You will have your chance to meet Him. Come, eat dinner with us." Mahir came back to get her and stood by her side as Sabirah waited. She added, "Grandfather isn't cooking." Her words cheered me a little.

I had forgotten He came again the next day. I felt a little bit of life come back into me at the thought of having the opportunity to see the Savior tomorrow. But because of my foolishness, I'd missed out on so much today. I'd missed seeing Samuel, missed seeing the angels, missed so very much. Though I'd see Him tomorrow, still . . .

I was upset with myself and not fit for company.

"You go ahead. I'll come later." I hadn't eaten since breakfast, but food was the last thing on my mind. I motioned for Sabirah to go with Mahir. "Really," I said. "I need to be alone."

Sabirah slowly turned, and together she and Mahir left.

I watched them go with the others. Filled with regret, I walked into the jungle. Sorrow penetrated deep, pressing like an anvil on my chest. My heart actually ached. Only one other time had I felt this incredible sadness.

Two years ago. When I realized I had no memory of Dad and Tyler leaving, I felt so alone, as though they had abandoned me, not only physically but in my mind, as well.

I felt I was the most wasted excuse for a human being. When would I ever learn? Some people needed a meteor to fall on them before they'd wise up to the truth. But me, I had been time warped to thousands of years before my time, been nearly eaten by crocodiles, imprisoned, nearly sacrificed, and even then I didn't learn. Well, I knew the truth about myself. I was a loser.

L-O-S-E-R. Big time loser!

I walked over to a fallen tree and sat down. What was a loser like me doing in Book of Mormon times anyway?

I no longer fit in anywhere. I thought of Mom and missed her more than breath itself. I missed the way her smile made me feel happy to be alive. I missed her telling me what to do. I missed the smell of the hospital that clung to her clothes when she came home from work. And even though I'd hated the smell back then, I'd give anything to get a whiff of it now or see her dressed in her scrubs, just coming home from saving lives. My mother had a gift for saving lives.

Dad came to mind. I loved to watch my father draw. My dad had the neatest hands. They were kind of like Sabirah's description of her father's: long fingers, clean nails.

I remembered one day at the lake when Dad, Tyler, and I were visiting Grandpa. *Dad drew a cartoon with me as the star. In the picture, I had bulging muscles and was dressed in a cape like*

Superman. Dad said he was going to use this character based on me in his cartoon strip. I was honored and happy. I'd forgotten that had happened, and now the memory wrapped around me like a soft flannel quilt.

Another memory latched onto the first. Dad had asked me to go sleigh riding with Tyler. I really didn't want to, but I went.

I remembered my brother and I sledding, the wind and bits of snow whipping our cheeks as we laughed all the way down to the bottom of the hill—down to the lake. The ice was melting. Trees were losing snow fast from their branches. Spring was coming. I even saw a robin. Tyler stepped from the dock onto the ice, testing it.

"Grandpa said the ice isn't safe," I warned him. He gave me the devilish grin he used when he had no intention of doing what adults told him to do. He stepped farther out.

"Come on, Tyler. Stop kidding around." A tickle of fear raised the hairs on the back of my neck, telling me to get him off.

I could hardly believe these thoughts tumbling into my mind. They were foreign and yet familiar. For so long, the past had been blank to me, as though my mind had erased it, but now I felt an urgent need to remember, even though it made me sick to my stomach with fear. Something deep inside warned me to keep the memories hidden, but they'd shadowed me far too long, always part of my subconscious. I had to face the past, no matter how painful it was, no matter what happened. So even though I desperately wanted to stop these memories from unfolding, I knew I couldn't stop them from surfacing and that it was time to face them.

"You're just a fraidy-cat." Tyler was at least twenty feet from shore, and that was when I heard it—the deadly crack of the ice. Before I could yell at him to stop, Tyler took another step—and as his foot pressed down, he broke through. He fell in slow motion. Fear widened his shock-filled eyes and held his mouth opened in a desperate cry as he disappeared beneath water and ice.

Filled with horror and fear, I couldn't move.

Then Tyler sprang up. Water sheeted over him. He screamed, "Help me! Tag, help me!"

I quickly searched for something he could grab onto. Though the snow was melting, it still covered the ground, hiding limbs and branches. Unable to find anything, I frantically looked back at him.

Tyler wildly grabbed at the edge of the ice, his gloved hands slipping as the edge gave way. Panic and desperation covered his face as he pleaded with me to do something.

I stood paralyzed as an ice sculpture, watching my little brother sink below the water, out of sight. I waited and waited for him to surface. He never came up again.

Terror erupted within me, and before I knew it, I was screaming uncontrollably. Dad was suddenly beside me. He took one horrified look at the hole in the ice and without reservation ran out to where Tyler had broken through, but long before he reached the edge, the ice fractured beneath his feet and the lake swallowed him, too.

Incredible silence filled the air. Only the swish of pine boughs danced in the warm breath of spring. This could not be happening. Any minute, I would wake up. But I didn't. Cold emptiness enveloped me, paralyzing me.

Grandpa huffed and puffed his way to my side. "Where's your Dad? Where's Tyler?" He ran up and down the dock, staring at the broken ice. His face reddened with each passing second, and his eyes teared up with the seriousness of the situation.

Unable to answer, I stood staring at the lake and the bobbing ice aimlessly floating about in the water. The lake laughed at me, daring me to tell Grandpa I'd let my brother and father die without doing anything. I'd stood there on the dock, not even wet.

"Come on." Grandpa grabbed me, pulling me away. "We need to call for help."

Then I remembered how I had pulled Rasha away from the temple, away from her mother who had disappeared in the terrified crowd, and to me the people became a lake filled with floating ice. At that time, with Rasha in my arms, I'd had a memory flash of this raw scene I'd just relived, but back then as the temple crumbled beneath our feet, I was worried for Rasha and had pushed this hidden ugliness further away.

Now, sitting here alone, I allowed the nightmare to play itself completely through. The blank spaces in my mind filled with mind-numbing pain. Because of me, my father and brother were dead. It suddenly occurred to me that the coward in me had made up the story that Dad and Tyler had merely left Mom and me. But the reality was that my father's and brother's deaths were my fault and mine alone.

I buried my face in my hands. Tears flowed freely. I sobbed like I never had before, until I felt a hand rest upon my head. Sabirah must have come after me. Didn't she realize I needed to be alone?

I jerked up to tell her to buzz off and abruptly stopped.

Standing before me was a man dressed in immaculate white robes. His loving, caring eyes peered into my soul. Warmth filled me from the inside out. All thought left my mind as I soaked in pure, white peace. He reached out, and I stared at His hands.

Holes cut through the middle of his palms.

Nail holes.

My Savior, Jesus Christ, stood before me.

32
The Blessing

Sabirah

As my family discussed the miraculous day and ate supper, my mind drifted to Tag. I sat a small distance away from the others so they wouldn't know how worried I was. I knew when I saw him leave the temple grounds today that I should have searched for him. But when the Savior arrived I couldn't pry myself away. As I pondered why, I realized my not leaving had more to do with a feeling that I wasn't supposed to find him, which didn't make sense.

"You're far away." Mahir sat next to me and took my hand.

"I'm concerned about Tag."

"Yes, he seemed upset that he missed the miracles today, but the Savior said He would return. Don't worry. Tag will meet our Lord." He rubbed my arm, trying to soothe me.

"There's something more that bothers him."

"More?" Mahir seemed surprised.

"Since the wayfarer arrived, I've felt he carried an unseen burden on his shoulders. As we neared Jacobugath, he told me a little about himself."

Mahir looked thoughtfully at me. "I've wondered about his story. What did he say?"

"He told me the reason why he fears snakes, about his mother and father. He has no sisters, only a brother named Tyler. The odd part was that his father and brother left."

"Left?"

"Yes. Parts of his story are similar to my own. Both our fathers and brothers had left; however, Tag has no memory of them leaving. I at least said goodbye to Father. And when Asim left to search for him, I watched him leave. Tag said his memory is blank." I looked at Mahir, hopeful he could explain.

"So he became a wayfarer searching for his father and brother, and his journey brought him to you." He paused, thinking, and then said, "Searching for your father and brother took the place of searching for his own."

My hand went to the wing-spread necklace. Tag had fulfilled my father's prophecy. "Yes. And now I'm afraid he must come to terms with his past. When the Savior arrived today, I should have searched for Tag, but something held me back." A deep sigh escaped me as I looked to my husband, wanting him to have the answer as to why I had that feeling, yet knowing he didn't.

"We all have inner struggles to overcome. The wayfarer is no different. Give him time. Only he can make peace with his past." Mahir smiled and rubbed my aching shoulders.

"What are the newly married speaking of over here by themselves?" Rasha came to join us, but she was looking down the path where we'd left Tag.

"Nothing a young woman with her future ahead of her would understand." I slid closer to Mahir, giving room for her to sit beside me.

"You're concerned about Tag, aren't you?" Rasha was smart.

"Yes."

"I should go to him." She started to rise.

"No," I said, pulling her back.

"Young men sometimes need to be alone." Mahir gave her a look, stating that this was something he knew about. As she settled down, he added, "Tell us of the young man who helped you in Tag's absence today at the temple."

Rasha again stared down the path, hesitated, but then her eyes lit up, and she told us how thoughtful and caring her new friend had been. I only half listened as I realized my cousin's future wouldn't be with Tag as I'd hoped.

And I knew the wayfarer's time with us was growing short.

∾

Tag

OVERWHELMED BY THE MOMENT AND humbled that Christ would appear to me, a lowly boy unworthy of such an honor, I dropped to my knees and bowed near His feet. His robes brushed my cheek as He bent over to pat me on the back. "Arise, Tag."

I had deliberately tried to avoid Him, deliberately tried to keep Him from knowing the truth about me. Now, here He was, asking me to stand.

Slowly, I peered up. He reached out His hand, giving me aid. Taking His kind offer, my fingers felt the nail prints in His palm. The touch bore witness to me and left no doubt in my mind that He was the living Christ.

What would He say to me, Tag Quincy, royal coward? What would He do? He knew I was responsible for my brother's and father's deaths.

"You suffer much." His eyes searched mine, and I remembered Dad's painting of Him. My father had captured the shape of the Savior's eyes. As I gazed into them, I knew He understood my pain, understood my grief, and understood the overwhelming guilt that had descended on me full thrust. I had no secrets from Him.

"You have been called to this time to help others and thereby learn your purpose." He smiled and motioned for me to sit down on a nearby tree stump.

I did so, never taking my eyes from Him.

"Yet, you have more to learn. May I give you a blessing?" His voice wrapped around me, filling me with hope.

"Of course." I bowed my head, ready for His touch. Never in my entire life did I ever think I'd have the Savior lay His hands upon my head to give *me* a blessing. What a miracle this truly was. He gently rested His hands—His carpenter's hands, His shepherd's hands pierced from nails—upon my head. I closed my eyes and waited for the blessing to begin.

Instead of hearing His voice, though, an image came to my mind. I found I was in a large cavernous building with marbled floors and no ceiling. A grand staircase, leading to the clouds, stood directly in front of me. I saw doors along the walls. I knew teaching was going on in those rooms. Curious to hear one of the instructors, I started for a door but stopped before I reached it.

Descending the stairs were Dad and Tyler dressed in white robes. Smiles brightened their faces. Eager to greet my father, I sprinted up the stairs two at a time and flung my arms around him. I could actually feel him, touch his hair, and smell his fresh scent that reminded me of the mountains. "You're alive!"

He hugged me back, lifting me up, kissing my cheek. "Yes. You knew I would be." He settled me on my feet. I saw Tyler and hugged him, touched him as though I couldn't believe that he, too, was here.

"Let's find Mom. She has to see you two." I pulled on Dad's arm, but he didn't budge. "Come on. She needs to know you're all right. So does Grandpa. We were so worried."

"Tag." Dad pulled me back. "It is true we live, but we are no longer part of your world."

"What?"

"You are strong now, and that's why your memory has been restored of that day." Dad gazed at me like he always did when he had to tell me something unpleasant.

"But I don't want to be strong. I want you to come back. You have to come back!" Tears came to my eyes, clouding my vision. For a second, I relived the torture of standing on the dock, alone, staring at the bobbing ice. And then flashes of a funeral with two caskets melted into empty days of Mom and me trying to deal with overwhelming sorrow so painful I hid them away in my mind, unable to live with them any longer.

"My son, you are strong." Dad placed his arm around me. "With the help of the Savior, you can face the truth."

Tyler nudged me as if he agreed. I smiled at my brother, whom I loved and missed.

His brows rose, and he said, "I've missed you, too, bro."

I wanted to say what had been heavy in my heart ever since the day they had left. Taking a deep breath, I said, "I'm sorry I couldn't save you. I didn't have enough courage."

My father stepped back. "No courage? My son, who stood up to King Jacob and lived to help guide others to safety? No courage? Tag, what do you think courage is?"

"But I didn't have the courage needed to save you."

"You were smart and knew you couldn't save us. You would have drowned if you had tried, and then what would your mother have done? You helped her through a very critical time in her life."

I thought of how rotten I'd been to Mom. Dad had it wrong. I didn't help at all.

"You helped in ways you'll never know." Dad stopped for a moment as if listening to someone else. He continued. "We only have a few minutes, and there is so much I need to say."

"Only a few minutes?" I didn't understand.

Tyler nodded his head. "You think once you've crossed to the other side all you do is hang around and play harps or something?"

I shrugged.

"Tag, I taught you that your mortal life is only part of your eternal progression. Don't you remember?" Dad's brows creased as he waited for my answer.

"Well, yeah, but . . . here's the deal, Dad. How can Mom and I progress without you? Why were you needed so badly here when Mom and I needed you more? I don't understand how Father in Heaven could take you from us. There's this Doctor Bradford who is trying to worm his way into Mom's life. You've got to come back." I hoped the shock of learning another man was taking Dad's place would be enough to make him return.

"Son, I know about Kenyon Bradford. Who do you suppose helped reveal to him what a wonderful person your mother is?" Dad looked at me, waiting for my answer.

"You?"

"I don't want your mother to be lonely. Besides, you need some fatherly guidance."

The thought of Doctor Bradford acting as my father sent a hot pang to my gut. How could Dad talk this way? Didn't he miss Mom and me at all?

"I miss you and your mother very much. I've been watching you. I know you've had a hard time dealing with our deaths, but, Tag, everyone must die except a chosen few."

"Who?"

"Elijah and Moses were translated. John the Beloved still lives as well as the Three Nephites. They roam the earth, helping people."

"Where were they when you and Tyler were drowning?" I needed to know.

"Tyler and I were meant to leave you and your mother. I don't know how to make you understand, but know this: Tyler and I will always be with you."

He grabbed me and held my head in a hammer-lock, tousling my hair like old times. When he released me, he took ahold of both my arms and looked me square in the face. "Always remember I love you!" Dad hugged me one last time, kissed my forehead, and then turned to walk away. Tyler slugged me in the arm and prepared to follow. I wasn't letting my little brother get away with that. I hugged him—and he hugged me back for a second before turning to leave with Dad.

"Wait!" I called. "There's something I have to know."

Dad gazed back at me.

"Does Grandpa really see Grandma when he's talking to her?"

"What do you think?" Dad smiled. "Oh, she wanted me to tell you to knock off the graffiti and work on your art the way you're meant to." He winked and headed up the stairs.

I stood transfixed to the spot, watching Dad and Tyler disappear as they walked up that grand staircase. And then, without warning, I was sitting on the stump.

Jesus was gone.

33
The Three

Tag

A VIBRANT FEELING OF WELL-BEING overcame me as I recalled gazing into Jesus' face, receiving a blessing, and remembering my dad and brother and how well they had looked. For the first time since their drowning, I felt as if everything would be all right. Mom would be all right. Grandpa and Ethan would be all right. And though I was a guy out of my own time, I knew I'd be all right no matter what happened, because Dad and Tyler would always be with me. And even though bad things may happen, there might be a higher purpose I didn't understand.

I really didn't care for that answer, but now I could make peace with it. I went straight to my hut. I couldn't talk with Sabirah or Rasha or anyone, for that matter. What had just happened was something so special that I wanted time alone to ponder and absorb it. Curling up on my sleeping mat, I closed my eyes and thought of the blessed event that had happened to me, Tag Quincy, nobody special.

I awoke feeling better than I had in a long, long time. I dressed quickly. Today Jesus would appear to the crowd again at the temple grounds. I wanted to be there this time to witness everything He did. Leaving my hut, I found Mahir, Sabirah, Asim, Lena, and Hashim by our village campfire. I wondered where Rasha was but knew she'd show up at any moment.

"Good morning, fair prince of the dawn." Hashim seemed entirely too cheerful, but that was okay. There was a lot to be happy about. Today we'd see Jesus again.

"We were just wondering if we should wake you." Sabirah stood as I came closer to them. "You slept a night, a day, and a night."

"What?" I couldn't believe it.

"I tried to wake you, Rasha tried, even Grandfather gave you a nudge or two," Sabirah defended.

"Yes, and when the nudge had no effect, I used my trick of the tickling feather across your brow. It did nothing to stir you from your slumber." Hashim handed me a piece of flat cornbread.

I took it and thanked him, plopping down beside Asim and Lena. "I slept that long?" They both nodded. "Then I've missed Him again." I was devastated.

"And what a sight, my boy." Hashim's face grew reverent with remembrance. "A mass of humanity crowded around the temple grounds. Jesus taught his disciples how to baptize. *We were all baptized*, not only by water but with fire, as well, because we were confirmed to receive the Holy Ghost. Another magnificent, glorious day spent with our Savior!"

I smiled at the old man. "How wonderful for you." I rose and started to wander away. Where, I didn't know and didn't care.

"Tag, where are you going?" Sabirah started to follow.

"I just need to be alone for a bit."

"Are you certain?"

"Oh yes." I took a bite of cornbread and made myself eat even though right at this moment my stomach felt as heavy as though concrete had been poured into it. Here I was in this miracle of times—and I was sleeping! Maybe my being with Jesus before zapped my energy so I needed more rest.

I knew I'd been blessed because I'd seen Him yesterday . . . no, the day before yesterday. He'd given me the very special gift of speaking with my dad and brother. How dare I feel bad about missing yesterday.

I thought of Nephi and how the day before Christ's first appearance he'd sought me out in our village to make sure I'd be at the temple. I needed to thank him and tell him what happened to me. He might find it interesting. Though he was probably extremely busy being the leader of the disciples and all, I had a feeling I needed to speak with him. I'd heard he lived not far from our settlement in a more established adobe home.

As I walked, I met Rasha on the path. "Tag, you are awake!"

Her dark brown hair curled around her face and over her shoulders; her doelike eyes searched mine as though she were truly happy to see me. "Yeah, I hear I missed quite a lot."

"Indeed, but you needed your rest. I was worried you'd fallen ill, but when Nephi visited us, he explained that he was certain you were merely exhausted."

The prophet had come to our camp? Knowing this, I wanted to speak with him even more than before. "Do you know where he lives?"

"Yes, I just left his home. The disciples are all there. Grandfather had me take them some cornbread." She pointed to a small modest house. I hugged her and kissed her cheek. She appeared surprised at first but then smiled.

"Don't tarry long, Tag. I want you to meet a friend I have made. He was helping at the temple." She waved and continued to walk down the path.

Nearing Nephi's home, I noticed no one was around. I mean, no one on the pathways or anywhere. Odd. While I'd been speaking with Rasha, people had passed us, at least I thought they had.

I knocked on Nephi's door. No one answered. I tried again. Still, no answer. Darn it. I wanted to talk with Nephi about my meeting with Jesus and what happened when He put His hands on my head. I decided to check in back of his home. Maybe he was in the courtyard.

Turning the corner of his house, I came to a dead stop. I could see a gathering of men, their backs to me, intently listening to someone out of my view. I recognized that Nephi and Timothy were among them. I moved closer to see better but still remained hidden. That's when I saw Him.

Jesus was talking with the Twelve. He was telling them He was sent to earth to give His life for all people. He told them to continue His work and help others keep the commandments. He asked what they, the disciples, would like from Him.

I couldn't see their faces, only the backs of their heads. Nine of them requested to be with Christ after their lives on earth ended. He promised them they would be together in heaven.

Three of them, who were kind of off to the side, away from the nine, held back. Finally, one of them stood and turned. I saw his face, and shock flooded my body.

John Doe.

My John Doe!

The John Doe who had talked with me in the Alpine Market, the John Doe whose cabin I had entered in the middle of a storm, and the John Doe whose stone I had taken.

The two other guys stepped beside him. Steve Smith and Bob Jones. They weren't dressed like they had been in their cabin. And Bob Jones didn't have a crew cut, but it was them.

Jesus asked what they wanted of Him. All three stood there, kind of looking down at the ground as if they were afraid to ask the Savior what was truly in their hearts.

Christ said, "Behold, I know your thoughts, and ye have desired the thing which John, my beloved, who was with me in my ministry, before that I was lifted up by the Jews, desired of me. Therefore, more blessed are ye, for ye shall never taste of death; but ye shall live to behold all the doings of the Father unto the children of men, even until all things shall be fulfilled according to the will of the Father, when I shall come in my glory with the powers of heaven.

"And ye shall never endure the pains of death; but when I shall come in my glory ye shall be changed in the twinkling of an eye from mortality to immortality; and then shall ye be blessed in the kingdom of my Father.

"And again, ye shall not have pain while ye shall dwell in the flesh, neither sorrow save it be for the sins of the world; and all this will I do because of the thing which ye have desired of me, for ye have desired that ye might bring the souls of men unto me, while the world shall stand.

"And for this cause ye shall have fulness of joy; and ye shall sit down in the kingdom of my Father; yea, your joy shall be full, even as the Father hath given me fulness of joy; and ye shall be even as I am, and I am even as the Father; and the Father and I are one;

"And the Holy Ghost beareth record of the Father and me; and the Father giveth the Holy Ghost unto the children of men, because of me."

Jesus turned to the other nine men and touched each one with His finger, but He didn't touch John Doe, Steve Smith, or Bob Jones.

All at once a glorious light descended from above and rained down on the three. The light became brighter and brighter until I couldn't see them anymore. My eyes stung and became blurry.

I backed away, trying to focus to see where I was going. Finally, the trees and plants on the pathway from Nephi's house came into focus, and I hurried down it, running as fast as I could. I ran hard, my mind tumbling over the events I had witnessed. I finally stopped and found myself at the spot where Jesus had appeared to me.

Sitting on the stump where He'd given me a blessing, I realized I'd just seen Jesus bless His twelve disciples. I'd witnessed the Three Nephites engulfed in heavenly light. I wondered what they were seeing. Could they be in the building I'd seen Dad and Tyler in? Possible, I supposed, but probably not. If I remembered right, at this moment, the Three Nephites were being translated so they could withstand the temptations of this world.

I felt very honored, loved, and humbled. I had witnessed a most profound event. And I actually knew the Three Nephites. I realized I probably didn't know their real names, only aliases used while helping me. No one knew their names, except the Twelve and Jesus. And I guessed that was how it should be.

Remembering I'd stolen John Doe's stone and lost it in the rubble of Jacobugath, I felt great remorse. I had no idea what I could say to John Doe if I ran into him. Then I remembered where I was. I was in a time where they didn't know me because we hadn't met. So, technically, I hadn't stolen the stone yet, right? I was rationalizing my sin away and becoming mixed up with time shifts.

I leaned over and rested my elbows on my knees, burying my face in my hands as I tried to think of the stone's journey while in my care: I had stolen the stone from John Doe, and in return, it sent me to Book of Mormon times. Then Princess Jamila stole the stone from me and gave it to her father, King Jacob. He had died with it around his neck. And the stone and the king had disappeared in the rubble of Jacobugath.

I would never get it back. I thought of its origin. The brother of Jared created the stone a long time before Christ appeared here in the Americas, but John Doe had it in my time period. So was it really lost? My head throbbed behind my aching eyes.

"Tag." I'd heard those soothing tones before and knew without looking up who was there. Swallowing hard, I gazed up.

My Savior stood before me once again. In His hand was the stone. I stared at it and then looked at Him. His rich brown eyes held only love for me.

"But how . . . where—" I was dumbfounded. My tongue felt thick and uncooperative. I couldn't put words together to make a sentence. All at once, a peace came upon me.

"There were sixteen stones made," He said. "I know where they all are. Instead of removing the stone from King Jacob, you saved Rasha from the quake. You sacrificed your own well-being to help another. And, yet, there is more for you to do."

Jesus handed me the stone. Tears pooled in my eyes as I took it from Him. I gazed down at the gem in my hand, marveling at its beauty.

Glancing up to thank Him, I found He'd left as quickly as He'd come.

And I knew.

I was going home!

34
Just In Time

Tag

I NEEDED TO SAY GOOD-BYE to Sabirah and her family. Clutching the stone close to me, I ran down the path as fast as my feet would carry me. The stone became warm in my hand. I abruptly stopped and gazed down on it. A glowing light grew within the stone.

Nooo! Not now! I had to say good-bye to my friends. The glow of the stone radiated beyond my hold, growing brighter and brighter. What would happen to Rasha? The light overcame my hand, crawling up my arm. I thought of the friend she'd told me about that she had wanted me to meet, and I knew she was meant to be with him. A giant bubble of light grew bigger and bigger until it engulfed me, becoming far brighter than the noonday sun, brighter than the sparkle of a starburst. I closed my eyes, giving in to its brilliance.

Light faded, and I chanced a peek. The glow only encased my arm, hand, and, finally, just the stone. Then the light blinked out. I was in the dark of night. Crickets and frogs croaked nearby. The air was scented with earth and pines. I was in the mountains of Idaho.

I had wanted to tell Sabirah that I loved her like a sister, that she had helped me more than I could ever say. I wanted to tell her what had happened to me and why I had acted crazy sometimes. And I wanted to tell Hashim how much I loved listening to his flowery speech. I would miss him—I would miss all of them.

But good-byes were not to be. I was back home, back where I belonged.

Excitement charged through me. Home!

I turned and looked up the hill. In the receding moonlight, I saw the small cabin where months ago—No, wait, I had the feeling that this was the same night. Had I only been gone moments? Had all that had happened to me during my Book of Mormon travels happened within the glow of the stone? Gazing at the cabin, I realized there was one way to find out, and I started up the hill.

I worried that when I opened the door, the Three Nephites would be sitting there, waiting for me. I decided if they were, I'd just tell them everything. Reaching the cabin, I turned the doorknob and slowly, inch by inch, pushed the door open.

Only darkness and the snores of guys deep in sleep greeted me. Leaving the door ajar so the moonlight could guide me, I quietly tiptoed over to the couch, squatted down, and ever so gently tugged out the heavy box.

Pulling off the lid, I set it down, reached inside, and opened the round, egg-shaped enclosure—the home of the stone. I gazed at the gem and realized how very precious it truly was.

This stone had helped light the barges as the Jaredites had sailed to America; this stone had transported me from one dimension in time to another, but, most importantly, this stone had been touched by the Lord. The reverence of the moment covered me like warm sunshine. I felt the profound love of my Savior, and my gratitude grew by giant leaps.

I wished I could keep the stone forever to have a physical reminder of the past events. But I knew I couldn't. To keep something so precious would be selfish and just plain wrong. I carefully laid the stone in the egg-shaped container, closed the dome lid, and then hefted the heavy lid of the stone box back in place. Sliding the container under the bed, my hand felt the side engravings. I thought of Malachi, Habib, and Josu—artists who had worked on carvings such as these. I would never forget them.

My fingers caressed the etchings for a moment, and I wished I could study them more closely. But there wasn't time.

Going to the door, I gazed at the three forms sleeping not far from me. I wondered, Did translated beings need to rest like other humans? Were they really asleep? Or were they pretending for my sake? I didn't know, but if they were pretending, that was fine with me.

Since Book of Mormon times, they'd experienced a lot in this world. They might have saved some of their people from the Spanish when they arrived in the Americas. They might have helped the Founding Fathers form the United States. They might have helped Joseph Smith as he restored the Church. And they might even have helped some of the inventors in the world. The possibilities were endless. The thought that I had spoken with them and even spent time with them was amazing.

I quietly closed the door behind me and started down the hill. My walk soon turned to a run. I wanted to get back to Grandpa's cabin. Unsure of the way through the woods, I decided to go down to the main highway that would take me to the road going up the mountain to Grandpa's. Tomorrow I planned to help Grandpa with his deck.

Grandpa, my grandpa!

I remembered how he looked at me as though I were an alien when Mom had dropped me off. First thing in the morning, I was going to get a buzz cut. And I'd be more than happy to wear overalls and flannel shirts the rest of the summer if it would make Grandpa happy.

I stopped and looked at the clothes on my body. I still wore the poncho and sandals John Doe had given me. This was proof of what had happened. I had physical proof!

Running, I came to the main road. On the other side was the trailhead leading to Grandpa's dock where my life had changed. Curious, I went over and looked down on the dock and the lake. In the gray tones of dawn, the water looked calm and quiet. For so long, I had hated to look at the lake, not really knowing why because my memory had erased what had happened. But now that I remembered that this was the spot where I'd last seen my father and brother alive, I was sad that they had died down there, but the haunting shadows were gone. As I was turning away, I thought I saw someone on the dock.

Must be an early morning fisherman. But as I started to leave, I realized that whoever it was didn't have a pole and bait box. In fact, whoever it was was staggering dangerously close to the edge of the dock as though ill. I quickly looked around to see if I could find the person's car or something, but there was only an empty highway and no vehicles parked at the side of the road. And I knew I had to go see if I could help.

I started down the trail to the lake. The filtered light of dawn cast the forest in eerie, surreal tones. I felt I'd stepped into an old black-and-white movie. Coming to the last big pine tree before the dock, I remembered how the paramedics had carried Dad and Tyler—covered entirely from head to foot with red blankets—on gurneys up this hill. I pushed past the memory and hurried down the trail. As I walked onto the dock, the mystery person came into view—my always-do-what's-right, in-my-face, pain-in-the-neck cousin, Ethan.

He looked wonderful. But something was wrong, very wrong as he staggered toward me. He was in the middle of a massive asthma attack. "Looking—" he sputtered, "—for you." And then, before I could answer, he fell into the lake.

35
Casting Fear Aside

Tag

EVERYTHING ABOUT ME CEASED TO be as my gaze turned to tunnel vision on the water. Ice formed before my eyes. Broken ice. Ice Tyler and Dad had fallen through. They were there in the water, and I was standing alone on the dock, watching. I needed to save them. I thought of seeing my dad and Tyler on the stairs in the vast hallway and how happy they were. I remembered Dad said the Savior would help me whenever I needed Him. Well, I needed His help now.

Casting all fear aside, I threw off my poncho and dove into the water.

The shock of the cold swallowing me in one big gulp only spurred me on. Opening my eyes, I barely made out shapes. Where in the world was Ethan? I had to find him.

I swam deeper and deeper. He was here somewhere. My lungs fought for air. I didn't know if I could hold my breath much longer, but I had to.

Pushing through the silt-filled water, I finally saw a dark, murky form. I quickly grabbed ahold and started kicking upward with all my might. It seemed to take forever to break through the water's surface.

There in my arms was Ethan. His eyes were closed. He wasn't breathing. I had to get him on dry land and out of the water. Swimming for the dock with one arm around my cousin, I saw someone waiting. Maybe someone had seen what had happened from the highway and had stopped. As I neared, I realized that someone was Grandpa. Only one strap of his bib coveralls was fastened, and his flannel shirt wasn't tucked in. He'd obviously dressed in a hurry. His face was pinched with worry and fear like I'd only seen one other time . . . the day Dad and Tyler died.

Without saying anything, Grandpa reached down and dragged Ethan up on the dock. I crawled out of the water beside him.

Ethan looked bad—he looked like Tyler had when they'd pulled him from the water—blue and pale. The look of death.

I knew in my soul it wasn't Ethan's time to leave. Not now. There would be no red blankets covering another member of my family, not if I had anything to do with it.

I rolled Ethan onto his back, made sure his airway wasn't obstructed, tilted his head, and pinched his nose, blowing into his mouth. His lips were cold, his body lifeless. I worked on him, thinking at any moment he would wake up. I thought of Mom and how she helped save people every day. I thought of her motto: "Do it, or get out of the way so I can." Well, I was doing it. No getting out of the way. I was determined!

"Tag." Grandpa kneeled beside me, sitting on the back of his heals. "He needs a blessing."

I knew Grandpa was right.

I watched as Grandpa placed his old gnarled hands on Ethan's head. I didn't know quite what to do so I folded my arms, closed my eyes, and listened to my Grandfather pronounce the blessing.

At that moment, in my mind I could see Jesus in His white robes looking down on us, and I begged Him, *Please don't take my cousin, too. I need him.* I stared down at Ethan, hoping beyond hope that somehow he would open his eyes. I didn't care if he teased me all summer long, I didn't care if he tattled on me to the principal, if only he'd wake up.

Still, he didn't move. I looked up at Grandpa. Sorrow bent his shoulders. He shook his head as if he were giving in.

No! This was not happening. I reached to work on Ethan again.

And then, all at once, Ethan's eyelids fluttered.

He began to choke and cough. I turned him on his side, and he threw up more water. Grabbing hold of my arm, he kept coughing, still in the throes of the asthma attack. Blinking as if he'd just been awakened from a bad dream, he looked at me. In between coughs, he choked out, "Tag?"

"Take it easy," I told him. I grabbed my poncho and snuggled it around his body.

I felt Ethan's eyes on me. I knew he was thinking about how Dad and Tyler had died in this lake, in this very spot, and I had been unable to save them. Despite his coughing and hacking, he smiled. I didn't know how he could smile while he was fighting for breath, but he did.

Grandpa dug in his overall pocket, pulled out Ethan's inhaler, and handed it to him. Ethan immediately sucked, drawing instant relief. He did it a couple more times and finally quit coughing. Relief in his voice, Grandpa said, "When I found that you two were both gone, I knew there was trouble, so before leaving the cabin, I grabbed his inhaler off the kitchen counter, just in case."

Ethan was going to be all right. I looked up at Grandpa and realized his blessing had worked a miracle. Ethan had been very close to death, and because of the power of the priesthood my grandfather held, he'd saved my cousin. One day if I became worthy, I, too, could hold the same priesthood. I, too, could give such blessings. Gratitude filled me.

Grandpa leaned over to help Ethan to his feet. "We need to get you to Doc's and make sure you're okay and everything."

Grandpa turned to me. "On the way, I want to hear what all this was about."

Ethan saw I was shivering, standing in only my briefs. He took the poncho from his shoulders and handed it to me. "You need this more than I do."

I pulled the poncho over my head. Grandpa gave me a curious look as if to say, *Where in the world did you get that?* I couldn't tell him now, but, boy, did I have a story to tell him once Ethan was all right and we'd returned to the cabin.

36
A Wonderful Gift

Tag

IT DIDN'T TAKE THE DOCTOR long to check Ethan over. He told him to take it easy for the rest of the day, but he'd be fine. On the drive back to the cabin, Ethan explained that when he woke up and found that I was gone, he was afraid I'd gone down to the lake, so he'd chased after me. I told both him and Grandpa that I was sorry I'd worried them. I knew Grandpa wanted me to fess up to what I'd done, but wise, old man that he was, he didn't press.

Once we were back at the cabin, Ethan camped out in front of the Franklin stove, warming up by the fire while Grandpa was in the kitchen making cocoa, toast, and oatmeal for breakfast. I dashed upstairs and quickly changed into the overalls and flannel shirt Grandpa had laid out for me the day before. I grabbed a dry change of clothes for Ethan and hurried downstairs.

"Thanks." Ethan eagerly took them and changed.

Grandpa brought in a tray of food. We all snuggled up close to the fire, mugs and bowls and all, eating in silence. Grandpa had slathered huckleberry jam on his toast and was eating it like it was chocolate or something. He sure liked huckleberries. Maybe even as much as Hashim liked peppers.

It drove me crazy not to tell Grandpa and Ethan about the people I'd met in Book of Mormon times. I had so much bottled up inside, so much to share. But I didn't know how to start. I looked at the picture Dad had painted of Jesus ascending from heaven in America, and I knew what to say.

"I have to tell you guys something. It's a long story, so hang tight until I get it all out."

Grandpa and Ethan looked at one another and then at me as if to say, *Get on with it.*

I told them about meeting John Doe in the market, which they already knew, but I wanted them to be really up to speed when I started in on the awesome part. I told them about sneaking out while they slept, about finding the cabin and John Doe, Steve Smith, and Bob Jones and the stone and how it sent me back in time.

Grandpa's bushy eyebrows rose quite high, but he didn't say anything. Ethan was very quiet, sipping his cocoa and staring at me over the rim of his mug. I told them about Sabirah, Princess Jamila, King Jacob, Malachi, and everything. I told them about meeting Jesus and about the blessing He gave me and about seeing Dad and Tyler.

When I stopped talking, there was silence. Only the ticking of Grandma's clock could be heard pinging off the cabin's log walls. The silence continued until I became very uncomfortable, until I couldn't stand it.

"Well?" I looked from Grandpa to Ethan.

Grandpa took a deep breath. "Well . . ." He rose, picked up our dishes, and muttered, "I don't know what to say, Teddy. I want to believe the boy." He was talking with Grandma again, as if she, too, were sitting there with us, hearing my tale. If she were, she'd tell him it was true.

The old, bent man headed to the kitchen. I stared at Ethan. He shrugged. "You've changed, so I know something has happened to you. I mean, you saved my life."

Grandpa came back into the room.

Inspiration hit me. "I need to return the poncho and sandals John Doe lent me and get my stuff back. You two can come, and you'll meet them."

Grandpa's forehead wrinkled skeptically, but he said, "Why not?" Ethan stood. "Let's go."

I knew they both wanted to believe me, and I needed to prove to them I didn't make up the whole thing.

Grandpa scooped up his keys to his Chevy truck. "Let's leave on out of here."

"Just a minute, let me get their stuff." I dashed upstairs and grabbed the poncho and sandals, but before hustling down, I knelt and said a prayer. I needed help. The prayer was short, and then I quickly left.

🙣

As Grandpa pulled up to the old deserted cabin where I knew the Three Nephites had stayed, I was taken aback. I hadn't noticed that it was really a sad looking shanty-type building. I opened the truck door and slowly crawled out. What was going on here?

A panicky, doubtful feeling flushed over me. I sprinted up the rickety steps and burst through the door. Only one room, no couch and no table. The place appeared long deserted, filled with cobwebs, and spiders.

Grandpa and Ethan walked in. They looked around, and I expected them to jeer at me, tell me they knew I'd been spinning a tall tale, but they didn't. Instead, their eyes were filled with worry as they stared at me.

"I don't understand," I said, searching the room for some scrap of evidence.

"I do." Grandpa pulled a sunflower seed out of the pouch pocket of his bibs and popped it in his mouth. "I've heard the Three Nephites don't hang around in one place for very long. They hit and run. Makes it hard to prove they exist."

"But they were here, and the place didn't look anything like this." I rubbed my hand across my face. "There was a couch there," I pointed to the wall. "And a room there, and John Doe hung his lantern there."

That's when I saw it. The lantern hung on the wooden peg behind the door.

"Yes!" I yelled and ran over to it. Carefully taking it down, I brushed cobwebs from the handle. This lantern had not been used for a very long time—but John had used it last night. I grew quiet.

"You're forgetting something that proves your point." Ethan stood beside me.

"Nothing proves my point. You must think I'm crazy."

"You have the clothes. They left you their clothes." Ethan wiggled his eyebrows. I looked over at Grandpa as if seeking confirmation.

"He's right." Grandpa nodded.

I'd left the clothes in the Chevy. Sprinting out, I leaped down the stairs and jerked open the truck's door.

The clothes were gone! My duffel sat in their place.

I stepped back from the cab and stumbled away. I gazed down the path where my journey to Book of Mormon times had begun.

There, about fifty feet away, stood John Doe. In his arms was the poncho and sandals. He smiled at me and waved.

Grandpa and Ethan stepped out of the cabin.

"He's there." I shouted, pointing down the trail without looking, knowing I could at last introduce them to my friend. Grandpa and Ethan strained hard to see something in that direction as they walked down the steps to stand beside me.

"Who's where?" Grandpa pulled his reading glasses out as if they would help.

Gazing down the trail, I saw that John Doe had vanished. I couldn't believe it. A numb tingling flushed over me, leaving me chilled to the bone, as though I'd jumped into the lake all over again.

"It's all right." Ethan nudged me with his elbow, much like Sabirah used to. "I believe everything you told us."

"The poncho and sandals are gone. He took them." I slugged my fist into my hand, feeling totally frustrated.

"But they left your duffel." Grandpa put his glasses back inside his pocket as he climbed into the cab of the truck.

I grabbed the bag and slid in, followed by Ethan.

Grandpa said, "You've been given a wonderful gift the three of us will always cherish. And maybe it's one of those things we don't tell everyone about. Telling the world might only weaken the gift. There would be nonbelievers, people who would say you dreamed it, or you hit your head and hallucinated—I mean, look at what the prophets have been through because they told the truth."

I immediately thought of Samuel the Lamanite, Joseph Smith, and, most importantly, Christ. They had all been persecuted because they told what they knew, but they were commanded to tell. I knew deep in my heart the experience I lived through was for me and not the world.

Epilogue

I SPENT THE SUMMER WITH Grandpa and Ethan. We rarely spoke of my experience, but whenever we sat in front of the fire and looked up at Dad's painting of Jesus, we remembered.

We finished the deck. It was a thing of beauty. Grandpa was so proud of our work that he treated us all to huckleberry shakes.

At the end of summer, Doctor Bradford and Mom came to pick me up. They were shocked to see the change that had come over me. I'd cut my hair. All the black was gone. I never wear black now. Nor do I wear a dog collar or lipstick or nail polish. All that stuff reminds me of King Jacob, and I want no part of it.

While I packed to go home, Mom seemed all nervous and stuff, but finally she sat on the bed. "Tag, Doctor Bradford asked me to marry him, but I told him I'd have to check with you before I gave him an answer."

I thought of what Dad had told me, that he had been the one helping Mom and Doctor Bradford get together. I gave her a hug and said, "It's fine with me, Mom."

She was stunned. "What's happened to you?"

I smiled at her. I wanted to tell her about my experience in Book of Mormon times and seeing Dad and Tyler, but the time was not right. Mom was looking toward the future, and I knew that's what we were both supposed to do, what Dad wanted us to do. "I'm just happy for you, Mom." Her eyes became all teary. A big smile came to her face as she hugged me tighter than I could ever remember, and I hugged her back.

When I finished packing, Grandpa and Ethan followed us to the deck. Ethan was staying another week. I gave them both a hug. Ethan told me he wanted to hang out with me at school. I was cool with that.

Mom and Doctor Bradford got into Mom's SUV. I stored my gear in the back. Shutting the hatch, I went to the rear passenger door to climb in, when Grandpa yelled, "Hold up there a minute."

He disappeared inside the cabin, and when he came out, he had the picture of Jesus Dad had painted. Walking toward me, a smile spread across his face, brightening his eyes as if he'd won a grand prize. He handed the picture to me. "I think your dad would want you to have this."

I couldn't believe he was parting with it. "Did Grandma tell you to give this to me?"

"Nope." He smiled. "Thought of it on my own, I did."

Taking the picture, I carefully set it on the backseat, next to where I was going to sit.

"Thanks, Grandpa." I hugged him and inhaled his scent of timber, earth, and a hint of huckleberry. I thought of Hashim and how he and Grandpa were kind of alike: both were short, stocky, quirky men, both liked the strangest foods, and, most importantly, both loved their families.

I climbed into the car. Doctor Bradford backed up so we could travel down the canyon. I checked to see if Grandpa was still watching. For a moment, I thought I saw Grandma, Dad, and Tyler on the deck. But then they were gone.

Had to be my imagination.

Or maybe not.

About the Author

Kathi Oram Peterson was born in the small town of Rigby, Idaho. Since childhood, she has loved reading and writing stories. After raising her family, she put her writing on hold to earn a BA in English and a minor in sociology at the University of Utah. Upon graduation, she worked for a curriculum publisher, writing and editing concept and biography books for children. Her first young adult time travel, The Forgotten Warrior, was number nine on Deseret Book and Seagull Book Stores bestsellers lists. Her Christmas book, An Angel on Main Street, was released in 2009.